Grace's Pictures

GRACE'S PICTURES

CINDY THOMSON

 TYNDALE HOUSE PUBLISHERS, INC.
CAROL STREAM, ILLINOIS

Visit Tyndale online at www.tyndale.com.

Visit Cindy Thomson's website at www.cindyswriting.com.

TYNDALE and Tyndale's quill logo are registered trademarks of Tyndale House Publishers, Inc.

Grace's Pictures

Designed by Beth Sparkman

Edited by Kathryn S. Olson

The author is represented by Chip MacGregor of MacGregor Literary Inc., 2373 NW 185th Avenue, Suite 165, Hillsboro, OR 97124

Scripture quotations are taken from the *Holy Bible*, King James Version.

Grace's Pictures is a work of fiction. Where real people, events, establishments, organizations, or locales appear, they are used fictitiously. All other elements of the novel are drawn from the author's imagination.

Library of Congress Cataloging-in-Publication Data

Thomson, Cindy, date.
  Grace's pictures / Cindy Thomson.
    pages cm. — (Ellis Island)
    ISBN 978-1-4143-6843-6 (sc)
1. Young women—New York (State)—New York—Fiction. 2. Irish—New York (State)—New York—Fiction. 3. Self-realization in women—Fiction. 4. Nannies—Fiction. 5. Christian fiction. I. Title.
  PS3620.H7447G73 2013
 '813'.6—dc23   2012045030

Printed in the United States of America

19	18	17	16	15	14	13
7	6	5	4	3	2	1

To my mother, Golden Peters,
and my mother-in-law, Eileen Thomson.
Voracious readers and cherished supporters.

Acknowledgments

I AM SO GRATEFUL GOD LOVES ME and embraces me as I am, working in my life day by day.

I feel very blessed to have had the help of a multitude of people while writing *Grace's Pictures*. Foremost the folks at Tyndale, who were gracious, patient, and incredibly nice to work with throughout the process. Many thanks to editors Stephanie Broene, Kathryn Olson, and Sarah Mason.

Thanks also to my agent, Chip MacGregor, for steering me toward writing about immigrants and for rooting for me along the way. While it was always a requirement that my agent be a baseball fan, I've been fortunate in so many ways to have Chip on my side.

To my fellow writers, many of them ACFW members. Thanks so much for sharing and caring. Specifically, I'd like to thank my blog team over at Novel PASTimes and a group of ladies we call Writer Sisters: Jenny B. Jones, Nicole O'Dell, Cara Putman, Kim Cash Tate, Marybeth Whalen, and Kit Wilkinson. Your prayer support and writing advice kept me going. I cherish you and look forward to your e-mails.

I'm so grateful to the Etna UMC prayer group for supporting me and also for these prayer warriors via a Facebook group: Scott and Dawn Brown; Cris Mantia Carnahan; Diane

DeGonia; Sandy Beck Drodge; Diane Harper; Robin Kane; Joyce Trowbridge; my sister, Beverly Wallace; Cindy Zudys; and Debbie Steele Woods (who knows a lot of interesting words for Bananagrams, like *yourn*).

Thanks to editor and friend Jamie Chavez, who helped me in numerous ways. Thanks also, Jamie, for consulting your Irishman Gerry Hampton when I had questions.

Several organizations and individuals helped immensely with my research: the National Library of Ireland; the New York Public Library; the Columbus Metropolitan Library; the Bowery Boys website and podcast; Eric Ferrara, executive director of the Lower East Side History Project; and Jeannie Campbell, LMFT, "The Character Therapist," who helped me better understand Grace McCaffery.

Finally, to my family, not only for your prayer support, but also for being the best cheerleaders ever. I'm so proud of my grown-up kids: Dan, Jeff, Kyle, and Kelsey. And the biggest thanks of all goes to my husband, Tom. Without his encouragement, support, tremendous cooking skills, emergency computer help, and occasional laundry duty, this book would truly not have been possible. I love you!

Seek his face evermore.

PSALM 105:4

1

"May I take your photograph, miss?"

Grace McCaffery spun around. She had passed through the inspections without a problem and was on her way downstairs, where she would meet the aid society worker. What now?

"A photograph?" A man stood smiling at her, next to a large camera. She'd only seen one of these machines before, and that was on the ship.

"Why?" She bit her lip. Was everything about to fall apart now?

"For prosperity. It's your first day in America." He handed her a small piece of paper. "My name and address, should you later wish to see it. It will only take a moment of your time, and then you are free to continue on."

Free sounded good. "What do I do?"

"Stand under that window—" he pointed toward one of the massive windows—"and look this way." Streams of late-afternoon sun shone in through the ornamental ironwork, tracing odd shapes on the tiled floor.

She did as he asked.

"Now look up, miss." He snapped his fingers. "Look toward the camera."

Her eyelids were iron weights, but she forced herself to look his way, wanting to get it over with.

After she heard a slight pop coming from the camera, he dismissed her. "Welcome to America!"

America! Ma should see Ellis Island and all the people milling about. Grace sat down on a bench just to the right of the stairs to collect the thoughts rambling around in her head like loose marbles. Imagine, a girl like her, now free in America. She would not have envisioned it herself a few weeks ago. Exhausted, she dropped her face to her hands as she relived what had led her here.

"Must go to the workhouse." Huge hands snatched wee Grace from her bed. "Your da is dead. Behind in your rent and got no means."

Grace kicked with all her might. "Ma!"

An elbow to her belly. Burning. She heaved.

"Blasted kid!" The policeman tossed her onto a wagon like garbage.

"Ma!"

"I'm here, Grace. Don't cry." Her mother cradled her as the wagon jolted forward. "Oh, my heart. You are special, wee one. So special to God."

Heat emanated from the burning cottage, the temperature torturing Grace's face. She hid against her mother's shoulder.

Later, they were pulled apart and herded into a building.

A dark hallway. The sound of water dripping.

Stairs. Up the stairs. Following other children. So many children. Was her mother dead?

The sound of heels clacking down steps brought Grace back to the present. She sat up straight and watched hordes of people march down the stairs. They were divided into three groups according to destination.

She knew her mother had loved her, but God? Her mother had been wrong about that. God loved good people like Ma. Not Grace. Grace knew she was not good enough for God.

So many of the people passing in front of her were mere children, most with parents but some without. Grace wondered if they were as afraid as she had been when she was separated from her mother in the workhouse, the place Irish folks were taken to when they had nowhere else to go. All these people now seemed to have a destination, though. A new start. Like her. In America she hoped she could mend her fumbling ways and merit favor.

A wee lass approached the stairs with her hand over her mouth, the registration card pinned to her coat wrinkled and stained with tears. Grace was about to go to her and tell her everything would be fine. After all, this great hall, this massive building, was not in Ireland. They were in the land of the free. They'd just seen Lady Liberty's glowing copper figure in the harbor, hadn't they?

But the lass, obviously having mustered her courage, scrambled down the steps and into the mass of people. Would the child be all right? No mother. No parents at all. It had happened to Grace. Free one day, sentenced by poverty the next.

She pulled her hand away from her own mouth. In the workhouse she'd had this nightmare and cried out. She'd been whipped.

Not now.

Not ever again.

She struggled to remember the song her mother sang to her at bedtime. *"Thou my best thought by day or by night . . ."* She couldn't remember any more of it. She'd forgotten. The truth was, she didn't know if everything would be all right.

She rose and followed the orders she'd been given right before the photographer had approached her. Down the steps to the large room where the lady from the charity would meet her.

She rubbed her free hand along the handrail as she walked, barely able to believe she was in another country now, far across the Atlantic Ocean. If it hadn't been for the miserable voyage in steerage, the stench from sweaty, sick passengers that remained even now, and wobbling knees weak from too little food, she might believe she was dreaming. Had it really been just a few weeks ago when she'd sat opposite the workhouse master's desk and twisted the edge of her apron between the fingers of her right hand as he spoke to her?

"Eight years you've been here, Grace," he'd said.

"Aye." She'd stopped counting.

"You are a young woman now, with some potential to be productive. Yet there is no employment in this country of yours. Nothing you can do." He was British and had little patience for the Irish.

She'd held her head low.

"And so, Grace, you've been sponsored to leave the work-house and go to America." He dipped the nib of his pen in an inkwell and scribbled, not looking up.

"What do you mean, sir?"

"America. You leave from Dublin in two days. I've got your papers in order. And this." He pushed an envelope toward her.

She remembered that at the time she'd worried about her fingernails when she'd held out her hand. She looked at them now. Grime on the ship had taken its toll. The master would not like that.

He is not here.

She touched that very same envelope now, crinkled in her apron pocket. It contained the name of the ship, the destination, and at the bottom, *Sponsored by S. P. Feeny.*

She mumbled under her breath. "Ma married him for this." To provide a future for Grace.

The line of people moved slowly. Grace sucked in her breath. Not long now.

"Mama!"

She turned and watched a red-faced lad scurry down the steps and into the open arms of his mother, who reprimanded him for wandering away.

Grace had begged to speak to her own mother the day the workhouse master told her she was going to America. He hadn't sent for her because her mother was no longer an inmate, but a free woman married to that lawman, that peeler named Sean Patrick Feeny.

But Grace's mother had come anyway, not to the workhouse but to the docks.

"Hurry along," the immigration worker urged her now.

Grace thought about S. P. Feeny's note again as she entered a room packed with people. Not knowing whether the charity lady would need to see it, she reached into her pocket and pulled it out. She glanced around and found a vacant spot on a bench.

"Wait until you hear your name called," a man in a brown suit said to the crowd.

There were more workers in that place than she expected. In Ireland only a handful of employees kept the inmates in line. She reminded herself again that she was in America. *People care about folks here, now, don't they?*

She opened the note and reread the part at the end, the words her mother's husband had scrawled there.

Your mother wants you out of the workhouse. With no other options, I have arranged for you to go to America, where you will find work and no doubt prosper. Pin this to your dress for the journey. It is the name of a man my connections say will take good care of you in New York and arrange a job. I have written him to let him know when you will arrive.
S. P.

The immigration official upstairs had told her not to expect this man to meet her, but rather someone who worked for him, mostly likely a woman from an immigrant aide society. "Don't worry," he'd told her. "They'll have your name."

As much as Grace wanted to crumple up the paper and toss it away, she dared not. Following directions had been essential to getting along in the workhouse, and she had no reason to abandon that thinking now. She had managed to survive back there, even though she was apart from her mother, who had worked out of Grace's sight until she got married and left the workhouse altogether. Surviving was a victory and perhaps the best she could have hoped for then.

She glanced down at the writing again. S. P. Feeny was a peeler, a policeman, like those who tore Grace and her mother from their home when Grace was but ten years old. Grace had thought her life was as good as over when she heard about the marriage. But now she was in America.

She blinked back tears as she thought about her unknown future. What if her father had been right when, so long ago, he'd told her she needed him to survive, could not do it alone? His death had forced them into the workhouse, and she had survived without him then, hadn't she? But now? Now she really was alone and she was not sure she could endure. And yet, she must.

She mentally rehearsed her instructions, the ones Feeny had written down. She'd done what she'd been told so far.

Now she was supposed to wait. But how long?

Running her fingers down her skirt to wipe away perspiration, she hoped she would not say the wrong thing when this stranger claimed her. Would they understand her in America? Did she speak proper English well enough? As much as her stomach churned, she mustn't appear sick, even though the doctor had already hurriedly examined her along with her fellow passengers. She'd heard stories. They sent sick people to a hospital and often they were never heard from again. Perhaps they executed the ones who didn't die. Or they put them back on the ship to return to Ireland. As bad as it was facing an unknown future in America, at least there was hope here that could not be found in the workhouse. So long as they let her stay.

She glanced over at a family. Mother, father, son, and daughter clung to each other. They would make it. Together they had strength. Grace had no one.

Soon a crowd of tall men jabbering in a language she didn't understand entered the room. Grace squeezed the note in her hand. As much as she didn't want S. P. Feeny's help, she'd needed a sponsor to start this new life. She had no choice but to trust his instruction. *If there is one thing a policeman like Feeny knows, it's the rules. Whether or not they abide by them is another matter.*

"Where you from?" a tawny-haired lass sitting next to her asked.

"County Louth." She thought it best not to mention the workhouse.

The girl nodded.

Good. She didn't seem to want to ask anything else.

After a few moments, sensing the girl's nervousness, not unlike her own, Grace gave in. "And you? Where are you from?"

The girl sat up straight. "County Down."

"Oh. Not far." Grace swallowed hard. They were both far from home.

An attendant stood on a box and raised his voice. "Mary Montgomery? Miss Mary Montgomery, please."

The girl next to Grace stood and went to him.

"I'm afraid there's been a mistake, miss."

A brief moment later the lass was gone from the room. Escorted off somewhere. Grace turned to the men seated behind her. "Where are they taking her?"

They shrugged. Only one of them met her gaze. "Don't be worrying, lass. Could be she's in the wrong place. Could be her family didn't come to claim her. Could be 'bout anything, don't you know?"

Grace tried to breathe, but the room felt hot and noisy. *"You can do this,"* she heard her mother say from the recesses of her mind.

In the workhouse, everyone was the same—wore matching gray uniforms, used identical spoons, slurped the same watery stirabout, marched together from dining hall to dormitory at the same exact time day after day, month after month, year after year. It was a routine she could count on.

She glanced around at the faces near her. Square jaws, rounded chins. Black hair, locks the color of spun flax. Brightly colored clothing, suits the color of mud. So many differences. And so many tongues. Where she'd come from, there had been no question of how to act, what to say, who to look at. But here?

She turned and kept her eyes on her feet and the trim of the red petticoat her mother had given her to travel in when she'd met her at the docks.

Oh, Ma! When Grace had been able to look into her mother's green-gray eyes, she found assurance. On the ship, Grace had tried to emblazon her mother's face on her memory so it would always be there when she needed to see it. She'd even sketched her mother on some paper with a charcoal pencil another passenger gave her. She had the sketch in her bag with her meager belongings. Not much, but all she had now.

"Thanks be to God." "God have mercy." "God bless our souls." "The grace of God on all who enter." . . . Her mother never failed to acknowledge God. She was a good woman. The best. Grace was so far away now from that umbrella of assurance.

She focused on the immigration official calling out names. Survival was human instinct, and humans adapted. She'd learned to do it once before. Perhaps she could manage to exorcise her father's voice from her head, the one that told her she was incapable, and actually make a life, a good life, for herself in America.

Grace's mother had held her at arm's length when they said good-bye on the docks in Dublin. She'd rubbed Grace's cheeks with her thumbs. "The best thing for you is to go to America. You are not a child anymore. I could not let you stay in the workhouse. Don't I know how hard it is for a grown woman to keep her dignity there."

Grace had tried pleading with her. "Take me home with you. I'll be polite to S. P. . . . I promise."

But her mother wouldn't hear of it. "There's no life here for you, Grace. Fly free, Daughter. Find your way. 'Tis a blessing you can go."

Grace had told her mother she couldn't do it. Not alone. Not without her.

"Listen to me," her mother had said, tugging Grace's chin upward with her finger. "I don't care what lies your father once spoke to you, darlin'. To us both. Pity his departed soul that he left us with no choice but the workhouse. But promise me you will not think of the things he said to you. Remember instead this: You are smart. You are important. You are able."

If she could prosper as her mother had asked her to, then perhaps her mother might choose to come to America too, a place where she would not need S. P. Feeny. Grace would make it happen. Somehow. She had to. Her hands trembled as she held tight to her traveling bag.

Grace's face grew hot. She lifted a shoulder to her chin, hoping her embarrassment didn't show. She didn't want to speak to a peeler—or whatever they called them in America. But she was stuck, shoved into a hot electric-powered car with more people than she thought it should safely hold. The man had addressed her and asked her a question. She had to respond. She spoke toward her feet. "I am well. I come from County Louth."

The large man leaned down toward her. "You say you are from County Louth, miss?"

"I am."

"Is that so?" He let loose a low whistle. "My people come from Tullamore. We might be neighbors or cousins or something."

The woman with Grace, who'd introduced herself as Mrs. Hawkins, chuckled. "You're all cousins, love, all of you from ole Erin."

Grace was no kin to men like that, and if she were, she would disown them straight away. *These are the men who force poor families from their homes and send them to workhouses the minute they can't pay rent.*

There was a lull in the conversation as the car pulled them through an intersection. She heard the peeler's breath catch. She dared to look at him. He was staring out at the street. He did not seem formidable at all and perhaps was even a little uneasy riding on the streetcar. Odd, that.

Grace glanced back down, studying the shoes surrounding her, trying to focus on the future instead of dwelling on the past. She was in the "Land of Opportunity," after all. She hoped not to associate with folks she didn't care to.

She clutched the bag containing her treasured drawing pencil, wee pad of paper, and a small card bearing the address of that Ellis Island photographer, Mr. Sherman, who had taken her photograph.

2

OWEN MCNULTY rarely took the streetcar, but he was late, so he'd made an exception, trying not to think about the fact that so many of them were involved in accidents every day. He had checked the street before he hopped on. Seemed safe enough.

After he'd ridden for a few minutes, the car had stopped near the Battery and he realized he'd gotten on going in the wrong direction. He'd be riding longer than he cared to, but at least now that the car was at the tip of Manhattan, it would be turning north again shortly. A crowd of people had gotten on, mostly new arrivals from Ellis Island, judging by the native dress he saw. Perhaps if he rode more frequently, he would be accustomed to seeing new immigrant girls like the one standing just beyond his right elbow. No longer on Ellis Island, she shouldn't be as frightened as she now appeared. She'd made it, and, he noticed, she was accompanied by a woman from his church.

Since the young woman seemed reluctant to exchange pleasantries, he turned to her companion. "Pleasant day, Mrs. Hawkins."

"Indeed it is." She smiled at the petite, auburn-haired young woman next to her. Owen followed the woman's gaze. When it landed on the girl's tattered red petticoat, she sighed. "I've begun a new outreach, Officer. Now that I have my house-keeper, I'm getting boarders."

"Isn't that fine." He glanced again at the girl, who did not look up. "And you, Miss From-County-Louth, what is your name, if you please?" Owen tipped his hat at the meek girl even though she refused to look at him.

She mumbled, "I was assured I passed the inspection."

"Easy, lass. Just being friendly." He looked to Mrs. Hawkins, who in turn stared down her large nose at the girl as they all gripped overhead rails to steady themselves while the trolley car maneuvered up the brick street.

"Miss Grace McCaffery," Mrs. Hawkins said, clearing her throat. "You may speak to police officers. There is no harm in it."

Owen chuckled to himself. The girl might not realize it, but he really was no threat to her. There was plenty of menace to be found in Lower Manhattan, however, and she was fortunate indeed to be in the care of such a kind protector as Mrs. Agnes Hawkins.

"Going to see Reverend Clarke?" Owen knew the man counseled new arrivals from time to time. He and Mrs. Hawkins and probably many others among First Church's congregants took seriously the need for missionary outreach to immigrants.

The girl named Grace finally glanced up in his direction but stared past his shoulder. He got only a quick peek at her wide blue eyes before she lowered them again. But that was enough time for him to see just how vulnerable she felt . . . and how attractive she was.

Later, while working his beat, Owen's thoughts wavered between that frightened immigrant girl and his job as he marched down a crowded street. He contemplated whether having a partner to work with would be beneficial. Like it or not, the captain had told him to expect as much when the new assignments were doled out. "You need someone with you, McNulty," the captain had said. "Someone folks might be more . . . at ease with." Owen worried that the captain might have lost confidence in him.

A group of vagrants clustered against a warehouse wall stood straighter when Owen approached. "Good day to you, Officer."

Owen nodded. His first anniversary on the force had passed, but he knew most of the locals still saw him as a college boy and not one of them.

He paused at an oyster vendor. "Packing up for the day. Here, Officer. Try?"

Owen accepted the sample handed to him on a half shell. He sniffed. "Ah, smells like the sea." He swallowed the salty delight. Even the Waldorf could not compete. Wiping his mouth with the back of his hand, he pointed to the seaman's wares. "Very good and fresh, Oliver."

"Thank you. Got a family, Officer? You can take some."

"No. But thank you."

It was a pleasant exchange. Most of the conversations he had on his beat were. But it was all superficial. He needed the local people to trust him and confide in him.

Oliver waved. "You should get married, Officer. Find a girl from home."

"I'll keep that in mind. Good night, Oliver."

The man continued shoveling ice from his cart into buckets. Owen moved on down the sidewalk.

Now that he'd passed his twenty-third birthday, Owen realized most of his childhood friends were married, some with children. Owen might have been too if he hadn't changed course. His life had turned out to be vastly different than most anyone expected, even the folks living and working in Owen's beat, who still seemed to think he belonged uptown instead of in their neighborhoods.

Before the night was over, Owen would head toward the mission, the late-night part of his rounds—for now, anyway, until his assignment changed, as it so often did. He looked forward to patrolling near First Church, where he was welcomed, a little island of respite.

Well, most folks embraced him there. He thought again about that new girl, Grace, who had avoided him like the smallpox. Definitely something amiss with her. Had there ever been a clearer expression of fear and uncertainty than what he'd seen on Grace?

He continued on his rounds. Buildings, being constructed further toward the sky month by month, threatened to suck him down into their shadows. There was much more light and fresher air up Fifth Avenue, where residents did not have to look at the filth lining the rivers on both sides of Manhattan. But if he were going to help where help was most needed, he had to patrol where the rats roamed like buzzards. He was needed here. He had no regrets about that.

Owen paused to watch some of the trolley cars pass up the street. Each one served to remind him that his role was not that of a rich son laboring ever so leisurely in his father's vast dry goods business. Not anymore. Owen believed God wanted him to be employed helping folks, especially those riding on trolleys.

3

When they left the trolley, Mrs. Hawkins took Grace's arm. "You'll learn soon enough, love. Be respectful to the New York police, and they'll be there when you need them. Treat them rudely, and spend the rest of your days looking behind you in dark alleys."

Och, nothing was different here. Grace would try harder. She did not want to be bullied. Not ever again.

They approached a brown brick building with *Irish Immigrant Society* painted on the side. Mrs. Hawkins rang a bell on the front door. A thin woman with gray hair pulled back in a tight bun answered the door.

"Good day, Edwina. I have Miss Grace McCaffery here to see the reverend. Grace, this is Mrs. Reilly."

The woman showed them in and bade them wait in a front room. Mrs. Hawkins smiled when Grace raised her head.

"You're most welcome here, lass. Do try to relax."

Grace let out a breath. "I'm sorry."

"Well, now. We know how unusual all of this is to you. Quite understandable. But before long you'll be all settled in and you'll be calling yourself American like all the rest."

This woman was as British as the workhouse master, but not nearly as coldhearted. Ma would like her.

When Grace heard someone approaching from the hall, a chilling thought gripped her. *Welcome?* She wasn't sure what that meant exactly. They might want something from her. There had to be a price for—

She gazed around the room. Clean, tidy. If S. P. had indentured Grace or sold her into servitude . . .

The woman named Mrs. Reilly returned. "Perhaps you'd like to tidy up, child? I'll show you to the washroom."

Grace hesitated.

"Go along, love. Leave your bag here with me."

Grace rose and followed the other woman down a hallway until she stopped. She flung open a door and pointed. "In here." She pulled on a cord and light lit up the room.

There was a basin and a stack of towels and a toilet. One toilet?

"Go ahead and clean up. There is soap in the dish on the basin. When you're done, come back to the parlor. The reverend is finishing up some business and he'll be with you shortly." She closed the door behind her, leaving Grace completely alone. She didn't think she'd ever been the only person in a room before, ever.

Tears sprang to her eyes as she rinsed ringlets of dirt from her arms in the washing basin. After she dried off, she hung the towel back on the rail fastened to the side of the basin stand. Whatever these people expected from her could not be as miserable as the workhouse or living with her always-drunken father before that, could it?

She noticed a small window in the corner of the room and drew back the curtains to study the moving shapes on the sidewalk outside. The folks in America were different. They walked faster, whistled less, and seemed so . . . so busy. But so far she hadn't seen any workhouses or locked doors. The sky might be darker, the air heavy with soot, and the city overcrowded, but she was safe, for now. Free to walk out that door and into that street if she desired. Free to talk to anyone she pleased. Free to lie down right now if—

A knock resounded on the door. "Are you all right in there?"

Grace opened the door.

As she followed the woman down a corridor that she said connected the reverend's residence to the church, Grace marveled at how elegant everything was. She must have gawked because the woman paused. "Different from where you are from?"

"It is." She thought there might be some scheme that allowed the reverend such a comfortable dwelling. "May I ask a question?"

"You may."

"Who pays for all this?"

The woman shrugged her narrow shoulders. "The church, child. You know. Tithes."

"The government . . . ?" Dare she even ask after the government-run house she'd come from?

"The church, I said."

"I just . . . ," Grace whispered. "Is this a workhouse?"

The woman cocked her head to one side. "This look like a workhouse? What are those castles like in Ireland? Palaces? If we don't meet your standards—"

"Nay. I do not mean that at all. This is very nice. Much better than from where I came."

"Odd one, you are, Grace McCaffery. C'mon. You'll meet Reverend Clarke now."

They stopped at a closed door and the woman tapped softly.

"Come in," a voice boomed from the other side.

Mrs. Reilly opened the door and waved an arm to usher Grace inside. A man sitting behind a polished desk removed his spectacles as she walked in. His blue eyes widened as though Grace were a long-lost relative. "Ah, a new arrival. Come in, child."

Such hospitality was not what Grace had expected, at least not from the man in charge. He must be hiding something.

Her escort left, leaving the door slightly ajar.

"I'm Reverend Clarke. Was your passage agreeable?" He pointed to a chair.

Grace folded her hands in her lap. "Thank you, sir, for allowing me to come here. I won't impose any more than necessary."

He smiled. "You are most welcome. We'll help you get settled." He tapped some papers on his desk. "Now, let's get some information about you and see what we can do about finding employment." He glanced up from the ledger in front of him. "You've eaten, haven't you?"

While Grace could have purchased food at Ellis Island, she'd chosen to hang on to her money because she didn't know what she might need to pay for later. "Nay, uh, no, but I'm fine."

"What!"

Grace pressed her back against the chair at his shout.

He bolted to his feet and scrambled around her to open the door wide. "Just arrived and you've probably been hours at the immigration station." He cupped his hands to his mouth and shouted, "Edwina, come here!"

Mrs. Reilly appeared, wearing an apron.

Grace blew out the breath she'd been holding.

"The poor dear hasn't eaten. Would you bring her a biscuit and some tea?"

"Certainly." She turned to leave.

The reverend snapped his fingers. "And some of that pork we had with breakfast. And an apple or two."

Grace's stomach rumbled.

Mrs. Reilly turned back. "Two cups for tea?"

He chuckled. "Well, I might have a bite as well. Can't let the girl sup alone, now can we?" He smacked his lips. "See that Mrs. Hawkins is served as well while she's waiting, won't you?"

"I planned to, but are you sure you want all that?"

"Indeed." He wiggled one hand in front of his chest.

The woman rolled her eyes, but the reverend didn't seem to mind her lack of respect. How different things were in America.

He turned his attention back to Grace. "We will help you find a good job. That's why you've come, yes?"

"Aye, yes, but . . . Reverend Clarke, may I ask a question?"

"Certainly."

"What is my obligation here?"

"You have none, other than to observe proper morals and help Mrs. Hawkins with chores. You'll be staying with her. You were referred to us as someone who needs a bit of help to get established, and that's what we do."

"Why?"

"Excuse me?"

"Why do you want to help me? Did my mother's husband pay you?"

"We don't accept payment, Miss McCaffery. This is a charity, an outreach mission. Mr. Feeny? That's it, isn't it?" He hurried back to look again at his ledger.

"Aye. That is his name."

"He asked if we could help you, and I replied positively."

She did not want to talk about that man. "So you want to help me?"

"Ah, yes. Well, we do expect you to apply yourself, but we are doing the work of our Lord."

Grace pondered that. Her mother trusted God. This was a man of God. Mrs. Hawkins was pleasant. Grace didn't know if God would accept her, but these people wanted to help, so . . . maybe, just maybe, things would work out.

Reverend Clarke tapped a pencil on his ledger. "Can you do laundry?"

"It was done for us in the workhouse."

"Cooking?"

"I did none."

"Well, then, sweeping up?"

"Aye. I can do that. I'm sure I can learn the rest, Reverend Clarke. I do a lot of watching; then I can do it. Like my drawing. I watched a lass and soon I was sketching with my own pencil."

"I suppose the tasks aren't too complicated to catch on to. I'm afraid drawing won't employ you adequately, though. We will focus on housekeeping."

Mrs. Reilly brought in the snack, and Grace and the reverend ate. The man had not asked why she'd been in a workhouse. Plenty of people on the ship had been as well, so it was likely he'd heard of it before. Neither did he ask about relatives back home, and she was glad she didn't have to relive the eviction after her father's death. He did, however, ask about the condition of her soul.

"Don't tell me if you're Catholic or Protestant," he said, waving a chunk of apple in the air. "Just tell me whether or not Jesus is your Lord and Savior."

His jolly manner made Grace feel more at ease, and that surprised her. "My mother was quite religious."

"Your mother." He nodded. "Well, if you have any spiritual concerns for yourself, I want you to feel free to come to me. We want you to feel at home here, Miss McCaffery."

Home? "Thank you."

She did want to ask a question, although it wouldn't change things. "I confess, Reverend, I do not understand why God allows misery in this world."

The man stood. "I confess the same."

She nearly dropped her china cup. "You're a man of the cloth." It might have been rude to point that out, but she could not help herself.

He turned to an overstuffed bookcase and withdrew a volume. He held it against his chest like a shield. "I've studied all the philosophers and read the Bible cover to cover. Many times." He shoved the book back in. "I have come to a conclusion, Grace. You don't mind me calling you by your Christian name, child?"

"I do not mind."

"Good, good. We're family here."

She swiveled in her chair to watch him as he strolled around his office.

He paused and held up a finger. "My conclusion is this: God does not reveal all. My mind couldn't comprehend it if he did."

"I don't understand."

He slipped two fingers between the buttons on his vest. "I don't either. Here is what I do know. In the book of 1 John—" He did not pick up a book. He was reciting from memory. "The Scripture says, 'We love him, because he first loved us.' And I ask myself, is there more love in the world because of what *I'm* doing? If not, I need to change that."

Well, as jolly nice as this man was, it seemed he was no

genius. But so long as he could set her up with a place to stay and a job, Grace could take it from there. She prayed he would not now ask about her life in Ireland.

He picked up his fountain pen. "Therefore, since I know you will need a bit of help, here we are to serve. Now, I am sure we have a family who would love to employ you in their household." He studied the ledger again. "I'll get to work on it while you take these things back to the kitchen."

She stood and collected the dishes and tray that Mrs. Reilly had brought. "Thank you. If you don't mind me asking, Reverend, how many girls do you do this for?"

"Oh, dozens, a hundred perhaps. I'm not quite sure."

She thought about the size of the houses they'd passed on the way there. Nothing like the workhouse. "Surely not all at one time?"

"Oh no. Only a few at a time. Then they move on and others come."

Move on. Grace looked forward to that.

When she got to the kitchen, she found Mrs. Hawkins there sipping tea. "Did you have a good chat, love?"

"Aye. Yes." She stood there with the tray in her hands, unable to form words. These people astounded her. She'd thought Ma was the only person God had found favor with.

Mrs. Hawkins rose and took the tray from her. "You're weary, and that's no surprise. We'll be on our way. I've a warm meal and a soft bed for you, love."

Hawkins House was lovely with a wide entry, carpets on the floor, and even a piano in the parlor. The staircase of polished mahogany was magnificent.

The reverend had escorted the women to the boarding-house, and now that they'd arrived, he did not remove his hat. "I'll let you get settled in, child. I will see you at services."

"You're leaving now?"

"You'll be fine here, child. I'll inquire on how you're faring later."

Grace tried to hold his gaze but he turned away. A hollow spot opened in her soul. People always walking in and out. She hated that. Things changed more swiftly in America than a swollen spring river, and she would have to get used to it.

After he'd gone, Grace rubbed her hand over the staircase spindles as she passed by, following the proprietor back to the kitchen. They paused halfway down the hall, where someone waited.

"This is Annie. Annie, Grace, our new boarder," Mrs. Hawkins said.

"Pleased to meet you," Annie said. "You're very welcome."

The lass spoke with a brogue. Grace held out a hand. "You're Irish."

"I am. Don't be thinking we're all as British as our gracious hostess." Annie winked.

The British built the workhouses. Grace was puzzled by Annie's nonchalant remark just as much as she was by Mrs. Hawkins's generosity. If this place was truly as nice as it seemed, why was Grace chosen to come here? There were others more friendly, smarter, more capable. Ma was praying for her. That had to be the reason.

Mrs. Hawkins turned toward the middle of the kitchen. "You and I will take turns with the chores, particularly the evening meal, until you are otherwise employed, love." She inclined her head toward a large gas stove. "And we still use coal for heat." Another stove stood in the corner.

"I shoveled coal in Ireland," Grace offered. The kitchen was incredibly huge, nearly as large as the one in the workhouse that served hundreds of people. Along one wall stood a table for informal meals. She had a peek into the scullery. It appeared well stocked.

The woman opened the back door, letting in a rush of cold air. "Out here is the washroom, love. There is a bathtub upstairs."

Grace took a quick glimpse at the washroom, which contained a toilet and sink.

The woman chuckled. "It's a bit dark in there some days. Take a lantern with you when you go."

Hawkins House, as beautiful as it was, had no electric lights. But that didn't bother Grace a bit. She had never lived with electricity before.

They doubled back to the entry and passed Annie polishing the banister.

Mrs. Hawkins pointed to a wee table in the foyer. "Mail, if we don't hand it to you personally, can be found here."

They moved toward one front room. "The parlor is for your enjoyment anytime you'd like."

The room was generous with a fine piece of furniture the woman called a breakfront cabinet at one end and a piano near the front window.

"We've passed the dining room. Evening meals are taken there, but otherwise you can be seated in the kitchen."

Grace followed Mrs. Hawkins up the magnificent staircase and then down the hall to a back bedroom. "Eventually you will share this room with another new arrival. But for now, you're the only boarder the Benevolents have."

"Who?"

"Just a group of friends who banded together to establish Hawkins House. We seek to answer the question 'Is what I'm doing making life better for others?' That's what we want to do, Grace. Help young immigrant girls like you."

"The reverend said something like that."

"Quite right. I expect we'll have another girl soon, but until then, you'll have the room to yourself. I hope you'll be comfortable here."

Grace could barely reply. Like the others in the house, this room was expansive. "Oh, aye. Extremely generous. Thank you."

The woman pointed to a door inside the room. "We use this for storage, and there is no wardrobe in here. But you can use this old trunk here at the end of your bed."

"Thank you, but I don't have many things."

"You won't need much. We have everything you'll need right here."

The room seemed chilly, being the upstairs corner bedroom, but Grace was not about to complain. The two beds were plump with quilts. Inviting. And decorated in pastel shades. Such an improvement over the lack of color she'd seen thus far.

"Let me instruct you about the bath, love."

Grace followed the woman out and into the room directly across the hall.

"So long as the weather's not too cold for the pipes, you can warm the water downstairs by the coal stove and turn it on here. That will take a few moments, however. It does not happen quickly, but a hot bath is worth it."

She watched as Mrs. Hawkins turned one side of the tub faucet and called it hot and the other cold. "Best to leave the cold one alone. Long as I've been here, it's never gotten too hot to need to cool it down."

"You haven't always lived here, Mrs. Hawkins? I mean, since you came from England?"

"Bought the place after my Harold passed away." She stood and clasped her hands together. "Hawkins House is a little project of mine, love, with help from my friends."

"The Benevolents."

"Correct."

When they joined Annie in the parlor, Grace sat on the sofa and admired a portrait hanging on the opposite wall. The man in the painting sported a long beard, darker than his hair, and was dressed in a military uniform. Grace pointed. "A handsome man."

Mrs. Hawkins rose and crossed the room to the wall where the photograph hung. "My late husband, Harold. He fought bravely for the Union." Tears glistened in her eyes. "He was a good provider. It's his prosperity that helps afford us this comfort today, love."

"You mean to say he worked to provide for your needs?"

"Indeed, love. Like most good husbands."

"My father drank his earnings at the pub."

"Pity. I'm so sorry. Thank the good Lord there are men who take their roles seriously."

"Like your Harold?"

"Like my Harold, love."

"'Tis an enchanting photograph. Was that the war where the South fought to secede?"

"That's correct. He fought to preserve the Union, love."

"Was he . . . ?" She wasn't sure how to ask.

"Killed in battle? My, no, thank the good Lord. He passed on a few years back. He was all I had until the Benevolents were formed. That and my girls here are my family now."

Grace could not believe her fortune. Never could she have

imagined such people existed. She wanted to believe this was real, but it all felt like a dream.

Grace examined the photographic image again. Just a bit of shadow on the right side of his face added depth, and the backdrop was soft enough to bring focus to the man's face. Exactly as it should be. This man, Mr. Hawkins, had the look of a kind, gentle person. And Mrs. Hawkins had apparently loved him deeply. Grace studied his face again, wondering if she could detect an element of compassion somewhere in his appearance. She turned back to the woman. "A man took a photograph of me on Ellis Island. I have his address."

"You should go see it, love. I bet it's handsome. I'd be happy to accompany you sometime and inquire."

This woman was very accommodating. "Thank you." She turned back to the picture of Harold Hawkins. "Who took this photograph, if I may ask?"

The woman raised a finger. "A man who works tirelessly for social reform. Maybe you've heard of him. Jacob Riis. He doesn't usually take portraits like this one."

"Mr. Riis is famous?"

"Well, he is certainly well-known."

"Why did he take this one? Is he a friend?"

"Not a friend exactly. Just someone who shares the convictions of the Benevolents. We met him at an event and he admired Harold's service to his country and offered to take the portrait. I haven't seen him since that time."

Later, after Grace retired to her bedroom, she collapsed on the bed, exhausted but pleased. She had a warm bed and a full belly. She was on her way.

With her head on her pillow, she should have dropped into a deep sleep after the tension of waiting at Ellis Island and then meeting all these strangers. But instead of sleep, thoughts pounded her consciousness. She was not sure she could let Reverend Clarke, as nice as he was, plan her prospects for her. The idea of handing over her future again, haunted her until she rose from her bed. She'd seen a newspaper in the parlor. Maybe it was still there.

Wrapping a thin blanket around her shoulders, she crept quietly down the stairs and let herself into the front room. A window faced the street, where the gas lamps still burned, allowing enough light to help her find what she was looking for. Tucking the paper under her arm, she wandered to the window. On the way here, she hadn't taken the time to properly observe her surroundings. She gazed out at the night. People still up, walking about. What were they doing? She leaned in until her nose touched the wavy glass panel. A large presence in a dark coat and hat lumbered by, something like a stick dangling from its arm. Seemed familiar somehow. She squinted her eyes. The man from the trolley.

He turned and stared right at her. She gasped and stepped back. Tugging her blanket tighter, she headed for the hall. A light rapping on the door made her freeze. It came again. If he woke the household, how would she explain herself?

She took a step toward the stairs. If Mrs. Hawkins woke, Grace would tell her she had gotten hungry and gone looking for a bite to eat.

Two quick knuckle thuds resounded louder. She darted to the door and peeked out the side window. It was him, all right. She cracked the door open. "What do you want?"

"Is everything all right, Miss . . . Miss Grace? That's it, right? I saw you on the trolley."

"Everything's fine, Officer."

"I saw you at the window. Are you sure nothing's up?"

"Just getting my bearings. I'm going to bed now."

"Good night, Grace."

"McCaffery's the name. Good night, Officer."

"Lock the door, then. I'll check again on my rounds."

"No need to come back. I am sure you have to be catching some robbers or some such villains, aye?"

He turned away, stopped, and then turned toward her. "Oh, and it's Owen. You can call me Owen."

She sighed, closed the door, and turned the lock. No one had told her that Americans were so . . . nosy. With the newspaper gripped securely in one hand, she took the steps two at a time. Grace tossed the paper to her bed, removed her blanket-robe, and whispered into the dark. "Can't leave my fate to others. I'm looking for employment." Grace turned up the oil lamp on the table by the window.

The stories in the newspaper were confusing. Where was Queens? The Brooklyn Bridge?

And the positions listed. She knew what a seamstress was, but she'd never sewn. A piece maker? A typographer? What strange factory names she saw. She wouldn't know what to do in a factory.

By the time Grace turned out the lamp, she had resigned herself to accepting whatever the reverend drummed up for her after all. Lots of people needed maids, it seemed. And since that's what the reverend had in mind, she might as well get some experience with whatever he found. Later perhaps she could expand her possibilities, but she had to get started somewhere.

She could cook, or at least she imagined she could. The cooks at the workhouse just stirred watered-down buttermilk into gruel and baked bricks of black bread. How hard could that be? Sweeping wasn't hard either. She could do that.

She was determined to. Becoming a maid instead of a workhouse inmate would mean she could leave her old self behind and become something different altogether. Someone much better, much more important.

She slipped beneath the cool bedsheets. As she settled down to sleep, she prayed, desperately hoping God would hear her, for Ma's sake. *God, change me.* The past eight years rotting away in a workhouse would not steal her hope.

She rolled over and thought about Ma again. Grace had gotten away to America like Ma wanted, though at a great cost to Ma since she had to marry a peeler to get Grace out. Feeny might not have been there the day Grace and her mother were evicted, but he was still one of them, and Grace had not an ounce of affection for any policeman.

The next two days were spent getting an acceptable work outfit together for Grace.

"Where did you get your clothes? If you don't mind me asking." Mrs. Hawkins was altering some donated clothing for Grace.

"My mother. The only proper skirt and petticoat I ever had. They were in better shape when I left. Not new, but they suited me fine." Grace flinched when the woman tapped pointed pins against her skin.

"The journey takes a toll. Even so, Grace, those clothes seem a bit old-fashioned to me, like what my Irish granny wore."

Mrs. Hawkins was perhaps a bit past middle age, sixty or thereabouts. Grace didn't see how her clothes could have been that old. "Well, I like the color, even a bit faded."

"Hmm." With pins sticking between her teeth, the woman kept working on the replacement dress that was the very shade of New York's pavement.

Although the reverend had not mentioned it, Grace felt disapproval from people on the street. Obviously Americans didn't like color. There was little of it on anyone's frame.

On Sunday, wearing the rather ordinary gunmetal-colored dress, Grace attended services at First Church.

"Did you have a pastor at home, Grace?" Mrs. Hawkins spoke from underneath her large-brimmed hat.

"I . . . uh . . . There was a father." She had a vague image in her mind of what the local parish priest looked like. She didn't want to admit that the bulk of her religious training had come from workhouse chaplains who read prayers in the dining hall.

She sat on a hard wooden pew bench between Mrs. Hawkins and Annie. First Church was as foreign an experience for Grace as anything so far, and she understood little of what was happening. Candles, choirs, robes, even the prayers and hymns were unlike any she'd ever heard. She bowed her head and tried to follow what the others did and absorb the feeling of the place, if not the meaning.

The reverend's voice rang out strong but still as caring as when he'd spoken directly to her. A kind of peace flowed from the pulpit and reached out to her. She liked it there, a place where no one stared at her, a calm in the midst of the squall of the city.

4

Just before Owen left for work Monday afternoon, his neighbor Otto knocked on his door. "Come, come. You have telephone call."

Otto and his wife had the only telephone in the building. Owen had given the exchange to his mother for family emergencies. He couldn't imagine any other reason she would call.

He was ushered inside and to the phone. He pressed the earpiece to his ear. "Yes, operator. This is Owen McNulty."

The reply came crackled, but it was clearly his mother.

"Mother, what is wrong?"

"Owen. I'm coming for a visit."

"A visit? Why? Is Father all right?"

"Oh, the old coot is fine and dandy. Always off at his club. A bit of indigestion at times, but with all that spicy food he eats, it's no wonder. I tell him all the time—"

"Why are you calling, Mother? I need to get to work."

"A visit, remember? Can't a mother visit her son? Listen, I'll be at the home of my friend, Amelia."

"Mother, Miss Amelia lives near Washington Park. I live in Lower Manhattan."

"For heaven's sake, Owen. They have trains, elevated ones.

I will come calling at your police station tomorrow at three o'clock. Mulberry Street, correct?"

"Mother," he shouted, making Otto jump back. "I go on the beat at four, and sometimes I pull a double shift."

"Very well. Make it two o'clock before you are on duty, then. We'll have tea or whatever it is one does down there. Now don't argue. I must speak to you."

"Mother, there *is* something wrong. What is it?"

"Nonsense. Good-bye, Owen."

He lowered the earpiece and stared blindly into space. He just knew his mother was coming to find fault and to urge him to move back to the family home. And she said she was coming to the station. He couldn't have that. He'd have to pay an early visit to Miss Amelia's house and cut Mother off before she got on the el.

As Grace expected, Mrs. Hawkins told her she would be given various domestic jobs so Mrs. Hawkins could observe and correct her housekeeping skills. When Grace was young and in school, she knew a neighbor lad who kept a toad in a glass jar. She was like that toad now, trapped and observed on all sides.

Monday, while finishing the dishes, she didn't know how much more she could take. With each plate she scrubbed, she renewed her will to learn and learn well. She needed money to bring Ma over. And then money for clothes, colorful clothes. Then she would be able to hold her head high when she walked the streets of Manhattan, despite the stares from the Americans, and not care if anyone said she was stupid and insignificant. One day.

"Aren't you finished yet, lass?"

Grace lifted her soapy hands from the washbasin and turned. Mrs. Hawkins's scowl made her look like a hawk somehow. That beak-like nose. Grace truly did not want to disappoint the woman, but frustration built inside her and threatened to boil over.

"I am finished, ma'am." She lifted the basin to take the wash water to the curb beside the back gate.

"Careful. Mind the floor, love."

Grace pursed her lips. If they didn't like her at this place, she didn't know where she would turn.

As she watched the water dribble down to the sewer, her gut tightened and tears choked her until she doubled over, tossing the metal basin on the paved sidewalk. The resulting crashing sound rattled in her ears.

"Are you all right? I was making my rounds and saw you here."

She covered her face with her apron and tried to regain her composure. Pulling the cloth slowly away, she eyed polished black wing tips and realized the man was waiting for an answer.

A firm hand helped her stand. She lifted her head to find Officer McNulty holding on to her arm. There was something in his eyes that for a moment reminded her of Reverend Clarke's caring gaze.

But, nay. This was a lawman. That just couldn't be.

Grace wiggled away. "I am quite fine." She scurried up the back steps, leaving the washbasin behind. She pushed past a startled Mrs. Hawkins. When she reached the stairs, she heard his voice.

"Here's your basin, Mrs. Hawkins."

"Thank you. Poor girl."

"There's something amiss with that one."

"There's always something amiss with immigrant girls, Officer McNulty. I'll tend to her. She'll be just fine."

Grace locked herself in the washroom and leaned against the wall, desperately trying to relax her breathing. Aye, she'd been foolish. To think she could survive all the way across the ocean and so far from her anchor, Ma. She put a hand over her eyes. Reverend Clarke, Mrs. Hawkins, that policeman. Could she trust any of them? She wasn't sure. She needed to hold on to something, someone. She wrapped her arms around herself.

Hold on. Breathe. You can do this.

As soon as she could, Grace retreated to her bedroom in hopes of getting a bit of time alone. But Mrs. Hawkins soon came to check on her.

"I'm fine. I'm sorry I caused a commotion." Grace hoped that would be the end of it.

"A commotion?" The woman clicked her tongue. "Not at all, love. But I sense an uneasiness around the police officer. You're not afraid of him, are you? Because there is no need to be."

Grace closed her eyes a moment, contemplating how she might explain herself.

Mrs. Hawkins grabbed her hands. "There, there, child. Like my Harold used to say, 'A trouble shared is a trouble halved.'"

Grace tilted her head to her shoulder, trying to figure the woman out. "Did your husband really say that, Mrs. Hawkins?"

"Indeed. He said many a wise thing. Funny, how once a loved one passes on, you remember things he used to say."

Grace remembered much worse things her father used to say to her. "You miss him?"

"Terribly." She smiled and patted Grace's hands, then

released them. "But I have you and Annie now and soon more boarders as well. I'm not lonely."

Grace felt a smile coming to her own face. "I'm glad for that."

"Well, now, I do have a bit of news for you. The reverend believes he has a family wanting to employ you."

"Me? Why? When?" Grace rose and began to pace.

"My, you're a worrier." Mrs. Hawkins rose as well and headed for the door. "This is fine news. Maids make a fair wage and some even receive room and board for free with the family. But for now you'll stay right here with us and travel uptown to work. The reverend will have news about your new job day after tomorrow. He'll give us the details then."

"I just want to make enough money for my mother to come to America."

"That's what every Irish lass who comes to America does, love. Send for someone in the family or else mail money home. You're no different."

Tuesday morning, standing in the hall bath he shared with the other tenants on his floor, Owen splashed cold water on his stubbly face to refresh himself. He was awake earlier than usual, and the late-morning sun coming through the bathroom window stung his eyes. He reached for the pocket watch he'd carelessly left on the edge of the tub last night. A miracle none of the others living on the floor had lifted it. This watch symbolized his dedication to police work. Thank the good Lord it was still there.

He listened for movement outside the door. No one was waiting for the washroom. He popped open the silver cover on his watch. Eleven thirty. He pinched his eyes shut. His mother would be on her way to Miss Amelia's. He had to hurry.

Dressing in his uniform because he'd have no time to change before his shift, Owen wondered what his mother would think of it. She'd never seen him so decorously attired with metal buttons from neck to knees. He had no time to shave, though, and she'd certainly offer comment on that. But better to head her off than to deal with her disapproval if she set foot in the station.

On the el he soon found himself among upper-class ladies on a mission to tour the department stores. They clustered together like hens as they discussed Siegel-Cooper & Company Dry Goods Store, a "Big Store" as the papers called it, and at least three times the size of his father's own business, which still was quite prosperous. The enormous white building, spread over an entire city block with pillars stretching several stories high, stood as a monument to the excesses of the rich in Owen's opinion.

"I simply cannot wait," one of the women proclaimed, swinging her mink stole over one shoulder.

"I know," her friend said. "We must certainly meet at the fountain!" They erupted into laughter.

Owen turned to gaze out the windows on the opposite side. The phrase "meet me at the fountain" had been propaganda perpetrated by company men to lure customers to the oversize fountain in the store's lobby. Colored electric lights frolicked between sprays of water, causing New Yorkers to stutter in amazement. Folks said the fountain's statue was a copy of the one from the Chicago's World Fair. Owen had seen it last year when he allowed an acquaintance to set up a date with a young lady who was promised to be a perfect match for him. Owen had no problem with monuments, and this one was stunning and laden with patriotic symbolism. Still he had found the whole experience—the fancy lady, the orchestra, the oysters, the gourmet dish called *croûtes aux champignons*—too close to the life of privilege he'd been born into.

As the train slowed, Owen could see the elaborate second-story windows. The keyed-up chatter of the women escalated. He was glad when they exited with all their furs, feathers, and jewels. He knew the disparity that existed in the city better than most. Born into high society, he now patrolled in some of the dirtiest and most desperate places on earth. He wondered if any of the shoppers had read Jacob Riis's *How the Other Half Lives* and if they'd be so eager to spend their husbands' income or their ancestors' savings on baubles and bric-a-brac if they had. Maybe they would. Some things never changed.

"Good day, ladies." He tipped his hat. Everyone, rich or poor, enlightened or a fool, was a child of God and no more or less worthy of his grace than another, according to his granny.

"Officer." They erupted in giggles. But Owen knew that as soon as the shiny, black heels of their shoes hit the polished marble floor of the department store, they'd forget all about him. And that was what was so intriguing about Grace McCaffery— her genuine smile and her ragged, red petticoat. She knew how the other half lived, and she was pulling herself out of poverty. Like most of the immigrant population he served, however, she saw him as an outsider, someone who didn't belong, like that wild ocean porpoise living in a tank inside the aquarium.

When Owen arrived at his destination, Miss Amelia's butler met him at the double leaded-glass doors. Owen extended his hand. "Ansel, good to see you."

"Sir?"

"Don't you know me? It's Owen."

41

Ansel narrowed his eyes. "The master Owen I knew didn't wear brass buttons and a badge."

It had been a while since Owen had even stepped foot uptown, let alone visited his mother's friend. "Kathleen's son. I'm a policeman now."

The man's eyes showed recognition even though he did not change his posture. "I see. Do you have official business here?"

Servants. One thing Owen didn't like was how unemotional, almost inhuman, they presented themselves. "I believe my mother is visiting today, and I planned to meet her here."

"Very well." With stick-straight posture, the man led Owen down a marble hall and paused in front of two slightly parted pocket doors.

Miss Amelia was in the parlor entertaining, and Ansel obviously thought Owen was intruding. The servant knocked sharply, waited just a moment, and then pulled the doors open a few inches. He cleared his throat. "Owen McNulty—" He grunted. "Mr.—" He paused again and shot Owen a puzzled look. "That is, *Officer* McNulty says he is meeting his mother here."

A whoop resounded from the room, and one door retreated into the wall. "Why, Owen, darling! Look at you. So handsome." Miss Amelia, rouged cheeks and a flower bouncing on top of her faded blonde bun, embraced him. She was so unlike his mother.

"Hello, Miss Amelia. Lovely to see you."

"Oh, honey. It's been too long. Come in; come in."

The butler retreated, and Owen stepped into the room of velvet-covered furniture. A delicate young girl rose from a seat near the bay window. He smiled at her. "Hello."

Miss Amelia grabbed his arm. "Oh, Owen McNulty, may I present my niece Tabitha Pierpont. She's visiting from Chicago."

"A pleasure to meet you." He held her tiny fingers in his much larger hand for a moment, as was proper etiquette. The girl blushed, her ivory skin turning frostbitten pink.

He turned to the other end of the room, where his mother sat, hands folded tight against leg-of-mutton sleeves. "I did not expect you here, Owen."

"Mother." He crossed the room and pecked her cheek.

She groaned as his beard brushed her face. "You've spoiled the surprise."

"Oh?"

"I hoped to properly introduce you to Miss Pierpont at a charity event Amelia is holding."

"I told you I'm on the night shift, Mother."

"Not tonight. On Thursday. That's why I planned to meet you at the station. To explain to your captain why you need to be released from duty that night."

What a disaster that would have been. "I'll check the schedule, but I do believe I have the night off."

"Splendid." She took a step back and regarded him. "What on earth are you wearing, Son?"

Owen spent the next few minutes explaining his job as best he could to three gentlewomen, including his mother.

Tabitha Pierpont pursed her lips as though she wanted to ask questions but thought better of it. And how could she, anyway? Owen's mother and her friend jabbered so much a candle didn't have a chance of staying lit in the room.

Miss Amelia pointed at Owen's side. "Just what does one do with a nightstick? I've heard rogue policemen slug pickpockets with those, but I'm sure such force is not necessary. What do you use it for, Owen?"

He'd tried his best to steer the conversation away from the

cruel realities of his job. He normally worked the night beat, and while it was daylight for the first few hours of his usual shift, most of the time he worked in the dark, when there were no puppies to rescue from fire escapes and very few respectable old ladies to help across the street.

His mother glared down her narrow nose at him. "Hmm? Answer the lady, Owen."

"I . . . uh . . . I . . . direct traffic with it. Folks have trouble seeing just my arm at night, so the nightstick—that's why they call it that—helps extend my reach." It wasn't too much of an exaggeration. The device did allow him to probe into murky corners where he was reluctant to stick his hand. And he'd motioned to a cart driver once with the thing.

"I see." Miss Amelia waved her ever-present paper fan in front of her face. "But have you ever—?"

"Tea?"

He glanced up to find Miss Pierpont already pouring him a cup. "Yes. Thank you."

Her interruption thankfully ended the interrogation. This girl was both lovely and smart. He noticed her black lashes fluttering on her white cheekbones as she looked down. When she spoke, her words were light, proper, befitting her. "Are you an outdoorsman, Officer McNulty?"

He chuckled. "You mean like Governor Roosevelt?"

"Well, yes."

Finally the old ladies were silenced.

"I'm afraid I rarely get beyond the sidewalks of New York anymore, Miss Pierpont."

She placed a butter cookie on his saucer and handed it to him. "The sidewalks of New York—not quite as quaint as the song implies, I'm sure."

"No, not really."

"Well, you simply must come to The Park on the Palisades in the spring. My brother has part interest in the establishment. He could take us there . . . if you're interested, that is. I have several friends you would enjoy meeting."

"How kind of you." He pulled the pocket watch out. "I'm afraid I have to go." He slurped the tea and then popped the cookie into his mouth. "I have to be at the station soon."

"Oh, pity." Miss Amelia snapped her fan shut. "A man like you does not have to work, you know."

He noticed his mother staring at the watch and quickly put it away. Their eyes met. His father didn't approve of his job. And his mother had not been in favor of his career choice either. "Lovely to have met you, Miss Pierpont." He winked at his mother when he bowed his head to kiss the young woman's hand.

"Thursday at seven sharp," his mother said. "Formal attire. I'll send your suit to your . . . apartment."

"Lovely. Thank you, Mother."

She took hold of his arm and whispered in his ear. "You must be there, Owen. It's a police benefit, and the O'Tooles will be there."

He gritted his teeth and then told her again he would come, knowing that neither Mother nor her friends would be there if it weren't foremost a social gala at which to be seen.

Miss Amelia patted her hands together. "Oh, I cannot wait."

On his way back to the station, the disparity between the society he was born into and those he sought to serve seemed as far apart as New York and the Philippine Islands he'd read about in the papers. It was as though he had been on a long voyage and now was headed home, when he had in fact not even left

Manhattan. No matter that the two worlds were close together geographically. He could not live in them both.

The train was not crowded because the working folks had not yet heard the factory whistle blow and the female shoppers were still engaged. Even so, a man in a brown tweed overcoat took the seat next to him.

"Good day, sir." Owen tipped his hat.

"Oh, it is that. Greetings."

As the Sixth Avenue el swung southward, Owen checked his watch.

"Nice-looking timepiece," the man said.

Owen glanced at the man and then quickly tucked the watch away.

"Mind if I see it?"

Reluctantly Owen handed it to the fellow.

"These are given to families of police officers killed in the line of duty." He raised his eyes, seeming to examine Owen's uniform. "How did you get it, if I may ask?"

"Someone gave it to me." Owen retrieved it from the man's hand. He should not have let a stranger touch it. He told himself to be more careful next time, not to check the hour in public, and never again to leave the watch in the bathroom.

"I'm sorry," the man said.

"For what?" Owen tried to study the architecture outside the train window.

"Well, you must have lost someone important in your life, and I'm sorry for that."

"You are very kind." Owen stood, even though his stop was blocks away. He still had time to make the walk, and it would be better than entertaining questions.

As soon as he descended the platform to the sidewalk below,

he knew he had made a mistake. Today Owen was heading for the main police station on Mulberry. He was only a few blocks away, but he was almost to Union Square. For two years he had avoided the very spot in which he now stood—Dead Man's Curve. The Lincoln statue seemed to gaze down at him, the two of them having witnessed the same awful event that day. The image of the streetcar barreling toward Broadway out of control, the little russet-haired immigrant girl, and the man wearing a blue wool policeman's coat running full speed toward impending doom. At the time the name Dan O'Toole meant nothing to Owen, but that day a stranger and his family forged the turning point of Owen's life.

A wave of sadness rose up from his belly. He tapped his fingers on the front of his own coat in an effort to remind himself. He was now a public servant. He was making a difference. He was doing what Dan no longer could.

Owen jogged across the street away from the statue, heading south. If only he hadn't been so slow to react that afternoon. If he had been a different person then, like he wanted to believe he was now, he might have been able to change fate. If Officer O'Toole's mother had known who he was—a member of the other half, the rich elite, the snobs—she never would have given him that watch.

Beads of sweat formed on his brow in the chilly air. The aroma of sausage and salty fish drifted to him from open windows and merchant carts.

Of course he would not court Tabitha Pierpont. *People like her are alien down here.* If his mother wanted to see him after Thursday's charity event, she would have to come to his apartment, and that had about as much chance of happening as the Queen of England taking a holiday in Battery Park.

5

Late Tuesday afternoon, Grace received her first task outside the house.

"Grace, love, I'm completely out of raisins." Mrs. Hawkins held the heel of her hand to her forehead as she stared at the batter she'd been mixing. "I cannot have bread pudding without raisins. Oh, and I've already sent Annie off with the laundry. Be a dear and scramble out to get some, would you? Just two blocks that direction." She pointed out the window. "I'd go myself, but I'm up to my elbows with flour and I have to get tonight's bread in the oven. Look in the second biscuit tin on the top shelf. There is a quarter in there you can use to pay for them."

"Oh . . . I suppose I could." Grace found the money, collected her cloak and a shopping basket, and hurried outside, telling herself she had to become accustomed to the city sometime. She willed herself to remember her mother's exhortation: *You are able.*

But once she set foot on the sidewalk, she lost her bearings. She glanced upward at the tops of the buildings. Two blocks . . . up or back? It could not be far. She chose not to go back and ask again lest her hostess think her inept. She could figure it out. She could.

At a crossroads she paused. Across the street stood several

vendors. That was probably the place. She hurried over and examined their offerings but did not find what she needed. "Raisins?" she asked one after the other.

"Not here."

"Sorry."

"Don't remember the last time I saw someone selling dried fruit from a cart on this street, miss."

She sank down onto the curb between an apple cart and a peanut roaster, barely noticing a cold wind swirling at her feet.

She heard a familiar voice.

"That *is* you, Grace. I spotted you wandering a block over and thought I'd better make sure. Are you lost?"

She looked up, shielding her eyes from a ray of sun that found its way between the two tall buildings across the street. Him again.

"I can help you." He extended a gloved hand.

"Thank you, Officer, but I can find my own way." *You are smart.* She stood and adjusted her shopping basket on her left arm.

"It's my job, you know. I don't mind at all."

Mrs. Hawkins's batter must be turning to soup by now. She needed to hurry. "I'm to buy raisins for bread pudding, only I can't find any."

"Oh, let me show you."

She reluctantly took his arm as he led her two blocks south. They stopped in front of a glass storefront painted with bright-blue letters: O'Malley's Market.

"They've got them in there, I bet. Go see. I'll wait out here. This is my area to patrol today. If I go in there, the owner will think something's wrong." He kept nodding and smiling, pushing her into the store with an insisting expression.

When she stepped across the threshold, the scent of cinnamon met her. She inhaled deeply.

"Help you, miss?" a man in a white apron asked.

"I'd like a quarter pound of raisins, please."

"Certainly." He began filling a paper bag from a barrel.

"I had no idea this place was here."

"Twenty-five years now." He smiled and handed her the bag. "I'm guessing you are a newcomer."

"I am. I . . . uh . . . have not been out much."

"Well, I do hope you'll come back."

She had so much to learn.

When she saw Owen McNulty waiting for her, she tried to be polite. "Thank you. I'll be on my way now."

"I will walk you back."

"Please, Officer. 'Tis not far. You go about your work."

He tipped his hat to two middle-aged women who passed by. They greeted him by name and giggled when he returned their hellos. Grace wasn't sure, but she thought they made light of him, whispering something about a wealthy boy. He let out a breath, impatient sounding, she thought.

He turned back to her. "I'm going your way anyhow."

She didn't want to encourage him. Not after Ma . . . "I'd rather go alone, if you don't mind—learn my way around here."

He bowed as though she were a princess. "Until we meet again, Grace McCaffery."

She did not want to like this man and hurried away before he could charm her any more.

She returned by the back door. "Sorry it took me so long."

Mrs. Hawkins hurried to her side and took the basket. "Oh, my. Did you get lost, love?"

"A wee bit."

"I am so sorry. I should have waited for Annie."

"No, no." Grace hung up her cloak and warmed her hands by the stove. "I found them all right."

"Indeed. Excellent! Did you ask directions? Always someone ready to help, love, if you ask."

"I did."

Mrs. Hawkins took Grace's shoulders and steered her toward the hall. "Look on the table, love. A letter just arrived for you. Reverend Clarke has informed the post office of your current residence. Go on."

Grace's heart leaped. *Ma!* She took the treasured letter into the parlor.

Dearest One,

I can scarcely believe this letter will find you in America. It warms my heart to know that you will be well fed, clothed, and your soul nourished in church. S. P. assures me the place he sent you to will take care of you. The only hope I have left for you that has not been fulfilled is that you will find a fine young man to marry.

I do hope you are still drawing. Ever since you were a wee lass, you liked to make pictures. Do send me something.

Work hard. I will continue to pray for you and love you with all my heart.

I also am well fed and attend church regularly. So do not be concerned. There is nothing I need besides word from you occasionally.

Love,
Mother

Her mother had to come to America. She just had to.

Grace refolded the letter, took it upstairs, and slipped it into the trunk at the end of her bed. She stared at the old piece of luggage for a moment. With its frayed leather strapping and scuffed exterior, the trunk might have crossed the ocean several times. Grace was not sure she could make that trip again to get her mother away from Sean Patrick Feeny, the man Ma was unfortunately married to. The peeler. She had to get Ma over. Without her mother, Grace was unsure she could make it.

6

Owen hoped Grace McCaffery had not heard the snide remark the women on the street made about him. The last thing he wanted was for new arrivals to get the sense that he was not who he appeared to be. He might have been born rich, but now he was a public servant, someone folks could count on. Many of the shopkeepers and upstanding citizens in Lower Manhattan did not trust the police—and with good reason—but Owen was working hard to earn a good reputation on his beat.

He swung his nightstick as he walked down a side alley and chuckled to himself. There might be another reason he hoped Grace didn't overhear. That petite redhead had caught his eye. He had no time for romance with the kind of schedule he kept, but he enjoyed pondering the idea nonetheless.

His mother would faint if she knew what her son was thinking.

Mother. If only he could separate the two sides of his life, build a dam between them. He'd tried and so far had not done a bad job of it. His mother usually had no inclination to come south of Gramercy Park. She'd never been down to Miss Amelia's place before today, so far as he knew. He would make sure she stayed away from his ward. Not only would she find the area repulsive, she'd blow his standing with the department, to say nothing of the folks on his beat. Once they saw the woman in fur and pearls, strutting the way only the rich do and snubbing her nose at everyone she deemed improperly attired, no one would take him seriously.

A noise at the end of the alley raised his senses. Rats? Maybe. But when he saw a figure move in the shadows, he knew it was human. "Who's there?"

"Whaaat?" A hobo emerged, clutching a glass bottle.

"Move along, fella."

The man tottered off and Owen continued on, kicking blackened leaves from his boots. He had no big job in the department, no cases to follow. All he did was patrol and chase away vagrants. Maybe someday, if folks would just trust him, he'd be able to do something bigger.

As they finished supper preparations, Mrs. Hawkins told Grace that she was invited to a lecture presentation that very evening.

"I don't understand."

"Jacob Riis, love. I thought you'd be delighted."

"The man who took your husband's photograph?"

"That's right. He's giving a lecture and presenting some of his photographs. When I heard about it, I thought you might like to go since you expressed an interest in that photograph. And Mrs. Reilly will be attending as well. You'd like to see her again, wouldn't you, love?"

"I would. I enjoy sketching, and photographs interest me greatly."

"Right after supper, then."

Later, as Grace tied her hat ribbons into a large, looping bow and followed Mrs. Hawkins to the carriage, she realized that even though she was less than enthusiastic about the lecture topic, the plight of immigrants—didn't she know what it was like to be one?—she was eager to see the photographs, examine the light and shadows, see how he positioned his subjects and what she could read in their eyes.

The carriage's sudden jolt as it halted to avoid hitting people in the street caused her to swallow hard just as a disheartening thought struck her. As much as *she* wanted to capture images and light and shadows, she wasn't very good at drawing a person's likeness.

You are smart. You are able.

She squeezed her eyes tight. The pencil sketch of Ma pinned to the wall in her room had brought Grace comfort, but Grace had not captured what she'd hoped to see. A camera could do that. Cameras froze a moment and forever captured the truth without bias. Photography was different from paintings, where the artist interpreted what he saw for others.

As soon as the notion of taking photographs herself occurred to her, she heard the long-ago voice of her father in her head. *"Weak. That's what you are. Pitiful. You're just lucky you've got a kind father, lass. There's not another would put up with the likes of ya. You or your mother. Yous would not survive without me, and don't you forget it."*

Weak. Pitiful.

She'd carried those messages with her to the workhouse, where no one retained a smidgen of self-respect. Grace could still feel her mother's hands cradling her youthful head as her father hurled hatred. "Shh, child." And then Ma would say those affirming words to her, words so smooth and even-flowing. Words that most times could not battle past her father's harsh, steely assessment of his daughter.

Grace leaned into the window of the carriage and gazed toward the tops of the skyscrapers. This was America. There need be no demise of aspirations any longer. Perhaps photography would suit her. It was worth finding out.

They entered an ordinary clapboard-sided building and made their way to some folding chairs. Mrs. Reilly was already there.

"Good evening, Edwina," Mrs. Hawkins said as she sat, causing the chair to squeak under her weight.

"Agnes, Grace. Lovely to see you."

Mrs. Hawkins motioned for Grace to take the empty chair between them. In front, a makeshift platform had been erected for the speaker, just a series of crates nailed together so the audience would be able to see Mr. Riis with ease. Grace glanced at the program bill they had been handed when they came in. *Mr. Jacob Riis* was boldly inscribed at the top, along with the description "Author of *How the Other Half Lives*."

Mrs. Reilly leaned over to whisper. "He's a very intelligent man, Grace."

"Who is the other half? Half of what?"

"There's the rich half and the poor half. You know." The woman turned her head away.

Grace thought surely there were more divisions in American society than that. She did not consider herself poor, not truly. She'd been poor. She'd gone to bed with gnawing hunger in her stomach. She'd lacked fresh water and combs for her hair. Now she had those things. She was . . . well . . . dependent. Who would write a book on the dependent masses? Grace started to ask another question, but the woman hushed her as a man in a suit came to the podium.

"Ladies and gentlemen, on behalf of the Children's Aid Society, I welcome you to tonight's lecture." He droned on about financial donations and the progress his charity was making until Grace had to cover her yawns with her palm.

Finally the man of the hour gingerly picked his way along the crate slats and turned to address the crowd. When he spoke about tenement houses, Grace knew that those were the places she had been fortunate enough to avoid. The most misfortunate of the lowly lived there.

Mr. Riis pulled on his coat lapels. "The poorest immigrant comes here with the purpose and ambition to better himself and, given half a chance, might be reasonably expected to make the most of it."

There! She'd heard it from someone who had been an immigrant and made something of himself. There was hope for her now, she supposed.

He went on. "Yet high rents for squalid living conditions and low wages depress the immigrant and squash his resolve."

Oh, so it wasn't so. Grace was confused, tired, and hearing her father's voice in her head again as Mr. Riis elucidated eloquently about the tenements and the immigrants' plight. "And these are the dungeons where crime springs forth, though it need not be. This, my friends, is where the line lies—that place that marks below it the dwelling of the 'other half.' My photographs will illustrate my contentions."

The words caught Grace's attention. She wondered if this man's photography was anything like Mr. Sherman's on Ellis Island.

An assistant dimmed the lights and turned on a tin box machine to project what he called lantern slides on the wall. Gigantic images. The crowd gasped. She was not the only one amazed. What a wondrous invention.

Grace strained her neck to see around heads. Scene after scene of dingy buildings and glum-faced families living in cramped quarters sprang into view in black and white. Instead of the creative compositions she'd expected, these images captured sullen faces and filth. Perhaps if the photographs were in color . . . but no, all of New York was mostly gray, as she had observed. Why he wished to capture faces so like the ones Grace had lived with in Ireland, she could not imagine. Grace longed for beauty. That spark of hope. That's what someone should capture. Mr. Riis had done that with Harold Hawkins's portrait. He had not accomplished it with these lantern slides.

She continued to stare at the images on the wall. As sad as it appeared, Grace couldn't help but feel that those children were more fortunate than many in Ireland. At least the children in Mr. Riis's photographs lived with their parents. In Ireland's workhouses the children lived in the attic, separated from parents they rarely got so much as a glimpse of, if indeed they weren't cared for in some far-off orphanage. She turned away, not able to summon a reaction as those around her did, bellowing with shock and indignation.

She glanced to her left. Mrs. Reilly sat stick straight, lips tight. She worked for a charity and likely felt that the indignation was appropriate, but she showed no emotion. On her right Mrs. Hawkins dabbed at damp eyes with a handkerchief. "Pity," she said to Grace. She reached over and patted her hand. "So happy we could save you from that."

Grace pulled her chin down to her chest, fighting her own

tears. She could not comprehend why anyone would want to save her. And there were so many immigrants. No one could save them all. But what struck her most in that moment was that these people even cared to try.

After the lecture, when cookies and punch were served, Mrs. Hawkins urged her toward the door. "We have some ironing to do before bed, and I have seen enough suffering for tonight, love."

In the carriage Grace pondered further. "How do you suppose he learned the trade?"

"Here and there at this newspaper and that, love. He worked with Governor Theodore Roosevelt back when the man was president of the police commission. If it weren't for Mr. Riis's photographs, the tenement situation would be worse than it is."

"Why is that?"

"He brought knowledge of it to people and then reform. We've a long way to go, but with people helping, change can happen."

"Is he why you and the Benevolents opened Hawkins House?"

"In part I suppose he was, love."

The influence an image could stir up enthralled Grace. She was unsure if she could afford photography equipment and doubted she could manage to use it anyway. But she could purchase pencils and paper. The possibilities were endless. *You are smart. You are important. You are able.*

The next morning after Annie had gone off to do the mending, Mrs. Hawkins reached for Grace's hand as the two of them sat at the breakfast table. "I see how interested you are in photography, love. Why don't we look up that man who took your picture on Ellis Island? Still have that card?"

"I do."

"Good. Go and get it. I'll go next door to telephone him, and if he's available, we'll go see him. I'm curious myself about the photographs he takes of immigrants. I wonder if they are anything like Mr. Riis's."

Grace honestly could not remember many of the faces of her fellow immigrants on the ship, but the poor people Mr. Riis had photographed had probably walked down the same staircase at Ellis Island that she had when they entered the country.

Mrs. Hawkins returned in short order. "He is available, love. Let's go now."

"Oh, I . . ." Just as soon as Grace got the courage to do something, it seemed to wane.

Mrs. Hawkins placed a hand on Grace's shoulder. "It is all right, love. Like my Harold used to say, 'Carpe diem.'"

Grace shook her head.

"It's Latin, love. It translates roughly: pluck the day when it is ripe. You understand. Seize this opportunity. You are interested in photography. You told me so, and it's clear from your admiration of my Harold's portrait. So here is your opportunity to learn more and to see your own photograph." She clapped her hands together. "Now, isn't this lovely."

"Thank you, Mrs. Hawkins." How could she refuse when this woman encouraged her so? And she certainly wouldn't want to deny the woman this memory of her husband. Grace had never heard a man spoken of so highly—and long after he was gone.

Right before Grace and her landlady were to depart to see Mr. Sherman, the mailman came to the door, whistling as always. Annie appeared, unforeseen like a ghost, and opened the door before he could place the letters in the mail slot. "Here's one for you, Grace." Annie held it out, but Grace hesitated, stunned.

"Another one?"

Annie bobbed her head. "Sometimes the mail gets backed up and you get letters on the same day that were mailed a week or two apart."

"But so soon?" Grace found this strange.

"Perhaps your mother wrote to you while you were still on the ship."

"I had not thought of that. I'm sure that explains it."

Mrs. Hawkins motioned to her housekeeper. "Leave it on the table, please, love. We've got to be going."

Annie placed the letter on the tray they kept on the hall table. "To see the Ellis Island photographer?"

Mrs. Hawkins put on her gloves. "That's right, but we're just going a few train stops north. He is not working today and couldn't see us if he was. The immigration station is remarkably busy these days."

"I'll take it with me." Grace snatched the letter. She could not wonder all day what was inside.

Aboard the el, she tore it open.

Dear Grace,

We are so blessed with a good crop of potatoes this year, thanks be to God. So all is well here. You and I had a difficult time once, but it is all past. Isn't that so, darling?

Tears sprang to Grace's eyes. While Grace was treated well and enjoyed enough to eat in America, her mother was still in the clutches of that man in damp, dismal Ireland.

"Is everything all right, love?"

Grace sniffed. "Aye. As well as can be expected."

"There, there. God has a plan." The woman patted Grace's shoulder.

God would not have planned this. Grace read on.

Do tell me all about your new home, Grace. Is the mistress there nice? Have you found work yet? Please write, even if you do not hear from me for a time. I need to hear from you and know that you are well.

Grace folded the letter and tucked it away. She would answer before bedtime that very night. She would let her mother know that help was on the way.

They exited at Christopher Street. When they approached a church, Grace paused. "Why are we here?"

"He's going to meet us at his church. He lives with his mother and several other boarders, love. He thought we could talk better here."

"But I thought I would be observing."

"To do that truly, we'd have to go over to Ellis Island. He doesn't have room for photography elsewhere. And you know what it is like there, love, all those crowds."

Grace frowned. She did not wish for mere conversation.

"Don't fret, love. He'll have his camera and his photographs. He's being quite generous to take the time."

They mounted the steps to St. John's. They stepped inside, their movements echoing in the cavernous building. Grace gazed at the stained-glass windows over the altar. She didn't hear the man approach until he spoke her name.

"Miss McCaffery, a pleasure to see you."

She turned to find the man with the receding hairline and a small bow tie that she vaguely recognized from her arrival on Ellis Island. "Thank you for agreeing to see me, Mr. Sherman."

"I'm most pleased to." He turned to greet Mrs. Hawkins.

The woman held his hand in both of hers. "You are looking fine, Gus. How is Stella?"

Grace stared at her landlady. Mrs. Hawkins obviously knew Mr. Sherman well. Of course Mrs. Hawkins was the reason he was being so generous. Not for Grace alone.

"My mother is fit," Mr. Sherman answered. "A bit of the rheumatism but otherwise sound."

"Glad to hear it." Mrs. Hawkins turned back to Grace. "I've been acquainted with Mr. Sherman's mother since before my husband passed away, Grace."

Grace narrowed her eyes. "Truly."

"There are some connections, very old friends, who will stick beside you through life's journeys, no matter if you see them often or not. The Benevolents, you know."

"Oh, I see."

Mr. Sherman rubbed his hands together. "Well, if you will come this way, I'll show you my camera. Normally I don't have it here, as cumbersome as it is to cart around, but I needed to do some repairs."

They followed him to a side vestibule where a camera stood on a tripod. The cloth the photographer blanketed himself in while operating the camera was pulled back, revealing the mechanical-looking box with a lens. She took a step toward it but stopped when Mr. Sherman hurried to stand in front of it.

"Please wait over there." He pointed to one corner. "The minister will be here shortly. I'm to take his photograph and you can watch." He smiled.

From another door in the room, a man entered wearing a black suit with large buttons and no collar other than a white clerical one with a protruding tongue, distinguishable from the Roman collar the Irish priests wore, a detail Grace remembered. It was the little things she noticed about people, the facets a photograph could capture long after memories fade.

The man dipped his chin toward them and then sat on a chair. Mrs. Hawkins grinned and nodded at Grace.

Mr. Sherman adjusted the shade on an electric light hanging from the ceiling. Someone must have lowered it earlier so that he'd have better light. Mr. Sherman held a finger toward the bridge of his subject's nose and drew his hand back toward the lens. When he seemed satisfied, he drew the camera's fabric over his head.

Grace stared at her shoes. This taught her nothing. She'd seen photographers take photographs before, even Mr. Sherman. She wanted to try it herself. The exact moment the shutter closed, it was done—an indelible moment solidified for all time. The photographer had to pick the precise moment to capture the expression, the light in the eyes, the meaning behind the face. That was what she wanted to learn.

When the session was finished, the minister retreated through the back door.

Grace stood. "May I have a closer look at your camera?"

Mr. Sherman froze as though she'd asked him for his soul. After a moment his expression warmed. "Of course." He wiggled his fingers at her.

She peered through the finder, amazed, but jumped back quickly when the man's shrill voice told her she'd looked long enough.

"You will allow that a camera is a very expensive piece of equipment, Miss McCaffery. I'm afraid I'm a bit protective of it."

"Of course you are, Gus." Mrs. Hawkins took Grace's arm and pulled her a step back.

"How expensive?" Grace asked.

Mr. Sherman raised a brow.

"I mean, could I perhaps find some old equipment to purchase at a secondhand shop and get started myself?"

"Young lady, do you know how much pigment-bearing colloid to apply to the photographic paper? Have you heard of the gum process? Do you know how to use a print roller?"

"Well, no, but—"

"I do have something to show you," he interrupted. "Shall we return to the chapel and have a seat?"

Reluctantly she obeyed his outstretched arm and headed back toward the sanctuary.

"Up here, please." He led them to the front pew, where a leather folder lay. "Please, ladies, sit."

They perched on the pew as he stood before them, untying the folder. "I thought you'd like to see the photograph I took of you the day you arrived."

He handed the photograph to her. Peering into the eyes of the girl before her, Grace felt as though she stared at a stranger. There was her usual unmanageable hair, her rounded chin, the subtle print of the dress Ma had given her. But somehow it just didn't look like her. This lass was terrified. She stuttered. "I look . . . I . . . I . . . Is that really me?"

Both Mr. Sherman and Mrs. Hawkins laughed. Mrs. Hawkins took the photograph from Grace. "It most certainly is. Shall we purchase this from Mr. Sherman, love?"

The man waved his fingers in a manner that was beginning to irritate Grace. "Oh no, ma'am. You may have it with my compliments. Look here."

He handed her several other photographs he'd taken of immigrants. A thickly bearded Russian Jew who, like Grace, stared off into the air. A side-facing image of a Hindu boy that featured his long locks and ceremonial headpiece. Lapland immigrant children dressed in odd hats with tasseled belts tied around the waists of their dresses. A gypsy woman in a headscarf and multiple beaded necklaces. If only the native colors of the clothing hadn't been grayed out.

Mrs. Hawkins put a gloved hand to her throat. "I've never seen immigrants in such clothing, Gus."

"That's why I photograph them on Ellis Island. As soon as they get to Battery Park, they shed their native trappings for more contemporary American clothing. Everyone wants to fit in and not appear foreign. But I think the costumes of their homelands are quite fascinating."

Grace saw more than that. Despite the lack of color, he had captured something vital. Poignant expressions. She admired his ability to capture them in all the photographs but one. Hers. He had not caught her indomitable Irish spirit, her desire to start anew. She did not want this reminder of the misery she'd endured.

She handed the photographs back and rose. "Thank you for your trouble, but we shouldn't tarry any longer. You've been most gracious."

Mrs. Hawkins stood too and embraced her friend. "Give your mother my love, Gus."

"Certainly." He handed Grace's picture to her.

"No thank you. I'm not worthy of such a gift."

"But—"

"Truly. It should stay with the others."

He seemed surprised. "Are you sure?"

"Quite."

7

Having finished checking doors on the west side of the street, Owen crossed to do the same on the opposite side. There was a "café" on this side, a place that was more of a drinking and dancing facility than an eating establishment. All Owen had to do was make his appearance known.

He was still a block away when he heard voices coming from a door well. Newsboys, he thought. He approached and called out so he wouldn't surprise anyone. He was not on a mission to catch illegal activities, just to help deter them with his presence.

A grunt.

He moved closer. "Who's there?"

He heard the scramble of feet, and then a man emerged, a dirty white handkerchief tied over one eye. "McNulty, aye?"

"I am. Who's with you?"

"Just a few mates."

"Send 'em out here."

He chuckled and turned toward the dark alley. "Mates, this copper wants to meet your acquaintance."

No reply.

The man pulled the collar of his coat to his chin. "They say they aren't coming out. Reckon you'll have to go get 'em."

"What is your business here? If you have none, you fellas better move along."

"I know who you are, and people don't like you snooping around."

"Just doing my job."

Suddenly someone sprang from the alley, a black-clothed figure with something in his hands. Before Owen could react, the thug whacked him on the knees with a metal pipe, and the bums lunged away like rats in the sewer.

Owen limped to the other side of the street. He wasn't hurt too badly, only his pride, but laughter bellowed from the dark buildings. "Pretty society boy! You don't belong here!"

Owen took a side street over to Broadway, where he met up with a couple of other officers. He told them what had happened and assured them he was all right.

"We'll check it out," the man he knew as Murphy said. "You stay over here, though. They're used to us, and they won't give us no grief."

"Used to you, huh?"

"Yeah, well, you might not be an official rookie cop anymore, but to the lowlife you're still a greenhorn, McNulty." He held up both palms. "I ain't saying you are, but they'll think what they want."

"They shouldn't be allowed to believe they can intimidate me. I'll go with you."

The man held a hand to Owen's chest. "No. Not a good idea. We'll let 'em know we're standing up for you. They'll understand we stick together."

Owen agreed and watched as the two men skirted down the street toward the alley where Owen had been jumped. As soon as they'd reached an intersection, Owen hurried, his legs throbbing, to get to the next block. He knew they would not be moving as fast as he was, and when he got to the next side street, he was not surprised to see the officers moving northward instead of toward the alley. Just as he thought. They had no intention at all of "standing up" for him.

An hour later Owen saw his fellow officers in a coffee shop. He stood gazing at the plate-glass window for a moment and then decided to go in. The warm smell of coffee mixed with the musty, furnace-heated air, easing the ache in his joints. No wonder the roundsmen preferred this place to standing on street corners in December. He approached Murphy. "Did you talk to those thugs? The fella with the white handkerchief tied on his head?"

"Oh." Murphy shrugged. "They'd already run off by the time we got there. You know how those riffraff are."

"Sure. I know."

8

ONCE THEY WERE ON THE TRAIN heading home, Mrs. Hawkins turned her beady eyes to look fully at Grace, reminding Grace again how odd it was that the woman's name reflected her appearance in some ways and her instincts perfectly. She was a sharp-eyed hawk for certain.

"It seems your years in the workhouse retarded the maturity of some social decorum, love," the Hawk said.

"What do you mean?" Embarrassment rose up like fire in her throat.

"You stood too close to his camera. You refused his gift."

"I did not mean to be rude."

"There's not another would put up with the likes of ya." She pushed away her father's voice, trying to ignore it. "You said I could learn about photography."

The woman smiled. "Well, you did learn how much you like photography, didn't you? I saw the way those images captivated you."

Grace drew in a breath. The woman wasn't truly angry. "I don't know how he does it. A moment forever preserved." She wished she had a photograph of her mother. She was beginning to forget what that light in her eyes looked like, and that left her cold and melancholy.

She blinked away the thought. "Why didn't you tell me you were acquainted the first time I mentioned Mr. Sherman?"

"I haven't seen him in years. I didn't want to get your hopes up in case I wasn't able to arrange a meeting. I thought you wanted to see your photograph."

"I did. Thank you."

Foolish, that was. She never wanted to see it again.

Mrs. Hawkins gave her a tight squeeze. "Well, no matter now. You said you liked to draw. Why don't we shop for some charcoal pencils, love? Perhaps some watercolor paints as well. We have time before Mr. Parker comes by."

"Mr. Parker?"

"Oh, my. Did I forget to mention it? Reverend Clarke believes Mr. Parker may want to employ you. Though he lives uptown, he serves at First Church as an usher. He's going to come by to meet you."

Grace checked the condition of her hair bun, suddenly self-conscious of her appearance. "I see." Grace's mouth ran dry. She still battled those voices but desperately wanted to squeeze them out. "I look forward to meeting him."

"Now, about those supplies."

"Uh, thanks. No need. You have done so much already, ma'am."

"You must cease from addressing me so formally, love. Mrs. Hawkins will do." The woman smacked her lips. "So no drawing supplies today. As you wish, love, but we will stop for some ice cream."

"Ice cream?"

"You're right. Too chilly. We'll get some fried pies from the little shop around the corner, then. My Harold always used to say, 'Life is uncertain, so eat dessert first.'"

"I'm beginning to grow fond of your Harold, Mrs. Hawkins."

Later, alone in her room, Grace pondered her visit with Mr. Sherman. Somehow she had in her head that she could take photographs as a hobby. But photography was a trade, much like being a blacksmith or a tanner. Learning how to prepare photographic plates and develop images would take many years to master and more funds than she could hope to come up with. She must try harder to improve her drawing if she really wanted to capture the faces she saw around her.

Grace rose from her bed to check her appearance in the washroom mirror. Surprised by the disheartened expression on her face, she pinched her cheeks and smoothed her collar. She could go about mending, sweeping, and preparing simple but tasteful meals. *That's all an American housemaid does,* she reasoned.

She swallowed hard. She had to meet the master of the house first.

She knew, in her head, that not all men were like her father or those awful peelers, but in her heart she feared that she might be wrong. It was one thing to speak to a merchant or observe a photographer. Quite another to work for a man and spend all her working hours in his house.

She stared into the mirror, watching her eyes go wide. She'd study his face, look for the expression, the nuances, something she could trust. If she could find that, she would be all right.

After forcing some resistant strands of hair back into place, she headed downstairs to wait in the parlor.

There she met Annie, who was dusting the breakfront cabinet. "Good luck with your interview."

"Thank you for that. You know that dance you told me about, Annie?"

"Aye. The *céilí*, the maid's dance on Thursday nights. 'Tis like at home—dancing, fiddles . . . every Thursday because the maids have the evening off."

"If I get this job . . . maybe I can't come." She let her gaze fall to the floor.

"Most folks follow the convention. Let's wait and see, Grace."

Just as Annie was leaving the room, a loud knock came from the front door. Grace got a glimpse of a man's coat as Annie took it from him. Mrs. Hawkins clambered up the hall from the kitchen to greet the man.

Grace stood as she was introduced.

"Mr. Parker, may I present Grace McCaffery."

The man smiled and crossed the floor with his hand out-stretched. He was perhaps a decade older than Grace, a half foot taller, and dressed in an expensive-looking wool suit. As he came closer, Grace detected the scent of a perfumed toiletry much like what Reverend Clarke used on Sundays. Well-to-do enough to afford to pay her salary, but not so rich as to employ numerous servants. Mr. Parker seemed pleasant enough, though she dared not look directly into his face. Not yet.

A quarter hour later the matter was agreed upon. Mr. Parker stood. "I wanted to see the nature of the girl before I decided. I do not care so much about your skills but about your disposition." He turned to Mrs. Hawkins, who nodded at Grace to stand as well. "I can see that your Grace is reserved and agreeable."

Mrs. Hawkins squeezed her fat fingers together. "I am so happy you are pleased. Do you have any further instructions for her before she arrives for work tomorrow?"

He held up a finger. "Ah, yes. The children's names. My wife is quite the horticulturist. That is why she needs domestic help, so she can spend more time in the garden. Small plot, being here in the city, but she insists, you know."

Mrs. Hawkins folded her hands. "Lovely. And their names?"

Children? No one had mentioned children. Grace didn't know if she could handle them. What if he mistreated his children? What would she do? Her stomach churned.

Mr. Parker shook out his calfskin gloves, preparing to put them on. "They are named after trees, you see. Hazel is ten, Holly is six, and the youngest for now is Linden. He is three. None are in nappies, but we are expecting in a few weeks. Big as a house now, my Alice. She'll need your help, Grace."

"Oh, delightful. Won't you enjoy that, Grace?" Mrs. Hawkins gave Grace a sharp poke with her elbow.

"Aye. Children. Three of them." She could barely find words.

Mr. Parker accepted his hat from Mrs. Hawkins. "And another coming. Either Willow or Douglas."

"Douglas?" Mrs. Hawkins escorted the man to the door.

"That's right. She agreed to the name because of the Douglas fir."

"Of course." Mrs. Hawkins called to Grace, "Say good-bye, love."

"Thank you, Mr. Parker. I look forward to the job."

As soon as he was gone, Mrs. Hawkins burst into laughter. "Trees in the park. Parker. See the humor in that, love?"

"Amusing." Grace slumped down on the sofa.

"Come now, love. Plenty of maids also look out after children. The two oldest will be attending school during the day. It won't be too much trouble, I'm sure."

"I am delighted you think so."

The woman sat down next to Grace. "I know you are troubled, but you'll see. Before long you'll be so busy you won't have time to fret. You have employment now. You can send money home."

"I know." She sucked back tears. "And I'm grateful."

The truth was, the only children Grace had ever been around before were the sick, troublesome peers she had shared the workhouse attic with. She had told herself that she would do whatever she had to, even shovel horse manure, to get her mother away from that policeman. Cleaning a stable might be easier than taking care of the Parkers' garden of children, though.

After supper, in the hour between kitchen duty and bedtime, Grace retreated to the parlor to find something to keep her mind off her anxiety. She picked up the Sears and Roebuck catalog lying on the sofa.

She flipped pages and paused at the photographic department. Amazing. It seemed she could order whatever she needed by mail, even an instruction book. She read further. No. The instruction book was free when you purchased a camera. Her fingers trembled as she turned to the next page. How would she know what to order even if she did have the money? Mr. Sherman had spouted off a list of equipment and supplies that she had never heard of. She wondered if this mail-order store would send her the instruction book first.

The Perfection Complete Viewing Outfit. The Empire State Photographic Outfit. These were inclusive packages with all needed supplies. She wouldn't have to order things separately. How much easier could it be? She'd show everyone that a woman could be a photographer.

Grace subconsciously tugged at her only Sunday dress. She did need new clothes, but that must wait. She glanced back down at the page. All she required, according to the catalog, was $15.35 to "start in a pleasant and good paying business."

There it was, right there in print. People did make extra money this way. The advertisement also said that if you had current employment, this camera outfit would allow you to gradually learn photography until you could start up a business. It did not ask if the person buying the product was male or female. Who needed an instructor when you had a free instruction book? She read further: "This will afford you a means to start until you can build up a business and satisfy that desire that constantly agitates the mind of every ambitious man." Well, she was an ambitious woman. She would just order under her initials.

She had only a small amount of the money S. P. had given her, and she wanted to pay him back. Her salary from Mr. Parker would only be five dollars a week. She had to save for Ma, and for what that camera outfit cost, she could send her mother a remittance for her travel. And Ma needed even more than that. She had to have money for other expenses—a trunk, traveling clothes, some American money so that when the immigration inspector asked to see what she had, she could produce something to show that she had a place in America. Grace could not risk sending too little and thus cause her mother not to come. Having a side business might help her reach her goal faster. If only it wasn't so expensive. She laughed at herself. A ridiculous idea. She closed the catalog.

Mrs. Hawkins came into the room toting a magazine. "I thought perhaps you'd like to see this." She handed it to Grace.

"*The Youth's Companion*. What's this?"

"It's a magazine a friend from Boston mails to me. I enjoy reading it. Mark Twain, Booker T. Washington . . . many interesting authors have contributed to it."

"I don't feel much like reading tonight." She handed it back, but the woman didn't take it.

"Turn to an advertisement in the back, love. Eastman Kodak. After our visit to Mr. Sherman, I recalled having seen some Kodak advertisements featuring a woman photographer."

"Truly?" Grace flipped the pages.

"No woman in this advertisement, but I think you'll be interested. Seems they are introducing a new type of camera."

Grace found it. *Eastman Kodak Co.'s Brownie Camera.* "One dollar?"

"That's right, love. Look at what it says right below that."

"'Operated by any schoolboy or girl.' Mrs. Hawkins, where can I get one of these?"

"You can send for it, love."

She had a dollar. She would do that.

Morning dawned earlier than Grace was prepared for.

"Hurry along, love. The early morning streetcars fill up fast."

Grace tried to straighten the stiff collar Mrs. Hawkins made her wear but finally decided it must be her neck that was crooked. She blew out a breath as she stepped from the kitchen washroom. Annie seemed to have taken up residence in the bathroom upstairs. *Please, God, don't let me ruin things.* She forced a smile as she turned to her landlady. "You really don't have to come with me." She didn't want Mrs. Hawkins to witness any mistakes she made.

"Remember when you went for raisins, love."

Grace was about to explain that she would be more careful, but she decided to take to heart the Irish expression: "'Tis not a trout until 'tis on the bank." She'd not proven herself yet. But she would in time.

"Just for today, love. It's better that we're both assured you won't get lost."

Grace agreed. Everything had to go as planned.

They found seats on the edge where they could watch the traffic on the street. Grace studied first the mission houses on State Street, their many windows and varied iron fire escapes wiggling up the facade like misplaced fence pickets. Rounding onto Broadway, they whisked past Bowling Green, which was more fountain than green, she thought.

The Hawk nudged her with an elbow. "Once there was a statue of King George there, love. Before independence."

America had not been a British colony for a century and a quarter. "What happened to it?"

Agnes Hawkins squinted her eyes. "Well, it's been said that it was hauled north and melted into musket balls for the continental army."

"That so?"

"Can't say for sure. But leave it to the Americans to do something so . . . so emblematic. As my Harold used to say, 'There are two sides to every question.'"

Grace turned back to observing traffic. As if the British were beyond symbolic gestures. Mrs. Hawkins was English born, though truly different from how Grace had judged the British previously.

Before long they passed the tenement buildings and then smaller clapboard structures and shops as they moved northward. When the view changed to the hue of bare tree branches and brownstones, Mrs. Hawkins turned to her. "Nearly there."

After exiting the car, they walked up the sidewalk along a partially treed lane. Grace spied a group of lads playing stickball in an alley.

"Even when Linden Parker is big enough, Mr. Parker will not allow his son to participate in such pastimes, love. Reverend Clarke told me the man is extremely protective of his children. We've never even seen them at First Church. He doesn't allow them that far from the house. You'll have to keep them all close."

"Where are we, Mrs. Hawkins?" The surroundings were unfamiliar, as though they'd left the city in only a few short blocks.

"Middle class neighborhood." She squeezed Grace's hand. "See why I wanted to come to show you the way, love? Look for landmarks. There is a flower shop one block south of the Parkers' house. See there? And a newsstand across the street. Follow the landmarks after you get off the stop, and you'll do fine."

"The wealthy live here?"

"We are still several blocks west of Fifth Avenue, where the wealthy live, love."

Grace drew in a breath as they marched up the steps to a limestone building bearing no fresco-plastered flowered facade. There apparently was not a servants' entrance. Mrs. Hawkins rapped the brass knocker three times.

A thin, pale lass opened the door. She turned her head to the side and hollered in a voice that should have belonged to a much heartier child.

A woman came lumbering up the hall. "Hazel, mind your manners. Invite the ladies in before they catch cold." Mrs. Parker was indeed heavy with child.

Hazel had to be the eldest, although she looked to be younger than ten. When the lass sighed heavily and shut the door, her actions betrayed her age. One thing Grace remembered— probably because she had been the same way—was that once a human being passed the decade mark, all childhood joys vanished. Innocence was fleeting. If this child was going to be difficult, she prayed the others would be more complacent.

The house was chilly—too cool, she thought. And the carpets and drapes too fussy and undoubtedly difficult to clean. Grace gazed about the room, taking in all the details. Since she would be in charge of the entire household, she would need to manage everything. A tall task.

"Please sit a moment, Grace. We will go over some instructions. And please stay for tea, Mrs. Hawkins." Mrs. Parker motioned to a brocade-covered sofa that Grace was sure held more dust than the street. With the woman's obvious lack of housekeeping skills, Grace could not imagine what instructions she could possibly give her.

Alice Parker grunted as though she had something stuck in her throat. "There will be general housekeeping, looking after the children, greeting guests, and the occasional social party to plan and serve . . . uh, Mr. Parker thinks hosting parties would be good for me." She pursed her lips and gave Mrs. Hawkins a sideways glance.

The woman didn't seem particularly pleased about hiring Grace. Her eyes bore shadows and her slumped shoulders gave her a depressed look. Maybe this wasn't a good idea. Grace gave the woman a cursory nod and then examined the room again.

"No, give it to *meeeeee*!" A child's hollering came from the hall.

"Oh, dear." Mrs. Parker eased from the armchair and waddled out of the room.

Mrs. Hawkins glanced around. "No tea?"

Grace shrugged. "I should go check the kitchen."

The Hawk wagged a finger in the air. "You should go help

with the children, love. That's what this dear woman needs the most."

"But you said tea—"

"Never mind what I said."

Grace gritted her teeth, pinched her eyes shut for a moment, and trailed behind Mrs. Parker. Just over the woman's shoulder, she saw a blur of arms and legs as a wee lad tussled with the thin lass who had opened the door for them.

"Linden, Hazel, Holly!" their mother shouted.

Grace had not even noticed the appearance of a third child.

Mrs. Parker turned back to Grace, a tendril of hair stuck to her forehead, her face beet-red. She sucked in her lower lip, obviously trying to regain her composure. "They just need a little discipline, Grace." With a clattering of footsteps in front of her, Mrs. Parker herded her children out into the backyard and warned them not to leave the premises and not to disturb her sleeping garden plants. Dusting her hands on the swollen belly covered with an emerald green skirt, she let out a low, whistling breath. "And I need just a moment to show you where the teapot is."

When Grace began filling the kettle with water, Alice Parker scurried back to the parlor, announcing her apologies to Mrs. Hawkins.

Grace peeked out the back door. Linden pouted, arms crossed over his reefer, while his sisters giggled and tossed a rubber ball between them. Poor chilly lad, his bare legs protruding from below the unfastened jacket. They had been swept outside like floor dust. Grace knew what that was like.

After she prepared a tray with bone china cups, a bowl of sugar lumps, and a plate of butter biscuits, she filled a matching china teapot with steaming water and let the tea steep. Then she called the children inside.

They stood just inside the kitchen door, rubbing their chilled limbs. Linden's cheeks bore damp tears of frustration, while the two girls stared wide-eyed at her under veils of stringy hair. Grace put one hand on Linden's shoulder and the other on Hazel's as Holly stood between them. "If you sit quietly at the kitchen table and don't speak a word while I'm serving tea, I'll find cause to bring you each one of those biscuits when I get back."

Linden gasped and bounced from foot to foot.

"I said sit, though. I'll not be tricked by the likes of fairies impersonating children."

They giggled at that and hurriedly plopped onto the wooden chairs around the table.

"Good, so." Grace whisked the tray away to the parlor. Right before she stepped into the room where her new employer sat with her landlady, she halted, their conversation bringing her up short.

"I did not want an Irish biddy, Mrs. Hawkins."

"Oh, I assure you Grace will be—"

"I know; I know. George told me he quizzed her thoroughly. I must be confident that her morals are beyond reproach. You know, the children . . ."

The teacups began to rattle on the tray.

"Grace McCaffery attends my very own church. She came highly recommended by Reverend Clarke himself."

Grace felt her shoulders relax. Glancing back down the hall, she noticed the children's faces staring at her, waiting in antici-pation. She sighed, licked her lips, and took one step into the parlor. Then she heard Mrs. Parker's voice again.

"Doesn't that policeman attend there . . . McNulty, is it?"

"Indeed. Why do you ask?"

"George has mentioned him. He's not like the other . . . uh, the average immigrant congregant over there, now is he?"

"I suppose not. He's from a prosperous family."

The mistress huffed. "Charity is one thing, Mrs. Hawkins, but why do some men feel like they have to devote their entire lives to it?"

"Are you speaking of Officer McNulty, love, or your own husband?"

No response.

The sound of the Hawk's taffeta silk–lined skirt ruffling filled a momentary silence. "Your husband attends to the tithes every Sunday. That right, love?"

"Yes. The children and I don't accompany him, though. They are too young to visit the immigrant sector."

Mrs. Parker's back was turned. Mrs. Hawkins's face bore worry lines when she glanced up at Grace.

Grace wanted to drop the tray right then and there. Her new employer despised transplants from Ireland and was only grudgingly accepting her. The woman was depressed and upset that her husband attended First Church. With the filthy condition of the home and the unruliness of the children, this bigoted woman had probably had great difficulty finding help.

But Grace mustn't drop the tea tray. As though she was tethered to the spot, she remained there, a smile glued to her face. She needed this job. She could not run away from the Parkers' house and their bramble lot of children no matter how badly she longed to.

Mrs. Hawkins waved her hand and Mrs. Parker turned. "Come in, Grace," Mrs. Parker said. "Show me how you serve tea. I do hope you've done it before."

"Oh, Grace is wonderful—"

"I will see for myself." Mrs. Parker interrupted Mrs. Hawkins.

Grace didn't know how she managed it, but she set a teacup in front of the lady of the house and poured without spilling a drop. Then she repeated the action for the Hawk, who kept twisting her handkerchief into a cloth snake. Grace offered sugar and biscuits and laid a cloth napkin in each lady's lap as though she were serving the Queen of England.

By the time she got back to the kitchen though, her hands trembled. To her surprise, the children were still in place, waiting.

"Not one word," wee Linden said, grinning.

If she hadn't understood before, she did now. These children. They were the reason she had to serve the family, not their mother. Grace couldn't bear not helping them, because no one had come to her aid when she was their age.

Grace returned to the scullery tin where she'd found the treats and removed three more. She placed each one on a small plate and then returned to the table, delicately balancing them all in her hands.

The children gobbled the biscuits down as though they'd missed breakfast. She was about to go looking for eggs to feed them when a gasp came from the kitchen door.

"What are you doing?" Mrs. Parker lunged toward Holly, who was putting the last bite in her mouth. "Spit it out!"

Horrified, Grace jumped to her defense. "'Twas only one. They were so well behaved. I just thought—"

"Foolish biddy!" Mrs. Parker glared at her until the Hawk stepped between them.

"Now, Alice. She's only trying to get along." She folded her hands as if in prayer. "The two of you will just simply have to come to terms. You need a housekeeper; Grace needs a job. You, dear Alice, are persnickety, and Grace here is . . . well . . . at times, impulsive. This can be worked out, and the way I see it, it's essential that it be."

Mrs. Parker narrowed her eyes, and the children darted away from the table toward the front room. "I will not have my children corrupted with sugar or any of this modern insensibility of coddling them."

The Hawk bounced her chin in agreement. "And Grace promises to abide by your wishes, don't you, Grace?"

"I don't see why I—"

"Good. She agrees. But, Alice, you must concur and show Grace kindness and not treat her as a common . . . well, you know, the way the upper class puts on airs with their servants. You must remember your place, dear woman. You are from the hardworking class, not too far removed from those like Grace."

"I protest, Mrs. Hawkins. My people are much further removed from the boat."

Grace huffed loudly. She should not endure such treatment. After her time at Hawkins House, she'd realized that people should be treated with respect, even herself.

Mrs. Hawkins patted Alice Parker's arm. "Be that as it may, Grace here is a child of God. Treat her as you would want to be treated."

Mrs. Parker bent her blonde head low. "I understand. I would never mistreat her, and I would like her to work for me, under my instructions."

The Hawk gave Grace a stern look. "And you accept, don't you, love?"

"Aye."

"And she certainly did an exemplary job of serving tea."

Alice Parker kept her gaze low. "She did well, I admit."

Grace caught a glimpse of Hazel in the hall. The lass stuck out her tongue and then vanished up the stairs. Grace guessed Hazel felt much the same way as she had, abandoned and angry. Hazel's mother was present in body but was likely absent just the same when it came to matters of the heart.

Grace bit her lip, wondering if she was up to the task. Of all the households in this enormous city, here she was, where complications grew like the mildew in the bathroom. This would be work—and plenty.

9

WHEN THURSDAY CAME, Owen had a sick feeling. He gripped the watch in his palm. Dan O'Toole had never married, so his parents had passed the watch on to the man who had probably, for them, become Dan's replacement. He should never have taken on another man's life mission. Especially one who had died before Owen could get to know him. Who could possibly expect to succeed at something so onerous?

He shoved the watch back in his pocket.

He licked his dry lips and drew in a breath as he rounded the corner to Miss Amelia's impressive house. He wasn't so sure he had the gumption to do this, pretend that he still had a place at these kinds of parties. He often didn't know where he belonged, caught between two worlds. He would keep reminding himself what he was called to do even while socializing within the circle he'd been born into.

He approached the door. "Evening, Ansel."

Miss Amelia's butler scrutinized him as though he could not make up his mind whether Owen was a common man like him or a rich guest he had to serve. The man bowed slightly and took Owen's hat and coat.

Inside, Owen smiled at two ladies and then found the hostess. "You are lovely as ever, Miss Amelia."

The woman's paper-thin flesh pinked. "Always the charmer, Owen McNulty."

"A charmer, you say?"

She patted his hand. "I meant it only in the most complimentary way. All the people from Tullamore are amiable, you know." She squeezed his fingers. "Oh, Owen, please come in. My niece is in desperate need of company from someone in her own generation."

He let himself be led away to the piano, where Miss Pierpont, dressed in canary yellow, a splendid contrast to her ebony hair, played a melody. He and Miss Amelia stood politely and listened. Soon Owen's mother joined them. He leaned down to whisper in her ear. "You look lovely tonight, Mother."

"Oh, pshaw. What about her? Isn't she exquisite?" She inclined her head toward the piano player.

"Mother, please. No matchmaking tonight."

"I have to look out for you, Owen. You are not doing that for yourself. I cannot take the chance my son will marry some gypsy on the street."

"Where is the smoking room?"

His mother glanced at the ceiling. "Your father is not here."

"Why not?"

"The man is positively exhausted. If you would just come and help out with the business . . ."

"I have a job, Mother."

"Oh, phooey. You don't need that job."

"I want the job."

She sighed loudly. "You can't fix things down there. There will always be disparity between the rich and the poor. Has been since the beginning of civilization, I suppose."

"I'm not trying to fix that. I'm doing what God wants me to do."

"What God wants is for families to stick together. Your father needs you."

"Is he that sick?"

"Sick and tired, I suppose." She wiggled her powdered chin. "But if your mind is made up, I suppose we will have to manage."

He excused himself and found a fellow serving canapés on a silver tray. He popped two in his mouth and intentionally looked toward the hall rather than the music.

But his mother found him. "Owen, I thought you'd enjoy meeting some people your own age and station."

He looked down at the top of her head as she greeted entering celebrants and attempted to hide the disagreement with her son.

"My current station? That would be someone who lives on the Lower East Side."

"Shush." She gritted her teeth and tipped her head in the direction of a councilman and his silver-headed wife. "You know very well what I meant. Stop trying to make it sound so callous."

How could he color it otherwise? "Is that the entire reason you invited me, Mother?"

She pulled a caviar delight from his hand and returned it to a waiter's serving tray. "Well, I did not invite you just for the canapés."

He might have argued with her about that, had she not drifted off to speak with some new arrivals about a masked ball they were planning. He drifted among the people, taking in a mix of scents—cologne water, sherry, and licorice. He had grown used to the earthy smells of horses, soot, and vegetable vendors. The sweet, refined aroma of Miss Amelia's party seemed a bit sterile.

Near the crowded corner of the parlor, he found an unoccupied chair and sat, but when an elderly lady made her way across the room, hobbling with the aid of a cane, he offered his seat.

The sound of stringed instruments replaced the piano music, coming from the direction of the large open area Miss Amelia liked to call her ballroom.

"Good evening, Mr. and Mrs. Stevenson." He nodded toward friends of his mother's and then shook hands with a stockbroker his father dealt with, along with the executive of a chain of department stores.

The night dragged. He chose to stay in the front room, as did many others who apparently held no fondness for dancing.

"Excuse me." A woman pulled her arm away even though she had barely brushed against him.

He caught a glimpse of yellow fabric as she wove her way through black suits. He trailed behind. When he caught up and captured her attention, he tipped his chin. "Lovely piano playing, Miss Pierpont."

Her ruby lips turned into a smile. "Why, thank you." She reached out her hand.

Owen spent the next hour chatting with the young lady and was delighted to find they shared an interest in Sir Arthur Conan Doyle novels and Southern pecan pie. He supposed he had been lonely and bored. His mother found them engaging in conversation on the parlor sofa.

"Come along, darlings. Come dance with us in the ballroom." She pulled Owen to his feet and, with a shrug of her eyebrows, suggested he help Miss Pierpont rise.

Thankfully, once they entered the ballroom, his mother disappeared. He took Miss Pierpont's gentle hand and led her to the dance floor.

"I must warn you that my mother plays matchmaker."

"Oh? And I suppose this does not please you."

"It does not. Uh . . . don't misunderstand. It's been lovely spending time with you, Miss Pierpont, and I've enjoyed our conversation. But let me be clear about something."

"Please."

She frowned, but he thought it would be better to set things straight. "I have a demanding job chasing down thieves and gangsters. I work most nights. I live in Lower Manhattan . . ."

He felt her sink back slightly.

"I am not suitable courting material, I'm afraid."

"I see." She pinched a smile. "I'm sure you are being too hard on yourself, Officer."

"Realistic. I don't mean to be rude. I truly have enjoyed your company this night."

"I'm flattered."

They waltzed to the edge of the crowd, and he released her. He coughed. The thickly populated house seemed to close in on him.

His mother appeared by his side. "Here come the O'Tooles. Say hello, darling, before they make their speech."

He turned to find the smiling faces of Mr. and Mrs. O'Toole. He had not seen them since the funeral. Mr. O'Toole shook his hand firmly, and Mrs. O'Toole leaned forward while he kissed her cheek.

"So happy you're here, Owen," Mrs. O'Toole said. "The night would not be complete without you."

"You are too kind."

"We are grateful for your service to the citizens, son." Mr. O'Toole thumped Owen's back.

"Well, I . . ."

The orchestra ceased playing, and Miss Amelia led the man and his wife to the center of the room.

Mr. O'Toole, dressed in an ordinary black suit, and his wife, wearing an unadorned navy dress and no hat, stood in the middle of the crowd, an island of ordinariness surrounded by wealthy patrons, the finest New York could attire. The contrast was more than just visible. It was palpable.

Mr. O'Toole began by talking about his deceased son and the plight of the poor in the city. The crowd nodded as though they understood. Owen knew none of them really did. Throwing money at a problem never solved it. The only way to make change was to roll up your sleeves and—

Suddenly the room erupted in applause, and the couple in the center waved to him. He drew closer. Mr. O'Toole continued on. "With the dedication of officers like Owen McNulty, much good is being done. This fine young man, who traded a life of comfort for one of service, utilizing good morals and avoiding the corruption of Tammany Hall, represents the spirit of servitude our own son possessed. We now award him the first annual Dan O'Toole Award for Excellence."

Had his mother and Miss Amelia only invited Tammany opposition, Mother might have endured this better. She stood at the edge of the crowd, fanning her pale face. She had been caught off guard just like Owen. As people congratulated him and asked to look at the silver-plated plaque he had been handed, he saw his mother and the hostess engaged in animated conversation near the swinging door the domestics used to bring in trays of champagne flutes. His mother waved her arms as she spoke. She never would have allowed the O'Tooles to give that speech if she'd known they were going to refer to her son as a servant. If Miss Amelia had previous knowledge of it, she must not have mentioned it to Mother.

Mr. O'Toole pulled him aside. "Did we surprise you, son?"

"Uh, yes, you did. This was very kind but not necessary."

"Of course it was necessary. I admire what you are doing out there." He glanced down at the plaque. "Besides, you'll pass the honor on to someone else next year and hopefully this will help encourage the honest cops out there."

Owen smiled. "I'm sure it will. It's a fine honor." He shifted his feet. "Sir, please know that I cannot replace your son. He was a great man."

"He was indeed. But you are your own man, Owen McNulty, and a good one too. Still got the watch?"

Owen pulled it out to show him.

"Good, good."

Owen pushed it toward him. "I think this should stay with the family."

"Absolutely not." Mr. O'Toole placed his hand on Owen's arm the way a father should, the way his father never did. "Not many men would walk into the path of an out-of-control trolley to save a wee child, even if such an opportunity arises again. You might, but whether or not you do is irrelevant. It's the spirit you have, lad. You may have been born into the upper crust, but make no mistake, you were meant to be a policeman in the immigrant wards. And thank the good Lord you've found what you were born for. Know what I mean?"

"I think I do."

He winked. "Now I'm off to lose this monkey jacket and get a pint at the pub."

Owen was leaving too. With his award and his watch and the confirmation he'd needed. He might be caught between two worlds as far as courtship was concerned. But he was in the right place, doing the job he'd been called to do.

When he stepped outside, a familiar face met him. Owen, being a tall man himself, stood nose to nose with New York City's police chief, Big Bill Devery.

"Nice award, son."

"Thank you, sir." Owen accepted the man's handshake. When it was evident the man had nothing else to say, Owen scrambled down the front steps.

Big Bill lumbered after him. "By the way, Officer McNulty, glad you weren't badly hurt."

"Sir?"

The man rubbed his large belly that stretched his tuxedo to the limit. "I hear you got roughed up a bit out there on your beat. A pipe to the knees?"

Owen stiffened. "I'm surprised you hear about such common occurrences down in Lower Manhattan."

"Oh, you'd be surprised what I hear." He leaned in close. "Every man on the force knows who's in the game and who's not. Roosevelt may have hired you, but you work for me now. Understand?"

Owen forced a smile. "Of course. You are the chief. Good night, sir."

As Owen sat on the train, he debated what he should tell Nicholson. The captain was trying to keep his own head on his shoulders, after all. Owen knew deep down inside that God wanted him to be a New York City policeman. Mr. O'Toole's encouragement was confirmation of what he already felt. And yet there was the matter of Owen's father. Owen had better find out what ailed the man. As his father's only son, he couldn't let the business fail. Stuck between two worlds indeed.

If Owen had thought receiving an award would make his beat more pleasant, he was wrong. He hadn't mentioned it to anyone, but word got out, Owen learned as he worked a rare morning shift. The precinct guys began calling him Most Excellent Officer. A few of the shopkeepers on the beat gave him the thumbs-up, but he could imagine what they said out of earshot. *"College boy. Thinks he's better than the rest."*

Why had Owen agreed to show up at that charity event in the first place? The O'Tooles meant well, but surely it hadn't been their idea. The concept of an award had to have been thrust upon them by socialites looking for a reason for a party.

And to make matters worse, the police chief himself had threatened him. Subtle, yes, but still a threat. He decided he would not tell Captain Nicholson, not just yet. He didn't want to be taken off this chase.

10

AT BREAKFAST FRIDAY, Annie showed Grace a page from the newspaper. "Owen McNulty, from our very own church. See his picture?"

Grace read the caption. It seemed he had been given some kind of an award at a fancy charity ball. "Officer McNulty? How could someone from down here end up in high society and be the honored guest at a place like that?" She knew America was different from Ireland, but still.

Annie pointed at the newspaper. "He did belong there. He's from a wealthy family."

The Hawk chewed the crust on her slice of bread and looked at both girls in turn. "Sometimes folks—even those who have a great deal of money—choose a simpler lifestyle. Sometimes God calls them to go somewhere, to do something that they didn't expect. You girls still have a lot to learn, it would seem." She rose and excused herself.

Grace exchanged glances with Annie. "What got into the Hawk?"

Annie tilted her head back and laughed. "I love that. The Hawk!"

"Seriously, Annie."

The girl rose and gathered the dishes. "I expect she is simply serious about aiding girls like us. That's all." She paused. "This Owen McNulty. He's quite a catch, isn't he?"

"He's a policeman."

"So?" She tossed her head. "Policemen don't marry?"

Grace drew in a breath. "He's nice, but I'm not interested. The police are not trustworthy, believe me."

"Some, maybe. But not him." She pointed to the newspaper again. "Look. He was honored by the police. So he must be an honorable man. Who could want more?"

Grace gave up. The last thing she wanted to do was talk about what the peelers had done to her. And her mother. There was no way Annie would ever understand. Besides, unless there were men like Reverend Clarke who were of marriageable age, she would stay single. And that would be fine with her.

After yesterday's adjustment, the children seemed willing to accept Grace as nanny, but that did not mean they were always cooperative.

Grace struggled to braid Hazel's hair while Holly complained loudly about having to wear woolen stockings. "Hold still, Hazel. No, Holly. 'Tis winter, so. Just put them on like a good lass."

Linden bounced a ball on the playroom floor. "I wanna go to school."

Even though both his sisters had been going to school for the last few months, Linden seemed especially disturbed about it now. Perhaps it was for Grace's benefit. Maybe the pending arrival of the new babe was making him sour. Or he didn't like having a nanny. Grace wasn't sure. "You're not old enough yet," Grace told him.

"Yeah, but *I* get to go." Holly glared at him, hands on hips. This was not helping.

"Not fair!" Linden was about to lose control. Grace had already begun to recognize the signs.

She took his hand. "Your time will come, laddie."

Linden, however, still seemed terribly aggrieved by it all. "Father says I have to be a man."

Holly twirled in her new school dress. "You can't go, Lindy. You're just a baby."

Linden marched over and delivered a blow to Holly's cheek before Grace could untangle her fingers from Hazel's hair.

"Oww," Holly wailed.

"Miss Gracie! You hurt me!" Hazel screamed, holding the side of her head.

Linden growled like an old dog.

The ruckus was enough to wake hibernating animals. It was all Grace could do to regain order before parading them down the street toward the school, a task Mrs. Parker thought she should have rather than a hired driver. She had almost gotten out the door before the mistress saw her youngest daughter's red face. Alice Parker rolled her eyes. "What happened?"

All three children tried to answer, sending up a squabble worse than the tower of Babel.

"Go on, now." Mrs. Parker kissed the top of each child's head and practically pushed them out the door.

Grace marched them down the sidewalk, prodding them toward the building side when a beat cop passed them. Thankfully, Holly took Hazel's hand when they got to the school and marched right up the steps with no more words to their brother. Linden pulled on Grace's arm. "Can we go home now?"

"Sure we can."

Once Grace had Linden alone, he transformed into a co-operative wee fellow. They set out straightening up the house.

"Here, Miss Gracie." He handed her his father's cold pipe left on a table. "Let me get the vinegar for the window smudges," he said, toddling off to the scullery.

Clearly his older sisters' teasing had been the trouble. Grace hadn't known about such things, being an only child herself and one who had not lived in a family since she was ten.

Linden carried his own dusting rag and followed her about, helping as much as he could. "Father says I will be the head of his company one day."

"That's a long ways away, lad."

Tears sprang to his eyes.

"Aw, now what's the trouble?"

"I'm not crying. I'm not a baby."

"You are a fine young man."

"And I don't cry. Father says. Or I won't be good enough to be the boss man."

But he was so young. Grace held his face in her hands the way her mother used to do to her. "You are smart. You are important. You are able."

He nodded.

Grace thought that if she, as wounded as she had felt when she left Ireland, could prosper, surely this lad born into a financially stable family could do the same.

By the time Hazel and Holly returned home, Linden had decided he'd rather they go to school without him. *Enjoy it now,* Grace thought, wondering just how unreasonably high Mr. Parker's expectations for this three-year-old might be.

Grace's first instruction at the Parkers' house after tidying up was to establish a day nursery. She was to get started before it was time to cook supper.

"But the children—"

"The children can play in their rooms while you're busy. Hazel and Holly can study their lessons," Mrs. Parker told her. The lady of the house was brief and to the point, just the way she was with the children. "Use the third floor, Grace. You know where the cleaning supplies are. I suppose you can sew? There is fabric for curtains in the bureau drawer in my bedroom. When it's clean, move the children's toys up there."

"Are you sure you wouldn't rather I start with the parlor drapes and furniture, ma'am? I haven't gotten to them yet."

"You agreed not to question me, Grace."

So she resigned herself to the attic. Even in the cool air, perspiration plastered her dress to her back as she climbed the narrow, steep stairs from the second floor. *This is not the work-house attic. 'Tis not the same.* This attic surely would not be as desolate and drafty as the place where she'd spent the last of her childhood. *Breathe. You're in America.*

A mouse scrambled over the toe of her boot as she entered, startling her. *Come on, Grace. You are able.*

She let out the breath she'd been holding. The vacant space was no plush American parlor, but there was nothing nefarious about it either. The walls did not reek of generations of suffering. This building held almost no age at all. Different. This was different.

There was but one window and a wee one at that. No electric lights either.

She dragged a broom across the wooden floorboards. Maybe with some lye soap she could freshen it. And if she could find some whitewash, it wouldn't be quite so dreary.

Curtains? She wasn't so sure. She vaguely remembered Ma teaching her how to thread a needle when she was a child. Sighing, Grace decided the woman would not notice if that wee window never got any curtains. Grace would press on.

Saturday morning Grace trudged up to the third floor again, this time with Holly and Linden in tow. They all wore coats. It was brisk up there, especially at that early hour. She gave them each a broom.

Whack! Linden smacked his against a beam.

"Whoo!" Holly circled hers in the air.

"Is everything a game to you?" Grace snatched the brooms away.

The two children stood before her, mouths open as though she'd thrown icy water on them.

"That's all right. You are not in trouble."

Their shoulders relaxed.

"But we do have to clean this place. Are you going to help or not?"

"Yes, Miss Gracie!" Holly reached for her broom and then Linden's.

Well, so. All they required was to feel needed. As they retreated to opposite corners to continue sweeping, Grace began to hum. "Say, let's make up a song." She began to sing, "You are smart. You are important. You are able."

Soon they were singing it with her, and she realized the

power of those words. If she believed it, perhaps she could pass that confidence on to the Parker children.

If . . . Grace was always saying *if* to herself. The unknown future sometimes paralyzed her. But perhaps having responsibilities and assigning tasks to the children would be a start, something real to grasp on to. And they seemed to have fun at the same time. Why not? *"Eat dessert first."* Harold Hawkins's advice could apply to many circumstances.

She found a carpet rolled up in a corner. After hauling it outside for a good pounding and then lugging it back to the attic, she unfurled it. A perfect floor covering to help warm the space. She'd changed her mind about whitewash, at least until spring. She found that if she lit the coal fireplace in the master's bedroom, the air warmed up some in the attic, enough to keep the children from catching cold, she thought.

Grace divided the next hour between trying to coax the children into behaving and cooking simple meals of boiled beef and roasted hens to see the family through Sunday, when she would not be there. While the meat simmered and roasted, she finished hauling the children's toys to the third floor. A rocking horse, a complete set of alphabet blocks, numerous dolls with miniature furniture sets, and an array of spinning tops filled out the attic room nicely. The children had been overindulged it seemed, except when it came to food.

Alice Parker clapped her hands when she saw the nursery. "Delightful, Grace." She never even mentioned the uncloaked window.

Beaming from the unexpected compliment, Grace dared to agree. "The children even helped a bit. They argue much less when they have a job."

"Right. Well, whatever you think."

"I'm thinking the children will be quite content to spend their leisure here when the weather's not pleasant."

"Oh, they'll be up here all the time, Grace." The woman turned to leave, careful not to snare her heel on the uncarpeted steps. She spoke again with her back toward Grace. "Except when the girls are at school, I expect you to keep them up here. That's what a nursery is for, now, isn't it?"

Mrs. Parker wanted the children out of sight. That had been the purpose of creating this space. Grace could not fathom how it was possible for a mother not to care for her children. A father, aye. But not a mother. She bit her lip and reminded herself that this woman made the rules and she would have to operate within those constraints. "Aye, that's what 'tis for—the children."

Alice Parker halted on the second floor and called up to Grace. "I almost forgot to tell you. I've invited two friends for tea today. Two o'clock."

Conveniently the mantel clock downstairs struck noon. Two hours? There were no more store-bought biscuits in the scullery. Grace only had time to make soda bread. "Certainly," she responded through clenched teeth, wondering how such an unpleasant woman could possibly have any friends. When she was beyond the woman's hearing, she spoke her mind. "Am I to be a miracle worker or what? A tea party two hours hence? That woman is as loony as a . . . a . . ."

"A loon?"

She jumped. Holly stood in the doorway. "Not a word of that, lass. Not if you want some of the tea treats I'm baking."

The lass giggled. Already Grace was winning their favor.

Thankfully the children did play in their new nursery while Grace worked in the kitchen. She only had to scramble up there once to break up a fight, which was less than she expected. As she scooped flour from the bin into a bowl, she could not dismiss the similarities. The Parker children were separated from their mother by two floors just like Grace had been from her mother. Of course, Grace's mother did not choose that division. It was forced on her. That fact made Grace resent her employer all the more.

Adding buttermilk, salt, and soda to the flour, she worked the dough past the stage of crumbs, something one should not do with soda bread. She knew full well to sift the dry ingredients together before adding the liquid, but she was in a dither and careless. The batter became the victim of Grace's frustration. Here she was working for a woman who did not love her children so that Grace's mother, who did love her daughter, could be freed from such tyranny.

The dough stuck to her fingers like river slime. She rubbed her hands together, dislodging as much as she could and wiping the rest on her apron. With a dust of flour on her hands, she turned the messy concoction onto a board and kneaded with fury.

She had just popped the bread into the oven when Linden came down the stairs, wailing. "Sissy kicked me."

She sighed and led him back up to the nursery. She found Holly sitting on a child-size rocker in a corner of the room, arms wrapped tightly across her wee chest. She knew Linden was telling on her. She stuck out her tongue.

"Now, now, lassie. Don't be that way. What's the trouble?"

Grace discovered that Linden had confiscated Holly's doll, Miss Margaret, to become a leader in his tin soldier army. "She's taller than the rest. I need her to see 'em all in battle."

Hazel had just arrived home, dropped off by the driver the Parkers had hired to take her to a special holiday choir practice at the school. Grace heard Mrs. Parker apologizing that her housekeeper had become too detained to greet him at the door.

Conversation wafted along the flower-papered halls like smoke in a chimney. And apparently Hazel had heard some of the commotion coming from the attic. She appeared in the doorway, hands on wee hips. "Girls don't fight in the army, stupid."

"Hey." Grace grabbed the stubborn lass's wrist. "No name-calling."

Hazel wiggled free and joined her sister in sticking out her tongue at their brother. Linden whimpered.

Just when it had been going so well. Perhaps the problem began whenever there were more than two together in the house. Grace was ill equipped to settle such juvenile disputes. She'd never had time for them when she was their age. Perhaps it was not all bad to have struggled for survival and skipped these foolish battles of wills. Despite all that, she had to try. It was her job.

After a time of hapless negotiating, she remembered the bread. "Linden, I'll help you make a tall general for your army." She tossed Miss Margaret back to Holly, who caught her by her blonde curls.

Much to her dismay, Grace discovered she would have to start over with the bread. *Pitiful.* What she made looked so unappetizing, Mrs. Parker's guests would never even taste it. She could not accept failure. Drumming her index finger against her forehead, she thought hard. The bread was still good enough to eat, so she put it aside for the children. Bribing them with food might prove to be advantageous, for now anyway.

In better humor after the children had a snack and settled down to play quietly, Grace began another batch of soda bread. This one turned out airy, and the caraway seed had mixed in perfectly. She sliced it and served it in the parlor with thick slabs of butter. She'd done it. All thoughts of her blundering nature dissipated.

"We can't stay long, dear," a lady in a maroon hat said, removing her gloves.

"You simply must have some authentic Irish bread," Mrs. Parker said, smoothing her gown over her pregnant belly as though she could hide it. "My maid recently arrived from the old country and she is a superb baker."

Did she mean it?

The taller woman spoke. "Very well. Have a seat, Doris."

The other woman dusted a chair with her gloves before sitting. Their disapproval of Alice Parker was apparent.

Grace served the tea and more than once was tempted to spill it on the snobbish ladies. But she had not yielded to that temptation.

When they'd left, she caught Alice in the front hall. "Why, may I ask, do you put up with that?"

Alice rolled her eyes. "Status, dear Grace. Status. I do not expect you of all people to understand. Besides, I can't get out in my state. This is better than nothing. I'm tired and my ankles are swollen. I'm going to retire."

"Very well."

Mr. Parker worked late and did not come home before Grace left. Once she had all the children tucked into bed, she waited a full hour to make sure they were asleep before locking the front door. She knocked softly on Alice's bedroom door.

"What is it, Grace?"

Grace whispered into the door. "The children are all asleep. I'm heading for home."

"Mr. Parker home?"

"He is not, ma'am."

"Fine. Go on."

11

A SUNBEAM BURST THROUGH the stained-glass window on the right side of the church, sending sprinkles of blue and green at Owen's feet. He glanced behind him and noticed Grace McCaffery sitting in Mrs. Hawkins's pew on the other side of the aisle three rows back. She seemed to notice him and glanced down. He hoped he hadn't embarrassed her.

When the services concluded, he made his way toward Grace and her companions. "Ladies."

Mrs. Hawkins replied. "Officer McNulty, how nice to see you. You are looking dapper as usual in your fine blue suit." She gave his lapel a tug. "I so prefer this to your police uniform."

He grinned. "As do I. Lovely to see you too, Mrs. Hawkins, ladies." He turned to Grace. "How are you getting along, Miss McCaffery?"

"Fine, thank you." She seemed to focus on the colored windows that had lost some of their illumination now that the sun was higher.

He cleared his throat. "If I can be of any help again . . . giving directions . . . anything at all, please call on me." He stood straighter and nodded toward Mrs. Hawkins and Annie. "That goes for all of you ladies."

Grace dared to look him in the eye. "I will not need anything, thank you."

She winced as Mrs. Hawkins's elbow nudged her side. He pretended not to notice.

"You are very kind, Officer," Grace said.

They said farewell and he watched them walk away, wondering if they felt the same way as those on his beat—that he was an outsider, someone who did not understand them or even care about the challenges they faced. Mrs. Hawkins did not seem like that. She always had an encouraging word when he needed it. But those Irish girls? Owen wasn't sure at all that they saw him as anything more than just another rich American.

He was still contemplating what he might do to change his reputation when Reverend Clarke extended his hand. "Always nice to see you in church, Owen."

"Always nice to be here when I'm not scheduled to work."

The reverend gave him one of his famous smiles, his sparkling eyes open wide. "You keep showing Christ to those you meet, Owen. This town needs more like you."

"Why, thank you, Reverend. I hope I'm up to the task."

"God equips those he calls, you know."

Owen basked in the reverend's blessing all the way back to his apartment. Some days, like today, it was easier to believe that than others. He needed to hold on to that, bank it for a rainy day. He could have used such encouragement at Miss Amelia's the other night.

On the walk back home, Mrs. Hawkins questioned Grace. "The day you were delayed with the raisins . . . was Officer McNulty the one who gave you directions, love?"

Grace tried to sound unconcerned. "He was. Why do you ask?"

"Well, as your guardian during the time you are adjusting to living here, I want to advise you to trust officers like Owen. He is a good man. I understand you are cautious. You didn't know. That's why I mention it." She linked arms with both Grace and Annie. "My Harold used to say, 'An ounce of prevention is worth a pound of cure.' Better to befriend someone like Officer McNulty in a big city like this, lovies."

After a day off, Monday hit Grace like a steam engine. Ever so grateful to be returning to Hawkins House that evening, she climbed the stoop like her shoes were lead.

"There you are, Grace." Annie helped her off with her cloak. "Look what came for you today."

"My camera?"

"Aye, 'tis. Over there."

Grace grabbed the package from the hall table and took it into the parlor.

"Open it. We have been waiting," Annie said, following her into the room.

Grace untied the string and pulled away the brown paper covering the box. On the outside she noted the words *Brownie Camera for Pictures 2 1/4 x 2 1/4 Inches. PRICE $1.00 Made by EASTMAN KODAK CO. Rochester, N.Y.*

No one would need to employ a photographer once these became popular. Grace pulled the lid off the box, eager to try it out.

"How does it work?" Annie asked.

Mrs. Hawkins clicked her tongue. "Give her time, love.

There should be instructions in the box. Even a child can operate it, you know."

The camera was a mere cardboard box, covered in black paper, nothing like the colorful box it arrived in. There was a lens on one end and on the top a winding mechanism she assumed was to advance rolled film. Grace could not imagine how something so simple-looking could take photographs. She began studying the instruction booklet and practicing with the shutter, which is what the booklet recommended you do before loading the film.

The Hawk cleared her throat. "Did you know, girls, the camera is named for the Brownie character, those darling little drawings Palmer Cox made for his stories in the *Ladies' Home Journal*? Maybe you've seen them."

"Like on the box?" Annie asked, picking it up.

The Hawk laughed. "Oh yes. There they are."

"Aye, like Irish fairies," Annie said, winking at Grace.

"The druggist down the street carries the film," the Hawk said. "Fifteen cents a box. You mail it back to Kodak and they will develop it for you."

"It doesn't get much simpler than that," Annie said.

Along with the camera, Grace had ordered two boxes of film, each with six exposures. The directions said the camera could be loaded in daylight. Amazing.

"Do you think you can operate it, love?"

She aimed the camera box at Mrs. Hawkins and clicked the shutter. The Hawk jerked back in her chair. "Don't waste your shots, Grace."

"Relax, Mrs. Hawkins. The film isn't loaded."

Grace and Annie giggled.

The woman put her hand on her chest. "Gracious. You

already know all about the thing. When you are ready, let us all know and we'll line up for portraits. What do they call these? Snapshots? Yes."

"I would be happy to."

It was Thursday and she'd gotten a half day off. But she was not anticipating the maid's dance. Grace had a new camera, so she was preparing for her first leisure outing alone. She was headed to the park with her newly purchased drawing supplies and her Brownie camera.

The sun set early on December days. She needed to remember that even on fairly warm days like this when she was tempted to forget. She hadn't loaded film in the camera yet, but she wanted to practice while she was alone. The chatter in Hawkins House didn't allow time to choose a fitting composition for her first snapshot. She thought that if she could first sketch the image of what she wanted to capture, she could then discern whether or not it was worthy of photographing. She did not want to waste her film.

When she passed Bowling Green, she was only steps from Battery Park. She had only moments to spare while the light was just right. She positioned herself under a tree and began to observe the activity around her. Finally she settled on a bicycle for her subject. Someone had leaned the contraption against a tree and she thought it made a wonderful image. Nature and man. She sketched the scene from two different viewpoints, then moved on, her fingers growing a bit numb from the cold.

Late afternoon rays of sun kissed her cheeks even if they did nothing to warm her. She rested on a stone bench near a statue of a man and pondered who it might be. A war hero? He did not wear a uniform. A statesman? Perhaps. Odd. He held something like a child's toy, a boat, in his hand. A fat pigeon interrupted her thoughts. She laughed as she watched it land on the statue's boat and bob its head.

She'd heard that America was a considerable country, much bigger than Ireland. New York was only one city, and there were fields and trees and vast open spaces somewhere. She inhaled, taking in the smell of the harbor, nearby food vendors, and even the sooty smell of burning coal.

"Did you know rain has no smell of its own?" a girl in the workhouse had once said. "It takes on the scent of whatever it falls on."

Grace now knew it was true. Rain on pavement and horses had a whole different odor than rain on grass. Thank goodness there was some green here in America—or would be come spring.

A discarded newspaper blew to her feet. She kicked it away. With all the crowds, garbage, and smokestacks in New York, the rest of America was hard to imagine.

She closed her eyes to try. But there was still sound. Lots of it. Trolley car bells, children laughing, people chattering, boat horns blasting.

She opened her eyes and rubbed her face. If she were going to survive, much less thrive, in this place, she would have to do what she had done in the workhouse. Look for the beauty—the lone flower, the glimmer of fresh raindrops, the carvings high on the facade of city buildings, the delicate differences in the shapes of people's noses, the shades of their hair, their expressions, the color that she knew had to be there somewhere. She looked around her and bemoaned the fact that her scribbling had nearly used up her only pencil.

As she contemplated the cost of fresh paper and charcoal

pencils, she removed her camera from her satchel. The low hum of a private conversation caught her attention. A trio of men, each one with a top hat and black coat, stood on the other side of the statue chatting with a more modestly dressed fellow. She began to wonder if there were enough differences in each individual's appearance to draw them uniquely. Was the cut of their coats the same? Perhaps one had deep-set eyes and another, freckles. Maybe one would dare to wear a red tie. Even if he did not, she could paint him that way or try to.

With her camera in hand she crept closer to the statue, raising a finger to her lips as she stared at the pigeon still perched on the toy boat.

"Fifty dollars, I'd say, Goo Goo," she heard one of the men mumble.

Businessmen, she assumed. Men in America had a strange way of doing business, here in a park. Surely there was a pub for such talk. She leaned out to sneak a look. The man's eyes met hers, rounded in surprise.

"Hey!" he called, pointing at her.

Embarrassed, she started to stutter. "I-I . . . uh, sorry."

"She's got a camera!"

One of the men lunged at her and she ducked under his arm. They wanted to steal her camera! She ran as fast as she could until she reached a round stone building on the edge of the harbor where a lot of people gathered. The crowd was large enough to allow her to escape by squeezing in among shoulders. "Hey," a plump lass with blonde curls said to her. "Wait in line like everyone else."

"Sorry. Someone was after me."

The girl shrugged her round shoulders and then pointed. "There's a copper out there, Red. Go tell him."

Copper. The word Americans used for a peeler. Grace stared at her. "Why would I do that?" No sooner had she spoken than she remembered the admonishment Mrs. Hawkins had given her after they'd encountered Owen McNulty on the trolley when Grace had first arrived. *"Be respectful to the New York police, and they'll be there when you need them. Treat them rudely and spend the rest of your days looking behind you in dark alleys."* Grace trusted the people who had helped her get settled, but how far should she take that dependence? Police—peelers—were some of the most unscrupulous people on earth.

The yellow-haired girl laughed. "I don't know. Maybe you need help or something?" She cocked her head to one side. "'Less you lifted someone's wallet and the cops are after *you*." She gave Grace a shove. "Go on and get out of here, Red. I won't rat on you."

Her first inclination had not been to find a peeler. It would take some time before Grace could talk herself into taking Mrs. Hawkins's advice altogether.

Grace touched a hand to her hair before wandering over to another crowd of people where she could stare out over the park. The area around the statue was now occupied by a group of lads playing a game of tag. She glanced up and down the walk that led around the water. The men were gone. The Hawk's warning rang true. Grace did need to look behind her in dark alleys and also in the park. There were plenty of evil people lurking everywhere.

She took a deep breath and held her camera to her chest. "Excuse me," she said to a young mother herding a group of children. "What would you all be waiting for?"

She smiled at Grace. "Why, to get into the aquarium. Are you coming in?"

"Uh, what is that?"

The boy next to her giggled. "The fish house. I'm going to see the whale."

"Where is the whale?" Grace leaned out to get a view of the water.

He tugged on her skirt. "In the fish house." He pointed toward the building. "They gots an octopus too."

Grace had to see that.

"Can anyone go in?"

The lass shrugged her shoulders. "There's no admission charge, if that's what you mean. Come on and wait in line."

When Grace got inside, she was amazed. Arched pillars and painted stucco walls gave the place a regal feel. Chattering children and giggling young lasses made Grace think of the great fairs in Ireland, a vague memory from before her workhouse days. The memory of light and color and life. The beauty she had not found out in the park.

She stayed with the flow of people and lifted her nose to breathe in the scent of hot peanuts. The lad she'd seen earlier inched past her, toting a small sack of the treats. He placed one nut in her hand.

"Thank you."

"A treat for a beautiful lady," he said, smiling without the benefit of a front tooth.

Beautiful? Not her. He was being polite.

His mother squeezed him to her side, smashing his cheek until he complained. "A charmer, I'm afraid." She gave Grace a half smile. "Like his father." She sighed.

A crashing sound turned every head toward the center of the building.

"The whale!" The lad tugged on his mother's pocket purse until she relented and moved in that direction.

Grace had seen a whale at sea and she could not imagine how one could be tamed inside a building. In Ireland, when she was a wee lass and her mother had taken her to visit relatives in the far west of the island, she'd seen whales dragged from the shore and cut up for blubber and oil and whalebones to be used in various ways. They were massive, magnificent creatures. She turned and clambered up the steps workers stood on to feed the animals, moving in the opposite direction of the crowd. When she reached the highest level where she could still see the pools below, she took in the sight, admiring how sunlight from the rooftop glinted on the water.

Someone bumped into her. She supposed she would have to explain herself to an aquarium worker. She had only wanted to get a better view and no taller than she was, it was difficult down below. But when she turned to the man standing next to her, someone she expected to be a spectator like she was, she noted the lack of a uniform and nearly fell off the platform. The man from the statue!

Just beyond him two fellows in tweed coats sat on the landing, dangling their feet. Sandwiched between them was a fellow wearing a black coat and holding his tall hat in his lap. He glanced at her, his deep-set, dark eyes serious. Even after he turned away, she remembered that face. In the park by the statue another man had called him an odd name. Something like glue. . . . Goo Goo.

He puffed continually on a cigarette as he stared at the opposite wall. The lot of them seemed wholly American to Grace from the cut of their clothes to the ring of their voices.

The man next to her suddenly pulled the Brownie from her hands, took it apart, and felt inside the box. Frowning, he turned the camera upside down and gave it a shake.

"What are you doing? Give that back to me."

He dropped it at her feet and she scrambled to pick it up.

"Where's the film?"

"'Tis not loaded.'Tis a new camera. I'm practicing." Before she could stand, he pulled her satchel from her arm.

"Hey!"

He grabbed her two boxes of unopened film and stuck them in his pockets. Then he tossed her bag to the ground.

"Nobody takes photographs of my boss, lady."

"I wasn't trying to—"

"Don't matter what you *try* to do."

Tears sprang to her eyes. As much as she didn't want to be bullied ever again, she felt weak and helpless. *You are able.* "Give me my film."

The curve of his lips and his low, dipped eyelids gave her a chill. His eyes were shadowed and beard stubble speckled his chin. The lines beneath his bulging eyes meant that he'd spent too much time in the pub. He rubbed his nose almost continuously. But despite his rumpled appearance, he was still properly attired for a gentleman, with smooth leather shoes and a finely cut suit, custom-made probably. He stared at her a moment, then scrambled down the opposite side of the metal stairs, following his companions, and disappeared below among the children carrying bags of peanuts and a troupe of women in colossal hats.

She examined her box camera and clicked the shutter. Some of the black paper was scuffed, revealing the cardboard underneath, but otherwise it seemed unharmed. All she'd lost was thirty cents' worth of film. This mugging could have been much worse.

12

OWEN REALIZED that the reason he was getting a partner was because of these extra assignments patrolling near the harbor. Things were boiling up in Lower Manhattan, and the force was not prepared. Either that, or there were too many corrupt police to find enough men to make headway against the criminal activity in this area. That new partner couldn't come soon enough. Cracking this gang could be just what Owen needed to earn respect and get a promotion.

Owen glanced up at the barren branches of a locust tree overhead and thought about his future. He was in line to be an inspector, a sizable promotion. He'd so far managed to avoid the long tentacles of Tammany Hall. That organization controlled and dictated much of the police department. Since joining the force, Owen learned to be careful not to draw attention to himself so that they would not interfere with his police work. He just wanted to do his job and move up to a more challenging position. Sergeant came after inspector; *Sergeant McNulty* had a nice ring to it.

He smiled at each face he encountered. If the people thought of you as a friend, you could get their cooperation and even information when you needed it. And like his Irish granny always said, "Every person's alike in God's eyes, laddie. They've all got worth, and better that you treat them that way." And of course, he'd received Reverend Clarke's blessing, and Owen took that to heart.

He'd tried to show Christ to everyone he encountered, like the reverend said, but being on the Lower Manhattan beat, he'd seen the worst of people—bodies mangled and bloody after being pushed from upper-floor windows, merciless men extorting money from ten- and eleven-year-old prostitutes, little paperboys beaten for the few pennies in their pockets. It was hard to grasp that God loved the downtrodden just the same as the fat aristocrats uptown. Some fared so well and others suffered. Owen had been called to do what he could for the poor folks, but it was often discouraging work, especially since he'd had no success so far moving through the ranks.

"Afternoon, ladies." Owen tipped his hat at two society women as they passed by him, taffeta dresses swooshing all the while. Today he was more interested in the faces of the men in the park. Word from headquarters was that Kid Yorke, Goo Goo Knox, and the like had moved on from their days with Battle Annie Walsh and were up to no good around the Hudson River docks, calling themselves Hudson Dusters. Knox was now the official head of the gang, but no one knew what that thug looked like. Just that he had a name that indicated he was not an old man, a baby face presumably. Owen's captain thought the gang was probably in Battery Park from time to time, and so Owen had to be vigilant. Those boys normally caroused in the darkness, but his hunch was that they might be emerging from their gutters to slink about this time of day.

He stopped a ball with his foot. A lad ran up to him, a stick in one hand and his cap in the other. "Sorry, Officer. It got away from us."

Owen handed him the ball. "Say, lad. Seen any bad fellows about today?"

"No, sir."

Owen ran his hand through the boy's tangled brown hair. "You come see me if anything's stirring. You hear?"

"Yes, Officer." The boy scampered back to his buddies who waited next to improvised bases—their discarded coats lying in a heap. Baseball was taking hold of New York's youth like nothing Owen had ever seen before. Better they aspire to be a New York Giant like George Davis or Amos Rusie than end up like Kid Yorke, Circular Jack, or Goo Goo Knox. If it was colorful nicknames the kids were after, baseball was a better choice. The sport had produced Old Hoss Radbourn and Bob "Death to Flying Things" Ferguson, after all.

He decided to move toward the aquarium, a place where families congregated, especially on winter days when they'd rather be indoors. The park with all the families and proper folks should not be soiled by gangsters, not if he could help it. He entered and gazed about, letting his stare linger in secluded corners and out-of-the-way niches. On a catwalk he noticed some young folks clustered together. Loitering in a public building was not permitted. He sighed and began to climb the steps, swinging his long arms. He paused halfway up and looked again. That young woman there with the red petticoat sticking out from under her skirt. Was that . . . ?

"Officer McNulty, what a pleasure."

He turned to look below him. Mrs. Morgan, a regular attendee of First Church on Rayburn Street, smiled at him.

"Enjoying the fish, Mrs. Morgan?"

She blushed, as women seemed to do in his presence. "Indeed. Have you seen the porpoise? It's new, I hear."

"No, ma'am. I'm working."

"Out here?"

"That's right." He inclined his head toward her. "Lovely to see you. I must move along." He thought he caught Mr. Morgan glaring at him from behind his wife's shoulder, but he couldn't linger. He had to find out what Grace McCaffery could possibly be doing up there. When he turned back, however, she was gone and so were the men she'd been talking to, probably exiting on the opposite side. He turned to look behind him but didn't see them.

He heard someone calling his name. Walter Feeny, a patrolman Owen didn't particularly like because of his gruff interactions with citizens the man seemed to despise, lumbered toward him. "Captain's called a meeting for the park patrol."

"Where, Feeny?"

"Main headquarters. Got a police wagon waiting. Let's go."

Captain Nicholson paced as he talked around the cigar in his mouth. "And so I've heard from three immigrant aid societies, men. They all said the same thing. Clean up that park or they're moving out. I expect the rest would follow."

Owen raised his hand. "Where will they operate from if they move?"

The man shrugged. "Don't suppose they will." He coughed and wedged the stogie between the middle fingers of his right hand. "And then we'll have more crime down there than we can handle. This puts me in a pickle. A pickle, mind you. Those Dusters might be lowlifes, but they have friends in high places. We got to chase 'em back to the docks, but to do that, we gotta get the big guy. I'm not asking for a roundup of all those thugs. Just the leader."

Feeny stood, his ruddy cheeks glowing. "Aw, surely they're not being that much trouble, Captain. We'll just make them uncomfortable for a time and they'll move on."

The captain waved the cigar. "Not good enough. These people, these charity workers, they won't wait. And think about it, men. If they don't protect those naive immigrants when they arrive from Ellis Island, there'll be pickpockets, shysters, and drunkards not only in Battery Park but all over Lower Manhattan."

Another man waved his arm. "C'mon, Captain. We got that already."

The captain resumed his pacing. "And tell me, Andy. You want more of it? Tell me you're not running holes in your shoes as it is."

Feeny again. "But why go after Goo Goo? He's a shifty thug if ever there was one."

The captain huffed. "A challenge, yes. But putting him in Sing Sing would break up the gang for good." He paused, turned face forward, and arched his thick black brows. "There'll be a fine promotion for the man who brings him in, not to mention the satisfaction of ridding Manhattan of a gang and protecting those poor immigrants."

The small gathering of beat cops whooped, although Owen was sure not many, if any of them, were actually going to put forth the effort required to catch Goo Goo Knox. These were the men who slept on duty, who visited dives when they were supposed to be working. Some, perhaps Feeny, even took protection money from the shopkeepers. But Owen would never do that, and he was working hard to make sure the local businessmen knew it. Owen's mission was to protect those poor immigrants, and if there were no aid societies, he'd have little hope of doing it. He couldn't house them all, not even one, in his tiny apartment. It was within his orders now to do something that could truly help.

On his way out, the captain stopped him. "McNulty, I know I promised you a partner."

"That's fine, Captain. I'm getting along all right."

"Well, that may be." He hesitated until the others left the room and then lowered his voice. "I've handpicked a fellow, just the same. He'll be here Saturday."

"Captain, why someone specific, if I may ask?"

"That's my business. Just be careful out there, McNulty. I trust ya. You're an honest cop. Trouble is, everyone else knows that too."

Owen headed back to his beat, wondering why it had been so difficult for Nicholson to find just one other beat officer he could depend on. Owen didn't know them all, but surely Tammany Hall didn't own the entire precinct save him and Nicholson.

Darkness fell early this time of the year. Owen pulled his collar up and began his rounds, checking for locked doors. The bakery, the shoemaker, the lunch diner—all secure. He checked on some newsboys who regularly slept in a doorway on Pearl. There they were huddled together like puppies. If only the aid society could do something for them. But they moved around and were reluctant to go into a home anywhere for fear they'd lose their jobs. "I'll bring you a blanket tomorrow," he told one who opened an eye to look at him.

"Thank you, Officer McNulty."

"Sure thing."

When he rounded the corner of State Street, he noted lit windows on all of the aid society buildings. Incredible how many people were coming through Ellis Island these days. Nicholson was right to be concerned about keeping crime out of this sector. Without those charity organizations, many of those folks would be lost in this vast city if they didn't have family or friends already in New York.

Several blocks north he passed a Chinese tea shop. He heard movement in the alley. Rats or dogs likely raiding the garbage. A gas lamp shone on the main street but the alley was dark and he had no lantern. He'd purchased one a couple months ago and then broke it during a chase of a pickpocket. He was just reaching for his .32 when someone grabbed him from behind.

"Officer McNulty, is it?"

Owen, being much larger than his attacker, gave the man a swift elbow to the gut. The man released him and coughed, but before Owen could spin around, he was struck across the knees with some kind of pipe. Not again!

As he lay curled on the ground in pain, a dark face drew near to his ear. "The Dusters don't want no honest cop snooping around."

Owen caught his breath. "Don't be on my beat then."

"We'll be where we want to be, copper. And we don't begrudge you your beat. Just stop asking little boys to spy for you. Turn a blind eye like everyone else. Then there'll be no more broken kneecaps. Got it?"

The pain burned up his thighs, but he was not going to answer.

"I says, got it?"

Thud! A blow to his right bicep this time.

As the toughs moved off, Owen heard him say, "Could take a lesson from that Feeny fellow, you know?"

Owen got to his feet; thankfully nothing seemed broken. He rubbed his legs and arm. He'd have bruises, but nothing too bad. Just like last time. It could have been worse. Another warning.

He'd no more gotten to the corner of Broadway when he spotted Grace McCaffery scurrying up the walk. He'd thought he'd seen her in the Battery earlier. She should not be out here. When she got close enough, he yanked her into the alley with him.

"It's Officer McNulty," he said before she could shout out a protest.

"You scared me."

"Better it's me doing the scaring." His sore leg wouldn't let him stand completely. He leaned against a wall.

"Are you all right?" She tried to steady him as he wobbled.

"I'll be just fine. Perils of my job."

"Someone attacked you? What should I do?"

"Nothing. I'm fine." He urged her back out to the street with him as soon as he regained his balance. "I only stopped you because . . . well, obviously it's not safe out here. What are you doing out alone?"

"I'm on my way home."

"I'll walk you back."

"Thank you."

She might have given him blank stares before, but she needed him now. He enjoyed that feeling and the closeness as she leaned against him.

When they arrived at Hawkins House, a much quieter part

of the neighborhood, they paused under the gas lamplight. Her large eyes bored into his soul, and he had to keep reminding himself that he was on duty. This was business.

She reached for his hand. "Are you sure you won't come in?"

They both glanced to the parlor window and saw Agnes Hawkins staring out at them. "Your guardian must be worried."

Grace did not release his hand. He leaned closer to her. "Don't worry about me, Miss McCaffery. I can take care of myself out here." He patted his nightstick for emphasis.

She smiled, still gazing at him. "Thank you for walking me home."

The front door opened. Mrs. Hawkins put her hands to her mouth. "Glad you took my advice, love. I was worried. Good thing Officer McNulty was available to see you home." She shuddered, wrapping a shawl tighter around her shoulders. "It's quite chilly, lovies. Come in."

"I must get back to work, Mrs. Hawkins."

Grace finally let go of his hand and said good night. When Grace reached the porch, he heard Mrs. Hawkins giving her an earful about not being out alone after dark.

As he returned to his beat, Owen wondered if that attack could have been random or, more likely, connected to the last one. Chaos was what Owen disliked about his job. He would much rather use his mind to track criminals than to make rounds. He only hoped he wasn't also fighting headquarters. He would get a photograph of the Hudson Dusters leader for that wall at headquarters, the one they called the Rogues' Gallery, if it was the death of him. They could try to intimidate him all they wanted. He'd just be more careful and steer clear of dark alleys so long as there was no apparent reason to enter them. *"God equips those he calls,"* he remembered the reverend telling him.

When the sun glowed a dim greeting over the harbor, he headed toward the Society. Reverend Clarke rose early, and Owen had to speak to him.

The clunky sound of the house mistress's boots echoed behind the door. Moments later Mrs. Reilly stood in front of him, blinking her eyes.

"'Tis awfully early, Officer. What brings you?"

"I want to see Reverend Clarke immediately."

"Is it urgent?"

"Of course it is. Sorry to intrude, but it could not be helped."

"Please, come in. He should be at morning devotions. I'll let him know you are asking for him."

Moments later the man shuffled down the hall, still dressed in his nightclothes. "Ah, Owen. What brings you by so early? Won't you have a bite of breakfast with us?"

"Thank you. No. I'm just off patrol. I came to have a word with you."

"Absolutely. Should we retire to my study?"

"No, no. I don't want to interrupt. I just want to warn you, Reverend."

"Warn me?"

Owen laughed nervously. "Well, inform you. You might not be aware. You should keep your charges closer to their house, especially late in the day."

"What do you mean?"

"I know she is at Hawkins House, but you are still concerned with her welfare, I'm sure."

"Are you talking about Grace McCaffery?"

"I am."

"Has something happened?"

"No, no. Thankfully she is fine. I walked her home last night myself. She had been out, in Battery Park, and did not begin her walk home until it was dark."

"So happy you saw her home safely, son. I'll insist she return home much earlier, and I'm sure Mrs. Hawkins has already addressed the problem."

"Well, that's not the greatest trouble, I'm afraid."

"Oh?"

"It's her presence in the park that I'm concerned with. That is where I first spotted her."

The man tightened the cloth belt of his robe across his belly. "You must tell me what happened. Come, sit."

"Uh, just for a moment."

They took chairs in the front room. Owen leaned forward, rubbing his sore thighs briefly, not wanting to reveal to the reverend what had happened to him that night for fear of causing him undue worry. He would be fine, just sorely fatigued. "The park near the harbor, Battery Park, is not as safe as it once was. I'm not saying not to go there at all, but young women should not go alone. The aquarium included."

"You are not saying she was there at night?"

"Late afternoon. Like I said, she failed to calculate how quickly the sun would set. I couldn't get away to speak to you until I got off duty. I came straight here."

"Oh, I see. Well, I'll be. I had thought since Roosevelt improved things . . . well, I thought we were all safer."

"We can't be too complacent."

"I understand, Owen. Thank you for coming to alert me."

13

GRACE WAS SURPRISED when Reverend Clarke showed up at the Parkers' Friday afternoon. "I've come to escort you home, milady."

"Truly?" His imitation of a knight amused her.

"It's dark out. I thought it best. Mind if we take the Broadway trolley? It's still running and I prefer it to the train. Less crowded this time of day."

"Certainly. Come in and have some tea while I put away the last few dishes."

The reverend sat and crossed his legs at the ankle. "Do you like it here, Grace?"

"Oh, I do. Very fine." She poured hot water over some tea leaves and let the pot brew upon a metal trivet on the tabletop.

"The master of the house treats you well?" He helped himself to a biscuit while she finished washing the dishes.

"I don't see him much. I'm not entirely sure he likes me."

"Well, don't be too concerned about that, child. Right now he only needs to like your work."

"Suppose that's the way of it. He asked me to steer clear of him at church."

"Did he?" The reverend used his thumb to wipe crumbs from the corner of his mouth. "My choice would be that when everyone crosses the threshold of the church, all would be equal, as they are in God's eyes. I don't always get my wish, though. George Parker is a fine volunteer, and he has a heart for the poor immigrants or he wouldn't be serving at First Church. Pride is all that is, and it's bred into people. Don't take it personally, Grace."

A quarter hour later Mr. Parker entered the kitchen and stopped them before they left by the back door. "I'm surprised to see you here, Reverend."

The elder gentleman grinned, his expression beaming. "I have the pleasure of escorting Miss McCaffery today, George."

"Very well." He slapped a white envelope between his palms. "I am aware of the extra time you've put in, Grace." He slipped the envelope into Grace's hand. "Mrs. Parker does not have to know about this. It's a bonus." He nodded his chin at Grace's escort.

The reverend put on his hat. "Mr. Parker. See you in church."

"Reverend."

Grace hesitated. "I'm not sure."

Mr. Parker urged the money toward her. "Go on. And remember what we talked about earlier."

She thanked him and hurried out the door as much as possible while waiting for the reverend to follow. On the way she peeked at the extra pay Mr. Parker had given her. This could pay off her bill with the seamstress. This could help her get Ma over sooner.

"Be careful of that," Reverend Clarke said, looking over her shoulder.

She stuffed the money in her pocket bag. "What do you mean?"

"Extra favors the missus doesn't know anything about. She might get angry."

"Maybe I should give it back."

"Up to you."

Alice Parker was the most aloof mother in all of Manhattan. Grace had worked hard for this. But something about it didn't feel right. "I'll leave it in his evening paper tomorrow."

"That's probably for the best. We've never seen Alice Parker at First Church. Can't say what the condition of that marriage might be, but you would not want the man to favor you."

Grace pulled her shoulders back. "Are you saying Mr. Parker is not an honorable man?"

"Certainly not. I would not put you in harm's way, Grace. I'm just saying he might not be aware of what he's doing. Just be careful is all."

She patted the man's arm. "Thank you for your concern."

"Um-hum." He turned his head toward the street.

The reverend's warning did trouble her. Alice Parker didn't seem any warmer toward her husband than she was to her children. Grace wondered why.

When they approached the trolley stop, Grace halted, momentarily taken aback by what she saw.

"What's the matter?"

"Someone's getting off that car. Someone I don't want to see."

He bobbed his head in all directions. "I don't see anyone. It's fine to go."

"Please, Reverend."

"You are safe with me, Grace."

"I know. 'Tis just . . ." *You are able.* "I've changed my mind. I am going to speak to him. Let's take the next car, if you don't mind."

"Are you sure?"

"Quite sure."

The reverend shrugged. "I'll be close by."

Grace set her bag down. "Wait here one moment."

She marched up to the man in the tailored suit, the one who had roughed up her camera.

He tipped his hat, revealing a shiner. "Hello, Rosie."

"You have me confused with someone else. We've not been introduced."

He was so drunk he couldn't find a hole in a ladder.

"I . . . I call ya that because of that red petticoat." He glanced down. "Where is it? I swear that's who you are."

She had been wearing the petticoat from her mother that day in the park.

Feeling especially brave with the reverend only steps away, she put on the most stern expression she could muster. "You stole my film." She was not as intimidated as before, mainly because of the state this man was in.

"I stole nothing."

"Listen, you. Don't come near me again or I will report you to the police." She didn't know if she intimidated him with that kind of threat, but she hoped that would keep him at bay.

He pulled his head back like a chicken. "Say, don't tell me you got pictures, photographs of my boss." His bloodshot eyes grew wide.

"What I have is . . . well, never mind," she bluffed.

The reverend joined them, Grace's traveling satchel containing her camera in his hand and his expression curious.

She would have to do something to save face. She addressed the odd man again. "I don't believe we were ever properly introduced, seeing as we just ran into each other at the . . . newspaper stand." She stuck out her hand and this time he took it. "I am Grace McCaffery."

"If you say so, Rosie." He bent awkwardly to kiss her hand. "And I'm Prince Charming, of the Hudson Dusters." He wobbled a bit on shaky knees and his breath smelled like a fermented bog.

The reverend had a distinctly puzzled look on his face, and she couldn't blame him. She tipped her head to one side. "We really must be going."

The fellow winked at her before leaving.

When they were seated on the trolley car, Grace whispered into the reverend's ear. "I really don't know that man."

Reverend Clarke whispered back. "How many times have you seen him?"

"Just a couple of times, but I hope to never again. I told him to stay away."

"Make sure you are always in the company of someone else, Grace. It's my duty to protect my girls."

"Don't worry."

They rode in silence for a few more blocks. Then he spoke again. "You say you saw him at the newsstand?"

"Aye."

"Not in the park?"

"The newsstand. I'm surprised he remembered me." She did not want to tell the reverend about the encounter at the aquarium. She'd been innocent, but she wasn't sure anyone would believe her.

14

THE NEXT AFTERNOON Nicholson called Owen into his office. A young man was already there, sitting in one of two chairs opposite the captain's desk. "This here is your new partner, son, Jake Stockton."

The man sprang to his feet and shook Owen's hand.

"Sit, McNulty," the captain said. "I've already filled Stockton in on the Duster problem and why I see the two of you as an important pair." The man lit a cigar and began the incessant pacing he was prone to. "We've got to stop this before it starts. Otherwise the criminals will be coming at us with hammer and tongs." He turned to look at them. "Know what I'm saying, boys?"

"Yes," they said in unison.

Owen looked over at his new partner. About his age, muscular limbs, straight posture. He was physically able. Owen had the aptitude they needed, although he might have to find some new informants.

"Pity I can't equip you boys any better," Nicholson said.

Owen caught the man's eye before he started pacing again. "Captain, the Dusters don't figure much into Tammany's interest, do they?"

"No. Lucky for you." He began pacing again, wearing down the floorboards behind his desk.

Jake patted the arm of Owen's chair. "I've tracked gang members before, only to have the night courts with their Tammany lawyers set them free. They depend on the gangs to round up immigrant voters and keep their boys in office."

Owen shrugged. "Sending the poor men to the barber's and shaving just enough facial hair to allow them to vote twice."

Jake laughed. "That's right. First the chin hair. Then the sides. Then the mustache. That makes for at least three extra votes."

Owen liked this guy.

Nicholson huffed. "Make light of it, but our resources are limited if we're going to be successful at this without Tammany getting involved." He stopped pacing and laid his hands on his desk. "We'll get this one. I know we will. Just steer clear of Big Bill over near Twenty-Eighth Street and Eighth Avenue."

"Big Bill Devery, the police chief?" Jake asked.

Owen spoke first. "That's right. No bigger Tammany puppet than him. Hangs out there past midnight glad-handing politicians and toughs. Far away from our beat, though." That's the way it had been in the past, and Owen hoped Tammany would continue to stay away, despite Devery's odd warning at Miss Amelia's party. Something told him not to bring that up just yet.

Nicholson coughed. "Right so. If we can get the head duck, our night court won't care to save him. We've got a chance with this one, but not all the men are on board, truly. Know what I mean?"

Jake groaned. "All too well. Don't worry. We'll work around the others."

The captain punched the air. "That's my boys!"

When Owen left the captain's office, he was surprised to find Mr. Parker in the headquarters building. "What brings you out here? No trouble, I hope."

"No, no, son. At least not yet. May we sit?" He pointed to a row of wooden chairs lined up in the hallway.

Sometimes these seats were filled with criminals waiting to be booked. Fortunately they were vacant at the moment. "What is it, Mr. Parker? Is Miss McCaffery all right?"

"Well, son, I did come to speak to you about Grace. Reverend Clarke tells me she should have an escort when she leaves my employ in the evenings. I would have her move in with us, but Mrs. Parker, she's a bit persnickety. You know . . . women."

Owen shrugged noncommittally.

"Well, I spoke to your captain earlier, and he agreed that you can take thirty minutes in the evenings to come to my house to escort her home. Hawkins House is on your beat, right? I didn't know who else to trust, and since the reverend speaks so highly of you . . ."

Owen scratched his head. He and Jake would not be scoping out the park too early in the evening. That was probably what Nicholson had been thinking. And Owen really wanted to help Grace. "Fine, then, Mr. Parker. Just tell me what time."

15

SATURDAY TURNED OUT TO BE a long day for Grace. Normally, she'd been told, Saturdays would be a short day, but there was plenty of work to be done at the Parkers'. By evening she felt satisfied she was doing well in her new position. She had not seen the master of the house much during her time there, only at dinner and when she brought the children to him to say good night before she put them to bed. It seemed they were to be entirely her charge, and truth be told she'd rather be with them, as misbehaved as they might be, than to endure the grumpy pregnant Mrs. Parker or the master of the house, and she thought it was probably best that she limit the children's interaction with him.

"Grace," he called out now, as she and the children headed for the stairs.

She turned.

"When they are tucked in, please come back. I'd like to speak with you a moment."

"Certainly."

Her heart pounded as she poked and prodded her charges up the stairs. He couldn't fire her. She was just getting started. And hadn't she done everything the Parkers had asked of her?

Failure. No one wants you. She battled with the foreboding notions rattling around in her mind, thoughts she could not afford to entertain any longer.

After getting the children into bed, Grace crept down the stairs. She could slip out the front door, say she forgot to return to the parlor, face this scolding later. Her arms ached; her toes pleaded to be released from her boots. She envisioned herself scrambling down the dim walkway toward the train, circles of light from overhead gas lamps guiding her way. But even though the last step did not squeak and give her away, she turned toward the room where the master of the house sat by the fireplace, the glow wrapping his silhouetted body. The heat of the room made her sweat, but still she forced herself to move toward him. She might as well face this. Bad news never got better with age.

"There you are, Grace. Please sit." He pointed the magazine in his hand toward an armless chair on his left. Mrs. Parker must have already retired.

She hesitated a moment, longing for Hawkins House.

"You must be tired. I won't keep you but a moment. Please."

She went to the chair and tried to sit gracefully, though she felt like collapsing.

"Please, Mr. Parker. I'm doing the best I can. Your children aren't exactly . . . uh . . . firmly rooted. And your wife? Well, she has no idea—"

He held up a hand to stop her. "I will speak, if you don't mind."

Her mouth was so dry she couldn't swallow.

"I must say that the morals the children are exposed to is utmost in my mind. That's why I inquired with Mrs. Hawkins before hiring you, you understand."

"I haven't done anything—"

"I'm not accusing you of anything, Grace. Let me be clear."

Please, get on with it.

"I want to keep you on."

She let her shoulders relax.

"Mrs. Parker, please understand, does not have the patience for the children's antics. Oh, she adores them, of course. She just needs her private space and time to garden once the baby comes. You understand. She is somewhat . . . shall we say, hermetical in disposition."

She did not understand, but she nodded anyway.

"I had hoped for a nanny, but Mrs. Parker sees the need for housekeeping as well."

Was the man blind?

"So I am willing to have you work these long days." He placed the open magazine on his lap to free his hands for expression. "But you are leaving quite late and unescorted. Reverend Clarke brought this to my attention. He's still very much concerned for your well-being, Grace."

"He is a fine man." The only trustworthy man she'd met.

"I agree. And we do not think it's best for you to be traveling back and forth alone."

A wee knock came from the front door. She stood.

"There he is now." Mr. Parker hurried to the door. Placing his hand on the doorknob, he turned back to her. "I've taken the liberty of arranging an escort for you. I've gotten permission from his captain to allow him to take the necessary time out from his usual duties. He's on the night shift."

Captain? Night shift? He didn't mean he'd hired a policeman, did he?

Mr. Parker swung the door open and in stepped Owen McNulty, flashing his famous smile. Of all the people, how did he . . . ?

"Mrs. Hawkins told me you two were acquainted, and I've met Officer McNulty at church," Mr. Parker said.

After what she'd overheard before she was hired, she couldn't imagine Mrs. Parker would be happy about this. "Does Mrs. Parker know?"

"She'll abide by my wishes."

Grace's knees went weak and she had to sit back down to recover.

Mr. Parker frowned. "I thought you'd be pleased to have the company."

He had no idea. He couldn't know. Grace was beginning to find Owen completely charming and that worried her. She did not yet know if he was cut from a different bolt of cloth than the Irish peelers. If he were another Harold Hawkins, all would be well. But she didn't know if that could be.

"He's on duty, you understand. So he's honor bound to deliver you to Hawkins House safely. He protects the citizenry. I know for a fact, Grace, he is reputable and an upstanding member of the congregation of First Church."

"Aye, yes."

"Good, then. Are you ready?" Mr. Parker was still holding the door ajar.

When they stepped out into the night, Owen did not seem any more comfortable with the arrangement than she was.

"I'm sorry to take you from your work, Officer. This was Mr. Parker's idea."

He rubbed his chin. "It's not that I mind. I've been happy to escort you home previously, Miss McCaffery."

"You do not seem happy about it. I understand."

He shook his head. "I would be very happy indeed, under different circumstances."

"I see."

"I'm on a special assignment. I just have that on my mind."

"I knew it was an inconvenience."

"No, no. I'll be handing this duty over to Jake." Owen stood in the aisle of the nearly deserted train while she sat.

"Who is Jake?"

"My new partner. Just transferred over from Brooklyn. He won't mind." Finally he looked her in the eye. "He's a fine fellow. Since you seem . . . uncomfortable with me anyway—"

"I am not uncomfortable." She shifted in her seat, knowing she'd not spoken the truth. "Thank you for your help. 'Tis just that I didn't expect this."

"You can trust Jake."

Truly?

He smacked his lips. "I would be happy to escort you myself. It's just that there is this special duty in the park. Well, I can't say any more about it, but I'll be engaged for some time."

"I see." The park? There were many parks in Manhattan. "You don't mean Battery Park?"

"Like I said, I can't say much about it." He lowered his voice. "I saw you there once. Don't go there alone anymore."

"You were spying on me?" Didn't she know as much? Her first instincts had been true. *A peeler is a peeler.*

"No. I . . . uh . . . I patrol there sometimes."

"I would prefer someone else to escort me. Like you said, the police are otherwise engaged."

"As you wish. But please don't misunderstand, Miss McCaffery. Under normal circumstances—"

"No. Nay. I do understand. Reverend Clarke might suggest someone for me."

"Whatever pleases you, Miss McCaffery. I really should be

about official business. You know, catching the robbers and such."

He referred to a snide remark she had once made to him. Her face hot, she kept silent for the rest of the journey.

Owen felt like kicking himself. Grace hadn't deserved to be the target of his frustration. How was she to know that he had been struggling between spending time with her and keeping his mind on his duties?

Owen eased his large frame down onto his bed. His legs throbbed. The slug he'd received in that Canal Street alley had bruised him up good. He was ecstatic to see his bed.

He rubbed both hands over his face and stared at the ceiling medallion. He rolled to one side.

Is this worth it, God? Did you make a mistake sending the rich boy to do this job? Who am I?

He knew who he wanted to be. A decent man with a wife and children. A family man. Someone worthy of the confidence Reverend Clarke put in him to show Christ to the downtrodden. He pulled his tightly woven blanket, the one his long-departed granny had brought from Ireland, over his head.

He reached for the watch chain on the bedside table and brought it close. Sighing, he put it back, wondering if he'd get any sleep.

And whose are you, Owen?

The question came to him in a jolt like a cold slap of wind.

He got out of bed and wandered over to the window. The elevated train stood demon-like. When the weather was better, he could lean out and get a view of the steeple on Trinity Church. But now only steel, steam, and black train rails rose stoic against gray structures. He had not been born here, hadn't lived here out of necessity like everyone else around him. Owen had come to the bowels of the city by choice. And at times it seemed to swallow him alive. Logic said he should get out, save himself. Go help his father with the business. But he still felt burdened by a desire to stay, to help, to do what Officer O'Toole no longer could.

Frustrated by the fact that Grace McCaffery and others like her still shut him out, he picked up the watch and flung it against the wall. He never should have insinuated that he was too busy for her.

The watch bounced and slid underneath his bed. Regretting his outburst, he retrieved it. The watch survived his temper.

He had no other direction for his life. Just one. The one the streetcar accident had pointed to.

The sound of screeching metal brought him back to the window. A train had stopped on the tracks. As though cloaked in disguise, black shadows of men slid from the train and moved back and forth on the elevated platform.

Owen went back to his bed, derailed, stuck, and in desperate need of One to drive his life for him. He drifted off to sleep in a cloud of prayer.

16

After church on Sunday, Grace requested a meeting with Reverend Clarke.

"An escort, you say?" He rubbed his watery blue eyes as he leaned on the desk in his study.

"Aye. To ease the mind of my employer, who does not want me traveling alone after dark."

"That's right. I suggested it. I hope you don't mind."

"I know you cannot see me home every night, Reverend, although I did enjoy your company."

He laughed. "As did I yours, child. And you say the New York police will not be sufficient for this job?"

She shifted on her chair. "I do appreciate your recommendation, Reverend." She inhaled before continuing. "I just think they are so busy doing more important work keeping the city safe."

"You are probably right about that. Hmm. Let me see. There is Mr. Crawley. He's a widower, quite lonely but respectable of course. He's an octogenarian but very ambulatory for his age."

"Perfect."

The reverend stood, steadying himself with his palms on the surface of his desk. "He should be in the sanctuary trimming the Advent candles. I'll go check with him."

"Thank you."

"Wait here, dear. I won't be a moment."

She helped herself to tea while she waited. Sipping the rich dark liquid, she gazed about the study. The man with the kind blue eyes had told her he didn't understand God completely. They had that in common. But he still professed a faith, like her mother's, that was foreign to Grace. She needed to be with people like that, draw from their strength. She wondered if she might someday take Reverend Clarke's photograph, the way she'd seen Mr. Sherman do with the minister at St. John's.

When Reverend Clarke returned, he brought an older gentleman with him. "Miss Grace McCaffery, this is Mr. Crawley."

He was tall and thin and wore wide black shoes. Despite his furrowed face, he had a smile that seemed to light the dark corners of the room.

"Pleased to meet you." She held out her hand.

Mr. Crawley had blue eyes like the reverend, although a bit more faded with age.

He patted her hand. "I'm the one to be pleased to be escorting such a pretty young girl." He bowed, indeed limber for his age as Reverend Clarke had said. "I vow to keep all ill-intentioned young men from your presence, my dear."

She laughed. "Lovely. When can you start? I can promise you a muffin most every evening when you pick me up and scones when I've time to make them."

He glanced to the reverend. "What a deal that is, Reverend. I'll be glad to help, once I finish the Christmas preparations here at the church."

The reverend gripped the man's shoulder. "And I do appreciate your help with that, Mr. Crawley. I'll escort Grace tomorrow. Then you can take over after Christmas. That all right, Grace?"

"Aye. Yes. But, Reverend, so close to your special services. Will you have time?" She should have realized how much she was imposing.

"Oh, I will have time, I expect. Deliver just about the same message every Christmas." He laughed. "I think I know it well enough."

"Are you sure?"

"Indeed. I am happy to oblige." His face lit up with sincerity not unlike the wee lad she looked after, Linden.

"Thank you both."

Right after the midday Sunday meal, Grace planned to spend some time outside with her camera. Remembering that daylight was limited, and because photo taking was nearly impossible indoors, Grace took her camera on a stroll through the neighborhood. "I won't be gone long," she called to Mrs. Hawkins.

"Take someone with you," she answered back. "Annie?"

Annie stared at her from behind a mound of dirty dishes. Grace realized she shouldn't run off and leave Annie with all the chores. "I should help you."

"I can manage. I'll let you scrub the bathtub later." She winked. "Taking your camera out?"

"I hoped to."

"Go along, but stay on our street and don't go more than three houses down. If you're not back in twenty minutes, she'll have my head."

"I'll hurry." Leaving her satchel behind so she could manage better, Grace slipped out the kitchen door. She had gone no more than five paces when a couple stopped her.

"Look at that, Charles."

The man tilted his head to examine Grace's camera. "I do believe that's one of those Brownie cameras. Am I right, miss?"

"'Tis. Excuse me. I have to—"

"May I see it?" The man reached for the camera.

Grace sighed and allowed him to hold it. Tapping her foot impatiently, she looked up and tried to determine how much daylight was left, but the towering tenements hid most of the sky. In Ireland she could tell time by the sun even without the workhouse clock ticking away the hours.

Annie had said to hurry.

"I must be going," she said, reaching for her camera.

The man handed it back. Turning to his wife, he said, "Cameras right on the street, dear. Imagine that. We could end up on the front page of the evening *World* just for walking down Broadway."

"Don't be foolish, Charles."

Grace hurried on. There was a druggist on the corner that Mrs. Hawkins had said sold film for her camera.

Once she purchased the film, she carefully loaded the camera and then returned outside. When she passed by an open door, the whooping and shouting erupting from inside made her pause and think of the games the workhouse master and the cook played in the master's office. Cards of some sort. She caught a glimpse of some men seated around a table. Was this American game anything like the Irish one? Curiosity killed the cat. She remembered Mrs. Hawkins telling her Mr. Hawkins used to say that. But Grace had no time to be cautious. She'd just take a quick peek.

She glanced at the box camera in her hands. A photograph allowed time to study the subject. Perhaps she could capture the scene on film and study it later. If she could do that, she might understand the Americans a wee bit better and lose the label of outsider all the sooner.

Standing out on the sidewalk, where there was more light, she hoped would bring her subject into focus. She didn't really know if it would work, of course, but if she didn't start experimenting with her Brownie, she'd never learn.

She nearly dropped the camera when a fellow plopped down from his seat in the open window. The sound of his feet hitting the floor inside the room rattled around in her head for a moment. She glanced around, holding her camera to her chest. No one seemed to notice her. People continued to stomp up and down the street and walkway, providing her a sense of anonymity. She looked around for something to stand on to give her a better perspective. A milk crate rested near the curb. She turned it over, and by perching atop, she achieved a clear view over the tops of the heads of the hoards of people passing by.

She aimed.

When she clicked the shutter, a bawl rang out from the room.

"Did you see that outside the window?" someone shouted.

They pointed in her direction, but had they meant her? She was sure she had been discreet, but if she could see over the heads of the passersby, then the people in the house could see her.

"Was that a camera? A nose from papers! Smokey, I warned ya they'd be looking to ruin me. Not even Tammany Hall can silence that."

"Not the papers, Mr. Middleton. Just a ragbag urchin girl."

What kind of English did these card players speak?

A scrambling sound came from the room, and although they could not have been talking about her, a desire to flee launched her from her perch. Her petticoat snagged on a fence post as she tried to rush away. She pulled at it, leaving some red threads behind before she scrambled to a trolley car and hopped on.

She thought she heard someone cry out the name Rosie, but there was so much commotion, so many people. Probably just in her head.

Sucking in breaths, Grace tilted her head against the back of the wooden seat.

"Sneaking up on a stuss game, miss?"

Grace bolted upright. A man on the seat across from her scowled.

"Are you speaking to me, sir?" Grace asked.

"I am indeed." He raised a thick brow and turned his head to one side. "Looked as though you were playing police detective with your Brownie camera."

Although Grace didn't understand what this man was implying, she knew she had to object. "I was not. I was just curious, and I thought I might—"

The man turned to the woman seated next to him. He crossed his gloved hands over the top of a cane that he repeatedly tapped against the trolley floor.

"Uh-huh," the woman said in answer to the man's stares.

The man puffed out his jowls. "Just as I predicted, Harriet. The advent of those little box cameras will mean that every John—or in this case, Jane—Doe on the street will be taking our photographs. There will be no privacy. Not just for lawbreakers, but for the gentlemen and women who wish to maintain their due right to privacy."

The woman nodded and smacked her lips, and then he pounded his cane harder.

Grace squeezed her eyes tight. Had everyone seen her blunder?

17

Owen sat in the department meeting, but his mind was not on the scheduling Captain Nicholson was speaking about. He was thinking about the Dusters and how he might find their leader. When Nicholson took a break to light a fresh cigar, Feeny, seated to his right, leaned over to whisper.

"Word on the street is Middleton was caught in a stuss game yesterday."

"The reformer?"

"That's the one. You know, the novelist, one of those fellas folks like to think know more than the rest of us so they're always quoted in the papers."

"Yeah, well, can't always trust someone's who they appear to be."

Feeny rounded his eyes like a cartoon character. "Someone took his picture. He don't like it much, I don't suppose. And to think he done it on the Lord's Day. Not good for his image, that."

"Suppose not. When did they bring him in?"

"Not an arrest, I'm speaking about, man. A civilian took his picture, all Jacob Riis–like. Just a wee lass, so I hear, with one of those newfangled box cameras. They say even a child can use those things."

"Well, I suppose a lot of people will be carrying those cameras around in the future."

Feeny always seemed to have something to jabber on about. Owen didn't much care about reformers who only wrote about the plight of immigrants but never worked in the trenches, and he certainly did not care to hear about those who demanded reform and yet still participated in the illicit activities the police were trying to clean up. Jacob Riis was an exception. He went out on the streets with Roosevelt and documented how miserable things were down here. But that was a few years past. Without the folks who did the real work out there now, things would be worse than they are. Kudos to the girl who took that hypocrite's photograph.

"I hear he's even sent thugs out after the photographer."

Owen turned back to watch the captain, sending a message to Feeny that he wasn't interested in the gossip.

Feeny tugged on his shirtsleeve. "'Tis the truth, I tell ya."

"Really, Feeny, where do you hear this stuff?"

"I know people. Important folks."

"Right."

During Linden's nap and while the girls attended to some needlework they were practicing in the kitchen, Grace decided to try to find out why the mistress of the house was so unhappy. Mrs. Parker sat in the parlor, a Burpee Seed catalog balanced on the top of her pregnant belly.

"Mrs. Parker?"

"What is it, Grace?" Alice Parker turned her shadowy eyes from the paper.

"I was just wondering, if you don't mind me asking, is there anything wrong, ma'am? Anything I can do to help you?"

"Wrong? What do you mean?"

"You are so . . . quiet . . . and you hardly want the children around you. Are you ill?"

Mrs. Parker slapped the arm of her chair with the catalog. "You are too nosy. I'm with child, if you didn't notice. George always says I'm grumpy when I'm with child. Well, so be it." She turned to look out the front window. "Nosy. This is what I get for hiring a biddy."

"I only wish to help. For the children's sake." Grace really wanted to slap sense into the woman. What was wrong with her?

"Don't be complaining to him about me, Grace. I'll have you fired."

"Oh, I would never." She thought about the money in her bag, money she would give back at the first opportunity.

Alice Parker rose and poured herself a sherry from her husband's decanter. "I despise my life, Grace." She twirled around and lifted her glass in Grace's direction. "And now you know. George thinks I'm not good for much else but birthing babies and growing flowers. He might not say so out loud, but I know that's what he thinks." She laughed. "What a life that is, huh?"

Grace retrieved the glass from the woman's hand. "The baby. You should not—"

Mrs. Parker collapsed on the sofa. "I suppose you are right, but don't get the idea you can tell me what to do." She mumbled under her breath. "Irish biddy."

The woman clearly had no fight in her. Grace urged her to recline and covered her with a blanket.

She lifted a finger. "I don't care any longer. Not about anything."

"Nonsense." Grace pointed to the catalog. "You care about gardening, now don't you?"

Alice Parker smiled. "Coralbells. I think I'll plant coralbells in the spring. The south side of the house. Don't you think, Grace?"

"Lovely."

When the woman had relaxed, Grace asked again. "Why don't you show the children more affection, Mrs. Parker? Children need it."

"Affection? Who showed me affection?"

"Your mother?"

She huffed. "I grew up in an orphanage."

"No, this is your family home. Your people go to church near here. Mr. Parker said."

"That's what he wants everyone to think, Grace. The nuns raised me." A stern look came over her face. "Irish nuns. And as you can see—" she waved her hand in the air—"as you can see, they didn't do a very good job." She pushed herself up on her elbows. "My biddy mentions this to no one, hear me? Do and I'll see you get no work on the entire west side." She whimpered. "He would not like that. Not at all. A miracle he even allowed me a maid."

"Not a word," Grace promised. "Are you crying?"

The woman wiped her eyes with her thumbs. "George says tears are a sign of weakness. You never saw me crying, understand me?"

"Aye. Yes." Grace instantly thought about what Linden had said.

Later in the day Grace busied herself in the kitchen. Grace

understood Alice Parker. The woman felt worthless, not unlike the way Linden felt. Mr. Parker had them under his thumb. Grace did not have her father around anymore and still he sometimes controlled her. She did not want to become defeated and depressed like her employer and certainly did not want wee Linden to be like his mother as a result of living with such a demanding and restrictive man.

Grace straightened the dishes in the pantry, folded some towels, and swept the floor—each task stirring up anger. Mr. Parker was a fake, pretending he had a happy life and hiding away among the immigrants probably because he liked how lofty and important he felt around them. Reverend Clarke did not know the man as well as he thought he did, but Grace had experience with his kind. George Parker might not be a violent man like her father was when he was drunk, but he was no good just the same. No wonder he didn't want his wife in church with him. It was probably bad enough that his nanny saw what was going on.

She blew out a breath. It just didn't seem right such people should exist in America. The reverend was right. Grace had to be careful. When no one was looking, she entered Mr. Parker's office and dropped the envelope of money on his desk. He'd find it when he returned from work. Maybe he would get the message and not bring it up again.

Grace muttered under her breath later in the day as she polished crystal glasses and placed them back in the dining room sideboard. Christmas Eve and she was expected to create such fancy dishes as she'd never seen before. "Spiced chutney and turtle soup and butter crème pie. How am I supposed to make those things? And why would anyone want to eat them?"

She closed the door on the sideboard and moaned softly

when she heard Linden cry out from his nap. She stood absolutely still, hoping he'd go back to sleep. The mistress had gone to her garden club's annual Christmas meeting at the house next door, a rare outing for the woman, and she'd only gone because the neighbor had promised to call the midwife if Alice had any problems. Mrs. Parker had potted a cutting from a violet she'd wintered indoors and was proud to be taking it to the Christmas gift exchange. If plants had not been involved, Grace was sure the woman would never have risen from the couch.

Hazel and Holly had gone with their mother to play with the children next door. They had a nanny who would supervise during the garden club gathering, thankfully. Grace needed to study the cookbook.

The house quieted again. When she opened her eyes, she looked down at her shoes. Ill-humored Mrs. Parker, before she headed next door, had insisted Grace purchase new ones—and at her own expense. "After all, they're on your feet, not mine. Why should I buy them? I pay you enough."

Grace sat on the sofa and let her legs dangle over the edge. If expenses kept gobbling up her pay, how would she ever get her mother over?

She thought about the extra money she had turned down. Tempting, that had been. Where did the man get all his money?

The postman turned the bell on the door.

She greeted him.

"Good day. Letters for the Parker family."

She took the papers from his hand and thanked him. Closing the door firmly behind her and glancing toward the stairs, hoping the sound hadn't awakened wee Linden, she placed the mail on a silver tray in the parlor near the chair where Mr. Parker reclined most evenings. The letter on top caught her attention.

Sanitation Department, Re: Chatham Square property. Grace had begun to learn her way around, and she knew that Chatham Square in the Bowery was a place to avoid. And Mr. Parker actually owned property down there. She questioned what she had gotten herself into by working for this man, and more importantly what he might expose his children to, the ones he so adamantly proclaimed he wanted to protect. There was definitely more to this man than what first appeared. She would have to be more than just careful. She would have to be vigilant.

She straightened the doilies on the furniture and picked up the cookbook. Ma would know what to do, but Grace could not risk putting this information in a letter.

Grace tried to shake the thoughts from her mind. She'd have to keep holding on to the confidence that had driven her thus far. She desperately needed to believe that she could get what she wanted if she tried hard enough. She would need to ignore the disparity between Mr. Parker's words and his deeds. One way or another she'd need to fan the embers of her certainty that she could survive in this place before it was completely extinguished.

Linden fussed and then burst into a full wail. She scrambled up the steps toward him. The poor lad had become almost as irritable as his mother. She wondered what he'd do once there was a baby in the house. She lifted the whimpering lad onto her lap and sat on the edge of his bed, pulling his sleep-damp curls up under her chin. "There, there, now."

"Sing, Miss Gracie, pleeeeze."

She crooned the song she'd learned on the ship to America. A fellow sang it over and over for days, so she'd had no choice but to memorize it. She'd let Linden believe it was the melody her mother sang to her as a child, but she'd had no lullabies in fact.

"The pale moon was rising above the green mountains,
The sun was declining beneath the blue sea,
When I strayed with my love to the pure crystal fountain,
That stands in the beautiful vale of Tralee.

"She was lovely and fair as the rose of the summer,
Yet 'twas not her beauty alone that won me.
Oh no, 'twas the truth in her eyes ever dawning,
That made me love Mary, the Rose of Tralee."

She stroked his fair hair. Grace longed for the truth in her mother's eyes, the way the songwriter had missed that something special in his love.

Grace was a good nanny, wasn't she? Finally something she actually could do well. "Linden, what do you say we go for a walk?"

He bobbed his blond head. She helped him dress, complete with mittens, boots, and a hat. She gathered a blanket to bring along. There were only dribs and drabs of gray snow on the ground. They'd have no trouble walking about.

She always brought her camera with her although she had little time to use it. The sun was out. Maybe today was a good day.

She held tighter to Linden's hand than he cared for, but she could not risk losing him in the crowds. Soon enough they found a small park, and she let him free to run among the tufts of dormant grass and chase a few pigeons.

Grace stood tall, her Brownie camera firm against her chest. When the right time came, she snapped the shutter. Those fleeting moments when the light was just right and the boy's face held an expression she wanted to capture were like wee gifts of joy to Grace. She wished she could see the photographs instantly to know if she'd captured what she hoped. She knew she needed a lot of practice.

"Many a little makes a mickle," she remembered Mrs. Hawkins saying. Another of Harold Hawkins's proverbs. This one, Mrs. Hawkins said, meant that wee bits of effort could add up to much, and Grace hoped that applied to her picture-taking practice. She was finally doing what she'd been dreaming of. Freezing a moment in time for future study. Linden had that light in his soul that beamed through other faces she'd noticed, the innocence that all too soon vanished. If only she had it too.

She snapped a couple more shots of the boy. Maybe these would cheer his mother.

She returned to the spot she'd selected for them on a bench and counted her remaining exposures. Linden ran up to her. "You are the most wonderfullest, Miss Gracie." He gave her a big hug. Maybe her job wasn't so bad after all. Maybe she really was able.

"Most wonderful," she corrected, blinking in the midwinter sun. She gave him another hug and sent him off. "Just a few more minutes, Linden. I don't want you to get too cold."

When they arrived home, she was surprised to find Mr. Parker waiting for them.

"Where have you been with my son?" His stiff posture and harsh tone ran through her like knives.

"Father!" Linden hugged his father's leg.

Mr. Parker bent down and pushed him away. "Be a man, Lindy."

The lad put on a straight face, then smiled when he looked

at Grace. "Miss Gracie is the most wonderful . . ." The lad paused to get approval from her. "The most *wonderful* nanny!"

"Is she now?" The man still glowered at her.

"She took me to the park."

"We were not gone long, Mr. Parker."

The man pulled off his son's muddy boots and handed them to her and then the lad's coat.

"Off to the washroom, Linden," she said, beginning to follow him.

"Hold on, Grace."

She cringed.

"I do not want my son out there among the city vagrants."

She turned. "'Tis a very nice park. I saw no one you would object to there. Lots of folks like yourselves."

He tugged at his shirtsleeves. "I will not argue, Grace. You've done a fine job thus far, and I see that you do not require any extra pay for that because you've returned the . . . bonus."

"I meant no offense."

"None taken. It's quite admirable on your part. In addition, we will need you here to help with the new baby. But my children will stay in the house when they are not in school or escorted by me or my wife."

She lowered her head, bit her tongue, and tried to remain calm. "As you wish."

"When they need fresh air, I will take them on a holiday to the shore . . . or someplace . . . where they may play in a suitable environment."

She hadn't seen that happen so far. "I understand. I'm sorry." A lie, may God forgive her.

With a jerk of his chin he moved toward the door. "I came home to pick up some papers from my desk. I'm leaving now.

Mrs. Parker and the girls are still next door. I checked. I will let them know you've returned home."

She glanced at the tray next to his chair. The letter on top was missing. His hat sat next to the mail. She handed it to him. When he was gone, she exhaled. These children truly needed her.

18

"I want you two to stick together," Captain Nicholson said, tugging on his mustache as he, Jake, and Owen stood in front of the assignment board after the group meeting. "Headquarters doesn't think the Dusters pose much of a threat, and that much we can use to our advantage."

Owen swallowed hard. There were thugs out there wanting Owen to back off—and Devery, who wanted Owen to realize he knew about it. Headquarters most certainly cared about the Dusters, though Owen didn't yet know why or why they wanted Captain Nicholson to ignore the cocaine-addicted troublemakers. For all he knew, headquarters might put the screws to Nicholson at some point for sending some of his men out after them. He and Jake would have to expedite things.

The captain went on. "I think you boys could make headway, seeing as Jake is a common man folks will relate to, and you, Owen, know the beat so well."

Jake and Owen returned to the locker room to prepare for work. "What's been going on in the park?" Owen asked, seeing as Jake had been there when Owen had the night off.

Jake shrugged on his uniform jacket. "The Hudson Dusters riffraff are stirring up some trouble as always, just like the captain says. But nothing I couldn't handle, not so far anyway." He finished buttoning his jacket and grinned. "Say, that little fellow you befriended has been awful helpful. I arrested two thugs on my solo night."

"No sign of Goo Goo?"

"Not so far."

When they reached the park, they found their young informant right away.

"Hello, there, Mikey. How are things?" Owen put a hand on the lad's shoulder.

"Fine, Officer. Seen two purse snatchings today."

"Well, that's down from the four you saw last time." Owen handed the lad a penny for candy. "Say, you see that fella we talked about much? Smokey?" He was the one Duster Owen could identify. Easy, because whenever he was about, he let everyone know who he was.

"Yeah. He hangs around a lot."

Jake bent low to talk to the lad. "Who's he with?"

"Mostly alone. Seen him talking to a few fellows but never the same ones."

Owen figured the meetings were drug exchanges.

"Heard any names mentioned when you were playing tag around the statue, Mikey?"

"Nah. Nothing."

"One more thing, Mikey."

"Sure, Officer."

Jake stood behind the lad to make sure he didn't run off before Owen was done with him. "Mention my questions to anyone? Anyone with a badge?"

The lad screwed up his lips and then answered. "Like who?"

"Man my size except much heavier."

"No, Officer."

"Sure?"

"Well, I never talked about you, but . . . maybe I did see a police fellow like that down here."

"Any of your friends talk to him?"

"Might have. Not me, though."

Owen put his hands on the boy's shoulders. "I'm your friend, right, Mikey?"

"Uh, yeah."

"You can trust me."

"I know."

"Just keep an eye out and let me know where you see this guy named Smokey. Don't get too close, though. Hear me? I don't want you talking to the fellow."

"Yes, sir."

"Swell. Run along, Mikey."

When he'd gone, Jake shook his head. "I'm changing my mind about that one."

"What do you mean?"

"I don't know. Something shifty about his answers just now. I'm not sure you can trust that ragamuffin, Owen."

"I'm not sure either."

"Who do you think talked to him? That fella Feeny?"

"Nah."

Owen walked with his partner, recalling the briefing at the precinct. "The day-shift officers closed down one party house run by the Dusters gang over on West Thirtieth near the Hudson River docks." He gazed toward the harbor. "That's more than an hour on foot from here."

Jake shoved his hands in his pockets. "Yeah. Doesn't make much sense, them all the way over here."

"Say, Jakey. You suppose those lazy bums have a rowboat?

The trip around the tip of Manhattan is much shorter on the water."

"Good point."

They moved toward the water to patrol around the boats. Nothing going today, though. Owen filled Jake in about his encounter with the police chief.

Jake twirled his nightstick. "Doesn't sit well that Big Bill knew about your work down here. Not well at all."

"I agree. But I've already talked to Mikey about Smokey Davis. That's nothing new Big Bill could pin on me. Let's just keep our eyes and ears open out here."

Jake nudged his hat back with the tip of his nightstick. "Heard plenty about these Dusters even over in Brooklyn. Folks, even well-to-do types, like to party with them. Would be good to keep those addicts out of a park like this." Jake tipped his chin toward the kids. "Over in the west village, one of the Dusters—they call him Ding Dong—roped street kids into sneaking into places he can't fit so he can steal goods from merchants."

"Despicable," Owen said.

They continued walking through the park, keeping an eye on happenings.

Jake broke the silence. "Tell me about your award. What was that about?"

"Embarrassing, mostly."

"Tell me about Dan O'Toole."

Owen sighed, licked his lips, and began to relate the details he did not like telling. Nicholson trusted Jake. Owen thought he could too. Jake might as well know the whole story.

"One day in '98 I tried to reach a little girl who was standing in the path of a trolley. Dead Man's Curve, they call that intersection, where the trolleys run out of control. Officer O'Toole was trying to do the same thing. We both failed."

"Oh, wow. The girl died?"

Owen pursed his lips and nodded. "And O'Toole. He was struck and later died too."

Jake wagged his head. "We see some awful things out on the streets, but when it's a child and a cop? Well, that's the worse."

"I wasn't with the force then. I didn't know O'Toole. I was just a civilian riding in a carriage. After that I realized I had a mission in life."

Jake slapped him on the shoulder. "You tried. Most folks would not have."

Owen rubbed a hand over his face, hoping Jake hadn't seen how emotional this was for him. His partner was right. They saw atrocious happenings all the time. But that day . . . he hadn't been prepared for it, not that he could have been. And no one else helped. Not even Owen's father. People had to help each other and if they just wouldn't . . . well, Owen had known he would have to wear a badge to make sure—to try to make sure—fewer horrible accidents happened with no one around willing to lend a hand.

Owen stared at the gray clouds overhead heralding the approach of sunset. It was only half past three, but a cloudy winter day in Manhattan could feel like nighttime. "Think we got a chance, Jakey?"

"Huh?"

"Nicholson thinks we can get these guys, but he doesn't know that Big Bill is on to us."

"Somebody's got to stand in the face of Tammany and show 'em what's right and decent. Might as well be us. And besides, maybe you getting that award, and it being in the papers and all, will get Big Bill to back off."

"Hope so."

Late in the evening, Owen and Jake stopped into a diner for coffee. "Surprised you're open on Christmas Eve, Joe. How are things?" Owen set his hat down on the counter.

"Slow as molasses in January. There's the occasional bum and cop needing to warm up, so here I am. I'll hang the Closed sign up in time for church." He poured black coffee into two white mugs.

Jake plopped onto a stool. "Quiet sounds good right about now."

Joe shook his head. "I'm closing up for good next week."

Owen joined his partner at the counter. "Why, Joe? Not enough business?"

"Oh, the lunch crowd's dandy. But the saloons do all the nighttime business. Got an offer to work in my cousin's shop in Buffalo. Suppose I will do that."

Owen lifted his cup. "We'll miss you, Joe."

"Me? You fellows come around once a fortnight."

Owen retrieved a doughnut from a cake stand. "We've been on the park beat. Probably be assigned there next week as well."

"Ah, shucks." Joe made a fist and pounded the air. "More reason for me to get out. Those coppers, the others? Ain't no more crooked fellows on the face of the earth."

Jake, unfazed, took a doughnut for himself. "Don't say that, Joe. We're all doing the best we can out here."

"If you say so." Joe disappeared into the kitchen.

Jake gulped down coffee as though it was no warmer than milk. "I hear you're up for promotion."

"You heard that?"

"Sure. And this park assignment could be just the ticket for you. I'm going to do what I can to make it happen. You know as well as I do that all this—" he waved the doughnut toward the plate-glass window—"can't be cleaned up. Not most of it. We do our job and trust that more folks are safe because we're here. We're a deterrent to some of 'em, you know. Think about what it was like down here even five years ago."

Owen was ashamed to admit that five years ago he couldn't have named a street in Lower Manhattan. He couldn't have offered an opinion about the police department because . . . well, back then he just didn't care. "Hey, Jakey, do you think a fellow can change his life?"

"What life? What fellow?"

"I'm just supposing. Do you think someone can truly care about things he used to never give a second thought to?"

"Ever heard of the Progressives?"

"Sure." Politics. But there did seem to be an awakening of sorts, and more charitable organizations were springing up all the time—real ones, not hypocrites like Middleton the writer.

"I know what you need, pal."

"You know what I need?"

"A night on the town. Anyplace. Just a time to relax. If I wasn't married, I'd make sure you had it."

Maybe that *was* just what he needed. But no more fancy uptown balls.

19

"I'M NOT FEELING WELL, GRACE. I think the baby's coming."

By Grace's estimation the baby was overdue. Panic crawled up her neck. Why couldn't this happen when Mr. Parker was at home? Yesterday was Sunday. Why not then? Tomorrow would be Christmas. Mr. Parker would be home tomorrow.

Alice Parker grabbed a candlestick from the dining room mantel and flung it across the room. Linden wailed and the girls clung to Grace's side.

"Didn't you hear me, girl?" She bent over, clutching her belly.

Grace spoke to the children. "To the playroom." They didn't hesitate. As soon as she saw the heels of their shoes disappear up the stairs, she hurried to help the mistress sit down in a chair. "What shall I do?"

Mrs. Parker gritted her teeth. "Call for the doctor."

"The midwife, Widow Brown, is right next door—"

"No!" She grunted and hung on to Grace's arm. "Something's wrong. Call the doctor!"

Grace had to pry the woman's fingers from her arm so she could leave and do as she was told. When she returned, she found the mistress trying to ascend the stairs. "I'll not have my child born down here in the dining room, Grace. Help me into bed. Did you tell the doctor I want chloroform?"

"I . . . uh . . ."

The woman swore. "This is all I need. An Irish biddy who's as dumb as a log. Just do as I say. For once."

"Shall I send for Mr. Parker?"

The woman's eyes went wide. "No. No, do you hear me? I don't want him to think I can't handle things."

"Aye, yes, ma'am."

By the time the doctor arrived, Grace was exhausted from running between the mistress's bedroom and the children's attic playroom. Grace had seen many pregnant women when she was in the workhouse. Obviously the separate floors had not kept men and women apart. None of those women had doctors or chloroform, and they'd survived. She couldn't imagine why Mrs. Parker wanted it so badly.

"Grace!" The doctor called to her from the hall.

Grace held a finger to her lips as the children gazed at her wide-eyed. She shut the playroom door behind her and rushed down the stairs.

The doctor stood with his bag in his hands. "I'm afraid you'll have to sit with her. The baby is reluctant to move down the birth canal. She is in for a long labor. Hurry and summon a neighbor to look after the children."

"Oh, the midwife—"

"Is attending another birth over on Eleventh Street."

Grace would much rather find someone to sit with the mistress than with the children. "I'll see to it. Will you stay until I get back?"

"Not possible. Be quick about it."

She had to first see him out and then hurry back to the children. "Hazel, you will have to look after your sister and brother."

She moaned. Linden looked worried.

"Just for a little while."

Holly began to twist a strand of her hair, something she did when she felt ill at ease. Mr. Parker had made it clear the children were not to go out alone. But it might be better, with Mrs. Parker in labor, for Grace to stay and Hazel to go. "Do you think you could just run across the street and ask Mrs. Wallace, the baker's wife, to come help?"

Hazel nodded eagerly.

"This is important, Hazel. You cannot go anywhere else. Your mother needs you." Grace hoped this would compel the girl to obey, but she knew the children held little affection for their mother. "I need you to do this, Hazel."

"I know." She hopped off the hobbyhorse and headed downstairs.

Linden was growing sleepy. Grace hoisted him onto her hip and led Holly down to the next floor. "Wait out here." She left them in the hall outside their mother's room.

She walked Hazel to the front door. "Go right out there to that house. Get the woman who lives there and then come right back. Hear me?"

She nodded.

Mrs. Parker moaned so loud that Grace had to hurry. She urged Hazel out the door and then ran upstairs.

Alice Parker continued groaning but otherwise seemed unaware. Grace dabbed her forehead with a wet cloth and then went back to the hall. Linden slumped on the floor against the wall, his eyelids at half-mast, but Holly wasn't there.

"Holly, come here!" Grace began searching the rooms. Finally she found the girl hunkered underneath her bed, clutching a blanket. "'Tis all right, lassie. Everything will be fine.

Don't hide." She could not lure the girl out. She finally gave up and plunked Linden down on his bed and sat in the room with them for several minutes.

Where is Hazel?

Grace bolted from the room, down the stairs, and out the front door. Soot glided from the neighbor's chimney and swam in front of her view. She dodged a carriage crossing the street and hurried to the Wallaces' house.

"I have not seen the little girl," Mrs. Wallace said, looking over her wire-framed spectacles. "I never see those children. I don't believe they are permitted out of the house."

"They are not, but I sent her over here to fetch you."

"What's the trouble, dear?"

"Mrs. Parker's baby is coming. Doctor says I'm to stay with her at all times. I just needed help with the children."

The woman wrapped a shawl around her shoulders. "Dorothy, I'm going across the street. Look after your brothers and sisters and don't let the bird in the oven burn."

"Yes, Mama," came a voice from another room.

Mrs. Wallace followed her back to the Parkers' house. "The others are napping, you say?"

"Aye. In their room."

"Well, I'll see to Alice. You better find that child."

The angle of the sun told Grace she did not have much time before Mr. Parker came home from the office. Why had Hazel not obeyed her?

As she peeked down alleys and studied the faces of children in the park, she wondered if Hazel had done the same thing Holly did—hide. Never being allowed outside alone before, anything could have distracted her and sent her down an alley. A cat. A milk wagon. A friend from school. It would not have taken much to be more appealing than returning to this house and listening to her mother moan.

As Grace passed house after house, she glanced under porch steps and behind coal bins, calling the girl's name. She thought about the time she herself had encountered a thug at the aquarium. *Oh, God, protect this child.* This might be a more affluent neighborhood, but there were folks everywhere who could not be trusted.

She passed a policeman, who greeted her and tipped his hat. "Everything in order, miss?"

Be respectful. Befriend men like him, Mrs. Hawkins had said.

"A little girl is missing." She gave a description, and soon the two of them were looking under shop awnings, between houses, in the candy shop.

"Wait a minute," Grace said. "We take the same path to and from the school. That is all Hazel knows."

"Public school one block over?"

"Aye. I mean, yes."

The man followed Grace as she retraced the path she and the girls took to school.

"That her?" the man asked, pointing to the building with his nightstick.

"Yes. Thank you, Officer." Hazel sat on the building's front steps, hugging her knees.

"Glad I could help." He crossed the street and continued on his way.

Grace was more than impressed with how helpful he had been.

"Now what would you be doing out here, lassie?" Grace brushed back Hazel's long hair, but the girl would not look at her. "Ready to go home?"

Hazel nodded. Surprisingly the girl clutched Grace's hand as they walked. Hazel was not normally cuddly like her little brother. She must be truly frightened.

"Did you get lost? Mrs. Wallace's home was right across the street."

"I was going there, but Millie called me from the corner. I went to see her new doll, but she lives on another street. Her mother called her inside and I couldn't find my way back. I saw the tailor shop, though. The one we pass on the way to school. I thought that if I went that way, I could turn around and come back. But then I didn't get Mrs. Wallace for you. I thought you'd be angry. Don't tell Father I was bad, please, Miss Gracie."

"Shh, so. Mrs. Wallace is with your mother right now. Everything's fine. Let's hurry along so the neighbor can get back to her home."

Hazel squeezed Grace's fingers. Mr. Parker had done the children no favors sheltering them so.

When they got back to the house, a hefty fellow in uniform stood blocking the door. He pointed a nightstick at them. "Is that little Miss Parker, Hazel Parker?"

Hazel flung herself behind Grace, nearly knocking her over. The child was only a head shorter than she was.

"'Tis herself. Let us by." Grace turned to the side to squeeze past him.

"She can go in, but you better wait out here."

"Hazel? Is that you?" Mr. Parker came running to the door, and Hazel fell into his arms.

"I didn't mean to, Father. I went to get Mrs. Wallace, and then I . . . I was afraid."

"Of course, sweetheart." He kissed the top of her head and sent her off inside. "Thank you, Officer. I will handle this now."

Handle this?

"Come inside, Grace. We'll talk in my study. Mrs. Wallace is with my wife."

"Yes, I know. I asked her—"

"Inside. We better have a talk."

She followed him down the hall to the back of the house, where he had a closet-size office, just room enough for a desk and two chairs. "There was no need to call the police."

"No need?" He pounded a fist on the surface of his oak desk. "My child is missing and there is no need to call the police? Why, may I ask, did you not do that straight away, Grace? Do you know what kind of people roam the streets of New York City?"

"A policeman helped me look for her."

"When I called the precinct, they'd had no report, Grace."

"Well, I know, but—"

She could tell she was not going to be allowed to speak. She kept her head low while he continued his rampage. When his voice pitched high, she squeezed her eyes tight.

"Would you admit this was an error of judgment on your part, Grace?"

She pressed her hands together and opened her eyes. "I would."

"Very well. It cannot happen again."

He was not going to fire her then. "I promise."

He sighed loudly. "After that incident with Lindy . . . well, I should have known. They are not allowed out alone, Grace. I've told you that."

"But perhaps if she knew her way around, then—"

"You will obey my wishes! Are you that pitifully stupid? I hired you because you were timid. I liked that. Don't go asserting yourself now, girl."

I am smart. I am important. I am able. "I am not stupid, Mr. Parker."

"Good. Then you'll know better not to violate my trust again. As punishment I'm docking your pay for one week."

"Sir?"

He stood. "Don't disappoint me like this again or you'll be out of a job. And from what Mrs. Hawkins explained, you don't have many options because folks don't want a maid who is completely . . . shall we say, backward? If not stupid, you are certainly without common sense. I'm trusting that you have enough intelligence to correct that, Grace."

Did he expect her to thank him? "I won't let the children out of my sight again."

"Right. Now go see to my wife. I've telephoned Mrs. Hawkins's neighbor and asked her to relay the message that you'll be spending the night. If you are able to sleep at all tonight—and according to the doctor, it's not likely—you may sleep with the children."

She stared at him a moment, not seeing the thin, sandy-haired American, but her father, angry, red-faced, eyes afire. *"Another blunder, lass! Is there nothing ya can do right?"*

Sucking in her breath, she nodded and left the room. *Don't listen.* She held her fists over her ears as she walked. *God, am I important? To you?*

Perhaps her worth was measured by someone with more authority and power than George Parker or her father.

Alice Parker lay in the dark room, softly groaning. Mrs. Wallace stood when Grace entered. She wrung her hands. "I really must be getting home now."

"Oh, aye, please." Grace backed away from the door. "Thank you kindly, Mrs. Wallace."

"I'm happy to help, although no one from this family ever asks. Come get me, Grace, whenever you need something."

"You are generous. We will get along fine now, Mrs. Wallace."

"Yes. Well, God bless." She turned slightly toward the bed, her brow wrinkled. Then she left, shutting the door behind her.

Grace checked. Mrs. Parker was sleeping. Grace darted up to the playroom to see the children and found Mr. Parker there, playing checkers with Hazel. He looked surprised.

"Oh, I forgot to ask if I should start the evening meal."

"I don't see how that's possible, Grace, when you are to keep a constant watch over Mrs. Parker. If she gets worse, call for me and I'll hail the doctor. Do you understand?"

"But the children's supper . . . ?"

"Is there cold meat in the icebox?"

"There is."

"I will take care of my children, Grace. Please do as I asked now."

Four sets of eyes glared at her. Were they safe with him? "I'll just be . . . uh . . . Come get me if you need me. Any of you."

"Go, Grace."

She didn't want to risk having him raise his voice any more in front of the children, but she also didn't want to sit sentry while Alice Parker awaited the birth of her fourth child. Grace was no midwife and didn't care to be one. "Shall I call Widow Brown? Surely she's back now from her other delivery."

He rose and stepped out into the hall. "We shall not alarm the children any more than need be. Mrs. Parker wants only the doctor and we'll grant her wishes."

"But the doctor is so busy. He might not get back in time."

"You let me worry about that. All she needs now is you."

He took a step toward her, effectively ushering her back toward the mistress's side.

Grace talked as she walked backward. "There are crackers in a tin in the scullery and some apples too."

"Thank you, Grace."

Alice Parker's face had turned deadly white. She still breathed but didn't speak. Grace wished Mrs. Wallace had stayed. Grace had counted at least five children roaming in and out of the hall in the Wallace house when they had spoken at the front door. She would know what to do. Grace was not the right person for this. She didn't know anything.

Grace moved closer. Mrs. Wallace had changed some of the bedclothes and pulled Alice Parker's hair away from her face with a green bandanna.

Suddenly Mrs. Parker wailed and rolled onto her side. She pressed the heel of one hand to her back.

"Your back? Your back hurts?"

No answer.

Grace rolled a towel and wedged it behind the woman, and she seemed to ease.

You are able.

Grace waited.

And paced.

And counted the hours chiming away on the clock.

At long last when the clock struck ten, loud footsteps erupted from the stairs outside the room. The door opened and someone pulled the chain to light up the room. The doctor and Mr. Parker hurried toward the bed.

"How is she, Grace?" Mr. Parker reached for his wife's hand.

"Wait outside, George." The doctor practically pushed him out. "We will keep you updated."

Grace told the doctor about Mrs. Parker's apparent back pain.

"It's the position of the baby." He lifted the sheets at the bottom of the bed and examined with one hand, modestly keeping his eyes focused on some spot on the far wall.

The woman tensed and cried out.

"Now, now, Alice," the doctor said. "We've been through this before. This baby's just being a little cantankerous. We'll convince him to turn."

Grace stared at the bespectacled man. "Isn't Mrs. Parker asleep? I mean, because of the chloroform?"

"Delirious. She'll hear me. I'll need my forceps. The baby's moved down now but needs assistance. In my bag there."

Grace followed his gaze to a carpetbag he'd left on the chair near the door. Inside she found bottles, capped needles, miscellaneous objects she couldn't identify, and one large mechanical article. She pulled it out.

"Bring it here now. I've determined the malpresentation."

Her hands shook as she held up the metal instrument. Was he going to . . . ?

"Now, girl!"

She rushed over and handed it to him.

"Get some clean cloths. We're going to pull this child out. Bring me my knife. I'm going to cut her to allow a smoother exit for the baby through the birth canal."

"What?"

He swore. "I'm not going to open her up, just make a cut. Why did my nurse have to visit her son's family and leave me with an incompetent Irish maid? Holiday? I never get a holiday. She's been away two whole weeks now." He rose and grabbed his bag. "Babies don't care about holidays—Christmas or any other."

Grace felt like she was about to faint or lose the contents of her stomach or both. She grabbed a stack of towels Mrs. Wallace must have readied and positioned herself at Mrs. Parker's head so she would not have to witness what the doctor was doing.

"Yes. That's good. Hold on to her shoulders, Grace."

Finally something she could do. The mistress's head dropped limp against Grace's collarbone. Grace held her against the doctor's pull and then, finally, the babe cried out. He passed the shivering, bloody baby to Grace after he clipped the umbilical cord. She quickly wrapped the baby in towels as he continued working on Mrs. Parker. Grace tried to coo to the baby. She dipped a cloth in a bowl of washing water and dabbed at his eyes and mouth. A pink, fat boy. Eventually the baby relaxed and she held him tight, thinking the naked child must be cold.

After some time the doctor took the child from Grace, and she worked at changing the drowsy woman and her sheets the best she could. When Alice Parker was snug and sleeping, the doctor handed the baby back to Grace. "Nicely done."

She hadn't messed up. Even the doctor thought she'd done well. A feeling of light rushed over her. She wasn't stupid, simple, or even incapable. She had helped with a birth and now held a new baby fresh from the hand of God, kissed by heaven.

Grace looked at the bundle in her arms. Sweet as the wee one was, there was something odd about his head. "Doctor, isn't his head shaped odd, though?"

He rubbed his weary eyes. "A tough birth, but he came through fine. Big lad, nine pounds likely. I'll bring my scales by tomorrow."

"But his head . . ."

He blew out a breath. "An infant's head is pliable, has to be to pass through the birth canal. It will regain its shape. Now see that the baby nurses just as soon as Alice awakes, which won't be long now. Take care that she stays warm and get her to drink some broth just as soon as possible. She's had a tough time of it. She's the one you should be concerned about."

Grace started to go with him to the door and then stopped, realizing she had the baby.

"I'll see myself out and find Mr. Parker. Good night."

"Thank you, Doctor."

He turned, a surprised expression blanketing his face.

"I mean, thank you for helping Mrs. Parker. She surely needed you."

He smiled. "I appreciate that, Grace." He twisted his neck. "I do sometimes feel as though folks don't appreciate my efforts. Kind of you to mention it." He nodded toward Mrs. Parker. "She needs you now. Good night again."

Grace sat in a chair next to the fireplace with the baby in her arms. Oh, the power of a kind word. She would try that on the Parkers later. *"A soft answer turneth away wrath."* While Mrs. Hawkins had said her husband had spoken those words, they actually came from the Bible, she said. And it did seem like something Reverend Clarke would endorse.

She glanced down at the sleeping babe. "Oh, Douglas. What odd parents you have, laddie." She smiled when she thought about his name. "Thankfully you are himself. If you'd been a lassie, you would have had a more evident tree name. Douglas is a proper name for a lad."

The baby slept. The mother slept. Grace fought to keep her eyes open.

Sometime later, Grace woke to Alice Parker calling her name. "Let me see my baby."

Grace went to the cradle, where she'd laid Douglas and brought him to her.

"A boy?"

"Yes, ma'am. A healthy boy."

The woman sighed and then worked at getting the baby to nurse. She looked up at Grace with droopy eyes. "You know, Grace, when I was younger, I thought I could grow children like I grew a garden." She laughed. "But plants are silent. They don't complain. You can just look at them and see how beautiful they are."

Grace went over and touched Douglas's downy head. "He is beautiful."

Mrs. Parker made a face as though the baby was hurting her.

"Are you all right, ma'am?"

"Yes." She lifted her neck and Grace hurried to put a pillow behind it. "Grace, light the lamp and bring me that Burpee catalog. I want to show you how to order the coralbells."

"Yes, ma'am."

20

In the wee hours of Christmas morning, Owen and Jake headed toward a dive where the Dusters hung out. They had not mentioned their plan to Nicholson or to the kids in the park. The fewer who knew where they were staking out the gang, the better. The walls had ears.

Jake dropped a banana peel on a pile of garbage at the curb. It did not take long for a rat to scramble out of the shadows and claim it. The sanitation department was supposedly cleaning up the streets of New York. Not in this neighborhood.

"Got a new informant," Jake said. "A new lad. Colin."

"Think you can trust the kid?"

They walked on together, dodging factory workers preparing to report for duty at the fish processing plant nearby. These men, like them, did not have the holiday off.

"Comes from St. Patrick's school over by the headquarters."

"So?"

"So the day shift says we can use him."

Owen halted. Jake took a few more strides before he realized Owen wasn't moving. "I know what you're thinking, Owen. Don't trouble yourself."

"Don't trouble myself? Jake, you know as well as I do half the cops in the station are crooked. What if Big Bill hears about this? This kid—If it's not a noose, he probably wants a big payoff."

"Right. Half. Half are *not* crooked. I checked. The fellas I talked to got no love for Big Bill."

"Not that we know of."

"Hey, I ain't no rookie. The patrolmen I talked to come from my old precinct. I know them."

"Fair enough. Half are not crooked. The other half love a good joke . . . or a bad one."

Jake pointed his lunch tin at him. "I scared the socks off the kid. He won't double-cross us."

"I hope you're right."

Owen gave his pocket a tap and felt the heavy lump of the silver pocket watch, his constant reminder of why he did what he did. Owen pulled the watch from his pocket and told Jake what the hour was.

"Ten more minutes and they'll rush out of there." Jake pointed to a pair of brightly lit windows glowing from the gray buildings like a beacon. Piano music and laughter pierced what was probably a peaceful evening for most civilized folks, who by now would be sleeping or returning home from midnight Mass.

"If only the Dusters kept a solid headquarters. Our boys run them out of one place and they set up another. We got a tough job, Jakey."

"Don't I know it."

As he crouched, hand on the .32 at his belt, Owen could not help but think about the contrasts within the city. Uptown folks dined on delicacies served atop a crisp linen tablecloth. Women donned feather-plumed hats. Men sported diamond pins on their coat lapels. He knew that life well. Just a short distance away, here he was kneeling in a grimy gutter and preparing to follow the lead dog of a vice-infested gang to the nest of its leader and arrest him.

"This would be a whole lot easier if we knew what Goo Goo looked like," he told his partner.

"Crying shame there's no picture of him on the mug shot wall. Makes our job all the harder."

They had spent a lot of time running down rabbit holes because they didn't have a clear idea of who they were looking for. "Well, Jakey, eventually all the worker bees return to the hive. Maybe tonight's the night."

"Come on," Jake called.

Owen looked up to see a fellow galloping down the steps of the house toward them, his unbuttoned overcoat flapping in the breeze. Owen crossed to the opposite side of the street as Jake trailed behind the man. They headed east, away from the docks. Either the hideout was camouflaged or they were being led on a goose chase.

The fellow turned the corner onto Centre and approached the open area politicians dubbed Mulberry Park. There were no lights there. Owen used only his somatic sense to estimate where Jake was and where the subject of their hunt had gone.

A few shadowy figures moved about. A lump leaning against a wall was probably just an old hobo trying to stay warm. Something whizzed past his head—a bat swooping for insects. He ducked his head, then spun around.

Couldn't be. It was winter. No bugs.

Who was he kidding? He didn't have good instincts. He'd never make a decent detective.

A grunt.

Jake?

Yes, a signal to move to the center of the lot. When a hand reached out and pulled at his jacket, he realized he had figured wrong. If he fired blindly, he might strike an innocent civilian. By the time he pulled out his nightstick, the thug had left.

"You all right?" Jake appeared at his side like a brownie from a children's tale. Incredible just how dark it was.

"Fine. Where'd he go?"

Jake spun in all directions. "I dunno. You were right. We were had. We're nowhere in Dusters territory. Better check your pockets."

Owen slapped his sides, then slid his fingers into his pocket. Nothing.

He tore off in the direction he thought the man went. His partner's footsteps echoed behind him. "What the devil?"

By the time Owen got to the nearest streetlamp, the fellow in the loose overcoat was nowhere to be seen. "He took my watch! That hooligan has my watch!"

Jake jogged up next to him, out of breath. "Sorry."

By the end of the shift Jake and Owen were tired, weary, and without an arrest. They parted ways outside the Old Slip precinct, where they'd been told to go. "Another thrilling night on the beat, huh?" Jake extended his hand.

"So it goes." Owen gave him a firm handshake and then turned to leave.

"Hey, merry Christmas. Sorry about your watch. You might check the pawnbrokers for it."

Owen thanked him and set off toward the sanctuary of his apartment. The hollowness of his pocket sent needles of regret through his whole body.

Early Christmas morning Mrs. Hawkins arrived at the Parkers'. Grace let her in the kitchen door. "I would have come last night, love, but Mr. Parker insisted that you had everything under control." She set a basket down on the kitchen table. "How is the mother?"

"Doctor says she's weak, but she's all right."

"And how are you, love? Tired?"

"Oh, Mrs. Hawkins. I was so frightened. I never helped with a birth before. But the doctor said I did well."

"Fine, love. I knew you could."

"You did?"

"Certainly. Sit now. I'll make us some tea. Where are the children?"

"Still asleep."

"The baby?"

"I just checked. Asleep in the cradle next to Mrs. Parker's bed. Mr. Parker slept in his study last night, and he hasn't yet come out."

"Fine. Sit, love."

Grace collapsed on a kitchen stool.

"The services last evening were inspiring. Here it's your first Christmas in America and you couldn't be there. Pity. Well, babies don't care about holidays."

"So I've been told." Grace was so tired she mumbled, unable to summon much of a response.

Mrs. Hawkins filled the teakettle. "What's that, love?"

"Oh, nothing."

"When I had Mr. Parker on the phone last night, he said you had been out somewhere with the oldest girl, Hazel."

"I was. She got sidetracked looking at a friend's new doll over on the other street and couldn't find her way home."

"Oh, my." The Hawk returned to the table and sat down. "Remember, love, Mr. Parker doesn't allow his children out without an adult."

"I know. I promised him it would not happen again." Grace leaned on one elbow. "I remembered what you said earlier . . . about who to trust . . . and a policeman helped me look for her."

"Good for you. Well, that's all fine now. I know you've been working hard here." She rose and pulled a bundle from her basket. She laid a red checkered napkin on the table and unwrapped two large buttermilk scones. "I have more for the children, love."

Grace felt a tear slip down her cheek. "So thoughtful of you."

"There, there, now. Don't you worry about a thing. I've insisted Mr. Parker send for his sister. She teaches at a women's college upstate. Edith is her name. It's the Christmas holiday, so she can come."

"You know her?"

"I have not made her acquaintance, but when I pressed Mr. Parker about getting family to help, he told me about her. Odd, since I thought Mrs. Parker had relatives in town."

"She doesn't, Mrs. Hawkins. She told me."

"Well, all the same, this woman will be here later today."

Grace wanted to tell Mrs. Hawkins that Mr. Parker was not at all the reserved polite churchman she and the reverend thought he was, but she couldn't summon the strength to start that discussion. Later. They could talk about it later.

The whistle on the kettle blew and Mrs. Hawkins rose to retrieve it.

The noise woke the children, who came lumbering down the stairs. They gasped when they saw a stranger in the kitchen bearing red-wrapped gifts.

"Mrs. Santa Claus," Linden cried.

"No, just someone to help, love." Mrs. Hawkins gathered the children to her like a grandmother.

An hour later Mrs. Hawkins said good-bye. "When Mr. Parker's sister gets here, call Mrs. Jenkins."

"Your neighbor?"

"Yes. She'll let me know, and I will have a carriage sent over for you. We've cooked a goose, and after you eat with us, you can take a nice, hot bath."

Grace nearly cried. What a lovely thought.

Later that morning, after getting some sleep, Owen went downstairs to borrow his neighbor's telephone. Mrs. Karila let him in. "You call doctor?"

"No, my mother, if you don't mind."

"Mind? No. But your face. You need doctor."

"I'm fine, Mrs. Karila. Just some bumps and bruises. Part of the job."

She frowned. "I have something for that." She made him wait while she went into the kitchen. She returned with a plate of pickled herring, a dish these transplants from Finland often tried to push on him.

"Thank you. May I use the phone first?"

"Yah, yah."

He dialed his mother's exchange.

"Oh, Owen. How did you hear?"

"Hear what?"

"Your father is in the hospital, Owen. I thought perhaps someone had told you."

"No, I just wanted to wish you a merry Christmas and see how he was. What's wrong?"

"Doctors aren't sure. You better go right over to Bellevue. I'm going back there myself shortly."

21

In the early afternoon, Mrs. Parker came downstairs and reclined on the sofa. Her husband had emerged long enough to kiss the new baby, deliver presents to the other children, and get a scone for himself. Then he returned to his study to read.

The children were remarkably quiet, probably because being allowed to play downstairs had become a rare occurrence and they didn't want their mother to send them away.

It was past noon on Christmas, but oddly the mistress of the house wanted Grace to decorate.

"I did not have a chance earlier, Grace, but I simply must have some decoration." She sniffed. "I never had Christmas as a child. And now I always insist on decorations in my own home. Greenery on the mantel, Grace. We simply must have some of the garden inside." Alice Parker pointed and then slumped back to the sofa. She could do very little in her weakened state.

Grace pruned some of the evergreen bushes outside and placed the cuttings around the parlor. Seemingly satisfied, the woman rose and headed for the stairs.

"Do you need help, ma'am?" Grace moved toward her.

"No!" She paused, looking from Grace to Linden, who sat at Grace's feet playing with a wooden train. "Carry on. I'm going upstairs to rest."

Grace returned to her work.

"Miss Gracie, did you get a stocking from Saint Nicholas like we did?" Linden pointed his wee chin toward her as she stood in front of the mantel and rearranged holly branches.

Thankfully their father had thought ahead to provide. He probably feared losing face should anyone find out the Parker children missed Christmas.

"Boys!" Hazel rolled her eyes.

"'Tis fine to ask. I did not, wee lad. Stockings are for children."

"That's sad." He stuck out his lip while he rolled the train engine in a half circle.

"I don't mind, laddie. We didn't much celebrate Christmas in Ireland." She stretched the truth a bit. Some Irish folks would expect visits from Father Christmas, but Grace held few memories of holiday traditions herself. Even before the workhouse, they'd had no time for it. They went to church and roasted whatever portion of lamb their neighbors could spare. Nothing more. But she was not about to tell all that to wee Linden.

At the hour for tea, Edith Milburn, Mr. Parker's widowed sister, arrived from Albany. Mr. Parker had picked her up from the depot. Dressed in a gray suit, she tugged a red scarf away from her neck. Grace took her coat and scarf and hung them in the hall closet. She already liked this woman who dared to wear Grace's favorite color.

Grace returned with a tea tray.

"No, no. Let me do that." She took the tray from Grace's arms. "I'm here to help and I intend to. I can only imagine how weary you must be, child."

What a relief—both that her exhaustion was acknowledged

and that this woman did not seem inclined to call her an Irish biddy.

Mrs. Parker, who had not long ago returned from her nap, sat in a rocker by the fire in the parlor, wee Douglas snuggled to her breast. She complained of soreness whenever she moved, so it seemed best for her to rest. Grace had been doing everything for her.

The children gathered at their father's command and he introduced them to their aunt. Grace wondered why they didn't already know her. Perhaps Mr. Parker had stayed away from his family because they would know who he truly was.

The woman bent low to speak to the children. "You all will call me Auntie. While your mother is recovering, you come to me if you need anything. I've brought books and paints. We'll get along famously."

Holly clapped her hands, but Hazel held back. "We have Miss Gracie."

Auntie Edith put an arm around Grace and squeezed her close. "Of course you do, children, but your nanny needs a rest. She's going home for a few days. But she'll be back. Won't you, Grace?"

"I will."

Hazel frowned. "What about our Christmas dinner?"

Mr. Parker grunted. Mrs. Parker was silent.

Edith whispered in Grace's ear. "Do you have anything prepared?"

"In the icebox there is a Christmas goose prepared to roast, cranberries cooked and jelled, and the ingredients for oyster stuffing."

Edith bobbed her head. "See there, children. We have all

we need. With your cooperation, I'll finish the meal and we'll all eat together."

A nurse in a starched uniform escorted Owen to his father's bedside. His father was asleep. "What's wrong with him?" Owen whispered.

"Heart trouble." The nurse backed away, fiddled with something on the side table, and then left.

Owen had never seen his father looking so old, so weak, so weathered. His forehead perspired and his breathing was labored.

A short time later a doctor stopped at the foot of the bed. "How's the patient?" The doctor, wearing a pince-nez, smelled of iodine.

"You tell me."

"I'm Dr. Thorp. Is this your father?"

"Yes. My apologies. I'm Owen McNulty." Owen shook the man's hand.

"Has he ever have heart trouble before?"

"Not that I know of. We . . . uh . . . we haven't seen each other in a while. Have you spoken to my mother?"

"No. I wasn't on duty when they brought him in last night. Do you expect her?"

"Yes. Shortly. How is he, Doctor?"

He held up a finger and then approached Owen's father and held a stethoscope to the patient's chest. Then he checked his pulse, looped the instrument back around his neck, and leaned against the bed's foot rail, arms across his chest. "What does he do for a living?"

"He owns a chain of dry goods stores. Very successful— perhaps you've heard of them."

"McNulty? Ah, yes, indeed. Does he have a staff of executives to help run the business, or do you do that?"

"Uh, no. He has one close associate, but mostly he prefers to handle operations himself. I am a New York City policeman."

"Well, he'll need a few days of rest here. Then some convalescing at home. After a month, if all goes well, he can return to work. He'll have to take it easy, though. Get regular fresh air outings and eat properly. No sausages or other spicy foods to upset the stomach. If he does that, I believe his heart will give him several more years."

"Thank you."

"Any chance you can take over the business duties until he's better?"

"I'll think of something."

After the doctor left, Owen considered his options. If he could get a leave of absence, he could help out, but he knew his father would use that opportunity to try to convince him it was his obligation to stay on. Maybe he should consider it. Owen had been so sure God had called him to police work, especially after Mr. O'Toole had expressed his gratitude and told him there was no doubt he was meant for the job. But losing the O'Toole watch made him second-guess himself.

The clanging of metal and a few groans somewhere down the hall interrupted his thoughts. He looked again at his father, so frail. A clattering of footsteps. He turned.

"Oh, Owen. How is he? Did you talk to the doctor?"

"Calm down, Mother. He needs to rest." He proceeded to tell her what the doctor had said, minus the suggestion that he help out with the business.

"How will we manage, Owen?"

"I'll think of something."

When Owen got to work late that afternoon, he discovered that Jake had the night off. He should have remembered. He was not surprised that the captain had scheduled him for patrol in the Fourth Ward instead of the park.

"Hey, McNulty." Nicholson motioned for him to come into his office. He shut the door. "Look. I'm pulling you and Stockton off the Dusters."

"What? Why?"

"Big Bill got wind of it. He's the boss."

Owen stomped his foot. "What reason did he give?"

"Says you boys would be better working Chinatown, where the folks like you better. Feeny and that unit will patrol the Battery."

"Feeny's in with the Dusters and you know it."

"Come on, McNulty. We can't prove that. Now collect your badge and be on your way."

"That's it? Captain, what about the societies pulling out? What about the crime that's going to spread down there like rabbits? You were worried about that."

"I still am." He leaned over to whisper. "What you and Jake actually do, I got no idea. You boys are out there in the dark. You might start out in the Fourth when it's daylight, but how am I to know where you go when it's too dark to see out there?"

"Gotcha."

"Tonight, no Stockton. You stick to the assignment."

"Yes, sir. Uh, Captain? What if I were to need a few weeks off?"

"Criminy! What do you mean?"

"I'm not sure. But what if I had something I had to attend to first?"

"No way." He swore and paced behind his desk. Then he looked up. "All right, then. I could try to get someone from Stockton's former precinct. But the time we'd lose . . . I don't know. We need you, Owen. For the first time since you joined us, we really need you."

"Never mind. I'm in." More important than the promotion was the fact that Big Bill could not be allowed to bully them over this and put innocent immigrants in danger.

Grace collapsed onto a dining room chair just as Annie was serving Christmas dinner. The smell of roasted meat made her mouth water. Grace had eaten so little the last few days that any meal sounded good.

"Mrs. Parker wears you out, doesn't she?" Annie set a large bowl of potatoes in the center of the table.

Mrs. Hawkins reached across the table and patted Grace's arm. "She doesn't need to answer for us to see that. Take a hot bath right after supper, love. It will relax you and help you sleep."

That sounded glorious. "Are you sure you don't mind? The coal it takes to warm—"

"We've enough. Take the bath, love."

Annie poured glasses of milk and then they all bowed their heads.

Mrs. Hawkins prayed. "On this most holy day of our Savior's birth, we give thanks and especially thank you for the safe arrival of the Parker infant. Bless this food, almighty Father. We thank you for your providence and the bounty you provide. Amen."

So weary were Grace's arms that even buttering her bread was a chore. The warm meat and gravy seemed to be the best thing she'd ever eaten. With her stomach full, she climbed the stairs and closed herself in the bathroom. Privacy at last.

Until someone knocked on the door.

"I forgot to give you this." Annie shoved a piece of paper under the door. "It came yesterday."

"Thank you."

Grace picked it up, hoping to see her mother's handwriting, but it wasn't what she thought. *S. P. Feeny.* Why would he write? She dropped the letter. *Please, God. My mother is a pious woman. You wouldn't let anything happen to her, would you?*

But she could not think of any other reason he would write. She dropped to the floor next to the letter, stared at it a moment, and then picked it up. Fingers trembling, she opened it. No greeting, no well-wishes, and thankfully no despairing news.

> *I got a nephew in the New York police. He's agreed
> to check in on you, Grace, assure your mother you are
> well. Expect to hear from Walter Feeny and give him a
> report. I will explain at a later date. Your mother is fine,
> although concerned about you.*

Grace closed her eyes. She had written to her mother as soon as she'd arrived in New York, but clearly she had not received the letter when S. P. wrote this note. She would write again tomorrow and hope to reassure her mother as soon as possible. There was no need for some relative of S. P.'s to get involved. No need for S. P. to stick his nose into her business.

22

WITH HIS FATHER RESTING COMFORTABLY in the hospital, Owen decided to meander the streets the next day before his shift and seek out a pawnbroker. He also needed information—and trustworthy sources—that he hadn't had time to search out during his patrol.

Shopkeeper after shopkeeper told him either they had no silver pocket watches or else they had some, but not his. As he neared Cedar Street, he stopped at a small shop with an array of jewelry in the window.

The shopkeeper rubbed his whiskered chin. "Got one, but . . . it's not available."

"May I see it?"

The man narrowed his eyes. "I've seen you around here. You're a beat cop . . . What is it? Oh yeah, McNulty. That's you, ain't it, college boy?"

The words rubbed like raw wool. Owen stretched out his hand. "Owen McNulty. But I'm off duty."

The man took his hand with a weak grip. "I don't deal in stolen goods."

"I assure you today I'm just a customer."

"So you say."

"May I see the watch?"

"Fine." He brought out a box from under the counter. "I don't sell to cops."

When he took the lid off, Owen saw that it was the O'Toole watch. "You can see that this is a police-issued piece."

He immediately slammed the lid back on the box. "You said no police work today."

"It's a private matter."

"I'm not getting in the middle of some dispute. Good day, Officer."

"I'll be back."

Owen wasn't sure how much to tell that man. He could have demanded the watch back. He could have paid him much more than it was worth. But neither of those things would earn him the respect he needed in that neighborhood to do his job.

That evening after nightfall, Owen and Jake were on their way to Battery Park. Owen had not even been thinking about the pawnbroker when they passed by, but Jake mentioned it. "Did you try looking for your watch?"

Owen glanced across the street to the sign with the three gold balls, the mark of the business. "I . . . uh, yeah. I believe I found it."

"That's great. I hope you didn't have to pay to spring it."

"Long story, but I couldn't get it yet."

"Let me talk to the fellow. I'll get him to give it up. It's stolen property."

Owen put a hand on his partner's chest. "Not just yet."

After several rounds through the park and up and down State Street, they rested on a bench and stared toward the Western Union telegraph office.

Laughter came from the shadowy corners near the water.

"C'mon." Owen led the way.

They approached two merchant sailors. "Public drunkenness is against the law," Owen said.

One staggered toward him, his breath smelling like rotting garbage. "Going to arrest me, Officer?"

Jake took hold of his arm.

"That depends," Owen said. "You sniffing the white powder?"

"Might. It ain't against the law."

It should be. "Public intoxication is, pal."

The other fellow said nothing but rubbed his nose in a way that told Owen he'd been partying with some of the Dusters gang.

"Tell you what." Owen put a hand on the pistol at his waist, just to make a point. "You do me a favor, and I'll do you one."

"What?" The subject chuckled as though this was some vaudeville act.

"Take me to the fellas who gave you the sniff, see, and I'll send you on your way, free and clear."

This time the sailor burst out into full laughter and his buddy joined him.

Owen's face grew hot.

Jake tugged the guy along. "We got a wagon over here." They did not.

"Hey, I did nothing."

"Disturbing the peace ain't nothing," Jake bellowed.

Owen had hoped not to use rough intimidation. He would have to communicate better with his partner in the future.

"I don't know where the guys went. I don't."

Jake shoved the man away. "Says you."

The man straightened his coat and the two of them marched off. Then the first man stopped and turned. "If I did, I sure wouldn't tell your kind of cop. If Feeny were here, he wouldn't care."

Feeny! That man grated on Owen's nerves like a starched collar.

"Come on, Jake."

"Where? There's nowhere else to look. They've gone."

"Suppose that pawnbroker is still open?"

Jake scrambled to catch up. "Let's go see."

The lights were still on, so Owen tried the door. It was unlatched, so they went in. The sound of boxes falling in a back room was followed by the appearance of the man Owen had spoken to earlier.

"Ah, come in." The man beckoned them in with a wave of his hand. "I don't want any trouble, Officers."

"Still have that watch?" Owen approached the counter with Jake at his heels.

"Oh, it's you. It's yours for fifteen dollars."

"What?" Jake nearly came out of his shoes.

"Hold on, Jake. I told you I'd handle this."

The man lifted his hands. "I run an honest shop. Like I said before, I don't usually sell to cops. I'm doing you a favor."

"Fat chance," Jake mumbled from behind.

Owen accepted a box from the man and lifted the lid to expose the O'Toole watch. He reached into his pocket. He'd brought some savings with him, what he kept under his mattress for emergencies. He hadn't decided until this moment whether he'd pay the man. "Here you go."

"What are you doing?" Jake slapped his hand on top of the bills on the counter.

"The man's just doing his job, and I did tell him it was not police business."

The pawnbroker grinned at Owen.

"But it was stolen while you were on duty. I don't see why—"

Owen grabbed his partner by the collar. "We'll be going now."

Jake complained loudly all the way outside.

"Don't you see, Jakey? We've earned his trust."

"Paid for it, you mean."

"Well, I suppose, but besides that I made him a promise and I did not go back on it. He'll be on our side should we need him in the future."

"You sure?"

"Instincts, Jakey. Instincts." Owen might be getting a handle on things after all.

Owen visited the shop the next day.

"You again?" The man sat on a stool examining jewelry and glared at him from behind a magnifier.

"A word, if you don't mind."

"Look, Officer. I pay off some fellows from your precinct and in return, they stay out of here. I think I pay out enough."

"I'm not looking for that. Something else."

"Information, I suppose."

"That's right. You know I'm a man of my word, an honest cop. It's my job to protect the hardworking citizenry, and I'm going to do it."

The man smiled. "Well, it's about time. It's about everloving time! Come into my office."

Owen followed the man into a back room and sat on a crate.

"What can you tell me about what goes on around here? I'm looking to find Goo Goo Knox. Know who I mean?"

"First, let me tell you about a little project some folks got going, businessmen and well-to-dos who don't like public debauchery. Folks who want to put some pressure on the police force to get things done."

"Go on."

The man leaned back in his office chair and tented his fingers. "They are calling themselves the Committee of Fifteen. You might not have heard of them yet, but I'll venture that in the future you'll hear plenty. They are doing their own investigations, writing up reports—stuff the cops ought to be doing. When they present the information publicly, they figure the department will have no choice but to follow through."

"Interesting. Citizens demanding the law be enforced. I like that."

"Thought you would. Now, as for that Goo Goo fella." He turned back to his desk and scribbled something on a pad of paper, tore it off, and handed it to Owen. "Go there. Ask for that fella. You probably have his face on your mug shot wall, so it shouldn't be hard to find him. He'll tell you what you need to know."

"Why would he do that? Do I need to pay him?"

The pawnbroker laughed. "Sometimes a fella likes to see a guy get what's coming to him, know what I mean?" He leaned forward, elbows on knees. "Look, McNulty. I know there's got to be good guys on the force. I figure you're one of 'em. You can trust what I gave you. Can I trust you not to muck it up?"

Owen stood and stretched out his hand. "You most certainly can."

23

"Help, Miss Gracie!"

Grace spun around before opening the oven, thankful she'd not caused the cake to fall with an unintended blast of cold air. "What is it, Hazel?"

"I can't find my blue hair ribbon and Carolyn Feeny always has a blue hair ribbon. I have to have mine!"

"What did you say?"

"I said I need my blue—"

"No. Who always has a blue hair ribbon? Feeny, did you say, lass?"

"Yes. Carolyn Feeny." She narrowed her gray eyes. "Why?"

Grace put a hand on Hazel's back and turned her toward the stairs. "In the top right drawer of your bureau."

The girl was halfway up the kitchen stairs when Grace called to her. "Is Miss Feeny's father or uncle, or grandfather, perhaps, a policeman?"

"Yes, I think so."

"Which?"

"Maybe all of them." She trudged up the steps.

Grace rubbed her tired eyes. Half the police force, maybe more, was Irish. But this was no coincidence. S. P. Feeny's nephew was on his way to interrogate her. She could feel it in her bones like the return of blustery winter.

Hazel reappeared, blue ribbon dangling from her hand.

"Give me that, lass." Grace quickly tied it in the girl's long, wavy brown hair. "Does Carolyn Feeny go to your school?"

"Teacher's pet." Hazel stuck out her tongue.

"Now don't be like that." Grace could not force a harsher reprimand. She knew what Feenys were like.

"I don't like her at all. She is always raising her hand when Teacher asks a question. Way before anyone else can think of the answer."

"Be patient and work hard. Your teacher will understand that you are a smart lass, Hazel Parker. Just as bright as the Feeny child."

As they began the hike to the school, Grace tried to remember the faces of the children she'd seen there before and the adults who escorted them. But she'd never before considered the possibility that a Feeny could be among them, so she wasn't sure. Today she'd look. She'd examine every face, looking for the roundness, the ruddy cheeks, the shifting eyes.

She saw it right after she'd dismissed the girls.

"Ouch, Miss Gracie. You squeeze my hand too tight."

"Sorry, Linden."

"Let go."

She certainly would not. Not with someone so closely resembling her mother's husband only a few feet away. "Let's go. Hurry. I have more baking to do, laddie."

They scrambled up the steps to the brownstone moments later. "Go get the pencils, Linden. You can draw at the kitchen table while I bake."

"Yes, Miss Gracie."

She pulled off his coat and mittens and he hurried off.

Breathe. He hasn't found you yet. He doesn't even know where you are.

She set Linden's drawing gallery up and began assembling the ingredients for bread.

"Grace, come here," Mrs. Parker called from the other room.

"I'll be back in a moment, Linden. If Auntie Edith comes back with the caraway seeds, ask her to leave them on the counter for me."

He nodded and continued his drawing of a man with a disproportionately sized head and arms sticking out where ears should be.

Grace answered the mistress's call from the parlor. Alice Parker lounged on the sofa while the baby slept in a cradle nearby. "I can't seem to find coralbells." Scores of catalogs lay scattered around the room. Mrs. Parker tossed one onto the pile. "See what you can do, Grace. I'm going to take a nap." The woman rose, her nightgown rumpled and her expression sullen. She waddled slowly toward the stairs.

"How are you feeling today?" Grace spoke to the woman's back.

She turned slowly. "Like it's all a waste."

"What do you mean?" The baby stirred. Grace went to the cradle and patted his back.

Mrs. Parker's gaze fell to the child and then back at Grace. "You are a better mother than I am."

Stunned, Grace tried to argue.

"No, no. It's true. One cannot give love when one is as unlovable as I am." She turned back to the stairs.

Grace hurried toward her. "That's just not true, Mrs. Parker. You are their mother. They love you."

The woman turned her gray face toward Grace. "I'm afraid I just don't care."

"Wait." Grace hurried over and snatched up a seed catalog. "Look." She flipped to a page of line-sketched daisies. "When you don't feel love, you turn to what's beautiful, don't you? I know you do, because I've done that myself."

Mrs. Parker walked to the mantel and took a deep breath, fingering the evergreen branches. "I suppose you are right. Nature soothes me. Every time I plant a seed and am rewarded with a bloom, I feel gratified that I'm a part of the process, a contributor to the beauty somehow." She turned toward Grace, gripping her gown to her neck. "Sounds foolish, doesn't it?"

"Nay. Not foolish at all, ma'am." Grace scooped up the baby. He nuzzled against her. "Don't you see? 'Tis the same. These children are beautiful creations. God created the flowers you delight in and also these children. And you are certainly responsible for bringing them into life, no less than the garden you tend. They are lovely. Look at them. I know when I do, my soul is uplifted."

For the first time Mrs. Parker smiled. "And why is that, Grace? Why do innocent things of beauty inspire us?"

"Reverend Clarke, in his sermon on Sunday, said that becoming childlike will draw one closer to God. He said Jesus himself told his disciples so. I don't know about such things. I only know what I see, but maybe . . ." She hesitated.

"Go on, Grace. I've never heard Reverend Clarke's sermons. Tell me."

"I'm not the one to be explaining such things, ma'am. Perhaps Mr. Parker—"

"No, no. You tell me what you think."

Cornered. Like that toad in a jar again. "I . . . uh . . . I just see something remarkable in the children's faces. Maybe we need them as much as they need us." Grace placed Douglas in her arms.

"I'll take him upstairs to his crib," his mother said, cuddling him under her chin.

When the mistress left, Grace turned back toward the hall and encountered Mr. Parker's sister. "Well done, Grace. Well done."

"You heard?"

"Indeed, and McKinley himself could not have offered a more poignant speech and certainly no truer one."

"Thank you. I don't know if it helped."

"Well, we often don't know. We just have to do our best to encourage others."

"I must get to the bread now." Grace's heart soared as though sunbeams shot through it, enlightening the truth and chasing away the lies she had allowed to fester there.

The woman followed her into the kitchen and patted Linden's shoulder. "A fine artist you are, my boy."

The lad beamed.

"I think you should take your paper and pencils up to the playroom and draw the general's portrait, don't you?"

"The one Miss Gracie made for me?"

"Yes, the clothespin one." Auntie Edith saluted like a soldier. "Every good general has his portrait made."

"He does?"

"Of course."

Linden grabbed his things and headed for the back stairs. "I'll do a good job. You'll see."

"Of course you will, sonny. You're a Parker, after all."

When he was gone, the woman chuckled and began

measuring the flour for Grace's bread. "I am afraid my brother has not done well by his wife."

A shiver ran up Grace's neck. She should not be having this kind of conversation. She remembered the reverend's wise advice. "He is a good provider. Nothing else is my business, Auntie." The woman had insisted Grace address her the same way the children did.

"You might say that, but truly, my dear, you run this household. You know this family intimately."

"I . . . uh . . . My job is to . . ."

"Fiddlesticks. I think you should know a few things. That way you will be more prepared to carry out your duties."

Grace didn't want to listen. She stirred the batter with abandon.

"It concerns the children, Grace."

Grace had been trying to compensate for the lack of parental affection in this house. Edith might be preparing to correct her for that. Perhaps that earlier compliment had not been what she'd thought. Grace bit her lip and dropped the seeds into the batter.

Edith wiped her hands on her apron and leaned against the sink. "My brother was an only son, and our father put high expectations upon him. I'm a bit older than George, and I noticed these things. He was a sensitive little fellow, and our father believed he had to toughen him up. I'm afraid he chose harsh words to do that, always telling the boy he was not measuring up. Father thought that would make him try harder."

Tears sprang to Grace's eyes. "'Tis the way most fathers are, I believe."

"Ah, probably so." Edith untied her apron and hung it near the back door. Then she seated herself in the spot Linden had vacated. "But in George's case, it only served to make him emotionally withdrawn and bitter. I study human behavior, being a scholar. I don't ascribe to many of the modern philosophies, but I know what I see and observe. Since I've been here, I've become concerned about his family. Do you know what I mean, dear?"

She did. "I know my place, Auntie."

"Oh, indeed. I'm not asking you to jeopardize your job, dear."

When Grace placed the loaves in the oven, Edith gestured toward a chair. "Sit a moment. You have time."

Grace took the chair opposite her. She liked Edith, but now she was wondering if she'd misjudged her. She had a soft, nearly creaseless face, and unlike Grace's, this woman's hair stayed neatly twisted into a bun, and her starched neckline gave her a proper, polished look, the way a school matron should appear.

"Dear, I just wanted to make sure you understand my concerns. I'd hate for Linden to learn to be such a disconnected human being. He's such a loving, happy child now."

"He is that."

"You've done a marvelous job thus far with the children, Grace."

Grace's face flushed warm. "I don't know about the girls. They quarrel quite a bit."

Edith clicked her tongue. "Girls are different. Don't I know that. At my school there is a squabble about some minor issue nearly every hour. But girls are emotional. It's their nature."

A long pause followed. Grace rose to pour them some coffee. She tried not to be emotional. Her own father had despised tears like Mr. Parker. A sign of weakness. She set a cup in front of Edith.

"But boys are taught not only to restrain their emotions,

which is critical in business dealings, of course, but also to restrict heartfelt expressions. I've heard my brother scold his son for trying to hug him."

Grace stiffened, remembering having been struck once for trying to merely touch her father's hand.

"You are a breath of fresh air for these children, Grace."

Oh, how she hoped so. Grace lifted her cup. "As are you, Auntie."

They toasted with their cups and laughed.

"But I'll be gone in a few days, Grace. I just wanted to encourage you to keep loving these little ones and showing kindness to their mother. Someone has to. Otherwise . . ." She paused.

"Otherwise what?"

"Well, let me just say that in my occupation I have seen girls who were neglected in childhood bloom into productive, happy adults under the proper care and tenderness. That can happen here as well, with you as these children's nanny."

The coffee, and Auntie's words, warmed Grace down to her toes. Grace had learned so much at the Parkers'. Life was different in America, but in many ways people were the same, both good and bad. She had once thought leaving her mother would be the end of feeling connected and loved. But there was another force at work, the source of the warmth streaming inside her right now. Others radiated the kind of affection her mother had for her, and that amazed her. *You are important.*

When Grace picked the girls up from school, Hazel could barely contain her excitement. "Carolyn Feeny wants to come to my house to play."

Holly bounced on the balls of her feet. "Can I play too?"

Hazel shrugged. "Do you think Mother will allow it, Miss Gracie? She just has to."

Grace glanced around but didn't see a Feeny face. "I thought you didn't like that lass, Hazel."

"Well, she's being nice now. Pleasant, so . . ."

"Are you sure you want her to visit?"

"Yes! If Mother says no, all the other girls will think I'm aloof."

"For the love of St. Michael, child, where did you hear such a word?" Grace hurried them along, hoping to avoid meeting any senior Feenys, even the lass's mother.

"Carolyn Feeny uses lots of big words. She said if you find words in the dictionary and use them, people will know how smart you are."

"A ruse, that is. Don't be trying to be someone you aren't, dearie."

"But will you talk to Mother, Miss Gracie? Please?"

"I will, so long as you get straight to lessons when we get home."

Grace was surprised to discover that Mrs. Parker was amicable. She had secretly hoped Mrs. Parker would not approve. "So long as they entertain themselves upstairs, it's fine."

Carolyn Feeny, a flaxen-haired girl bearing no resemblance to the Feeny Grace knew, appeared on the doorstep. Grace smiled at her. "Hello."

"I've come to see Hazel." She pointed behind her to the sidewalk. "My cousin walked me over."

"Oh, delightful."

The man tipped his hat back, and Grace saw that he bore the same moon-shaped face and red hair that S. P. had, the face she thought she'd glimpsed earlier on the walk to school. And he was dressed in New York police blue.

"A word with ye, ma'am?"

Grace led them in just as Hazel scrambled down the stairs.

"Do you like checkers?"

The two girls disappeared upstairs before Grace could turn back to the other visitor.

"Are you Grace McCaffery, by chance?"

She wanted to lie but thought better of risking her position for being untruthful with guests. He'd never believe her anyway. He'd been looking for her. "I am. Did someone tell you my name?"

"I knew yer stepfather back in Drogheda. Ole S. P. Feeny."

She swallowed hard. "Are you Officer Feeny, then?"

He bowed. "Walter Feeny, at your service. Was just about to pay a visit to your boardinghouse, but you saved me the trouble, lass."

"You should know I've no fondness for that old peeler."

He laughed. "Is that the way of it? Well, so. Just a moment, please?"

"In the kitchen."

"After ye."

He pulled up a kitchen chair, making himself at home. "He's supposed to be related to me, so I hear. Don't know him well, I don't." He stretched his neck like a goose, taking note of her. "I think I've seen ye before, Miss Grace McCaffery."

She turned toward the sink. "You're mistaken."

"Ye might be missing the red petticoat now but 'tis herself all right. I'd know yer pretty face anywhere. Ye were with those

Dusters, now weren't ye? Carrying a box camera? That was yer-self now, wasn't it?"

"What? I don't know what you're talking about."

He chuckled. "Don't get coy."

"Dusters? I don't know what that is."

He squinted at her. "Ye mean it, don't ye?"

She turned, hands on hips. "S. P. sent you to check on me. I am fine. I have written to my mother. There is no need for any other questions, Officer Feeny. What time will you pick up your cousin Carolyn?"

"In the park. At the aquarium. I saw ye talking to a fella called Smokey Davis." He snapped his fingers. "A known crimi-nal, don't ye know?"

"I did not know. I'm friendly enough to folks."

"Well, ye can't be too careful out there, miss. But ye can count on me. I'll not be mentioning this wee . . . uh, indiscre-tion to the Parker family. Wouldn't want this to cost ye yer posi-tion here. I hear Mr. Parker is quite . . . uh . . . sanctimonious when it comes to his family. And since ye did not know to whom it were ye were talking . . ."

"Thank you." She might have gritted her teeth, but she got the words out.

He stood and placed the chair back against the wall. "Well, I would appreciate it if ye'd repay me for this kind turn I'm doing ye. Just a dance or two."

She faced him, her hand at her throat. "Excuse me?"

"At the maid's dance on Thursday. Over at the Hibernian Hall near yer boardinghouse. Ye know the one?"

"I do."

He lowered his chin. "See you then, aye?"

"Well . . ." A trapped toad once again. "I will be there."

When he left, she doubled over with nausea. Things had been going well, but now a peeler—named Feeny, no less—had the power to threaten her job.

24

WITH THE INFORMATION Owen received from the pawnbroker, he was eager to get back to work. But unfortunately a disturbance at a canning facility in Chinatown took up his time for days. And with daily visits to his father and phone calls back and forth, he had not been able to follow up on his tip. A week later he was determined to get back on the Dusters case. But first there was the organizational meeting at headquarters. Walter Feeny walked close to Owen as they traveled on foot from the precinct closest to headquarters. Owen didn't think Walter suspected anything, but he hadn't expected the police chief to turn up at Miss Amelia's either. Owen constantly had to watch his step.

"Surely ye like Irish music sessions, being that yer family is from Ireland," Walter Feeny said as he and Owen maneuvered past a strolling accordion player singing "Rosie O'Grady."

"I suppose so." The truth was, not much of the old country was in Owen's upbringing. Only memories of his granny's brogue and her kind spirit. None of his surviving family had ever been across the sea.

"Ever been to one of those maid dances?"

"Me? No."

"Owen rarely goes anywhere," Jake added, popping up on Owen's left.

Thanks, Jake.

"I invited a pretty lass to come tonight. Ye fellas might remember seeing her around the Battery when ye were patrolling."

Jake groaned. "Not one of those ladies of the evening, Walter. What are you thinking?"

Walter reached around Owen to slap Jake's back. "Not the typical one, anyway. Yous might have seen her loitering some time back, but she didn't stay around. This one is maid for my wee cousin's school chum."

"Swell." Jake attempted to steer Owen on ahead of Walter, but the man kept trailing right along with them.

"The Parkers over on Fourteenth. Nice house. Real nice."

Owen waited up for him. "You don't mean Grace McCaffery?"

"Oh, and you do remember her, so." He whistled. "Fine-looking lass."

Jake tugged on Owen's arm. "Let it go. None of our concern."

Owen put his hand on Jake's shoulder before they ascended the stairs at headquarters and muttered in his ear. "You know how Walter treats the ladies?"

"Yeah. Chews 'em up and spits 'em out. He's always trying to one-up you, Owen. Haven't you noticed? It's his problem. Ignore him."

"Reverend Clarke would want me to do something for that young lady."

"Sure?"

"Absolutely."

"So do something. Hey, Walter, hurry up."

The man jogged up next to them.

Jake slapped the Irishman on the shoulder. "Where's this dance held?"

When Owen entered the hall Thursday evening, he wondered if he'd made a mistake. The building was familiar. He'd passed it every day on his way to the station. "Are you sure this is the right address, Jake?"

"Yeah. These kinds of dances are pretty plain. The musicians will be here soon."

"Your wife all right with you coming?"

"Sure. I told her I had to look out for you."

"You didn't have to come."

"And let you deal with Feeny alone should something brew up? No way."

Inside the wood frame building, a row of folding chairs lined one wall. A few people mingled about. Jake found someone he knew and left Owen sitting alone. That old feeling of not belonging swept over him again like a murmuration of black-winged birds, back and forth, in and out. He thought he'd be fine; then he wanted to run out the door. But of course he couldn't. Grace might need him.

He sipped on a fizzy drink as five men carrying instruments pulled chairs together in a circle. Two fiddles, a round skin-covered drum, an accordion, and a small flute. Owen sat on a chair across from them while Jake continued to talk with a couple of fellows.

Owen was still there much later when the music was in full swing and dancers twirled about. He'd tried to strike up conversations with folks sitting nearby, but the music made that nearly impossible. When he stood to refill his refreshment, his eyes fell on a petite girl dancing in the center of the crowd.

Grace McCaffery.

Feeny swung her around on one arm. They clapped their hands and stomped their feet. Owen kept his eyes on them.

Someone leaned toward him. "Lose yer date, did ye?" A wiry old gent glared at him over the top of spectacles.

"Uh, I didn't have a . . ."

"Don't need a partner to dance." The man shrugged and looked toward the crowd.

Owen smiled and stuck a hand in his pocket to check for his watch. Still there. "I was just going to get . . ." He held up his cup. He didn't know what the Irish called their fountain drinks. "Would you like something?"

"Thank you, no. Enjoy!" The old man winked and then wormed his way into the crowd, singing at the top of his voice.

Owen had never had trouble making friends, but he was in foreign territory, and it seemed everyone knew it. They parted when he walked by. One or two folks acknowledged him as a cop in their neighborhood but then moved on.

Leaning against the refreshment table, he caught another glimpse of Grace. Her normally pale cheeks flushed, and while those around her seemed to be having a good time, Grace appeared as annoyed and uncomfortable as he felt. When the music stopped, he approached her. He overheard their conversation.

"I told you, I don't care for any of the Feenys." Grace tried to pull away from Walter but he held fast to her sleeve.

"We Feenys are just friendly, that's all. You don't know what's good for ye, simpleminded as ye are. New York's a big scary place for weaklings. Let me help ye."

"Let go of me!"

Owen pushed his way in and towered over them both. "Walter. Enjoying the dance?"

Grace did not look up at him. "I don't need your help, Officer."

Walter sneered. "Hear the lady, McNulty?"

Owen gripped the man's shoulder. "What's the trouble?"

Walter huffed. "You see this here lass, McNulty? We know her kind, don't we?"

Grace ducked between them and inched away.

"Whoa, now." Owen caught her arm before she got two paces away.

"I told you I did nothing wrong," she whispered. "Now leave me alone."

"I didn't say you did. Is he bothering you, Grace?"

"He is. And so are you."

She managed to get through the crowd and out the door to the street before he could stop her. When he caught up, he found her leaning against a vacant hitching post, chest heaving as though she couldn't catch her breath.

"What's wrong, Grace? Feeny's gone. He won't bother you."

She gazed at him, wild-eyed. "You can't take me away again. I won't let you! Any of you!"

"What are you talking about? No one's taking you any-where." He placed his hands gently on her arms, hoping to nudge her out of whatever trance she seemed to be in.

"Peelers. The cottage. Burning. Pulled me away." She turned her face toward him, swollen with tears. "How could he do this all over again? He married my mother!"

"Walter Feeny? No, Grace, you're confused. I told you, he won't—"

She broke away from him and tore down the alley.

"Wait!"

She turned. Owen rushed toward her. She ducked into a cross alley and he tore after her. A dog, barking an alarm, chased him for a few moments until he reluctantly kicked it away. Ahead he saw Grace trip over discarded tin cans and reach for her knee.

"Wait, Grace!"

They emerged at the bottom of a set of stairs leading to the elevated train.

She scrambled up the steps and threw herself onto a train seat just as the car lurched forward, bellowing steam.

Jake pulled up next to Owen. "What happened? I heard a commotion, and folks said you were following the McCaffery girl out here."

"I'm not sure what happened. Feeny had his hands on her. She didn't like it much, and I was steering him away when she just took off like a shot."

Jake smacked his lips together. "Odd. She's disturbed in the head, Owen."

"I don't know. Something has traumatized her, that's for sure, and Feeny, despicable as he can be, didn't have an opportunity to do any harm. She got on the el."

"Well, you accomplished what we came here for. You kept her out of Feeny's clutches. I'm ready to head home now."

Owen knew Jake needed to get back to his wife, so he didn't mention that he had some promising information from the pawnbroker and would be headed down to the park, especially since he knew Feeny wasn't on patrol tonight. "See you tomorrow, Jake. Tell Sandra and the kids hello for me."

Owen pulled his collar up and hailed a cab. Not in uniform, he could be an ordinary citizen and not draw attention to himself. "Night fishing," he explained to the driver.

The man laughed. "Oh, sure. But not the kind you'd do in the Hudson, I don't suppose."

It was a lame excuse, but Owen didn't need to explain himself.

After he paid the driver and gave his horse's nose a pat, he lumbered off toward the benches near the center of the green area. A quick check of his watch told him he'd arrived in time. Goo Goo Knox himself had been making personal visits to some of the cops in the Battery according to the pawnbroker. Tonight Owen would just observe. He had to determine if the pawnbroker was trustworthy.

A few moments later a police wagon stopped on State Street. A couple of cops jumped out and headed straight for him. Owen glanced around. Seeing no one near, he realized they were coming for him. He darted behind the statue into the shadows.

"McNulty! Come out here. We've had an emergency call from your mother."

Owen considered the possibility that Big Bill had set him up, but when he recognized one of the men, he came out of hiding.

"Captain Nicholson, how did you know where—?"

"C'mon, McNulty. You can use the phone at the closest precinct."

"Mother? Calm down. I can't understand you."

"Owen, yesterday the bankers called. Maybe that brought it on."

"What, Mother? Brought what on?"

"Your father's heart trouble. Oh, Owen, your father is ill and now the business might fail. You must come home."

"Is he . . . all right? Are you at the hospital?"

"No. We are home. He's stable."

"I'll be there in thirty minutes." Owen hung up the phone and returned to the wagon where his captain waited. "Thank you, but how did you know where to find me?"

"You were not at home. Telephoned over to Stockton's place and he said you were going home. Figured you took me up on the . . . suggestion. Know what I mean? And sure enough you were in the Battery."

"Yes."

As Owen hailed another cab, this time headed uptown, he pondered what Nicholson might be up to. From the time he left Jake to the time Nicholson found him in the Battery . . . well, no. Nicholson could not have been blindly searching for him. He'd found him too quickly. But why would his own captain, a man who'd told him he wanted to go against headquarters and run the Dusters out of Battery Park, be trailing him?

A young Irish servant Owen had not seen before opened the door of his parents' house for him and led him upstairs to his father's bedchamber. Owen's mother sat dozing on a chair. In the dim room he could barely see his father's face, but he heard his snoring. The servant quietly closed the door behind her. Owen tapped his mother's shoulder. "Mother?"

Her eyelids rose and then she sat up, dropping the book she'd been reading to the floor. "Owen. When did you get here?"

"Just now. How is father?"

She stood and took his father's hand. "Resting. The doctor was just here."

"Son?"

"I'm here, Father." Owen moved to the opposite side of the bed and leaned down.

"Good, good. Listen." He licked his lips.

"Rest, Father. We can talk in the morning."

"No. Listen. In the morning, go to my office. Bring the books home with you."

"Father, I do not think now is a good time—"

"Can't trust Blevins. You hear me?"

"I will. Now rest."

His father sighed, closed his eyes, and drifted off to sleep.

When Owen and his mother got to the parlor, Owen had plenty of questions for her. "Since when does Father not trust his closest colleague, Mother?"

"Since the bankers threatened foreclosure. Please, Owen, you've got to go look into it."

She was right. But he was just about to root out the leader of the Hudson Dusters. He could not be in two places at the same time. He stood. "I'll handle this. Get me Father's keys."

Grabbing his coat, he kissed his mother and then rushed down the four blocks to his father's office. He let himself in, flicked on the electric light, and headed toward the file cabinet behind his father's desk. After retrieving the account books for the last several months, he locked the office door and turned toward the entrance.

A light shone from under another door. He knocked.

"Who is it?"

"Owen McNulty. Who's in there?"

The door flung open. His father's associate, Alvin Blevins, blinked bloodshot eyes at him. "Glad you're here, son. I've been going over my salaries and such, trying to see where we can cut expenses."

"That's not your area of expertise, Mr. Blevins."

The man shook his head. "I know. I always follow your father's direction and carry out his orders, but in times like these . . ." He glanced to the books in Owen's hands. "Ah, the accounts." He reached for them. "Perhaps I can cut expenses there as well. Maybe return some of our stock."

Owen backed away. "I'll be handling that."

"Fine, fine. Let me know if there is anything I can do."

"There isn't. Go on home now. I'll lock up."

"Well . . ." He sputtered his lips. "Yes, very well."

Owen waited until the man was properly attired and then followed him out, where they said good-bye. He had never even asked about Owen's father's condition.

25

THE HAWK SPUTTERED through her lips when she saw Grace's scraped knee but made no other comment. Somehow that woman knew when to speak up and when to keep silent. Grace tried to explain. "I just wanted to leave sooner than everyone else. I was tired, you know."

"Yes, yes. You work hard, love. When Annie gets home, we'll give her your skirt. She'll have it mended before you need it again."

Grace went to her room and shut the door. She'd messed up . . . again. If this Feeny complained about her to the Parkers, she might lose her job. He'd spoken what she was afraid to acknowledge. *Simpleminded.* She closed her eyes tight. *God, if you hear me, help me understand. Why have the Feenys followed me all the way to America?*

Grace relived her outburst in the alley. Owen had been there. He had always been there when she needed help, but this time she had pushed him away. He was not like the Feenys. She knew that. She'd just failed to believe it before. Mr. Parker liked Owen and Owen would stand up for her. Mr. Parker did not know Walter Feeny. She'd been foolish to think Feeny could get her fired over seeing her in the park. She'd done nothing wrong. *Oh, God, why do I keep listening to people like the Feenys?* Like her da?

Grace lit the gas lamp on the desk and sat in front of it. She needed to do something. Take action. Not allow Walter Feeny to bully her out of her job. Hazel, Holly, Linden, the wee babe Douglas. They needed her now. Springing from her chair, she retrieved her camera and checked to see how much film it held. If Mr. Parker saw for himself evidence of how happy his children were with her, he would have no reason to let her go.

She couldn't sleep, so she wandered down to the kitchen for a snack. Noting that the garbage had not been taken out, she picked it up and stepped outside.

There were always people out and about in New York. She thought nothing of the figures milling about in the alley until she caught the outline of a police helmet. Walter Feeny in uniform stood leaning against the adjacent house.

"Got McNulty's shift for tonight. Captain called me in right after the dance."

"How nice for you." She emptied the can she had in a trash barrel and turned toward the door to the kitchen.

"Ye left the dance in an awful hurry."

"I . . . wasn't feeling well."

"Well, I'll be seeing ye about, Rosie."

She spun around. "Why did you call me that?" Rosie was the insulting moniker that man in the park had given her.

He crossed his arms. "Ain't that what old Smokey calls ye, or is that a name—" he came toward her—"just between the two of ye?"

"You're making that up just to scare me."

"What's the matter, lass? Don't like cops? Just McNulty?"

"Don't be ridiculous."

He laughed. "We're not all the same, ye know. McNulty's just a soft ole college boy."

She set the can down and crossed her arms to match his authoritative stance. "What does that matter to me?"

"Smokey is a lookout, protection for his gang boss. Sometimes he takes jobs from folks to . . . intimidate their enemies. I suppose ye didn't know as dull as ye are, but some of us on patrol observed ye speaking to him."

"You mentioned that before. I told you, I don't know him."

"He quite certain knows ye." He winked. "Do ye recall spying on a card game, lass? With that box camera of yers?"

How does he know about that?

"I can see from yer face ye do. Smokey recognized ye from that night, lass. There's folks don't like their picture made. Makes 'em real mad, it does. Ye probably don't even know ye took a photograph that night of a reformer, a fella that preaches against gambling."

"I . . . uh . . . I don't know anything about that."

He held up his palms while his nightstick dangled from a leather cord around his wrist. "I understand. Blameless folks can get caught in the webs they don't see, don't ye know? But nothing for ye to worry about. Just give me the photograph, and no one gets hurt, see? No need to worry about Smokey being after ye."

"He's after me?"

"Now didn't I just say so, lass?"

Photograph? She was not at all sure which roll of film that shot might be on. "I don't have it."

"Now, don't be putting up a fuss about it. I'm trying to help ye."

Fat chance. "I sent the rolls off to Kodak. I haven't yet received the prints."

"I see." He lifted his round shoulders as he turned away. "Don't say I didn't warn ye."

She glared at his despicable wee round head and noted the smell of the garbage still clinging to her hands. "And why aren't you out there right now looking for that Smokey fellow, Officer?" she shouted at his back.

He laughed. "So little ye know, lass. It's all about favors."

"And Officer McNulty—"

"Aw." He waved a hand behind his head. "He's not part of the game, ye see. Davis knows that. Only some of us know what's going on, lass."

So Owen McNulty truly was different. Mrs. Hawkins had tried to tell her. She thought back to that day in the park. She'd interrupted some discussion and startled some men by that statue and again in the aquarium. She hadn't meant to and certainly hadn't heard anything about a gang boss. She should not have been there, as she well knew now. Best to stay out of it.

"Wait." He trotted up the back steps and stood next to her. "Ye got troubles with Smokey Davis. Be sure of that. I can keep him away, not to mention shield all this from your employer's attention." He whispered in her ear, "For an exchange of favors, if ye know what I mean."

She gave him a shove and ran to the door.

"Ye don't know what you're dealing with, Grace McCaffery. Remember what I said."

Mrs. Hawkins surprised her in the kitchen. "It's late. Were you speaking to someone outside?"

"I, uh . . . I . . . I noticed the kitchen trash had not been taken out."

"Oh, that's right. I told Annie I would do it and it slipped my mind. Thank you, love." She turned the lock on the back door. "Was there someone out there?"

"No one, really."

The Hawk reached out for her arm before Grace could escape upstairs. "Something upset you. Wouldn't you like a nice cup of tea, love? Coming home from the dance early and all." She clicked her tongue. "I'm here to listen, love."

Grace gasped for air, but too late. A horrific sob burst from her lungs.

"Oh, love. Come sit down." The Hawk guided her to a chair.

"I'm always messing up, Mrs. Hawkins. I'm going to disappoint my mother, and if I do, she won't come to America, and if she doesn't come to America, I don't know what I'll do." Once she started, Grace could not hold back.

The teakettle whistled, sending a shrill blast to Grace's aching head. "He can't dismiss me. Those children need me. And Mrs. Parker. She sees no value in living, not even for the children."

Mrs. Hawkins removed the teakettle, and soon the smell of mint rose to Grace's senses. "Why would Mr. Parker fire you, love? I'm sure nothing so horrid has occurred."

"Not yet. But I don't know how to keep bad things from happening. Without my mother, even without that awful workhouse, I'm like a ship at sea without a rudder. Don't you see?"

The woman patted Grace's hand. "I do see, love. That's what the Benevolents are for. To guide you girls until you feel strong enough to set out on your own. And you will, love. You most certainly are able with the help of the One who will guide you through troubled seas."

"Thank you." Grace wasn't sure she believed the Hawk, but the woman believed it herself, and that alone was something to cling to.

In the warmth of Hawkins House's kitchen, Grace began to recover from the cloud of despair she'd tried to leave behind in

Ireland. She would stop taking random photographs because, as Feeny had said, some folks didn't like that. Instead she would photograph the faces of those she truly cared about. There was something they all had in common, and she needed to find out what that was.

26

THE NEXT NIGHT when Owen got to the station, he secured his father's account books in his locker along with his civilian clothes, figuring that was the safest place he had for them. Then he sought out his partner. Instead of blurting out the information the pawnbroker had given him, Owen decided to wait until he could be sure it had been a good tip. No sense looking foolish.

Owen and Jake headed out to Battery Park. When they got to the corner of Morris Street, they noticed a police wagon. Jake elbowed Owen. "Feeny's on wagon patrol, ain't he?"

"That's what the captain said. Him and Murphy and Green. Let's go say hello. Tell him we were just on our way over to the Fourth. Wouldn't hurt to know what he's up to."

They strode over, and seeing no driver, Owen tapped on the closed carriage door with his nightstick.

No answer.

He opened the door. "It's empty, Jakey. Now that's not right. They should not leave the wagon unattended."

Owen gazed down Morris. He and Jake had gotten a late start, having had to walk a lost child home and speak to the owner of a bookstore who was worried about break-ins over in their assigned ward, the Fourth. He grabbed the lantern from the side of the police wagon. "Something's wrong. Go around the back side of the block, Jake, and work your way around Greenwich. I'll start knocking on doors, beginning right under the el. We'll wind our way to the docks." Owen handed him the lantern.

Jake put a finger to the brim of his hat and disappeared.

"Evening." Owen greeted some hoboes. "Seen some cops around here?"

"Nope."

There was no reason for them to help, but it was worth a try.

Owen got only shrugs from the first two doors he knocked on, but at the third a hunchbacked woman answered. She held out her hand.

"Know something, then?"

"I do."

It was a moment to use his best instincts. He reached out and held her hand. "I have to have more than your word, ma'am. A detailed description."

The moment he touched her wrinkled hand, the corners of her mouth trembled. She gazed at him, eyes sparkling as though no one had touched her in a long time. "Three cops?"

"That's right. Can you describe one?"

She scowled. "Round-faced Irishman tugging a girl along. Filthy cop."

Feeny. Owen pulled out a quarter and placed it in the fingers that still held loosely to his own.

"They're at number 505."

"Thank you." He placed one more coin in her hand and gave her cheek a kiss.

Counting off the doorways, he paused outside 505. If there was trouble, he'd need Jake. But Feeny would just tell him to go mind his own business, maybe even tell him to take charge of the wagon. These were policemen, after all, not gangsters.

Owen charged up the steps. "Feeny, Green, Murphy? You in there?"

The sounds of boots scurrying on wooden floorboards came from inside. Then the door flung open.

"Feeny. What is going on? You left the wagon."

Walter Feeny closed the door, grabbed Owen by the sleeve, and urged him off the stoop and into the street. "You should not be here. Davis don't like no college boy cops."

"Davis?"

"Never mind. Do the rounds with the wagon, will ya?"

"Yes, but—"

"No questions."

Owen glanced up at a window where Smokey Davis glared out at him.

Feeny turned him away. "The fella's a wee bit concerned about yer connection to Grace McCaffery. He thinks she tried to identify his boss, but I'll get him off course. Ye just get out of here."

"Grace? What are you talking about, Feeny? You and the boys have to get out of that house."

"Mind yer own business, fancy-pants. I'm trying to save yer hide. Best listen to me." He grinned. "Look, we'll discuss it over a pint after our shift. I'll buy."

"Grace has no connection here, Feeny. You better leave her alone."

"See there? I told him you didn't know nothing." He gave Owen a shove. "Go along, boyo."

Owen found Jake at the docks. They made their way back toward number 505 and stood across the street in the shadows while Owen told him about finding the missing cops.

"Feeny? That scum. I'd tell the captain, but it won't make any difference. And if the Dusters are in that house, they'll be moving along to another before we can get back there, like they always do. I say we keep watch. What if Goo Goo is in there too?"

"Jake," he said, "Davis knows who I am."

"That's no surprise, seeing as even Big Bill knew you were after the gang."

Owen scratched the back of his neck. "Worse, I once saw Grace McCaffery, innocently enough, talking to Davis. Now he thinks she is a spy for me or something."

"What a mess that is."

Owen rubbed his temples. "How are we gonna hide here, then? There's no way we can bring them in, even if we do spot Goo Goo."

"We could wait until the cops leave and then raid the place."

Just then a man in a long coat left the house. He paused to gaze at them and gestured with a nod of his head. Then he kept walking.

"I don't know, Jake." Owen held back his partner with a hand on his shoulder.

"We won't follow him into no dark alley or nothing."

Owen had to rush to keep up with Jake. They headed up Greenwich, catching some temporary light from the el as it passed. "What happened to the lantern?"

"Dropped it."

"And why didn't you pick it up?"

"One of those sewer holes. So black I couldn't see a thing."

Suddenly the man halted, turned, and waited for them. "Officers, I'm with the Committee of Fifteen."

"What?" Jake reached for his gun.

Owen shook his head. "Uh, I was going to tell you about that, Jake."

Jake held up both hands. "Would someone tell me what in thunder is going on here?"

The man pulled out a stack of papers, forms with the title *Disorderly House Report.* "I work for a group of private citizens concerned about the debauchery in Manhattan and the failure of the police department to do anything about it. I was just in that house, playing the role of cocaine buyer."

Jake took one of the forms to examine it and then looked to Owen. "What do you know about this?"

"The pawnbroker told me. It's a way folks are trying to take back their neighborhoods from gangs and vices." Owen urged the man and Jake to keep walking as they talked. "If Goo Goo was in that house, and illegal activity was going on, this fellow's about to write a report." Owen asked the man for a pencil and wrote down his name and police precinct. "Make sure you talk to no one but me or Officer Stockton here, understand? We'll get our assignments at four o'clock tomorrow. We can't loiter around here much longer without tipping off the Dusters."

"I'll be around to see you tomorrow afternoon as soon as you go on duty, then." He darted off toward a hired carriage on Broadway.

Shouting erupted from somewhere in front of them. "Cops! We need cops!"

They tore off as fast as they could until an invisible force bounced them backward. Ropes! Owen landed hard on the street. "Jake! It's a trap. Where are you?"

In the cave-like dark he heard his partner gasping for breath.

"Jake!" Owen scrambled on hands and knees as shadowed voices mocked them.

Someone kicked him in the side. He sprang to his feet, fists ready. A rock whizzed past his head. "Lay off or I'll come find you with my gun, you street rats!"

When no one else bothered him, he crept toward the sound of Jake's wheezing. He found him sitting in a garbage heap, clutching his throat.

"Easy, Jake. I got you." He put his hands to Jake's throat. No blood.

Jake relaxed a bit. The rope must have caught him full against his voice box. Owen was taller than his partner. The rope had struck him in the chest. "Idiots!" Owen cried out. "Come on."

He pulled Jake to his feet and helped him lean against him. They ducked under the rope. Owen used one hand to extend his nightstick. There didn't seem to be any more barriers. "We let our guard down, Jakey. We should have been ready for this as many times as we've encountered it on dark streets like this one."

Jake continued to sound like a pipe full of holes.

"Just a little farther to the corner where the wagon is. Hang on."

But the corner at Morris Street was vacant. "Blasted Feeny!"

When they got to the nearest substation, the lantern-free wagon was parked outside. Feeny stood at the desk when they entered. "You two smell something awful."

They'd stepped into a few of those sewer holes on their way off Greenwich and tussled with street rubbish during the attack.

"Where were you, Feeny? We needed you." Owen gave his partner over to a police matron who had come to help.

"I was where I was supposed to be, unlike the two of you, apparently."

Owen glanced at a closed office door, wondering what authority might be on duty in that place.

"No captain there," Feeny said.

He grabbed Feeny's collar. "I've been trailing Davis for some time. Why are you protecting him?"

"Lay off, like I told you."

Owen pushed him away like the repulsive lug he was. Feeny motioned to the back door.

"What?"

"Let's talk."

Owen followed him out. The back alley air was warmed by steam coming from a factory building, but the change of space did nothing to placate Owen.

"Look, McNulty. I've been trying to help you. You know as well as I do there's fewer good men here than crickets at the North Pole."

"Yeah. So?"

"So give up on Davis. He's small potatoes anyway. I know you're trying to do your job. I'm trying to help you, man."

Owen opened the door to go back.

"You know I kid ya, right? Just a wee bit of fun?"

"Right. I gotta check on my partner."

Owen found Jake with a bandage on his neck. "He's hoarse," the matron said. "Needs to rest his voice. He should see a doctor in the morning." She waddled back toward the women's ward.

Owen told Jake what Feeny said. Jake began wildly shaking his head.

"You think we should go back to Battery Park tomorrow and look Davis up despite it all?"

Jake slammed his fists together. Then he reached for a pad of paper and scrolled the words: *For Grace's sake*.

"You're right."

After the kind of night Owen had had, he could have slept for hours. Instead, he pored over the account books his father had told him to pick up. As far as he could tell, there were no discrepancies. However, there was way too much inventory. Blevins was probably right after all. If they could liquidate much of it, they might save the business. He could take a look at the expense reports, but it was obvious the business operated with little overhead. His father had few employees besides the clerks in the stores, and the office itself was quite modest. Owen's father had always said his meager outlay was the key to his profits. No gold-leafed fancy facade buildings for McNulty Dry Goods. Unless Blevins was embezzling, and Owen could not fathom that, the overpurchasing had to be the problem. And it could be fixed.

Owen shut the last leather-bound journal and turned out the light, for little good it did. Morning sun, even on a cloudy winter day, lit up his bedroom. He pulled down the shade and collapsed on his bed, not bothering to take off his shoes.

Owen slept so late that he would have to wear his uniform when he went to visit his father. He shoved his pocket watch away just as someone pounded on his apartment door.

"Missus Varga! Laundry!"

A quick glance around his tiny dwelling told him he needed her services badly. "Come in." He opened the door. "I'm afraid I haven't gathered up the laundry yet, Mrs. Varga."

"No matter. I get it. And straighten up for you."

"Here." He pressed two dollars into her hand. "I'm sorry I'm so late paying."

She smiled. "You busy man. You catch the bad boys in the Battery, no?"

He set the account books down on his table and gave her his full attention. "Where did you get that idea?"

"Oh, everybody know. You the good cop out there. You and your partner."

"Everybody?"

"Oh yeees. You keep the aid workers from leaving. That's what people say."

"Me?"

She nodded her sky-blue-scarfed head.

"But the Battery is blocks from here. How could you know anything about what's happening down there?"

She laughed. "Officer, you so amuse me. You think I live in your nice neighborhood?" She waved the air as she scurried from corner to corner picking up his clothes. "I come here on the el."

"I see. Well, we are just doing our jobs. Trying to, you understand."

"Ah, yes. And we know."

He bowed as he backed out the door. "Thank you, Mrs. Varga. Thank you."

When he got to the house, he realized he was going to have a difficult time leaving. His father stared past him as he spoke, a man whose mind seemed so burdened he could not pull his focus back into the room. "I made mistakes, Son. I don't want your mother to have to pay for them."

"It can be fixed, Father. I'm sure of it."

"You don't have the time, and I certainly don't if you believe the doctors."

"Don't say that. We'll hire someone. Some fresh-faced graduate of City College."

"I'm afraid it's all hopeless. I should never have trusted so much to Blevins."

"Why? He's your friend."

Owen's father's chuckle turned into a dry cough. Owen found a pillow on the chair nearby and put it behind his head. "Why, Father? Do you think Blevins cheated you?"

"Heavens, no." The weary man wiggled his bony fingers in the air. "He's just incompetent. In over his head, so to speak. And I did not realize it until it was too late."

"But you've been in business together for years."

"Yes, uh-huh."

Owen checked his watch. "I have to be going."

"Go on, then."

"I'll be back."

"Did you bring the accounts?"

"Yes." Owen pointed to the bedside table where he'd left them. "But I don't see anything out of the ordinary. Just too many orders. More than your chain of stores could hope to sell if they stayed open twenty-four hours a day."

"That's what I feared. Blevins tried to help too many merchants." He clenched his fists. "I had hoped to retire and leave you the business and instead I trusted a man with a dough-soft heart instead of a mind for business."

"We'll fix it." Owen thought about the informant from the Committee of Fifteen. Jake would not be back on duty, so Owen had to get to Mulberry in time to meet the man. If he said anything to Feeny first . . .

"Try not to worry, Father. It's not good for your health."

"That's what I've been telling him." Owen's mother, looking

only slightly better than his father, stood at the foot of Father's bed. Owen hadn't heard her approach.

"He will be fine, Mother." He kissed his mother's cheek.

She rolled her eyes.

Owen had to go.

27

GRACE LEFT EARLY FOR WORK the next morning, just as the sun was rising. Her knees wobbled as she took a seat on the train. No, she could not survive in the city without help. Mrs. Hawkins, Mr. Crawley, the reverend . . . they were all nice enough folks. But what did they know about Dusters and the likes of officers like Feeny? She sucked her bottom lip and watched the city flitter past the train window. *God, if you are out there, why don't you help me? You know how little I can do. You can help me. You are divine. Why won't you? Do you hate me too?*

The train jerked to a sudden stop and the passengers moaned.

"Lousy train! Stuck again?"

A porter began hollering for folks to get off. Grace followed the crowd of people. When her feet reached the icy sidewalk, she skidded about but found her footing again and rushed past surprised street vendors and rag pickers who were just beginning their long workdays. She stopped a newsboy. "Where are we?"

"Chatham Square, miss."

She glanced around. "Do you know of a building around here owned by a Mr. George Parker?"

He shrugged his shoulders.

People huddled around fires built in metal cans. Infant wails pierced the sooty air from upper windows that were wide open despite the cold. A nearby alley saluted with lines of dingy white laundry, but other than that the buildings appeared to be shuttered shops or were otherwise unidentifiable. There certainly were no welcome mats to indicate where people might live. How alarming that she had ended up in the very place she supposed Mr. Parker owned property. She took out her camera. True, she'd vowed not to take random photographs, but how was she to know she'd end up here? Did Mr. Parker truly know what it was like in Chatham Square?

The newsboy posed for her with a toothless grin. She gave him a penny and made her way northward to the next el stop. On impulse she stopped and turned. Aiming her camera carefully, she snapped a few tenement scenes.

As she sat on the next el train, she recalled something Mrs. Hawkins had said to her. *"My Harold always said if you find yourself off course, look around. God may be directing you to something."* And hadn't she just asked God to help her? She didn't know why she'd landed in Chatham Square that morning, but perhaps the reason would become clear later.

Hazel met her at the front door.

"What's wrong, lass?" Grace dropped her bag at the door and pulled off her gloves.

"Nothing, Miss Gracie. I'm to invite you to breakfast." She collected Grace's things.

What a transformation the aunt had made with the oldest Parker child. Hazel had been much more courteous to Grace now that a member of the family had insisted she exhibit proper manners. "Well, that's very kind of you, but your father doesn't approve of the help eating with the family. You know that. I'll have to tell your aunt."

"But Father is not here." Hazel took Grace's hand with a gentle touch and led her to the dining room.

Seated around a green tablecloth, Edith, Holly, and Linden smiled at her. The baby cooed from a basket at his aunt's feet, and Mrs. Parker, still wearing her nightgown and a dour expression, sat in the corner of the room. Candles glowed from the center of the table, and the aroma of egg soufflé invited Grace to come closer. "What is all this?"

Holly bobbed up and down on her chair. "We wanted to surprise you, Miss Gracie."

Linden joined in the chorus. "Surprise! Surprise!"

Grace removed her coat and Hazel took it from her. "Father had to go in early to help the accountant with the books today. We planned this all week."

Grace turned to Mrs. Parker, who shrugged. "The children seemed entertained by it all."

Grace wrapped her arms around her chest and faced the others. "I . . . I don't understand. Why did you want to . . . ? I mean, you could have just told me. I would have made raisin bread."

"Don't have to," Holly chimed in. "Me and Auntie already did."

Hazel must have made a face at her sister because Holly stuck out her tongue.

"Now, girls," Auntie Edith said. "You all helped. What did I tell you about humbleness?"

"Yes, ma'am," they responded in the chorus they'd repeated plenty of times before.

"Mother ordered flowers from the florist," Hazel said,

stretching her brows. "Mother says they grow them in winter in greenhouses."

Grace touched the edge of a delicate pink lily. An extravagance that she hoped cheered the mistress. "Very lovely indeed."

Edith inclined her head. "Please sit, Grace. The food is getting cold. Alice is only having coffee."

At least that was the excuse so she would not have to sit with the biddy, Grace thought. Still, it was a monumental step for the woman to allow this.

"Sit, please. Sit," Linden echoed.

Grace pulled out a chair opposite him and gave him one of her this-is-a-special-treat looks.

Edith gave thanks, and just when Grace thought she was about to say amen, she added, "And we thank thee for Grace and what she has done for this family as we celebrate her birthday today. Amen."

"Were you surprised, Miss Gracie?" Holly asked.

"I'll say I was. 'Tis not my birthday."

Hazel, sitting next to Grace, placed Grace's napkin on her lap for her. "We didn't know when your birthday was, so we just decided to pick a day. If we asked you, it wouldn't be a surprise."

"Well, this is a delight. Thank you." She turned to the children's aunt. "I don't know how we would have fared if you had not come to help."

The woman fanned the air in front of her face. "You were doing a fine job without me, Grace." She leaned in to whisper, although clearly Mrs. Parker could hear her. "Don't you despair. I'm working on my brother and his excessive vigilance."

Alice Parker cleared her throat and left the room.

Grace cut into her portion of the egg dish and savored the moment. Things were certainly improving at last.

Linden started to talk with his mouth full, but after Grace shook her head at him, he understood. After he swallowed, he said, "You are older than Hazel. Are you twelve, Miss Gracie?"

She laughed. "I'm a bit older than that, lad."

"How old?"

Edith reprimanded him. "Now, Linden. Only children are asked their ages."

"I don't mind. I hardly even remember being twelve. 'Tis not my birthday, but in June I will be nineteen."

The boy's mouth formed an O.

"That's old," Holly said.

Auntie Edith rolled her eyes. "Oh, to be that young again."

After they cleaned up, Grace had a moment while the girls brushed their teeth to prepare for school. She found Mrs. Parker in the parlor. "I do hope you don't mind, ma'am. I'll tell Edith we won't be having any more breakfasts together."

Alice Parker turned her dark eyes toward Grace. "You are more of a mother than I've ever been." She'd said that before.

Grace stepped closer. "Oh no, ma'am. You are their mother. Only you."

A tear dripped down the woman's face. "Truth is, I don't know how to be a mother."

"But you can learn. I mean you can get better. 'Tis not hard. I had no experience with children before I came here."

Mrs. Parker shook her head. "Do you still have your Brownie camera, Grace?"

"Aye. Yes. I bring it with me every day. But I promise you I do not let it interfere—"

"A portrait. Just me and the children. Can you do that?"

"I can try. They are wee prints, though, ma'am. Nothing you can hang over the mantel or anything. They are called snapshots."

"Capture the moment. Isn't that what the advertisements say?"

"Aye. Yes."

"Very well. This afternoon. It might take me that long to get ready." She sighed.

"As you wish."

Grace wasn't sure about photographing the Parkers. What if Alice Parker hated it? What if Grace could not get a good shot? She'd never photographed a group before.

After the girls came home from school, they all assembled. Grace removed the shades from the electric lights and pulled back the heavy draperies, hoping that would create enough light. Alice Parker put a gentle hand on Holly's shoulder and she looked up at her mother, perhaps a bit surprised.

"Look this way," Grace called out.

The baby opened his eyes at just the right moment, cradled in his mother's left arm. Linden sat straight up, and even Hazel smiled, just a bit.

"One, two, three." Grace held her breath and clicked the shutter.

Mrs. Parker was quiet, but the way her eyes lit up when she looked at the children, who celebrated as though Grace had just shot off fireworks, seemed to suggest that the ubiquitous thundercloud hanging over the woman's head was beginning to break up. Perhaps there was hope for this family yet.

As Grace and Edith were preparing supper, she brought up the topic that had been bothering her all day. "Auntie, you know what you told me about Mr. Parker and his growing up?"

"Yes. You haven't spoken of it to anyone, have you? He's very sensitive."

"Oh, nay. No. I was wondering . . . if you don't mind . . . where you all grew up. Was it in this city?"

"Sure enough. We moved from the family home when I was a baby. If you think the Bowery's bad now, it's nothing compared to then. Filthy, so sad. But when my grandfather bought the home, it was a respectable place. We moved close to Washington Park, not too far from here in fact. George sold the place when I got married and moved away."

"The Washington Park residence?"

"Yes."

"So he spent most of his life right here in this neighborhood, then?"

"That's right."

"What about your grandfather's place? Does he still own it?"

"Oh, I hope not. All the old homes, chopped up into tenements. Such a shame. It's a sewer down there."

"Tell me more."

She clicked her tongue. "The tenements? Sad places."

"Aye, but how did they get that way? I've heard that the people who live in them mostly have jobs and make money, but they spend most of what they earn on rent. Mr. Riis said so too, but how can living in those places cost so much?"

Auntie sighed. "Such an intelligent question but I'm afraid it has no good answer. Greed, child. It's just greed. The owners know all those immigrants have to live somewhere. You are overcrowded here in Manhattan. Demand means they can charge what they want."

"That's just not right." As ornery as she thought Mr. Parker was, she had not imagined him to be so horrible.

"No, it's not. Wish we had more reform. Tear those shacks down and build proper houses."

Yes. Grace had seen it for herself when the el train broke down. Now she wondered, was she supposed to see that for some reason?

Auntie set the kitchen table with bowls for the children's stirabout, something the woman liked to call porridge. "I must tell you, I'm preparing to return home. I'll hate leaving that little Douglas, though. And all the children."

"They will miss you, too."

Edith pinched Grace's cheek. "You are doing fine here, girl. Maybe I can convince that brother of mine to let you come up to my school for a few weeks in the summer. You'd love the library, a smart girl like you. You could bring the children for a holiday."

"That sounds lovely. Thank you." *A smart girl like her?*

28

By the time Owen got to the precinct, he was too late.

"There was a man here inquiring for you earlier," the desk officer said.

"Did you ask him to wait?"

"Hey, what do I look like, McNulty? Your secretary?"

Owen leaned over the desk. His size could intimidate, but he only took advantage of that when he needed to. "Look, I know they only put greenhorns at the desk, but try to be more helpful. Did this man talk to anyone else at the precinct?"

The fella would not look at him. "I . . . uh . . . I don't think . . ."

"That's the problem, now isn't it? Think, Jones! I know you can do it if you try hard enough." Owen pounded a fist on the desk.

"Let him be, McNulty." The captain appeared at Owen's side. "The kid can't keep track of every visitor who's not here on official business." He put an arm around Owen's shoulder, though he had to reach high to do it. "In my office."

The man shut the two of them in before he spoke. "I told you word would get out." This time the captain did the desk slamming. "If I could fire that Feeny, I'd do it in an eye blink."

"Are you sure you can't question him, Captain? Or at least let him know you don't sanction colluding with gangsters?"

"Talk is cheap, McNulty. Tell me. The fella you were expecting. Who was he and why did you plan to meet him here?"

"I don't know his name but he's working with the Committee of Fifteen."

Nicholson wandered to the left side of his desk to begin his usual pacing. "Oh, is that so?" He stroked his mustache thoughtfully. "You mean those wealthy businessmen and the like who want to take law enforcement, and even interpretation of the law, into their own hands?"

"I don't know, Captain. All I know is he was in a Dusters' dive and he can identify Goo Goo."

"You don't say?" The captain rubbed the stubble on his chin and then stroked his muttonchops, considering.

"I thought it would be no trouble to meet him back here, but then I got detained."

"What detained you?" Nicholson sat and lit a cigar.

"Family matters."

"Look, son. When you came on, we all made it clear that a police officer in this ward will need to put his personal life second. You work long, tough days. Don't tell me you didn't know you'd signed up for this."

"Yes, but my father's business is in trouble."

The captain shrugged. "Like I told you before. I'll have to replace you if you can't give us all you got here. Things are shaking up." He took a long puff.

"I want to do my job, sir."

"Good. The Committee of Fifteen, I've been told, meets tonight at eight on Worth Street."

"You knew about them, then?"

The man smirked. "The building right next to the Italian mission. Know the one I mean? Limestone front?"

"Yes."

"Stockton's not operating on all cylinders yet. Doc says I can't schedule him as much as I'd like. I'm depending on you. And not just me." He shoved a newspaper across his desk. "Take a look at that, second column on the right."

Increase of Criminal Element. Charities Threaten to Abandon the Battery.

"Just like you thought." Owen laid the paper back down on the desk.

"I'm not making this up, McNulty. We'll have a much bigger mess on our hands in ninety days if we don't catch that goon."

"Ninety days?"

He poked at the paper with his index finger. "That's what they said. They'll leave in ninety days when their lease is up. One of the mission houses. Won't take long for the others to follow." He waved his cigar in front of his face. "I got two choices: patrol there more or get rid of the problem. Both are nearly impossible. I simply don't have enough trustworthy men to put in the park all night long. Catching Goo Goo would be the better fix."

"I agree. But ninety days? I'm not sure that's enough time." Investigations and arrests could take much longer.

"That's all we got. You'll have to pull some double shifts until Stockton gets back full-time. Can you do it?"

"There's no one else?"

"No one I can find that quick. Look, I know I'm bucking the system. I know Devery put me down here because he wants me out of Tammany business. Reckon that's why you're in my ward, McNulty. But God willing, we can do our job down here."

So the captain knew Devery wanted Owen to back off tracking the gang even without Owen telling him. He should have figured. "Captain? How did you know to find me in the park that night my mother telephoned the precinct?"

He leaned back in his chair and crossed his arms against his chest. "Think I was born yesterday? The Committee of Fifteen. Some of their inspectors were in the area and telephoned to tell me you were there. Wanted to know if I approved. Sometimes they're meddlesome; sometimes they're helpful. The citizenry is often my secret weapon. Now keep that under your hat, son."

That evening Owen slipped away from his rounds to get over to the meeting Captain Nicholson steered him to. Night classes were in progress at the Italian mission house next door. The windows were lit up and you could see rows of tables with people huddled over them. The quicker immigrants learned the language, the money, and the customs of this country, the easier time they'd have of it. There was no shortage of schemes to separate a newcomer from his money.

He tapped lightly on the front door of the limestone building. A man with a handlebar mustache opened the door. "May I help you, Officer?"

"McNulty. Captain Nicholson sent me."

"Sent you why?"

Owen whispered. "To attend the meeting."

The man made no sign of recognition.

"The Committee of Fifteen? I was supposed to meet a man at the precinct today, and I was late."

His eyes widened. "Ah, yes indeed. Come in, young man."

He was led to a room lit by a single lightbulb hanging over a long oak table. Owen guessed there were fifteen men seated around it, counting the man who had risen to answer his knock. "Take my chair," the mustached man said, pointing to the lone empty spot.

"I can stand."

"Oh no. We all want to speak with you. Please sit."

Owen felt the stares as he took a seat. A gentleman seated at the head of the table grunted and twiddled his thumbs. After an awkward moment of silence, the man spoke. "I am William Baldwin, chairman. McNulty, is it?"

"Yes, sir."

He proceeded to introduce each man by name. About halfway through, Owen recognized one of them. Blevins, his father's friend and business associate. He stood, halting the introductions. "Owen, let me explain. I'm here solely because of what the criminals are doing—"

"As we all are, Blevins," the man to his right said. "Sit down, please."

He acquiesced, and the introductions continued until they ended with the man at the head. Owen barely heard the names. They were wealthy concerned citizens—railroad men, university presidents, lawyers, publishing giants—just as the pawnbroker had said. But Owen had never imagined Blevins would be involved.

The committee chair spoke. "Nicholson sent you here?"

"He did. I was supposed to—"

"I understand." The man turned to his right. "Edwin, is this the man?"

"Yes, that's him."

Owen wasn't sure he recognized the man who confirmed

his identity. "Were you the man I spoke to over by the Hudson River docks?"

"No, no, but I consulted with the gentleman a few hours ago. We hire these men . . . investigators of a sort. We thought you'd changed your mind about bringing in that Dusters gang leader when you didn't show up for your arranged meeting."

"Oh no. I apologize. I have not changed my mind. My father . . . Well, I was detained."

The man stood abruptly and slammed a fist into his open palm. "There can be no dereliction of duty here."

Owen's neck began to sweat. "No, sir. I assure you I am committed to this end."

The man remained standing while the others shifted on their wooden chairs and murmured to each other. The man began to shout. "Gentlemen, gentlemen, please. Time is of the essence." He passed around a paper. When it came to Owen, he saw that it was the Disorderly House Report the other man had filled out that night. Goo Goo Knox was clearly written on one line. The man seated next to Owen cleared his throat, and Owen passed the paper on.

After they all had examined it, the man called Edwin demanded order again. "I am prepared to give you all the information we have, Officer McNulty, with one condition."

"Yes, sir. What is it?"

"You must see to the matter immediately. No delays for any reason. If the settlement missions move out, Lower Manhattan will be overrun with debauchery. Can you tell me you will do so, Officer?"

"I give you my word."

The man twisted his jaw before he spoke again. "With the current condition of the police force and the Tammany

Hall machine that controls much of it, I'm afraid that is not enough."

His word wasn't enough? "What more can I offer, sir?"

"Tell us here why you are committed to this. Do you have any compulsion other than the orders of your precinct captain?"

"I do." Owen explained the day he'd tried to help Officer O'Toole and the little girl when they were struck by the trolley car. His voice caught, surprising him. He thought he had been controlling his emotion. He swallowed hard and continued. "I didn't understand how miserable conditions were for people just a few miles from where my family lived. And I just knew that day, felt more sure of it than anything before or since, that God called me to the profession." He paused and lifted his gaze to the ceiling. *Please, God, let me get this story out.*

"Go on, son," someone encouraged.

"I imagine you all have various motives for being on this committee, both business and moral God-fearing reasons. And these aims drive you to do this, I suppose. Like you, I have no choice, gentlemen, than to answer that call, and I am accountable to a much higher power than my captain, you understand."

"Hear, hear!" The room erupted with applause and approval.

"That will do fine," Chairman Baldwin said.

Only one face in the room appeared less than pleased. Blevins gazed at Owen with a look that seemed to say, "But what about your father?" And Owen felt ashamed, wondering if he had really been seeking the approval of men rather than seeing to the responsibilities of an only son.

29

"ANOTHER TENEMENT FIRE. When will something be done?" Mrs. Hawkins tossed the newspaper on the tea table and wiped her eyes with a napkin.

Grace picked it up. "Anyone hurt?"

"I suppose so, but by God's mercy it appears no one died this time." The Hawk wiped her nose and returned to her chair without her tea.

Grace looked at the newspaper. "Where?"

Mrs. Hawkins sighed. "Chatham Square. Thankfully the fire department put it out before it spread very far. Those buildings are as flammable as cardboard."

Chatham Square? Grace had never learned the exact location of Mr. Parker's property. She wondered if she brought up the subject with him—it was in the paper, after all—she could find out.

"Maybe I could take pictures. With my camera."

"Now why would you do that, love? No, stay away from that area. Think before you leap, as my Harold always used to say."

Grace turned to the breakfront cabinet to choose a book. She'd already taken some shots, but no one knew that. Had Mr. Parker seen what she saw? Did he have any remorse over cheating those people by charging high rents?

Annie bolted into the parlor. "People are in the streets, yelling and protesting. Even the mission workers, Mrs. Hawkins."

The woman twisted in her chair. "What are you talking about? Where?"

"On State Street. Nora, the housekeeper at the Mission to Irish Immigrant Girls, was just here to tell us. She's run off to warn the others."

"Ridiculous. Protesting what, love?" The Hawk was standing now.

"They say the police have to do something about the gangs in the Battery or they'll move out. Mrs. Hawkins, are we going to move as well?"

The woman walked to the hall in a huff. "I'll say not. Get my coat, love."

⁂

When Grace and the others arrived, the sound of a brass band made the protest sound more like a carnival. Mrs. Hawkins stopped a lad with a megaphone. "What is going on here, young man?"

"The police must act. We will not be bullied." He darted away.

Grace noticed a group of young people laughing and smoking in the narrow alley beside the Irish mission house. Annie noticed too. "That's what they are talking about," Annie said. "Even the rich take part in alcohol and cocaine parties, but these church-sponsored mission houses will not put up with it happening on their doorsteps."

Grace removed her camera from her bag and snapped a photograph of the revelers despite her earlier vow not to take strangers' photographs. Before long, she realized she had wandered away from the others while observing what was happening beyond the rambunctious protesters.

An overwhelming feeling of dread filled her as she scrambled down the street between milk trucks, carriages, and people on foot. Too many times she'd been warned not to be out alone after dark. Stupid of her.

She tucked the camera back into her bag and looped the handles tightly around her arm. Fear like spiders crawled up her arms as she could not find Mrs. Hawkins and the others.

When she approached an alley, she wandered toward it to avoid a band of drunken soldiers. A hand reached out from the unlit recesses and grabbed her. "Gotcha!" A man with breath worse than three-day-old cabbage in a pot spoke into her ear.

"Let me go!"

"What's a pretty lassie like you doing out here alone?"

She squirmed until she was able to shove her knee where it would incapacitate him the most and he let go. She bolted away as fast as she could but managed to run into another man, this one much bigger.

"Whoa there."

"Let me go."

He released her. "Just trying to help."

She continued rushing down the street, tears streaking down her face. As bad as the workhouse had been, there had not been this many people to maneuver around. She felt like a salmon swimming upstream. A very small, foolish salmon, not the wise one in Irish folktales.

"Hey, stop!" Three thugs blocked her path.

She started to turn down the cross street, but one of them caught her.

"Steal from a shop, did ye?"

"What's it to you?" She would not be intimidated even though this dark-eyed thug could see her tears.

"What'd ye get?" He grabbed her arm.

She screamed.

He held a knife to her cheek, drawing blood.

Suddenly a whistle blasted from somewhere behind them.

"Cops!" The thugs took off.

Grace put a hand to her chest to steady her breathing. Not seeing anyone else around, she scurried out into a mass of people, where she felt safer. She hadn't known such terror existed so close to Hawkins House. No wonder the people were protesting. She wondered if Owen McNulty and that horrible Feeny peeler were doing their job in the slightest.

She edged toward a building to free herself from the flow of people so she could think and get her bearings. Across the street two men tussled. *The truth.* Someone had to show the truth of this place. She pulled out her camera and found a vacant spot near a lamppost where she had enough room to extend her elbows and aimed.

Whack! Someone struck her arm.

Owen left the meeting conflicted. Yes, he had to go after Goo Goo right away. Yes, he had to help his father right away.

He pulled out his pocket watch as he rounded Water Street. Only half past nine. This was going to be a long night, and there was not much he could do alone except keep an eye out for the gang boss and watch where he went. That is, if folks didn't register minor complaints for him to follow up or he didn't spend all his time rounding up prostitutes, which was becoming a larger problem of late as the missions had said.

He encountered Feeny just east of the Battery. "A protest going on right in front of those mission houses."

"What?" Owen started to move, but Feeny stopped him.

"Got some fellows containing the crowd. Don't worry about it. What are ye doing down here anyway?"

Rats! He wasn't supposed to let Feeny see him. "I . . . Nicholson gave me an assignment over on Worth and since I was done there, and things are quiet on my rounds, I just thought I'd check in with you fellas over here."

"We're fine. I'm betting things won't be quiet over yer way all night. Better head back before Big Bill finds out ye were off your post."

"I'm not off my—"

"Beat it, McNulty."

Yeah. Who but Walter Feeny would tell the police chief about a lowly beat officer wandering a couple of blocks from his rounds? "I'm going."

Owen turned and headed back, but out of sight he turned left to trudge up the crooked path of Stone Street. Better check out this protest. He wasn't needed in his patrol area because a sergeant and two roundsmen were near there, but Feeny didn't need to know that.

Owen spotted a man and a woman standing in front of a building.

"You came out here for a reason, Rosie. You and that camera!"

The man stepped backward into a crescent of light under the streetlamp. Smokey. This was not how Owen had hoped to encounter him.

"Let me go!" the woman wailed. "I didn't come here to see you. How was I to know you'd be here?"

"I w-w-won't be panned."

"Smokey, that's your name, isn't it? Let go of me. I got lost, is all."

"I'm to teach you a lesson, Rosie, and I aim to do it!"

She kicked him but that only fazed him for a brief moment. This was just the kind of distraction Owen had hoped to avoid. There were no other Dusters around that he could see, and he would have to arrest these two and bring them in for disturbing the peace and the usual public drunkenness. "Halt. Don't move," Owen called out.

Smokey flung the girl away from him and she landed in a seated position on the icy sidewalk. The thug tried to run off, but he was truly pickled, so Owen had no trouble handcuffing him. "She's a liar. No matter what she says to you, she's lying."

"Yeah, yeah." Owen snapped the handcuffs and yanked Smokey to his feet.

Owen glanced at the girl. "Hold on, Miss Rosie."

"That's not my name."

Now that he was closer, Owen recognized that voice even though her face was shadowed and partially covered by her dense, disheveled hair. "What are you doing out here?"

"I got lost."

"Lost? This time of night?"

"That's right. I . . . uh . . . We . . . left Hawkins House. There is a protest . . ."

"You better come with me."

"All right. I should have known better. I don't know why I keep—"

"You're all right now. Just come along."

She trailed behind Owen as he lugged Smokey along. "Isn't Hawkins House the other way?"

"We're going to the precinct. There's a patrol wagon a few blocks north."

"Uh, no. I'll find my way." She stepped out from the curb, but he pulled her back with one arm while still struggling with the criminal with his other hand.

"Let go."

"Look, Miss McCaffery. You should not be out here."

"As I well know. I'm going home."

"I can't let you go on alone. Why don't you come with me, and I'll call over to Hawkins House and they'll come get you."

"No."

He had to squeeze tighter on her wrist. "I don't mean to frighten you. I'm trying to help."

Suddenly she gasped for air. Owen thought she might faint.

"Need some help, McNulty?"

Walter Feeny.

Grace took a step closer to Owen. "I'll come."

Owen shouted as they plodded down the dark street. "No, Feeny. I'll handle it."

"I don't think so." Feeny pulled out his gun.

"What are you doing, Feeny?"

"This is my beat, Owen. Let the man go."

"Public drunkenness. Surely you can see that."

"I'll take care of it."

Owen stared at the man's face. He was serious, although probably showboating for Grace's benefit. Owen didn't want Grace to be in the middle of it. "I'd let you if I hadn't already used my cuffs on him."

Smokey's eyes rolled heavenward. He was clearly unaware of what was happening. Feeny seemed to notice it too. He put his pistol back. "You don't know what yer messing with,

McNulty. But . . . because of this delicate lass here, I'll let ye carry on."

"Noble of you, Feeny."

"I'll just escort Miss McCaffery home."

Owen felt her shudder against him. "I already made arrangements, Feeny."

"That so? Unmake them." He took Grace's arm.

"Let go of me! Officer McNulty is taking care of me."

Owen saw the man's red face turn a shade darker.

Feeny leaned close to Grace. "I warned ye, now didn't I? Don't ye forget I was the one."

Owen tugged Grace forward. "Leave her be, Feeny."

Walter raised both hands in surrender. "Fine, fine. But let me give ye a tip. If this fella wasn't so snickered, he'd have done ye some harm, Miss McCaffery."

Owen pulled Grace tighter while Smokey slumped against his shoulder. "She understands she should not be out here alone at night."

"Yeah? Well, so. Let me tell ye something ye both don't know."

"Get lost, Feeny."

They left the man stammering on the curb.

Back at the station, Smokey sat in a jail cell. They would charge him with disorderly conduct and he'd be back on the streets in less than forty-eight hours, likely with no memory of the faces of those who had arrested and questioned him. Now fallen down drunk, possibly also dazed by cocaine, rampant among the Hudson Dusters, Smokey Davis would scarcely even realize he was alive by morning. When he was able to stand on his own feet, the captain would send him off. He was small potatoes but still a lure to follow. With any luck Smokey wouldn't remember Owen. Feeny? He was all talk and nothing else.

Tammany Hall boss Crocker and even Big Tim Sullivan—the politician most folks liked because they didn't know how he did business—might have their greedy tentacles over most of Manhattan and her ubiquitous illegal businesses, but not the night court in the First Ward. The judge would send Goo Goo up the river, if Owen could catch him.

But he had precious little time to do it.

"None of my girls should be in such a place!" The short, stout woman with the British lilt to her voice stomped into the main office, her chunky heeled boots pounding loudly against the tile floor. Owen had never seen Mrs. Hawkins so out of sorts, but he couldn't blame her.

Grace stood, but Owen motioned to her to sit. She ignored him and called out to the woman. "Mrs. Hawkins, I assure you 'tis all a mistake."

The middle-aged woman tried to wiggle past a patrolman who stopped her. "Let Miss McCaffery go. I'll take her home straight away."

The captain, alerted by the commotion, flung open the door to his office and marched up to Owen's desk. "Let her go, McNulty."

Grace was angry with him, although she'd come willingly. It wasn't his fault she'd wandered off during the protest. Whatever life she'd escaped in Ireland had obviously filled her with mistrust. "I'm happy you were not hurt, Miss McCaffery."

"Thank you, Officer," Mrs. Hawkins said as she hugged Grace to her and moved toward the door.

Nicholson motioned to him. "Let's talk about that meeting on Worth Street."

30

Grace scrambled up the front steps, Mrs. Hawkins at her heels.

Annie met her at the door. "What happened?"

"I don't want to talk about it." Grace covered her face with her hand and ran upstairs to her room. Behind her she heard Annie and Mrs. Hawkins mumbling together. Whether or not they thought she was a complete nitwit to have gotten lost and ended up at the police headquarters way over on Mulberry, she'd learned something. She knew who *not* to trust: Feeny.

Sleep would not come easily after all the evening's commotion, so she might as well warm some milk and try to calm herself. Slipping out from under the quilt on her bed, she crept from the room and made her way downstairs.

Carrying a small oil lamp, she stopped at the front door. A piece of paper lay just beyond the mail slot. She hadn't seen it earlier. Mail was not delivered at night. She picked it up. Her name was scribbled on the outside, but no return address and no stamp. She peeked into the parlor. Empty. She set the lamp down on a side table, slid onto the sofa, and opened the letter.

Dear Rosie,
  I'm watching you. I should have smashed that camera.
Whatever goods you got better not show up in public.
Cross me and you're dead, little lassie.
Davis

He knew where she lived. She crumpled the note and held it against her chest. She didn't have any goods, as Smokey put it. Why had she pretended she did when she approached him that day at the trolley? Because she was no smarter than a toad, that's why. *"Another blunder, lass!"*

Looking to Mr. Hawkins's portrait, she silently pleaded, *Who will protect me?*

Sunday passed all too quickly, and before she knew it, she had to leave the secure confines of Hawkins House to go to work. She had not mentioned the note to anyone, hoping a solution would occur to her so she wouldn't need to worry anyone. Grace studied every face on the streetcar that turned in her direction. Every muscle in her body tightened whenever a new man boarded. When she exited to make her walk to the Parkers' house, she paused at a newsstand to let those behind her go ahead. As unlikely as it might be, she found herself wishing the Parkers lived on Owen's beat. But he would be nowhere near here if she needed him.

A gust of wind blew debris along the street. The smell of musty, decaying leaves made her nose twitch. The stormy day whistled in her ears. *You can't survive.*

"Stop it," she said aloud, alarming a few people near her. She smiled at them and then continued walking, holding her hands over her ears to block out her father's voice. She'd been tossed into a stormy sea without her permission and now she had to swim. And she would. She had to.

Grace kept walking and looking. She did not see Smokey Davis, thankfully.

When she was in sight of the house, she rushed toward it and ran up the steps. Only when the large door closed behind her did she allow herself to inhale deeply. For once she would have no trouble keeping the children in the house. As she hung up her coat and hat, she wondered if she would see Officer Feeny when she walked the girls to school. He'd wanted Owen to let that scum Smokey go, and hadn't he offered to protect her from him? They were in cahoots of some sort, apparently. She bit her lip.

"Good morning, Miss Gracie." Linden stood in his union suit gripping a glass of milk.

"Has Auntie gone, Linden?"

He frowned. "Father took her to the train. They woke me up to say good-bye."

"And your mother?"

"Still in bed."

"Come along. We'll make some breakfast."

"I want sugar in my porridge."

Grace scooted him along toward the kitchen. "You know how your mother feels about giving you sugar, Linden."

"Please?"

"Molasses, so. Hurry along. Maybe we'll make hotcakes instead."

He toddled on down the hall and set his milk on the table just as Hazel and Holly bounded down the rear staircase into the kitchen. Hazel set the table and Holly placed a linen napkin at each spot. Routine. The children were more comfortable with it and so was Grace.

Once the kitchen filled with the smell of fresh hotcakes and creamy butter, Grace glanced out the back door. No sight of Smokey Davis. She turned back to the children. "Where is your mother this morning?"

Holly started to answer with a mouthful, but Hazel stopped her. "She went back to bed after she fed Douglas. I don't think she's feeling well today, Miss Gracie."

"I'll check on her. You all behave and finishing eating, aye?"

They nodded. Grace pointed a finger at Linden to remind him of his promise, and then she scurried up the steps.

She found Alice Parker under the covers in her bed, a magazine open near her face. "Oh, Grace." She pushed herself up on one elbow. "You should read this."

"What is it?" Grace pulled back the drapes. The baby stirred in his cradle and she patted his belly.

"An old issue of *Ladies' Home Journal*. Edith gave it to me before she left. There is an article in here about children's nurseries she wanted me to see."

"Oh?" Grace took a quick glimpse out the window to the street below. Nothing seemed out of the ordinary. She returned to the woman's bedside. Alice Parker's complexion was unusually sallow. Grace picked up the magazine.

"Edith says most people today think children need more stimulation. See what you think. I don't think we'll put in an indoor pond so Linden can float his boats like the article suggests, but an indoor garden seems like a good idea. And a skylight, so that the third floor will receive more light."

Grace tucked the magazine under her arm. "That sounds delightful. Does the baby need a change?"

"No. Edith changed him right before she left. That was close to the hour of eight, I believe."

Grace glanced to a mantel clock. She had about twenty minutes before she had to walk the girls to school. "Would you like some hotcakes?"

"No. Nothing."

"I'll make you some tea. You're looking peaked."

"I'm not feeling real well."

"Well, stay in bed. If Douglas wakes, I'll bundle him and take him with us."

Later Grace found mother and baby slumbering, so she gathered the other children and set off toward the school. Her knees were weak, but they made it fine. No sign of any gangsters and no peelers either. A good morning.

When she and Linden went to pick the girls up, he began tugging on her arm as they squeezed past a crowd of people on the corner across from the school. "Miss Gracie, why are we walking so fast? I'm tired."

"Sorry, Linden, but we must hurry."

"Why?" He began the whining that she had been trying to break him of.

"You know your father doesn't want you children out for very long. Now come along."

He began to cry.

They stopped at the front steps of the school, where they always met the girls. "What's the matter, Linden?" She sounded impatient, even to her own ears.

He cried harder.

"Stop that."

"I don't want to be a big boy."

She bent down to look him in the eyes. "'Tis all right, Linden. I just . . ." She glanced around. No Feenys or that evil Smokey. "'Tis all right. I won't tell anyone, and I'm sorry I scared you."

He wiped his face with his coat sleeve and nodded.

She pulled a handkerchief from her bag. "Blow."

He puffed up his cheeks and blew his nose. He grinned when she stopped wiping. "You won't tell Mother or Father I was crying?"

"They should not care. I don't. But nay. I won't mention it."

On the way back, she lifted her eyes to the sky and wondered silently, *Have you protected us this day, Lord?* She wanted to dare to believe.

31

As soon as Owen got to work, he found Feeny. "What was that all about?" He gave the man a shove against the police lockers.

Feeny straightened his jacket. "Ye don't know the game, Owen. Smokey wants that camera-toting lass to know her place."

"You oughta know your place, Feeny. Smokey doesn't care about her. Who put him up to this?"

Feeny sneered. "Didn't I tell ye? Middleton didn't like gettin' his picture made. Was that Rosie girl who done it."

"Well, if she did, she didn't know what she was doing. No harm done, right? It's not like she sold it to the papers or made Wanted posters with it."

"Well, she can't be trusted. Next thing ye know, she'll take a picture of Goo—"

"What?"

"She'll take a picture of some thief who'll shoot her for it. Someone needs to warn the wee lass."

"That's not what you were going to say."

"Buzz off, McNulty. I got work to do."

"You listen to me, Feeny. I'm looking out for that girl. If you've got connections like you think you have, you'll make 'em back off."

"I could, if I wanted to."

Owen was just about to deliver a punch when someone grabbed his arm. He spun around. "Jake?"

"Not the way to get things done, Owen. Trust me."

Jake steered Owen back to the lobby, where he was working at the desk. "We'll find Smokey. And when we do, we'll lock him up with his leader."

"She's innocent, Jakey. She was in the wrong places at the wrong times."

"I know that."

"Why does this happen to people? Life is so unfair." Owen was relieved he had someone to complain to, even if his complaints were useless.

"I know. Good thing she's got you to look out after her."

"Am I wrong, Jakey? Am I letting my personal feelings interfere with my job?"

"I think you're the just the guy she needs. What could be wrong about that?"

Grace tried not to think about the note from the gangster as she went about her usual duties. That evening, shortly before Mr. Crawley was to arrive for her and after the older children had gone to bed, she went to the parlor to get Douglas to put him in his cradle.

She lifted the sleeping baby from his mother's arms as they both dozed in front of the parlor fireplace. He barely stirred when she placed him in his cradle upstairs. She took in the sight of his plump cheeks, the smell of talcum powder, the peaceful wee smirk his lips made while he slept.

She retrieved a wool blanket from the chest in the upstairs hall and returned to the parlor to cover Alice Parker. The woman's head tipped backward and her mouth hung open. Grace expected she would stir when the warm blanket covered her, but she didn't. Grace tapped her arm. "Mrs. Parker, I'm leaving now."

No response.

"Mrs. Parker?" Grace put the back of her hand against the woman's neck. Cold. She pulled the blanket off and the woman slumped at a peculiar angle. *Oh, dear God.*

She dropped the blanket and ran to the kitchen when she heard Mr. Crawley's knock.

"Good evening, Miss McCaffery. How was your . . . ?" He dropped his hat and gripped Grace's shoulders. "What is wrong, child?"

Grace's lips felt like jelly. "M . . . m . . . She's . . ." All she could do was point.

The man rushed to the front of the house. A few moments later he shouted to her. "Grace, get on the telephone and ring Mr. Parker. Now, child!"

Her fingers shook, but she finally managed to get the operator and place an emergency call, instructing the operator to insist Mr. George Parker return home immediately. Then she collapsed in a kitchen chair.

Mr. Crawley came back. "Did you call?"

"Aye."

"I'll phone the doctor as well."

She didn't recall what happened after that. The house filled with people. Footsteps clattered by but she didn't care to notice who they belonged to. Finally someone shook her by the shoulders. Mr. Crawley.

"Get on upstairs and make sure the children don't come down here, Grace."

She pulled a slumbering Linden from his bed and lifted him to her shoulder. Wee Douglas still slept peacefully in his cradle. When Grace stared at him, she sucked back a sob. He didn't know. None of them did, but soon would. Their mother was dead.

As she tucked Linden into bed with Holly and then climbed in beside Hazel, Grace wondered. Had she done something wrong? Should she have insisted Alice Parker not be so sedentary? Should she not have given her tea so late at night? She could not pinpoint just why this had happened. Surely Mr. Parker would blame her.

Sometime later someone woke her. "Shh. Come downstairs, love."

"Mrs. Hawkins? Where am I?"

"Still with the Parker children. Don't wake them. Come on, love."

When they got to the parlor, Mr. Crawley sat in Mr. Parker's chair, long legs crossed at the knee. Reverend Clarke sat on the sofa. They both gave her a sorrowful look. Grace turned in all directions. "Where is Mr. Parker?"

"Locked himself in his study, love. I believe he'll sleep in there. Sit down."

Grace couldn't move. This looked like an inquisition. "I didn't do anything."

"Of course you didn't, love. Arrangements have to be made . . . and . . . Well, we'd just like to hear what happened."

Grace sat next to the reverend. He reached out and patted her hand. "Let's say a prayer for this family."

Grace bowed her head but could not remember the words he spoke. She wanted to ask if God heard, but this man had once admitted he didn't have all the answers, so she didn't bother. Instead she told them how she had found Mrs. Parker.

Mr. Crawley shifted in his chair. "The doctor was here. It's his opinion that a blood clot formed sometime after the birth and burst tonight. Death was instantaneous."

"A blessing she did not suffer."

"Aye. Yes." Grace could not find the words and doubted there were any to explain this.

"I've telephoned Edith, love. She'll be on the next train."

"Oh, good. The children . . ." The tears came then. Grace covered her face with both hands. The others wrapped their arms around her.

"God will provide," Reverend Clarke said.

Grace wiped her face with the handkerchief Mrs. Hawkins gave her and looked at him. Those crystal eyes still held the same light she'd always seen there. "But, Reverend Clarke, you once said you didn't understand God."

"I said I didn't understand why he allowed suffering, and that is still true. What I do know, Grace, is that he is here with us, guiding and providing, and he never changes, though the world around us and the people in our lives do. He is the same today, yesterday, and tomorrow."

"Amen," Mr. Crawley said.

They held a memorial service for Alice Parker in Grace Church on Broadway, a place where respectable people, in Mr. Parker's opinion, would come to pay last respects. While it was true that Alice Parker never attended First Church, Mr. Parker did, so this arrangement made no sense to Grace. But it was none of her affair anyway.

Alice was not buried there, though. Grace had been told it would be several hours after the service before the mourners would return to the Parker home because the graveside service was a distance away. Grace had stayed at home with the children and the baby to prepare a meal for their return.

Wee Linden played at her feet while she cooked. The girls were in the playroom and the baby was asleep in his cradle. She pulled meat from the carcass of a goose and consulted the fancy cookbook Mrs. Parker had given her. Aspic jelly with cold slices of goose meat would have to do. Grace was finding it difficult to navigate her way through her duties, and Mr. Parker would just have to accept whatever she could manage to put on the table.

The man had barely spoken to her since his wife died. Grace had expected him to lay blame, but so far that hadn't happened.

A sad hush hung in the house. The children didn't argue or complain or even cry, only the baby, who had to get used to a glass bottle feeder and infant formula. Grace would speak to the midwife as soon as she could. Certainly she would know of a wet nurse Mr. Parker could employ.

When the food was ready and the table set, she took Linden up to the playroom to read the children a book. They stood together staring at the bookshelf. Finally Grace pulled one down and Linden settled into her lap while the girls scooted close. The Brothers Grimm. "Here now, *Twelve Brothers*. Doesn't that sound fair?"

He nodded.

"'Once upon a time there were a king and a queen. They lived happily together and had twelve children, all boys. One day the king said to his wife, "If our thirteenth child, which you are soon going to bring into the world, is a girl, then the twelve others shall die, so that her wealth may be great, and so that she alone may inherit the kingdom." Indeed, he had twelve coffins made . . .' Uh, let me find another."

Hansel and Gretel? Nay, the witch wanted to eat the children. She kept looking while Linden twirled one of his army men in his hand. Story after story was about children and the evil adults in their lives. No good. She gave up.

"Just tell us a story, Miss Gracie," Linden pleaded.

Hazel agreed. "One from Ireland? Please?"

A story did occur to her just that moment. *The Dagda's Harp.* "Long ago, before the time of Saint Patrick, there was a leader of a great tribe in Ireland. His name was the Dagda. His greatest weapon was not a spear but a harp, a special harp that obeyed only him. Its beautiful music made the seasons change, so they say. I don't know myself."

The children giggled. They loved stories that defied logic, Grace assumed.

She continued on. "There came an enemy one day, and they stole away the Dagda's harp and took it to a faraway place. The Dagda went after it, and it took a very long time to reach the hiding place."

"Did he get his harp back?" Holly asked.

"Wait for her to tell," Hazel scolded.

Grace patted the wee girl's head. "This enemy tribe had a great many warriors with long spears and snarling dogs, and the Dagda had no such weapons for his defense."

Linden lined his toy soldiers up on the floor. "How did he get his harp back, then?"

"He spoke to the harp, just in time, before the warriors had him in their clutches." She tickled Linden and he squealed in delight.

"Tell the story, Miss Gracie," Hazel said.

"Well, the Dagda instructed the harp to play three tunes. The first was a slow, sad tune, and the room full of warriors fell to the ground sobbing in misery until the floor was soaked with their tears."

"Then what?" Linden asked.

"Then the harp played the second tune, a merry piece that had everyone chuckling and dancing and holding their bellies because they laughed so hard."

She might not have gotten the Parker children to laugh, but they smiled, so that was better.

"There was a third tune, Miss Gracie?" Hazel asked.

"There was. This was the sweetest tune of all, very gentle and soothing. Soon, man by man, heads began to nod and shoulders slumped until the warriors were all curled up on the floor snoring away."

"And he got away with the harp?" Linden asked.

"Oh, aye, he did. See? Didn't I tell you he had the most powerful weapon? The Dagda, only one man, stood up against a powerful army with only his harp."

"I wonder," Hazel said, resting her chin on her arm. "Did he know the harp could make the men go to sleep or did that just happen?"

Grace gave her a quick hug. "I suppose he had to have faith that it would work."

"I wish I had a magic harp," Holly complained.

"Magic harps are only for stories, lass, but you have us, and we love you." Grace kissed the top of the girl's head, and it occurred to her that perhaps God would provide what these children needed, despite the loss of their mother. She prayed that she would have as much faith in that as the Dagda did in his harp.

But sadness was not so easily dismissed. Sitting on the floor with a pile of blocks the children used to make a castle, Grace fought back tears. It was unthinkably sad that these children no longer had a mother nor grieved as Grace might have if it were her own mother who passed away. "Wait here."

She hurried down a floor and crept into the Parkers' bedroom. She found the Burpee catalog in a pile under the bed. The snapshot she'd taken of Mrs. Parker and the children lay on the mantel. Grace picked it up. Somehow Alice Parker had known to ask for this. The photograph was sure to be a treasured memento for the children. She brought both things back to the attic.

"Children, I want to show you something."

They gathered around her. She flipped a few pages. "Here, coralbells."

Hazel touched the illustration. "Beautiful."

"Your mother wanted these in the yard. We are going to plant them in the spring. What do you think?"

They agreed and each one took a turn holding the catalog.

"Remember this?" She let each of them hold the tiny photograph. "We'll get a wee frame and keep it in the day nursery. She wanted you all to have this photograph because she loved you."

Tears rolled down each child's face, even Hazel's.

"Now, now. 'Tis a good thing to miss your mother, but you have these memories of her. Be happy when you look at them."

Linden sniffed. "We will, Miss Gracie."

"And don't hide those tears," Grace said. "Tears are God's way of washing your hurting hearts."

The sound of the front door opening brought her to her feet. "Stay here, children. Hazel, come get me if the baby cries. Do not try to pick him up. You can rock his cradle, but that's all."

"I will, Miss Gracie."

Grace scrambled down the back stairs and began pulling

plates from the icebox. Auntie Edith came to help her. "I'll be staying for a while, Grace. To help."

The poor woman had barely left before turning back to come to Alice's funeral. "Are you sure? I wouldn't want you to neglect your own affairs."

The plump woman sliced the butter into pats and placed them on dishes. "I love those children." She blew out a puff of air. "Alas, I cannot stay more than a week. I have the new term beginning."

"I'm grateful you will be here. This will be a difficult adjustment for them all." She knew all about the horrendous turns life could take.

Edith paused and gave Grace a hug. "You all right, dear?"

"I believe I am." She remembered what her mother had told her before she left for America. *Fly free.*

32

When Owen heard the news about Mrs. Parker, he waited until the day after the burial and then paid a visit. Grace answered the door.

"It was very nice of you to come. I'm sure Mr. Parker will appreciate it. I'm afraid he's not taking visitors now, though."

Owen searched for words. He had not anticipated that Grace would assume he'd come only to offer George Parker his condolences. "I'm sorry. I mean, I will leave my regards for you to pass on, but may I speak with you, Grace?"

An older woman came up behind her. "Who is it, child?"

"Edith Milburn, may I present Officer Owen McNulty. He attends First Church. Officer, this is Mr. Parker's sister."

"Glad to meet you, madam."

The woman flung the door wide. "Come in, Officer. So nice of you to stop by." She ushered him into the parlor. "Grace, get our guest tea." She took his hat from him. "You are off duty now, Officer?"

"Yes, I hoped to speak to Grace. That is . . . if she is not too busy."

The woman winked. "She is not. I'll get the tea."

A few moments later Grace returned. Owen stood. "This had to be difficult for you."

She nodded and sat gingerly on the edge of the sofa.

He returned to the chair he had been sitting on. "I just want you to know, you don't have to worry about things . . . you know . . . that thug and Walter Feeny."

Her head popped up. "Why? What do you mean?"

"I don't know if you realize it, but some folks thought you were snapping photographs all over town, and they didn't want their pictures made."

She wrung her hands in her lap. "Who said that?"

She seemed inappropriately nervous. "Grace, is there any more to the story? Anything I should know? I mean, I'm hot on Smokey Davis's trail. He's not going to—"

"You mean he's not in jail?"

"Well, no, but you know that business I said I was involved in, in the Battery?"

"Aye."

"Well, Jake—my partner—and me . . . we're getting close to shutting down Smokey's gang."

She was visibly shaken. "Officer?"

"Call me Owen, Grace. I believe we're friends."

"Owen, I got a note from Smokey. I didn't tell anyone, but he threatened me."

Owen's jaw tightened. "Was it the Middleton business? The photograph of the stuss game?"

"I believe so. Do you think I'm in trouble? Am I putting the children at risk by being in this house?"

"No, not so long as I draw breath."

She looked surprised.

"Do you have the photograph?"

"I don't know. I got a package from Kodak, but after I found the photograph I took of Alice and the children, I put the rest aside. They are right here in my bag."

She opened a cardboard envelope, and they both looked at the small photographs. There were two of Linden romping in a park. Another of a newsboy and some tenements. Grace set those aside on a tea table. Then she pulled out one of the card game.

"Say, this is a nice clear shot." He took it and held it up toward the light coming from the window. "There's old Middleton. Well, no one would care about this photograph except him. Mind if I take it?"

"I don't mind."

"Don't worry about that threat, Grace. Smokey's bark is worse than his bite. I'll see that he gets this. It's all he wants. But don't be snapping any more photographs in this neighborhood, all right?"

"I promise I won't."

The worry on her face was still there.

"Is there something else?"

"I'm not sure." She squeezed her hands together in her lap.

"Just tell me. Even if you think it might not matter. Let me be the judge."

She glanced up at him. "It was some time ago, when I first got my camera. I was in the park and heard some voices behind the statue. You know, the one of the man with the boat?"

"Yes, the Ericsson statue."

"I was curious, and when I saw the men on the other side, they thought I was spying on them. I thought they wanted to steal my camera and I ran."

"Was Smokey among the men there?"

"He was. He found me in the fish house."

"Yes, the aquarium. I saw you talking to him there."

"He thought I was trying to take someone's photograph. Someone who was with him there. But I wasn't! I didn't even have the camera loaded."

"Did you hear the man's name, the one who didn't want his photograph taken?"

"Something foolish-sounding." She wrinkled her brow and gazed at a corner of the ceiling while she considered it.

"Goo Goo, perhaps?"

"Yes, that's it."

"So you did not take his photograph?"

"I did not. I didn't take any that day."

"But you saw this Goo Goo?"

"Well, briefly."

Owen rubbed his chin. "Can you draw?"

"I try."

"Do me a favor and practice a bit. See if you can recall what that man looked like. Don't tell anyone you're doing that, all right? I'll check back with you in a couple of days. Can you do that?"

"It would help you catch that mean fellow and keep Smokey from bothering people?"

"Most certainly. But it must be our secret, Grace."

"All right, so."

"Good."

They smiled at each other for a moment. It felt fine. "I should be going."

She walked him to the door.

"Tell Mr. Parker's sister thank you, but I could not stay for tea."

"Another time?"

"Yes, thank you. And, Grace, don't worry. I'm looking out for you."

33

GRACE WAS SO BUSY the next day that she could only spare a moment here and there to practice with her pencil. When Officer McNulty came back, she'd have to tell him she needed more time. Memories could be hard to summon. If only she *had* taken that thug's photograph that day.

Edith had helped Grace prepare some meals in advance, and she did all the mending of the children's clothes Grace hadn't had time to do. But she would be leaving soon, and Grace expected Mr. Parker would want her to stay permanently with the children. She would miss her comfortable bed and Annie and Mrs. Hawkins, who were becoming her family. But the children needed her.

But to her surprise, Mr. Parker made no mention of her staying when Mr. Crawley arrived to escort her home that evening. "Maybe I should ask him," she explained to Mr. Crawley.

She made her way to the parlor, where she'd last seen Mr. Parker after bringing the children in for good night wishes. He was still in his chair, but unlike other nights, he had switched on the globe lamp next to his chair. "Grace, come here a moment."

She stepped into the room. He was holding the snapshots she had forgotten to retrieve from the table. "Are these yours?"

She dipped her head and went to take them from his

outstretched hand. "They are. I'm sorry. I forgot I left them there." She licked her lips as she turned to leave, wondering if he was going to ask about the ones taken in Chatham Square.

"Grace?"

She turned back.

"I want you to take tomorrow off. That will give you Saturday and Sunday off. I need to spend more time with my children."

"Your sister is leaving."

"She is, but she'll be coming back frequently. The children like her."

"So do I. But are you sure you don't need me? The baby?"

"I have a wet nurse arriving in the morning."

"Oh, all right. If you're sure."

"I am. Good night."

When Grace returned to Hawkins House, she found a telegram waiting for her. She almost squealed aloud in delight. From Ma!

She rushed upstairs to read it. Flinging herself on her bed, she carefully slid a fingernail under the seal and pulled the message out.

S. P. inquired by way of nephew if you can receive
visitors. Answer is yes. Will be visiting in time for
St. Patrick's feast day.

This was not what Grace had expected, but her mother was coming to see her!

She rolled onto her back and lifted her arms toward the ceiling. *God! Did you hear me after all?*

She clenched the letter in her hand.

"Oh, that's wonderful, love!" The Hawk clapped her hands when Grace told her the news. "St. Patrick's Day, you say? Even though that's a ways off, I'll reserve a room for them at Miss Hall's boardinghouse. We want to make sure it's available to them. It's very nice and popular with visitors. Just a few blocks from First Church."

"But my mother will stay here." Grace held the letter against her heart. "She can share my bed."

"Her husband is coming, right, love? They will want to stay together, and I don't permit men to board here, not even fathers."

Grace gritted her teeth. "He is not my father."

"Sorry. Stepfather. Just the same—"

"Fine. Reserve a room for him."

"But won't your mother want to stay with him?"

"She will not."

The Hawk shrugged and reached for a butter biscuit on the tea tray near her chair. "We will let them sort that out. I'll reserve a double just in case. Of course, your mother is welcome here, should she choose."

"Thank you. You'll need money for that room. How much?"

The Hawk pursed her lips and shook her head. "I will take care of it. You don't have to worry about a thing."

"I have a job. Just tell me how much."

"No, no. When my girls get visitors from home, the Benevolents provide the guests' room and board. That is our way. Do not argue with me."

"But—"

The woman held up a hand. "I said no argument. It's settled. So long as they are not permanently staying on. Your mother said a visit, yes?"

"She did, but I expect she will stay on and her husband will go back." Grace fought hard to keep disgust from her voice. "He has a job to return to, Mrs. Hawkins. Responsibilities."

The Hawk poured Grace a cup of tea. "Your mother is welcome to stay with us as long as she wishes, love."

Grace inhaled the flowery smell of Mrs. Hawkins's special brew. She wanted to say that the man was definitely not worth the Benevolents' concern. *Let him sleep on the floor at the police precinct.* But she held her tongue. Grace had to admit that she was relieved there was now a means to separate her mother from that man, at least at night.

34

OWEN NOW HAD TWO GOOD SOURCES FOR LEADS: Grace's potential drawing of the suspect and the name the pawnbroker had written down for him, a man called Michael Taggart, a fellow who had left the gang and held a vendetta of some kind.

After discussing the note with his captain, Owen surveyed the wall of mug shots until he found the one he wanted: Michael Taggart.

"Shift's up, McNulty. Follow this tomorrow." Nicholson leaned over his shoulder. "Ugly mug, huh?"

"At least his pockmarked face is one I'll remember. See you tomorrow."

Murphy tapped Owen on the shoulder. "Message for you. Jones has it at the desk."

"Thanks." This could not be good. He hurried over to pick it up. From his father.

Arrange to see Blevins immediately. He is spending
more money.
John McNulty

Owen dismissed sleep in order to catch Blevins when he arrived at the office. Fatigue caused his mind to swirl. He could have used a cup of coffee, but Joe had indeed closed up shop, and he had no time to go looking elsewhere.

The Sixth Avenue el slowed at the Fourteenth Street station, and Owen stood to get off quickly. Marching past the white limestone department stores, he made his way a few blocks down to his father's building. No one would suppose the great McNulty Dry Goods Store held their business office in such a modest structure.

He let himself in and was pleasantly surprised to find a secretary there brewing coffee.

"How is your father?"

He accepted a cup from the plump, middle-aged lady he'd not met before now. "If he could lessen his emotional stress, he'd be much better." He could have kicked himself. He should not give such personal information to an employee. He was not good at this and told himself to use his detective instincts from now on.

"Isn't that the way with us all? Mr. McNulty, are you here to see Mr. Blevins by any chance?"

"I am, as a matter of fact."

"He just telephoned and said he wasn't feeling well today."

"Do you know where he lives?"

"Oh, I don't think you should—"

"Look, madam, both the principal owner and his second in charge are under the weather. Do you truly think I should leave the company's welfare to chance?"

She set the coffeepot she'd been holding down on her desk. "Well, when you put it that way . . ."

"I'm in a dreadful rush, if you don't mind."

"Certainly. Mr. Blevins lives at number 105 East Seventeenth Street in Gramercy Park."

Thirty minutes later Owen rapped on the door.

Blevins, rather than a servant, opened it. "Mrs. Miller let me know you were on your way, Owen. Please come in."

Owen didn't move. "What is going on, Blevins? I've just come off my beat and had no sleep. Shall we get right to it? My father thinks you are spending him out of business."

The man's smile disappeared. "He thinks that?"

"He does."

"Please, my boy, come in. We have much to discuss."

They sat in a well-appointed receiving room, not as plush as Owen's parents' but much more comfortable than the dwellings in Owen's neighborhood. Alvin Blevins leaned back in a fat leather chair and folded his hands over his chest.

"Mr. Blevins, I have to say you don't look ill to me."

The man laughed. "I did not tell the secretary I was ill, just that I wasn't feeling well and that is true enough. This mess we are in is quite disturbing."

"We?"

"Well, my boy, you are making it your business now, aren't you? And that's the point."

"Please, cut through the bacon fat and get to the meat of the matter, would you?"

"Hmm." Blevins leaned toward a small round table on his left and poured himself a shot of whiskey.

Drinking so early in the morning. This must indeed be a mess. "You thought you could clear things up by returning some stock and cutting some positions, right?"

The man rubbed his mustache. "That's what I said, yes. And I will do that. But the trouble goes beyond finances. Let me explain."

"Please."

"Would you like a drink? Some coffee perhaps? My wife is in the kitchen. She could make you some biscuits."

"I'd rather not take the time, if you don't mind."

Blevins glanced at the mantel clock and kept his focus there while he spoke. "When I first came to work for your father, I was mesmerized by his business sense and his sheer intelligence." He smiled, still gazing into space. "He built his business from the dust to become one of the most successful in town."

"I understand. Please, Blevins, what is the trouble?"

"Oh, it's true that I overpurchased at times. Hard to turn away some of the folks I heard hard-luck stories from, I tell you. But that is not the mess, not really." Blevins took another drink. "I am not sure how to say this. Your father does not . . . Well, he's not himself lately, I daresay. His judgment is . . . well . . . skewed a bit."

"What do you mean?"

"Oh, long before the problems with his heart, he . . . well, he's not making sound choices, son."

"What? My father's not that old. His mind is fine."

"I'm just answering your question, son. If you choose not to believe it . . ." He shrugged.

Owen didn't believe one word of it. "Tell me about your association with the Committee of Fifteen."

Blevins straightened his vest. "An entirely different subject. I am a reformer in my off hours. Running into you at the meeting was quite the coincidence."

"Was it?"

"Indeed. My status is well lauded in New York, Owen. I was invited to join. Those other men and I banded together because we don't like the vice and crime in our neighborhoods." He lifted his glass. "And you will see. We'll make a difference. We're not trying to supersede law enforcement, just aid you men."

"So this committee business has nothing to do with my father?"

"It does not. I will say, though, that if your father continues in this vein, on this foolish venture of pride, the company's lost, son, and the debtors will come after us all unless . . ."

"What?"

"If only he had listened to me years ago and incorporated." He pounded a fist on the arm of his chair.

"Blevins, unless what?"

"Unless you take control or give me authority. Your father is not fit." He stared at his hands in his lap. "There. I've said it."

Owen stood and paced between his chair and the front window. "That can't be."

"If you think there is any discrepancy in what I've said, you better go talk to your father."

"I will."

"But be aware. Things might not be as he presents them."

He left Blevins's house and walked west on Seventeenth Street. He could get to his father's house if he went to Union Square and caught a Broadway trolley, but he always avoided the area of Deadman's Curve whenever he could. And he was bushed. He turned and caught the Second Avenue el heading south instead. He had to get some rest. Nothing Blevins said made any sense at all.

When he got to his apartment building, he met Mrs. Varga on the stairs. She was carrying down laundry for another tenant.

"Let me help you." He took a basket from her and toted it down to the bottom step.

"Thank you, thank you." She joined him at the door and

reached up. She could not touch his face because she was so short, so she waved her hand until he lowered his head. She patted his cheek. "You catch bad men, Officer. You catch them!"

"Yes, ma'am." He wearily climbed back up the steps.

After he'd slept, he borrowed his neighbor's telephone. "You said he was stable, right?"

"I know, but, Owen, he's distraught. Did you talk to Blevins?"

"Put Father on the telephone."

"I . . . uh . . . I better not. He's not exactly making himself clear, Owen."

"What do you mean?"

"Oh, he's just upset. You better get over here."

"I have to go to work."

"Pshaw. You have a partner now, don't you?"

"He was injured and is not working a full shift yet."

"Owen, *you* need time off."

He blew out a breath. He could never make her understand. "I'll telephone the doctor and get a report. I'll come up after my shift is over in the morning. Good-bye, Mother."

He didn't let her protest and hung up the phone. Then he telephoned Bellevue and asked for the doctor in charge of his father's diagnosis.

"His heart is recovering fine, although he works himself into a frantic state. I've suggested that your mother take him on a holiday—Florida or somewhere warm."

"I see. And, Doctor, what about his mental state?"

"Do you have concerns?"

"No, no. It's just that sometimes . . . when folks age . . . they lose their . . ." He could barely say it. His father was only fifty years old. "Their good sense, if you know what I mean."

"Ah, well, if you have concerns about that, bring him in for an evaluation."

"Thank you, Doctor."

When he hung up the receiver, he almost picked it up again. He stood over it, rubbing his fingers.

"You eat?" Mrs. Karila said.

"Yes. I'm fine. Thank you very much." He went back to his apartment, still not knowing if he should have telephoned Nicholson and told him he could not go in to work.

35

GRACE WAS MORE THAN RELIEVED to receive two full days off. Yesterday had been spent mending her clothes and helping Mrs. Hawkins with meals. But now that Sunday had come and she was sitting in church staring toward Owen McNulty several rows in front of her, she realized she had not done what he asked. Neither had he come asking her for the drawing. Maybe he had changed his mind.

After services concluded, the Hawk turned to her. "My Harold was strong for me when I could not bolster myself, Grace. There is a young man God has in mind for you, I'm sure."

Had her staring been obvious? "What do you mean?"

"You might be thinking of courting, and you should, a young attractive girl like you."

"Mrs. Hawkins, I'm much too busy to even think of—"

"Just don't miss what the good Lord has planned for you, love." She glanced past Grace. "I'll wait for you outside."

Grace turned around to find Owen McNulty standing there. "I'm sorry I haven't had time to—"

He held up a finger, and she remembered that she'd pledged secrecy about the drawing.

He touched the tip of his finger to her elbow as he guided

her down the aisle toward the door. "I've been otherwise occupied myself." He paused and greeted a few parishioners and then leaned down to speak quietly to her. "I still need you to try. Today, perhaps?"

"I will. Right after supper."

"Fine. I'll stop by on my night rounds."

Grace gnawed at her pencil. Was the man's nose full or thin? She wasn't sure. But he did have full cheeks, she remembered that, and deep-set eyes.

Mrs. Hawkins joined her in the parlor. "What have you got there, love?"

"Just trying to remember what someone looked like."

"You have a camera, love."

"I do, but I did not take a photograph—" She realized she had probably said too much. But how was she going to explain the reason for Owen's visit later?

"Well, try drawing me, love. Maybe the practice will help."

"Truly?"

"Certainly. I'm just sitting here with my tea. Nothing else to occupy me right now."

Grace stood. "Wait a moment. I'm going to take your photograph so later I can study them both."

"I'd hate for you to waste your film on me, love."

"Oh no. Don't say that. I want to take your photograph, if you don't mind." Grace retrieved her camera and instructed the Hawk to sit in front of the window. "Outside would be better, but it's frightfully cold out."

"I agree. Perhaps if I light the lamp."

Grace nodded, although she doubted that would help.

Pulling back the draperies did allow more light in, and a coating of snow outside helped brighten things up.

She held the camera waist high and found Mrs. Hawkins's image in the viewfinder. She held her breath and clicked.

The woman clapped her hands. "Well, what do you know. I've had my picture taken in my very own parlor. Harold would never have imagined such a thing when he sat for his portrait."

Grace returned to her seat on the sofa. "Mrs. Hawkins, this morning, what you said to me at church . . ."

"Ah, yes. I was wondering if we'd get back to that."

"What I really want to know is, do you think God chose Harold for you?"

"Absolutely. And he's chosen someone for you, too."

"You believe that?"

"I believe it with my whole heart."

Grace picked up her pencil. She wanted to believe something that much.

Much later, after sunset, a knock came at the door, followed by the tinkling sound of the doorbell. Annie answered it, and Grace put down her notebook. She had achieved a fairly good likeness of the Hawk, she thought, but the other sketch she worked on had not turned out as well.

Owen entered the parlor. "Greetings, ladies." He turned to Grace. "What is this you've been working on?"

She handed him the pad of paper.

"Of course. It's Mrs. Hawkins."

The woman beamed.

"It's a perfect likeness, Grace." He turned the page to where she'd been trying to work on the Goo Goo fellow. She shook her head and frowned when he looked at her.

He handed the paper back. "Well, fine work. Even though you have a camera now, I hope you'll continue on with your hobby. You're quite talented."

Grace let the compliment flow over her like a welcome winter sunbeam.

"She certainly is talented," Mrs. Hawkins agreed. "Officer, won't you sit a while and have some biscuits and tea?"

Grace took every opportunity in the evenings to practice. Mr. Parker was true to his word, and during the weeks that followed, he did spend more time with the children. He dismissed her immediately after the evening meals so she had time to draw, and even take more snapshots, when she returned to Hawkins House.

One Wednesday evening Grace entered the parlor to find Mrs. Hawkins sitting with the *Times* in her lap, weeping considerably.

"What's happened?"

"The Queen! Oh, the Queen has died."

"Queen Victoria?"

"Oh, love. That's so sad."

"Did you know her when you lived in England?"

The woman wiped her face with a lace handkerchief. "Oh, my, no, of course not. But she was a benevolent leader and such a gracious woman. She enjoyed the longest reign in English history. She's been on the throne since 1837. Have you seen her photographs, love?"

"I have not."

The woman reached to a basket of reading material she kept under the side table by her chair. "Look at some of the copies I have of the *Illustrated London News*, love. You'll find some of her."

Grace was amazed. This publication had numerous drawings of people. "May I study these for a while?"

"Certainly." The woman blew her nose loudly.

So many faces and expressions. The ones she saw of the Queen seemed to show her thoughtful and reflective. And there were many, many photographs in those pages. The images of men might be helpful, she thought, to determine which features were like Goo Goo's and which were not.

She leaned back against the sofa and stared at the ceiling to collect her thoughts. As wonderful as this was, it was limiting. She had seen that man in the colors of life, not shades of black and gray like photographs and ink sketches. She would have to think harder.

36

OWEN KNEW GRACE could come up with a fair representation of Goo Goo. Her sketch of Mrs. Hawkins had proven that. She had the ability, but he wondered if too much time had passed for her to remember. *It's probably much easier to sketch someone you know well.* Even so, police had been making suspect sketches for decades, and they'd proved helpful. With any luck, Grace would come up with something close. And of course he still needed to follow up on the pawnbroker tip.

The decision he still had to make loomed large. If he continued with his police work and made sure innocent immigrants like Grace were protected, his parents would disown him, and his father's business might fail. But if he left his beat and took over his father's business, the Dusters would flourish and the immigrants would be left without the aid they needed when they arrived from Ellis Island. And, he realized, Grace McCaffery might continue to get herself into trouble with no one to rescue her but Walter Feeny, and he was no savior of vulnerable women in Lower Manhattan.

The more he considered it, the more he thought the scales leaned toward staying at his job. He was absolutely certain God had led him to this post and was not telling him to abandon it. All that he knew about God, however, did not point to having

Owen abandon his family in their time of need either. If God was good, how could he let McNulty Dry Goods go bankrupt and put his mother and father out on the street?

Owen struggled with his dilemma as he sat at his window and watched the elevated train go by. He remembered the night he'd equated a stalled train with his life, and noted the ease with which this train now traveled. The difference between a moving train and a still one was the presence of an engineer. Owen had a driver for the train he called his life. He'd been struggling against God, a modern-day Jacob wrestling with an angel. That was why he was feeling so exhausted. He could not do that anymore. The most important decisions in life were difficult, and this was certainly that.

He picked up his Bible. He'd been reading the Psalms lately. With a job like his, he needed the calm assurance that God was active in the world, and he often found that in the Psalms. He turned to Psalm 106 and began to read a summary of the story of the Israelites in Egypt. It seemed to Owen that those people could have escaped their desert exile much sooner if they had just listened to Moses, who in turn was getting direction from God. Running his finger down the page as he read, he stopped when he got to the words, "They waited not for his counsel." That was how the Israelites went wrong. They did not wait. Waiting was not easy. But Owen realized that even if he couldn't see the answer to his dilemma now, it was there.

While Jake healed from what turned out to be severe bruising but no permanent damage, he'd been on desk duty. Owen walked his normal beat alone and talked to the folks he'd befriended, asking them all if they knew where Michael Taggart was. No luck until he talked to an old gent in a cigar shop.

"I like ye or I'd not be telling ye this, son."

"I appreciate that." Owen bought the man's nickel cigar even though he wouldn't smoke it.

"No one calls the man Taggart. Ask for Dasher. More likely to find him that way, although I haven't seen him myself."

"Thank you."

Owen hurried out to the newsboys, his most reliable informants thus far.

Stevie, a freckle-faced kid who sometimes slept on the precinct steps, grinned when Owen asked him. "Why didn't you say so before, Officer? I just saw Dasher walk into the Old House at Home."

"McSorley's pub?"

"Yes, sir. East Seventh Street."

Owen hailed a cab. He could not let this opportunity pass. On the way he shrugged off his coat and placed his badge, hat, and gun firmly inside and wrapped up the bundle. "Hey, driver. Might you have some rope?"

The man reached into a box on the seat next to him and handed Owen a short length. "Planning on tying up your suspect, Officer?"

"Tying my things, is all."

McSorley's place was fairly filled to the brim, so he took a stool close to the door, keeping the bundle under his arm. All the seats close to the old stove were taken, but since that was where the regulars resided, Owen figured he'd probably find Dasher there. Owen studied the men's faces in that spot.

Before long he recognized him. Owen took his bundle over and stood behind the man. "Dasher?"

"Who wants to know?"

"Someone who wants to help you get back at a fella called Goo Goo."

The man spun around on his stool, nearly spilling his dark ale. That was Taggart's pockmarked face, all right.

"Let's talk outside."

As Dasher spoke, Owen wrote down the highlights on a small notepad.

"I got no use for him, ye know?"

"Yeah. Go on." Owen didn't care what had transpired between this man and Knox, only that he was willing to give a description. He'd pay Grace another visit and see if this sparked her memory.

"A wide nose, yeah. You know, what it looks like when a fella's had it broken."

Finally he had something credible.

"Won't do you no good, at least for a while."

"What do you mean?"

"Ole Goo Goo's not in Manhattan."

"Why not?"

"Aw, it's winter, see. He'll be back early March, but for about a month or so, he's out of the city."

"Where?"

"Cocaine run. Where else?"

"You mean he's the one who brings in the drugs?"

Taggart turned Owen away from the pub's entry and whispered, "A deck of the stuff brings twenty-five cents on the street. Sure, he can make a profit by buying it from the druggist and reselling it like everybody else. But Goo Goo sees a big future in the drug, even bigger than opium and morphine. He goes down to South America to buy it all cheap-like and make a bigger profit. He thinks the price on the street's gonna rise. Know what I'm saying, copper?"

This was a bigger mess than Owen had realized. "Thank you." He pointed his notebook at him. "Thank you very much."

He hurried to the station house to fill Nicholson in.

The captain closed his eyes as Owen told him what his contact had revealed. "Well, then. We'll wait for him to return to the city. No doubt we have to get him now." He sighed and then looked at Owen directly. "I think he could be right."

"I think he's a trustworthy source."

"Yeah, and he's probably right about this drug becoming a bigger menace than anyone realizes."

Owen no longer needed to rush Grace's memory in sketching Goo Goo's likeness. The old Owen would have feared this delay would cause the trail to grow cold. But he wasn't concerned. A prevailing feeling that all would unfold properly boosted his confidence. *A good detective is patient, waiting for the ideal moment to catch his suspect.* In the meantime it seemed he had been given a breather, time to look into the problem of his father's business. *God's timing is perfect.*

37

On the first of February, knowing her mother would arrive sometime in the coming weeks, not even the chilly and gray skies could dampen Grace's mood. Because it was St. Brigid's Day, she planned to teach the children how to weave crosses from straw after she picked the girls up from school.

They sat around the children's table in the nursery. Even Linden wanted to give it a try.

"Your mother taught you?" he asked.

"She did." It was the one thing she was able to retain in the workhouse. She'd woven the crosses from the bed straw after carefully picking away the bugs.

"Children make these in Ireland?" Hazel asked.

"They do. Every February 1. Now hold one piece like this." She demonstrated, stopping to do Linden's for him because his chubby fingers couldn't hold on to the pieces.

"And St. Brigid's Day means spring is coming?" Hazel asked, glancing to the window.

"That's right," Grace answered. "It's when we usually see the first snowdrops in Ireland, a wee white flower that blooms early."

"Like scilla and crocus?" Hazel asked, still gazing out the window. She had apparently learned something from her mother.

"That's right. 'Twon't be long before we can plant the coral-bells." Grace gathered up the leftover straw and stuffed it in a bag. "Help me clean this up, so, and then we'll hang your crosses."

When they were done, she tied them with string and each child hung a cross over their bed. Grace put hers over the baby's cradle. The exercise had kept the children busy for . . . oh, ten minutes or so. They were active and needed to be outside.

Some days Grace wished the school had longer hours so she had more time to work alone when the wee lads napped, but mostly she was beginning to enjoy the children. Wouldn't her mother be surprised to know that?

When Mr. Parker returned home from the office as usual, a quarter hour before Mr. Crawley picked her up, Grace cautiously approached him. "May I have a moment, Mr. Parker?"

"What is it, Grace? I've plenty to worry about without complaints from my maid."

Like how to press more rent money out of immigrants? She squeezed her fingers together. "My mother is coming next month for a visit."

"From Ireland?"

"Aye."

"I suppose you want time off?"

"Well, aye. Yes. If . . . that is . . . if you don't mind."

"Of course I mind. I'm not sure when my sister will be back."

"Could my mother come with me? At least for part of the day? She could help. For no pay."

"Hmm. We will see. I'll inquire of Edith."

"Thank you." She darted out of the parlor before he could create some kind of an objection.

The weeks that followed were as routine as Grace could have expected, being the nanny of a busy household. Even so, the days drew out excruciatingly long. Mrs. Hawkins had given her a calendar to mark off the days. She had admonished her to remember her late husband's words: *"Count not the days on the calendar, marking them off number by number, but instead note the time spent with those you love."* Grace had been counting the days without her mother. Now she would count them toward an end to that separation. Mr. Hawkins had probably meant something more, though. She'd remember that to ponder later.

Even though she didn't know the exact date her mother would arrive, she knew it would be in early March, so when she turned February's page over, her heart soared. All the city seemed abuzz with talk about McKinley's second term and the inauguration of New York's former governor as vice president of the United States. But to Grace, the really important news was that her mother would be arriving any day.

On the eighth day of March, Grace got word that her mother and S. P. had arrived in New York. Grace had cleaned her room and emptied a corner of her travel chest for her mother's things. Here, among these Americans in this modern city, Sean Patrick Feeny would not be able to come between Grace and her mother. Finally.

Mrs. Hawkins met Grace in the hallway and grabbed both her hands. "I've prepared a shepherd's pie, love. I do hope your mother and her husband will enjoy it."

"I'm sure my mother will adore your cooking, Mrs. Hawkins." Grace was tempted to tell her that in Ireland they ate little more than boiled potatoes and gruel. Grace's mother would be as famished as Grace had been when she stepped ashore. "But the process at Ellis Island takes hours, Mrs. Hawkins. They probably won't be here in time to eat your meal."

"Oh, didn't Mabel tell you?"

"The neighbor? Tell me what?"

"Your mother's husband telephoned. They are already in New York. After a brief stop to speak to someone at the hospital, they will be here."

"What?" Grace should have known S. P. would find a way to get favors and speed through immigration. "Why the hospital? Is my mother all right?"

"He assured Mabel everything is fine. She wondered also. Now, we just have a few things to get ready."

"Special, you are." Grace kissed the woman's cheek and then headed to the kitchen to check on the meat pie she smelled cooking. Just as she pulled the Dutch oven out, Grace heard voices at the front door. As quickly as she could safely do so, she set the pot on top of the stove and scrambled down the hall.

At the front door she saw her. Ma's face beamed. Running into her arms, Grace was overcome with sobs. "Ma, Ma! I've missed you so." She tried to squeeze her mother tight, but there was a bundle between them. Grace heard a gurgle. *A baby?*

Ma lifted the bundle, and Grace saw a crown of bright-red hair. Feeny hair. "Grace, I'd like you to meet your wee brother, Patrick."

Grace looked back to her mother. "What? You were expecting?" As thin as her mother was, and with a heavy cloak and shawl, Grace had not realized her mother was with child when they said good-bye in Dublin. The thought had never entered her mind.

Ma just smiled and nodded.

Grace gave the man standing next to her a curt nod and then turned back to her mother. "Why didn't you tell me?"

Mrs. Hawkins and Annie gathered up coats. "Please come in by the fire. We will serve tea while you catch up."

Grace stood to the side so her mother and S. P. could enter the room. S. P. approached the fire and rubbed his hands in front of it. "Give me the boy, Ellen. 'Tis a bit warmer by the fire."

Her mother handed the child over, and Grace watched as the man gently took his son and cooed to him as he rocked him in his arms.

Grace and her mother sat on the sofa, holding hands. Ma gazed toward the baby. "He's doing much better, he is. Born with a lame foot. The doctors at the American hospital said there is hope that treatment will enable him to walk. Isn't that fine, darlin'?"

That's why they went to the hospital. Maybe it's why S. P. agreed to come to New York in the first place. "Fine, 'tis very fine." Grace took her eyes off the lad for a moment. "Ma, you should have told me."

"I didn't want to worry you, lass. I wanted you to do well for yourself in America, and you have." She squeezed Grace's hand. "You have indeed."

S. P. had pulled up the stool Annie sometimes used when she mended by the light of the fire and sat on it, cradling the babe. "Walter says you have a fellow sweet on you, Grace. An American copper, he says."

"Walter Feeny is a busybody."

S. P. tilted his head back and laughed the way only an Irishman can. "Why do you think I chose him to check on you, lass?"

She wanted to say the man's nephew was worse than that, but she truly did not want to engage the man. She turned back to her mother. "You don't have to go to the boardinghouse with him, Ma. You can share my bed here, you and the baby." She hoped Mrs. Hawkins would approve.

"S. P. and I have a fine room to stay in, Grace."

Grace lowered her voice. "You don't have to. Not anymore."

"Have to what, darlin'?"

When the Hawk returned with a tea tray, Grace stood. "Ma, I'd love to show you the house and the kitchen. I'm sure the lads won't mind." She glared at her stepfather. "Will you, now?"

"Go along," he said.

As soon as they were in the kitchen, Grace repeated herself. "You are safe here, Ma. You don't ever again have to live with S. P. Feeny."

Ma put her palm on Grace's cheek. "He is my husband, child. I'm not leaving him and my son."

"I'm your daughter." Tears flowed freely down Grace's cheeks.

"Oh, darlin'." Ma wiped Grace's cheeks with her thumbs. "You are all grown up. Just as it should be. I have my life in Ireland. You have yours here."

"But . . . you only married him for me, so that he could sponsor me to come to America."

Ma wearily sat on a kitchen chair. "I don't expect you to understand. But I'm a woman with a mind of my own. I'm comfortable being the wife of an R.I.C. officer."

Grace fell to her mother's feet. "But 'twas a peeler like him who pulled us apart. Don't tell me you don't remember. He yanked me away from your arms. He made me march up those stairs in the workhouse to the attic. He is the reason I did not see you for months at a time. Tell me you haven't forgotten."

Ma's eyes reddened. "I remember, aye. How I wish those things hadn't happened. My poor *babaí*." She looped her arms around Grace's head and rocked back and forth. A moment later she let go and lifted Grace's chin. "But you mustn't blame S. P."

"Why did you marry him? Why did you allow him to touch you and give you that child?"

She let out a breath. "We care for each other. You don't understand."

"He sent me away from you, Ma. S. P. sent me here."

"I asked him to. If he hadn't sponsored you—"

Grace pulled away and stood at the sink.

"Grace, if he hadn't married me, if he hadn't gotten you out of that place, who knows what would have become of us?"

Grace covered her face with her hand as she heard wee Patrick crying for his mother, her mother.

Ma came to her. "Don't you see I wanted a better life for you?"

"You don't have to put up with him, Ma."

"Aye. I don't. He's not bad to me." She wiped away her own tears. "And like you, I will make my own choices."

Grace pulled her mother into an embrace. "Are you sure? Are you fine? He doesn't hurt you?"

"He's a good provider. He paid for our passage, second class, and for Paddy to see the American doctors. And here." She drew an envelope from her pocket. "Here is the American money you sent me in your letter, child. I've saved it all for you."

Grace gasped. "That was for you. I was going to send more, in time."

"I know. And no daughter shows that she loves her mother more than to send money from America. But S. P. has his own sponsors now, American ones. They are helping him because he is what you might call an ambassador for them over in Ireland. He works for the British government, yet he secretly supports the United Irish League."

"I don't know what that is."

"'Tis because of what he had to do, evict tenants, that he now supports the UIL. They are pushing for reform, for large landowners' holdings to be split up among tenant farmers. Perhaps one day no Irish children will ever be forced away from their parents again." She held Grace at arm's length. "But besides all that, you should see him with that boy. I do believe the child has given the man back his faith in humanity. 'Tis a frightfully difficult job, that of the Irish peeler."

"Ma, you could stay here, you and Patrick. We could get a place to live together, the three of us."

"You didn't hear me, Grace. My place is with S. P. And his work is in Ireland."

"Well, he could work here in New York. Why would anyone want to go back? You are here now, safe in America."

Her mother closed her eyes. "Not everyone's future is in America, darlin'. Some of us will stay in Ireland. Some of us will work to make our homeland what God intended." She opened her eyes again. "Not all. Like you. But some. Like me."

"I don't understand."

"'Tis not like before. Folks have hope now. The crops are prospering again. S. P. himself is an important force there, Grace. The link between the common Irish folk and the British law. He is not who you might suppose him to be. He and Walter are raising money here in America for the Irish. That's why we're here right now and will stay through St. Patrick's feast day, for the parade."

"Walter? It can't be good if he's involved. You don't know him."

"True enough, I don't know the man. But we were able to visit you because of those American benefactors."

"I don't know all about that."

"'Tis true, thank the good Lord. Have you not heard of the St. Patrick's Day parade in New York City?"

"I know there are police marches uptown, but I don't pay attention. They do not appeal to me."

"No matter. But you've got to trust me. Ireland's my place. Yours is here. As much as it breaks a mother's heart to do it, she's got to let her girl grow up and take flight like the wild goose." She squeezed Grace's hand. "And you've made me proud, you have."

Grace liked that, making her mother proud. Grace, an American family's nanny, a resident of Hawkins House. She pondered whether it was possible that God could have ordained all of this. She imagined herself to be a transformed swan, free to be who she really was and not what her father had told her she was.

Grace linked arms with her mother. "Help me get to know my wee brother, so."

Grace did not find it any easier to look S. P. in the eye, but seeing Patrick made her think of Douglas, a baby who no longer had his mother. Grace's mother took the infant and retreated to the kitchen to nurse him. Grace had thought of Ma as only being hers. But Grace wasn't a child anymore. Hadn't she been trying to convince herself she was as strong and independent as any American woman? The time had come to let her old life go like feathers in the wind. The wild goose taking flight.

38

OWEN HAD SPENT WEEKS poring over his father's account books. Even consulting with Blevins had not turned up a major crisis in the business. Finally he came to a conclusion and made the difficult trek uptown. Waiting to tell his mother he would not be taking over his father's company would not make delivering the news any easier. Best to get it over with.

When he arrived, he found his father sitting in a rocker next to the front window, muttering.

"The bankers, Father. Give me their names and I'll talk to them."

The man's face tightened. "Bankers? What bankers? I'm so very tired."

"Father? Tell me which bank has threatened foreclosure."

John McNulty shook his head.

Something wasn't right. Owen did not sense the man was out of his mind. He seemed to be playacting. Owen motioned for his mother to join him in the hall, and he shut the pocket doors for privacy. "I think he needs medical attention, Mother."

Owen's mother bristled. "No. They'll stick him away in some institution."

"I don't think so. The doctor said he could be evaluated and that you should consider going to Florida."

"What? Whatever for?"

"Rest and relaxation, of course. I'm going to mention the idea to Father."

She blew out a breath and fingered the cameo at her neck. "You've forgotten about the bankers, I suppose."

"No, I haven't. Mother, have you spoken to these bankers?"

"Of course not. Your father handles the business."

"Tell me, does it make sense that after all the years he has done business with the bank, they would so suddenly foreclose?"

"Owen, what are you suggesting? That your father made this crisis up?"

"Not entirely. Blevins does have some work to do. But in part, yes, I'm afraid he has stretched the truth in an effort to manipulate me."

She took a step back. "Preposterous!"

"I can't do any more, Mother."

"Oh, you could, but you won't." She looked away and dabbed at the corners of her eyes with the handkerchief she always had in her left hand.

"I don't expect you to understand completely, Mother, but I hope you'll try. I believe everything will work out."

"How, Owen?"

He turned away, pulled open the doors, and approached his father, who looked up at him with sad eyes. "Tell me about Blevins, Father."

The older man sighed but said nothing.

"If I summon him, will you two speak to me, together?"

His father shrugged.

"Good. Mother, telephone Mr. Blevins and ask him to come over immediately."

"Owen! Why on earth?"

"Mother, please. It's better to get everything out, and I'm too tired to argue."

Her face whitened and her eyes bulged. She was unaccustomed to her son giving her orders and likely still reeling from Owen's accusation. "No. I will not."

Owen crossed the room to her. "We must talk to Blevins."

"He's . . . well . . ." She whispered even though his father showed no signs of attending to their discussion. "He thinks your father is going mad."

"I doubt that, but yes, he has concerns. Look at him, Mother. This might be a temporary breakdown, but you cannot argue that he's in his right mind."

As proper as always, and obviously in hopes of keeping up appearances, his mother refused again.

Owen breathed in the musty, fire-warmed air of the gilded parlor, praying that he had the will to say what he must. "Then I have done all I am able. If you still believe the bankers are threatening the business, I suggest you call Blevins. If you give him authority, he'll trim expenses enough to make the proper payments to the bank and then give you an allowance to take Father on a temporary leave from the company."

He went to the door and halted. Turning, he softened his voice. "I may not be able to follow up to see that you've done this, Mother. But I must insist. If you need me, come to my apartment. I will welcome you." He had his hand on the door latch before the servant could escort him.

"Owen, wait."

He turned.

His mother's eyes blazed. "Don't go."

He held her gaze a moment. "I will pray for you both."

On his way down Broadway, he fought the dismay that

boiled up. His father's business was not really in danger of failing. Whatever mismanagement had happened, Blevins was willing and adequately able to remedy. Owen had nearly fallen for his father's ruse. He kept telling himself that his father had suffered a mild breakdown. It wasn't his fault. He was not that manipulating under normal circumstances.

It had been a damp and dreary few weeks, and when Owen had checked with Dasher, he'd told him Goo Goo had not arrived back in the city yet.

The day after Owen told his mother what action she should take, he'd called and discovered she'd allowed Blevins to take some initiative with the business. That, at least, was a relief. Owen had not pushed too hard but had allowed the train conductor of his life to take control of matters.

And finally Jake was back on regular duty.

Owen met his partner under a streetlamp on the corner of Wall Street and Broadway. They had been sent again to guard against gang activity near the park, although clandestinely so no one from Feeny at the bottom to Devery at the top would hear about it. Owen would be ready when Goo Goo showed up.

Jake pulled his collar up against the rain. "Ready?"

Owen shrugged. "Ready. Let's rid Manhattan of those thugs we've been trailing; what do you say?"

"What's changed? We've had no luck so far."

"This will be easier now."

"And why would that be?"

"Wait until you hear what's been happening while I was waiting for you to get better, Jakey."

They strolled south toward the Bowling Green. Owen

talked excitedly. "Got a new contact. Someone a bit older and more reliable than those kids we've been talking to and a little less shifty than Smokey Davis."

"How is that?"

"What would you say about a fellow who survived drug withdrawal and now wants to see the Dusters done in, a fellow who up until a few months ago was the runner for the big man himself?"

"For Goo Goo Knox?"

"That's him. This fellow was his, um, secretary. That's what he called himself."

"Excellent. You've done well." Jake patted Owen's shoulder. "But how do we know Feeny didn't set us up?"

"Easy. This guy's got a mug shot. Saw it myself. It's him, all right. And he didn't come find us. I sought him out. Followed a tip from the pawnbroker who had my watch and met up with him at the Old House at Home."

"McSorley's?"

"That's the place. It's the best we got, Jake. Now's the dirty work. Hope you're up for it."

"I'm up for it, partner. Good job running down these clues."

"Well, folks are beginning to trust me in this neighborhood."

"'Bout time."

"All we need is hard proof that Goo Goo is involved in illegal activity. That's the word from the judge."

"You should have let me come with you to McSorley's, Owen."

"When I found out he was there, I had to hurry. I've kept in touch with him since then, though, dropping by McSorley's when I could. He's still on board."

Owen paused to scrape some wet leaves from the bottom

of his shoes. "If we could just find out where this Goo Goo character is."

"Won't your contact say? What's he calling himself?"

"Dasher. Makes me think of Saint Nicholas's reindeer."

Jake shrugged. "Grown men with kid names. Never understood it. So where does Dasher say his boss is?"

"Doesn't know. They move around from the tenements to the houses near the docks. But we have something now we didn't have before, since Goo Goo's never been arrested."

Jake slapped his partner hard on the back. "A description. What did your contact say the man looked like?"

Owen pulled the description from his pocket. "Something like this. Grace is working on a sketch for us."

"Grace McCaffery?"

"That's right. She's a much better artist than me, and we just can't trust opening this up to the whole department right now. What do you say we stop over at Hawkins House and see if she's got anything ready?"

"Take the trolley?"

Owen moaned. "I suppose."

It only took them a few minutes to get to Hawkins House, and when they arrived, Grace let them in. "I just got home from work. My mother came with me."

"Your mother?"

"She's staying for a while. She's back at her boardinghouse now or I'd introduce you."

Jake cleared his throat.

"Oh, Miss McCaffery, may I introduce my partner, Jake Stockton. We're here on official business."

Mrs. Hawkins came lumbering down the hall. "Official or

not, you'll come in and have tea, gentlemen. You may talk in the parlor." She headed to the back of the house.

Owen took a seat under the portrait of a distinguished-looking man. He noticed Grace kept glancing between him and the portrait. "We are in need of the sketch now. Whatever you've come up with will be fine."

Grace sighed, went to the breakfront cabinet, and retrieved her drawing pad. "I wish it were better."

Jake peered over his shoulder. "Hmm. Don't know that we've seen that fella, but we have a better idea of who we're looking for."

Owen held up the pad. "May we keep it?"

"Of course." Grace tore out the page for them.

"Thank you so much for your help, Grace. We have to be going."

"You are most welcome. I'm not completely sure that looks like him."

"It will help."

On the way out, Grace whispered, "Walter Feeny is my stepfather's nephew, and my stepfather is here now with my mother. I'm not sure if they're up to something."

Owen gave her a grin, hoping it would ease her concern. "Feeny's always up to something, but don't worry. The captain has him occupied in a different ward."

Owen and Jake spent the next hour roaming the paths in the park and discussing the gang boss and his likely mannerisms. *A short man walks with a quick stride. A tall man takes longer steps. A man trying to hide doesn't wear flashy clothes and, in fact, would probably dress like the most common man on the street.*

This intellectual banter was what Owen really loved. Trying to outsmart a criminal was far more stimulating than running him down and tackling him on the cold ground. Owen was ready whenever duty required him to use his agile and strong body, but now he was ready to use his brains and be the detective he was primed to be.

During a break Jake paused and opened his coffee tin for a snack, offering Owen an orange. They sat in silence, and Owen decided his partner was probably also weighing in his mind the chances of catching the gang leader. Finally Jake spoke. "These Dusters. Captain says they are not known for the particular level of brutality other gangs are."

"Not so far. Still, pushed against a wall, who knows what Goo Goo might do."

Jake licked his fingers. "That's why they pay us the big bucks, right, partner?"

They laughed and then set out on rounds again, staying close to the shadowy buildings in case Feeny was around, but they didn't see him. Even if Nicholson hadn't been able to divert him, Feeny would likely be goofing off on the clock again.

All was quiet near the harbor. By the end of their shift no one matching Goo Goo's description had shown up. Tomorrow was another day.

They returned to the precinct building to discover where their next assignment would be and when. "We're on it," Owen told the captain. "No matter how long it takes."

"Got no detectives to spare on this right now," Nicholson said, leaning back in his creaky office chair. "You and Jake just do the best you can down there."

"And Feeny?"

"Feeny's busy with the parade and all."

Owen tried not to show his satisfaction with that answer. There were politicians counting on the Hudson Dusters to creatively influence voters in their district. Thankfully they were tied up with the massive St. Patrick's Day parade that distracted Feeny as well. And with no authorized detectives in Ward 1 to contend with, Owen would be free to use his own smarts.

Jake met back up with Owen at the assignment board. "I want to meet this contact, Owen."

"Like I told you earlier, he's skittish. But with all the focus elsewhere, he might agree to it."

Jake shook his head when he saw their names on the board. "Looks like we're back on days, at least for now. See you in a few hours."

Owen didn't feel a bit tired. "Yeah. And hopefully with news from Dasher."

When Owen got home, he had only three hours to rest before heading back out again. When he reached the top of the stairs, he noticed a light shining from under his door. Grabbing his nightstick, he kicked the door open and barged inside.

His father stood white-faced at Owen's kitchen sink. "Blazes, Son. Is that how you enter your own house?"

"When I'm not expecting anyone to be here, it is." He quickly shut the door.

"I don't know what kind of ludicrous schedule you keep. Your neighbor let me in."

"Otto." Owen slumped down on his sofa. He smelled coffee. "How are you feeling? You seem to have made a wonderful recovery."

Owen's father handed him a steaming cup. "I have been ill. The doctor told you that."

"Yes. Well, why did you come?"

"I had to have my say." He sat on the only kitchen chair Owen had, placed his own cup on the small round table, and leaned forward, elbows on knees.

"Please, go ahead. I have to be back at work in—" Owen pulled the watch from his pocket—"in less than three hours. If you're here to make sure I get fired, do me a favor and wait a few days. I'm on a case."

"I'd hoped you'd give it up on your own. But I stayed out of it."

Owen pinched his lips together. "What did you want to say?"

"Steer clear of any Tammany Hall business. You'll be better off that way, and I won't have to console your mother if you wind up dead in an alley somewhere."

"I appreciate the concern, but I can take care of myself."

"I confess I never understood why you chose this path, Owen. I suppose it had to do with that little girl and that O'Toole fellow, but that wasn't your responsibility."

Owen stood with the morning sun from the front window shining in his eyes. "You're right."

"Am I?"

Owen poured himself some more coffee. "Oh yes. You are undeniably correct. Becoming a policeman was not something I had to do because that officer died trying to save that little girl. It was something I had to do because God used that moment to tell me I had a mission in life, right here in Manhattan. I can't change what happened. I can't even save most folks, if the truth is known. Dead Man's Curve will still take lives, no matter how many times I or another cop blow a whistle. But whatever I can do, I will. The pity would be if I didn't try."

"I hope you don't hold this against me, Son."

"Is that an apology?"

"You can't blame a man for wanting his only son to take over the family business."

So it wasn't an apology.

"Tell me you are going to Florida, Father."

"Texas."

"Well, fine. Try to relax. Blevins is a good man."

"I agree."

They parted ways, and Owen had to admit that at least his father had taken the door Owen had left open for him. Perhaps their relationship could be mended someday.

39

THE NEXT EVENING AT HAWKINS HOUSE, as Annie passed around the lamb stew and buttermilk biscuits, Grace outlined her hopes of taking the Parker children on an outing. Aunt Edith had returned, on leave from her teaching position, and she was hopeful of succeeding where Grace had failed in obtaining permission for the children to leave the house. "I would love it if you and baby Patrick could accompany us, Ma," she said.

"I would love that, dear." Grace's mother sat next to her, the baby sleeping on her lap. She'd been able to join them at Hawkins House most evenings, while S. P. was occupied with whatever business brought him to New York. "Where do you think you will take the wee ones?"

"Central Park, perhaps."

The Hawk grunted and picked up her water glass. "Probably not a good idea with the parade about to take place up that way."

Annie agreed. "Aye, too close to St. Patrick's Cathedral."

And too close to where S. P. and his awful nephew would be. "I'll find a place," Grace said.

The Hawk picked up her silver spoon and held it over her bowl. "Best to let Mr. Parker choose. Remember what I said about how protective he is over those children."

Grace's mother patted Patrick's back. "And just after losing his wife, too, poor man."

By Thursday, Owen was growing discouraged. He'd met up with Dasher again at McSorley's, and he'd told Owen he knew Goo Goo was back in town. But despite the cooperation of many of the shopkeepers and laborers around the Battery, there had been no clues to follow.

Before he left for work, Owen knelt beside his bed, the silver watch in his hands. *Oh, God, I know you are directing my path. Give me patience and keen instincts. Help me to catch the villain that could soon be bringing the curse of addiction to scores more poor immigrants.*

When he rose to his feet, an idea came to him. Dasher had told him which newsboy would pass messages to him securely. It was time. Jake needed to meet Dasher, and they had to see if the fella would truly finger Goo Goo. He needed Dasher to be in Battery Park.

On the corner of Mulberry and Grand, Owen found the newsboy he was looking for. Sad little guy, with tattered trousers and shoe leather so thin he might as well have nothing on his feet. He was identifiable by the reddish birthmark on his right cheek. "Give him this, Henry." Owen handed him a paper with instructions to meet behind the aquarium at three thirty the following day.

The lad nodded and was about to dash away when Owen stopped him and handed him a quarter. "Go buy yourself some shoes, all right?"

He grinned. "Right after I deliver your message, Officer."

When Owen left his apartment the following morning to pick up milk for his coffee, Henry was waiting for him outside his building. "What are you doing here, son?"

"Got a message for you."

"Where is it?"

The lad pointed to his head.

"Before you tell me, Henry, how did you find me?"

"I got smarts, is all."

"Keep it to yourself and I'll fill you with as many bakery rolls as you like."

"Truly?"

Owen would have to move. *Such is the life of an undercover detective.* "I said so."

"Say, Officer. Any fella that gives newsboys blankets like he promised gets my loyalty. From us all."

"Fine, lad. Appreciate it. Now what's the message?"

"Penguin pool. Very important you meet Dasher there and thirty minutes earlier than you said."

"You sure?"

"Yep." He held out his hand.

Owen gave him fifty cents. He had to be sure he could trust this kid.

On Friday morning when Grace greeted Auntie Edith in the kitchen, she found her to be unusually cheerful. "We're going on an outing, love. Telephone your mother over at her boardinghouse."

"Mr. Parker agreed?"

"He did. School is canceled for the day. So many families preparing for St. Patrick's Day in the neighborhood, I suppose. The weather looks lovely, and the children are already chattering about it." She smacked her hands together.

"Did he say where we could go? It's the eve of the parade uptown, being that the saint's day is on Sunday this year, and I'm told we should not go to Central Park. Oh, I'm so amazed, Auntie. Are you sure you heard him right?"

Auntie Edith's smile spread across her chubby face. "I did indeed, Grace. I spoke to him about an hour ago before he left for the office."

"But did he say where we could go?"

"Oh yes. I tried to get him to go with us, but he said he always tries to stay out of that part of town. Sunday mornings are the sum of his visits to the old neighborhood." She jittered her head. "Wish I knew why it's so painful for him to be down there."

Well, with the parade and all, they did have to stay south toward the immigrant wards. Grace thought she knew why Mr. Parker scoffed at coming. Because he didn't want to face the fact that he was a slum tenement owner.

Edith put a plate she had been drying on the pantry shelf. "My brother says he will allow you and me to take the children to the aquarium this afternoon."

"The aquarium? Well, I suppose if we go soon." Rabble-rousers slept late, Grace figured. If they got there early in the day, they'd be less likely to encounter anyone like Smokey Davis. And Owen had said she was safe enough. Besides, she would not be alone, so perhaps it would be all right. "I hear there is a new octopus there. I would love to see it. I could bring my camera, take pictures of us all. The prints are small, but I've done fairly well with them thus far. Even took a photograph of the children and their mother before . . ."

"Bringing the camera is a wonderful idea, Grace," Edith said. "Can you take photographs indoors?"

"Only if the sun is bright through the skylights. But we can always get some shots before we go in. Wouldn't Mr. Parker adore photographs of his children at the aquarium?" Perhaps it would help for him to see the delight on their faces and know they'd been safe while on an outing. He'd probably looked at the ones she'd taken earlier, but more couldn't hurt.

"Surely. Now telephone your mother. We'll stop over and get her on our way." Auntie Edith raised the baby to her shoulder. "After this one's nap, of course."

The woman was upstairs with Douglas before Grace could say boo. She'd rather go now, this very minute before Mr. Parker could change his mind and before any thugs might enter the park. She hurried to the playroom to collect what they would need: hats, a bag to carry formula for the baby, and some crackers in case Holly and Linden got cranky.

Linden was waiting for her. "Miss Gracie, Miss Gracie, we're going to see the fish!" He hopped from one foot to the other.

"We are. Where are your sisters?"

"Getting dressed. Look, I got ready all by myself."

Grace stopped what she was doing to look at the lad. She stifled a laugh. His shoes were on the wrong feet and the buttons of his shirt were fastened but misaligned. "You did a fair job, Linden. Just let me help you a wee bit."

He grimaced as she removed his shoes and put them on his feet correctly. When she was done lacing, he wiggled like a worm while she unbuttoned and rebuttoned his clothes.

She checked off a list of what she needed to bring along. She had the things she'd come upstairs to gather, and her camera was in a bag she'd left downstairs.

When everyone was ready and Douglas was awake enough, they met up at the front door to take an inventory and to urge the children to visit the bathroom before they left. "Oh, diapers." Grace started to go upstairs, but Edith stopped her.

"Right here, child." She held up the bag Grace had put the canned formula in. "I stuck the nappies in here and even thought to bring extra pins. The formula was a good idea just in case. The things for the older children I put in your bag with your camera. You don't mind?"

The woman was so organized. "I do not mind. Thank you."

"I think we are all set. Come along, children. Promise Auntie you will be perfect angels on the trolley."

"Maybe we shouldn't take the baby," Grace wondered aloud. "The baby is too young to enjoy it, and one of us will have to look after him and keep him out of drafts. And won't he get heavy?"

The woman cuddled him under her chin. "My dear, no. We aren't taking Douglas to the aquarium, just across the street to Mrs. Wallace."

"Oh. Mr. Parker agreed?"

"He listened to me, Grace. He's going to have to accept more help now, and the neighbors are hospitable."

"Are you sure?"

"Absolutely. George said it would be fine, so long as we are not gone too long. And I spoke to the neighbor this morning. She is delighted to look after him." Edith slung the baby's bag of things onto her free arm. "You needn't worry, Grace. The wet nurse knows to visit and the midwife is at home should Mrs. Wallace need anything. I checked."

"All right." Grace grabbed her bag and suspended it from her elbow. She took Linden's hand and then Holly's. Hazel followed behind. "Off we go."

When they got to the boardinghouse, Grace's mother was ready. "Such a pleasure to meet you," she said to Edith, extending her hand.

"And you, my dear. I think you will enjoy the outing."

"Any outing with my daughter is sheer delight." She gave Grace a hug.

"Are you sure you don't want to bring Paddy, Ma?"

"No, no. Miss Hall will look after him. I've left a bottle. I've had to leave him overnight at the hospital before. I know he'll be fine."

The trip on the trolley was delightful. The children, not used to outings, were quiet and well-behaved.

"Let's get off early," Grace suggested to Edith. "The weather is so pleasant and the children and my mother would enjoy seeing some of the sights."

"Fine idea." The woman pulled the cord, and when the trolley halted, they got off and trotted up the sidewalk.

They paused in front of St. Paul's Chapel, where Edith told them President George Washington had worshiped. "He even took his oath of office here, right out front," she told them.

Only Hazel was impressed, having studied about America's first president in school.

They continued up Broadway, dodging pretzel vendors and lads as young as Linden hawking trinkets. When the Bowling Green was finally in view, Grace scrambled them all to a trot. So many people had bundled up and ventured out to Battery Park, where the trees were beginning to bud and the grass was greening up nicely. Businessmen spilled out of their towering office buildings to inhale the open air like swans seeking blue water. Several groups of families also populated the park. As they entered, she led the children to the bench where she had once sat and admired the statue she had since learned was inventor and engineer John Ericsson. "Sit right here. I'm going to take your picture."

Only Hazel's legs were long enough to reach the ground. The others dangled their feet.

Grace held her camera at her chest. The sun was so bright she wasn't sure she had them centered in the finder, but as soon as she got their attention away from someone selling flags and whirly toys, she shouted orders. "Chin up. Now, when I count to three, I'm going to hold my breath to keep the camera steady and you all look right at the box. Ready?"

"Ready, Miss Gracie," Linden replied.

"Now, don't say anything or the image of your face will come out fuzzy. One, two, three." She clicked the shutter and then released them from their pose.

So easy, as they said, that a child could do it.

40

When Owen met Jake at the park entrance, he realized that on a fine early spring day like this, hordes of people came out to enjoy the weather. He pulled Jake to the side of a passing crowd of giggling girls. "I don't think it was a good idea to meet Dasher here."

"You said the kid told you he'd be here. Said to meet him at the penguin pool."

"I know, but do you know how many people are going to be crowded into that place?"

"I'll say. But what choice do we have now?"

"Let's just try to get him outside, all right?"

They smiled and greeted mothers with babies and ladies in silk gowns and Gibson girl hairstyles waving paper fans in front of their faces. The last thing Owen wanted to do was create panic. No one must know they were meeting a former Duster gang member in a place so popular with children.

Jake took a stand near the penguin pool while Owen stood on the opposite side of the spacious hall. A fish with oversize eyes swam by, wiggling his head from one large-eyed side to the other.

"Is there trouble, Officer?"

Owen jerked his attention from the fish tank. A fellow in a light-gray set of clothes wearing a cloth cap, the uniform of aquarium workers, stood next to him with a broom. He did not make eye contact.

"Not at all. Carry on."

The man didn't move.

"You should get back to your duties," Owen told him.

The fellow grinned with tobacco-stained teeth and nudged his cap upward. "I will when you do. What kind of detective are you, anyway?"

"Taggart?" Owen glanced in Jake's direction, but he was no longer there. "Excuse me one moment. I need to get my partner." Owen started toward the middle of the hall when Jake caught up to him.

"In disguise? That rascal." Jake tugged Owen back in the direction of the janitor. "So you're Dasher?"

"Hush." The man turned his back on them and headed for a rear hall.

Jake and Owen followed. When they were away from public ears, Jake let him have it. "We are not here to play tricks. Now just tell us what we need to know."

Dasher pushed the bill of his too-big cap with the handle of his broom. "I'd like nothing more than to see Knox get locked up, but I value my life. You think his toughs don't hang out here once they wake up from their stupors?"

"I know they do." Owen did his best to glare at the man. He'd seen that low-life Smokey at the aquarium before. "But they're usually too wasted to cause much trouble." He stared into the man's eyes. "Is that your problem, fella? Come on, Jake. He's got nothing."

The bluff worked. Dasher apologized and begged them not to go. "The only reason I led you here is because he's coming. You can catch him today."

"In here?" Owen motioned toward the center of the aquarium, filled with people.

"You don't think he'd make his deals where he could be easily snagged, do you? He figures no city cop would risk the lives of well-to-do children to catch him."

Endangering kids was not in the plan. Owen would have to think of a way to either get the criminals out or force the civilians to leave. The foolish man should have given him warning so they could have more police at the ready.

"Stay here," Owen ordered. "I'm going to check out the exits."

Just beyond a wall of embedded water tanks, he noted a locked door. One had to weave around the tanks to get to the front exit. He was trying to imagine all the scenarios that could go wrong when he heard a familiar voice.

"We can't stay too much longer, children," Grace called out.

"Have to see the penguins," Linden said as he bobbed along the whale tank railings.

"All right. Then that's the last thing," Edith said.

They'd been in the aquarium almost an hour, the happiest hour Grace had spent since coming to America.

"Let's get another picture outside the door." Grace gathered up the hands of her charges. "This one with everyone."

"Auntie Edith too?" Linden asked.

"Oh yes."

The woman huffed. "Don't need a photograph of me."

Linden broke from Grace and embraced his aunt. Then he reached for Ma's hand and stood between the two women. "Everyone! Everyone!"

Grace laughed. "All right, so. Let's find the right spot."

She steered the children toward the harbor. While the water would make a nice backdrop, she needed the sun at her back for the light to be right. She had them stand under the budding trees but then changed her mind. "Let's try to get one of the boats in the edge of the photograph. Stand right here." She stood in the spot where she wanted them to assemble.

Edith pulled Linden up against her and placed one hand over each of the lad's shoulders. The girls stood next to him, and Ma took her place behind them. *Perfect.*

Grace peered into the viewfinder. Just a smidgen to the left would get a bit of the boat into the picture, just to show where they were. She nearly gasped when she noticed the lettering on the side of the boat. Just in case it might help Owen later, she moved her camera just a hair more to make sure she got it in the picture.

She held her breath.

Ready.

Click.

"One more," she called out to the group. This time she'd actually get them all in the shot. She wound the film, aimed, and clicked.

What was that?

She had the impression someone else had gotten into the background. "One more. I don't think I got it—" Someone gripped her shoulder from behind. Her body jerked and she turned around. His large, warm brown eyes bored into her. "Officer McNulty, what a pleasant surprise."

He wasn't smiling. "Take the children home now, Grace."

"Oh, I'd like you to meet my—"

"Can't talk now. Take them home."

He'd never spoken to her like that before. "What's wrong?"

"Grace, move along, please."

"We were just going."

He snatched the Brownie out of her hands. "But I'll need this. I'll return it."

"But—" She wanted to mention the boat, but he hurried off toward the aquarium.

"What's wrong, Miss Gracie?" Hazel asked. "Why did the policeman—?"

"Everything's fine. He's just . . . borrowing my camera."

"Did you get his name or his badge number?" Edith asked.

"No. 'Tis all right. I know him. You met him when he stopped by the house right after Mrs. Parker . . ."

"Oh, I remember that young man. He was so polite." She worried her lip. "I think we should follow his instructions."

Ma held on to Grace's arm. "Well, so. We should do as he says now and get along home."

"Uh . . . aye, let's go." There could be people about they should avoid for sure. "Hurry. Let's go now." Trying not to look behind them, Grace heard a scuffle as they headed toward the Bowling Green.

Then some cursing.

"Faster! Come along!"

She glanced back at her mother and Edith, who wobbled along, trying to keep up. Grace had to make sure the children were safe. She rushed them into a trot. Too many people wandered about, crossing their path this way and that.

"Hold Holly's hand tight, Hazel."

"I don't wanna . . . ," the younger girl wailed.

Grace hoisted Linden on her hip and reached out for Holly. "Don't argue, lassie." Her hands grasped air as the child wiggled away.

"She won't let me hold her, Miss Gracie."

Grace turned. The older women were too far away. They would have to wait for them. *Please, hurry!*

A group of men approached from the side and then stood in the path in front of them.

"This way," she called, weaving a path to the right.

The black-coated men mirrored her detour.

Her stomach knotted.

The park is crowded. No need to worry. No one would bother their small party. No one was after her.

But Owen's warning rang in her ears. *"Take the children home now."*

A face appeared among the gaggle of folks just as all the others faded. Smokey!

He stepped toward her. "When I saw that copper talking to you, Rosie, I knew you had to be in deep. Didn't I tell you to mind your own business? Didn't I give you fair warning? Goo Goo don't want his photograph taken, and you did it anyway, Rosie. Just like you did with Middleton." He nearly growled his words.

"Is he talking to us, Miss Gracie?"

"Hush, Hazel." Grace pulled the rebellious Holly closer. "I only photographed the children. Leave me alone. I'm not involved."

"Oh, but you are. See, my boss don't like the cops knowing what he looks like. Don't even have his photograph up on that wall at police headquarters." He scratched his head. "What'd they call it? Oh yeah, Rogues' Gallery." His voice took on a mocking tone. "He's not on there. It's my job to make sure no one knows what he looks like. Middleton, he only wanted me to rough you up, teach you to mind yourself. But Goo Goo, that's another story entirely."

"What's he talking about, Miss Gracie?"

"Hush, Hazel."

Smokey turned his beady eyes toward the girls as he spoke, sending shivers down Grace's spine. "And you with your box camera. Think you can take us on? Well, we can't have that."

He raised a shoulder to his face and rubbed his nose while he gripped a metal pipe in both hands. "I warned you plenty, Rosie, like I said."

She yanked the children behind her. "I was taking photographs of the children, I tell ya. That's all."

"Gimme that camera." He thrust his chin out.

"I . . . I don't have it anymore. Officer McNulty took it from me." She drew up her strength. "He's going to run you out of here. If he finds out you were threatening us—"

Smokey turned abruptly toward his punks and began bobbing his head up and down. "That's a swell idea you just gave me, Rosie. McNulty's as soft as any cop we ever knowed. He'll give the contraption back to us with a . . . trade."

The children began to sob. *Please, God, don't let me show my fear.*

She glanced behind her as the women finally caught up. No cops anywhere. When she truly needed Owen's help, he had vanished.

Edith gasped. "What is going—?"

"Now!" Smokey shouted, and the men ran toward them, scooping the girls off their feet. Another man had Linden before she could blink.

"No!"

Edith screamed.

Ma yelled for help.

Grace managed to grab hold of one thug's shirttails, but she was no match for him. He gave her a sharp rap on her thigh with his weapon. She wailed and tried without success to limp after them.

Grace fell to the pavement, screaming for help, shards of pain coming not only from her leg but from deep inside her heart.

Her vision blurred as masses of color streaked and throbbed before her eyes.

Shrill police whistles stung her ears and then the pop of a pistol.

She gasped and crawled to her feet. She didn't know where he came from, but Owen appeared and embraced her, squeezing tight. He was too late.

Grace squirmed. "Let me go! Someone took the children."

"Ten policemen are on their heels, Grace. The captain must have guessed we'd have trouble and he sent help. If only I'd known your plans today, I would have warned you away." He turned to the women. "Are you all right?"

"Yes, yes," Edith answered. "But the babies! Do something!"

"Yes, ma'am. Can you give a description?"

Edith started to describe Smokey's pallid looks and rumpled hair. Ma added a few things as well. Grace reached for words from her dry throat. "'Twas that fellow Smokey. The very same one you arrested a while ago."

"Are you sure?"

"I am sure. Had some others with him." Grace clenched her fists into tight balls. "What did they want? Why did they do that?"

"I don't think they wanted their picture taken."

"That's what he said, but I didn't take a photograph of his boss. Not now and not before. I told you that."

Owen turned her away from the women and whispered. "When you saw him in the park weeks ago, he thought you took his picture. Didn't you tell me that?"

"Yes. I had my camera then too, but on the grave of Saint Patrick I did not take any stranger's photograph just now. I did take—"

"He thinks you did, Grace. And you might have, without knowing. That's why I took the camera."

She glanced behind him. "Where is it?"

"At the station, in case it's evidence. Sent my partner over with it right after I took it from you. I saw you aiming and I thought it could be possible you'd inadvertently snapped the scum's mug."

"You saw him? The sketch I made . . . You saw *him* here?" Her mouth went dry.

"I thought so. Then all the commotion started . . . Well, come along, ladies, and I'll take all of you over to the station."

The police station. Peelers. Not again! Why, God, won't you help me?

Owen spoke in a quiet voice, meant, she supposed, to calm her. "When they realized you didn't have possession of the camera, they turned desperate."

Ma, regaining her composure, tapped Owen's arm. He turned and she reached for Grace. "We'll go get S. P.," she sniffed. "He'll know what to do."

"No." Grace's voice rang out like broken glass. "We don't need his help. A telephone." She glanced around her. "We have to . . . Oh, Edith. We have to call Mr. Parker."

Edith embraced Grace. "Are you sure your men will catch up with those thugs, Officer?"

"We're doing our best." Owen pointed toward Broadway. "The police precinct. I'll take you over."

Grace cringed. "Oh no. We don't want your help." She meant to say they didn't *need* his help but it came out all wrong.

"Grace McCaffery," her mother scolded. She turned to Owen. "My name is Ellen Feeny. My husband is with the Royal Irish Constabulary, and we are visiting my daughter. I'm sure he can help. We accept your offer and need to make several calls. To Mr. Parker and to Miss Hall's boardinghouse on Rector Street. And if my husband is not at Miss Hall's, then to Tammany Hall."

"It will be my pleasure to assist you, Mrs. Feeny. Try not to despair. We are on the case. There is a police wagon over here. We'll take you straight to headquarters."

41

THIS TIME IT WAS OWEN pacing in the captain's office. They'd been forced to endure the presence of a Tammany Hall sympathizer, an Irishman here for the parade. He was probably gathering American funds for some Irish cause. But because he was Grace McCaffery's stepfather and a police inspector in his own country, they could not put him off easily. Problem was, he was related to Walter Feeny. Grace had warned him earlier, but he hadn't given it a second thought until now.

The captain twiddled his thumbs. "You say you're with the R.I.C.?"

"That's correct, Captain Nicholson. Done years of criminal investigation in Ireland, and I'm here to lend my support."

"When you left Tammany, did anyone ask you where you were going? Your nephew, perhaps?"

"I didn't mention it. Walter was in another planning meeting. Should I have?"

"Uh, no. We have all the resources down here we need."

"I just thought I might help."

"Appreciate that." Nicholson tapped a cold cigar on the edge of his desk. He didn't offer any details about this case or the Hudson Dusters. Wise man.

"Look," the elder Feeny said, tapping his tented fingers

together. "I don't want to get into your business. Wouldn't want anyone in mine, you understand."

"Yes, I understand," Nicholson said.

Owen cracked open the door and peered into the hallway. "How long does it take to develop snapshots?"

"Couple hours, I'd say," the Irishman answered.

Owen was dying to know the strategy. If only they could get this fella out of the office. "Hey, maybe you could tell the fellas at the board how you track kidnappers in Ireland," Owen suggested.

"The men in the hall in front of the blackboard?" Feeny twisted in his chair.

"Uh, that's right." Nicholson stood. "They're trying to brainstorm ideas for some leads."

"Be happy to, if that's where you need me most."

"Oh, it is," Nicholson answered.

Feeny rose and hurried out of the office.

"Good thinking, McNulty." Nicholson shut the door.

"What do we do about him?"

Nicholson shrugged. "I think he's harmless. He's just in town to raise money. Tammany will help him do that, but I doubt he has any influence over there. Now . . ." He sat down and leaned his elbows on his desk. "We have to make sure Devery doesn't get wind of this." He turned to Jake, who had been dead silent in the corner of the room. "So Smokey thinks we identified Goo Goo, right?"

Owen glanced at his partner. "Our contact took off like a shot after he pointed him out to us. We only got a quick glimpse, but I think Grace's drawing was on target."

"Not much to go on," Nicholson said.

"I believe Smokey thinks we got 'im, Captain." Jake tapped

the heel of his shoe on the polished floor. "And whether his face is in those snapshots or not, we gotta make the Dusters think we have 'im or we'll have nothing to negotiate with." He stood and clenched his fist. "How did the boys lose those kidnappers in that tiny park?"

Owen slapped his partner's shoulder. "You know how. We talked about it before. Our boys did not have a boat. The gang slipped a rowboat in among the coal barges and steamships, I'd guess, and then rowed away into the fog that was rolling in."

"Aw." Jake gazed at the floor and shook his head. "Could it have been any simpler? And we still couldn't nab 'em."

Owen looked to the captain. "A boat, right?"

"That's right. Had to be. They could be anywhere by now."

At the station Grace sat down and tried to calm her queasy stomach. Where were the children? How frightened were they? *Oh, God, hold them in your arms.*

Ma and Edith sat with her, silently wringing their hands and wiping their eyes.

The sound of Owen's heavy footsteps made Grace look up.

He spoke softly. "Mrs. Feeny, your husband has arrived from Tammany. He is consulting with the men now. He'll be with you shortly."

"Thank you, Officer." She hugged Grace again. "You'll see, darlin'. S. P. will locate those children."

Owen stammered. "I . . . uh . . . I have to get back. I'll come back as soon as I can."

"Thank you again," Edith said.

Grace could not find the words to respond. How could this have happened? She knew Smokey hung out at the park. She should never have endangered the children by agreeing to go there. "I'm a hopeless failure," she muttered.

"Oh, darlin'. 'Tis not your fault." Ma rocked slightly, making Grace feel like a child again. But not comforted. Cruel men had burned their home when she was a child while Ma rocked her. Nay. Ma could not fix this either, and S. P., a peeler from across the sea, surely could not.

"Don't blame yourself, Grace," Edith added. "We were all with you, and none of us could have stopped those pipe-wielding toughs."

No one understood the voices in her head. *Weak. Pitiful. You will not survive.*

Grace gritted her teeth. She would not accept those messages anymore. She'd done fine with the children before this, and she would not surrender to self-doubt. She had to be strong for the children. They needed her.

Mr. Parker burst through the doors, his face red as hot coals. "Where are my children?"

Edith stood. "Now, George, try to remain calm."

Grace could not meet his eyes. Owen emerged from his meeting again in time to put his tremendous hand on the man's shoulder and convince him to sit down on a bench. Just as soon as he was released, Mr. Parker lunged toward Grace. "How could you allow this to happen? I trusted you."

Owen stood in his path, once again her protector.

Grace stammered. "It . . . it . . . uh . . . happened so fast. They just grabbed them."

He pointed his finger over Owen's shoulder. "You! If any harm comes to them, it's your fault, young lady."

"George!" Edith shook her head at him as if that would shut her brother up.

"Calm yourself, Mr. Parker." Owen managed to wrestle him back down on the bench. "No one meant for this to happen. Our men are out there right now looking for your children."

Mr. Parker's voice was tight. "And why are you in here, Owen?"

"I'm keeping you from accosting your nanny, sir. If we could all keep cool heads, I could get on with my business."

That seemed to subdue Mr. Parker. Owen was called back into an office. The air between Grace and her employer lay heavy with tension even in the silence. She left and found her mother pacing the hall. "I have to do something," she told her.

"What, darlin'? 'Tis the job of the police now."

"No, none of them can help. I must think of something." Her voice faltered. She swallowed hard. "Only someone who knows what those children are feeling can help. No one rescued me when I was a child. I can't let it happen again."

Ma grabbed her arm so hard, pain shot to Grace's shoulder. "This has nothing to do with that, Grace, and you better know it. Get ahold of yourself. Listen to me. Those police *want* to do their job. They *want* to find the children, God bless 'em. This time they're working for the wee ones, not for some landowner." She shook Grace's arm. "This is not about what happened to you."

Grace caught her sob with her hand. "But what can I do? The children . . ."

"Pray. And thank God you've got Officer McNulty on your side and S. P. here as well. They are trained, equipped, and know far more than you and I how to track kidnappers. God has sent the help we need, Grace."

Grace turned to find her stepfather moving toward them. S. P. gave Ma a kiss on the cheek and then turned to Grace.

This time Grace dared to look into his eyes. His face was creased with worry lines and his eyes were soft. "Are you all right, Grace? Are you hurt?"

"I'm well. All but my heart." She put a hand to the hollow in her chest.

"I know, Grace. I've talked to Owen. Not a Tammany man, and he let me know it. Still, I believe they are capable. I'm staying here to lend whatever assistance I can. There is a hansom waiting to take you all home."

An indignant surge leaped to her voice. "I can't leave."

He touched her shoulder. "There is nothing you can do here."

She glanced back to the hall where Mr. Parker sat, head in hands. "Maybe there is." She had misjudged Owen and probably even S. P., who truly seemed concerned. But perhaps the worst thing was how she had believed Mr. Parker didn't deserve his children. The thought of the pain he had to be in now stung like nettles in her heart. She gestured to her mother. "You and Edith go on along. There are two babes that will be needing you. I'm going to sit with Mr. Parker."

"Are you certain, darlin'?"

"Aye. I am."

Ma hesitated. "I'm not sure I should leave you."

S. P. huffed. "She's a grown woman, Ellen."

Ma shook a finger at him. "Don't be telling me what I already know."

Grace patted her mother's shoulder. "He's right, Ma. Patrick needs you and I can handle things here. You always told me I was smart, important, able. I've been able to do much more in America than I ever imagined I could. You're right. I did not cause this."

"You can depend on it, Grace. I am so proud of you. Telephone if you need me, darlin'."

"I will." She kissed her mother, hugged Edith, and sent them off.

As she moved toward the man she worked for, Grace was unsure how he would respond. He might still be angry.

She sat next to him. He didn't stir.

Shadows paced beyond a frosted glass door. Owen and some others met inside. Plotting. Planning. Preparing. Doing the work that police did in criminal cases. Ma was right. She had no idea how such things were done. *Thank you, God.*

Behind the door, hands waved; men marched back and forth. She watched as S. P. entered the room. All the while Mr. Parker sat silent.

Soon a young lad emerged from the meeting carrying her Brownie camera.

"Hey!" She leaped to her feet. "Where are you taking that? That's mine."

"Going to find someone to develop the pictures, miss."

Owen must really think she took the gang boss's photograph. He'd be disappointed when he saw the shots. Unless the boat could help in some way. It was worth finding out. "All right." She reached for the camera. "Let me take the film out for you. You don't need to take the whole camera with you."

He rushed off with the roll and she returned to her vigil.

Eventually Mr. Parker looked up. "Your camera?"

"Aye. Yes. The police think I may have taken someone's photograph unintentionally. Maybe something will show up that will help them."

He blew out a breath. "I suppose that caused all the trouble."

"I am so sorry. I should not have brought them to the park."

He wagged his head. "You didn't know. It was my suggestion, seeing as the big parade is drawing so many folks uptown. I'm sorry I yelled."

"You were upset, of course. Anyone would do the same."

"But it's not your fault."

Even Mr. Parker did not think she had messed up.

They sat for a few more quiet moments.

"Grace?"

"Aye? Yes, Mr. Parker?"

"I saw the photographs you took in Chatham Square."

"Oh." He hadn't mentioned it and she'd figured he hadn't noticed.

"I'm not the man I seem to be."

"You don't have to explain."

"Those snapshots woke me to what I'd been doing, pretending I was someone I wasn't and all the while collecting high rents for . . ." He put his head in his hands. "I suppose I had turned a blind eye to how bad it was down there. But snapshots do not lie."

"They do not," she answered softly.

"I . . . I'm afraid my actions may have caused this. God does invoke punishment, doesn't he?"

"Well, I don't—"

"You see, I never wanted to let the children go far from home because . . . well, I know there are . . . dangers, Grace. Dangers I know about."

"Aye. Yes. I understand. You wanted them to be . . ." She could not get the word out. Were they safe now? *Please, God. If you can hear me, please help!*

He grunted and sat up straighter. "I held too tight and still lost my wife. You see, I never told anyone this, but she did not come from a well-to-do family. She was raised in an orphanage. I wanted her life to be safe and secure, a cocoon, and I wanted that for my children as well."

"I know." She'd never told him how Mrs. Parker had confided in her.

He hung his head. "And I could not do it, keep anyone safe. Not myself when I was a child. Not Alice and now not the children. I'm a failure." He caught a sob in his fist.

"Oh no. I don't think—"

"Oh yes. Chatham Square was not good to me. I could not bear to go back there and so . . . I let the building rot. I was a coward."

"Nay, Mr. Parker."

"My father told me to be strong. It was what I learned, what I was trying to teach my children. I was wrong. I want to tell them that and hold them and . . ." He sobbed into his hands.

"No one is perfect, Mr. Parker. I should know that. But you are not a failure so long as you keep trying."

He mumbled into his hands. "I want to, Grace."

"I'd be happy to call Reverend Clarke for you, if you'd like."

He flung his head up to look at her. "I declare now before you and God that if my children return unharmed, I will become a better person."

Grace bit her lip. Hadn't she bargained with God if he would just let her mother come to her? She hoped Mr. Parker would become a better person. She hoped she would too. But bargaining with God over the children? That did not feel right.

"Your wife wanted to plant coralbells," Grace said, hoping to lessen the awkwardness in their conversation. "I told the children about that, and we ordered the seeds. When they return—and they will, safe and sound, you'll see—we'll plant them like their mother wanted."

The precinct doors flew open, sending a breeze down the corridor to the place they sat. Two figures scurried toward them, Mrs. Hawkins and Reverend Clarke. They embraced Grace and then the reverend took Grace's chair next to Mr. Parker.

"Edith telephoned us, love."

"Oh, Mrs. Hawkins. The children!"

"I know. I know. We'll pray and ask God to send his angels to protect them."

42

ON THE WAY TO THE HARBOR, Owen commandeered eight more men and positioned them along the pier, in an adjacent fishing boat, and in the park near the statue in case anyone tried to escape that way. Twilight fell, bringing both a help in cloaking them and a hindrance in hiding the suspects. *Dear God, give us skilled instincts.*

He held his breath a moment before he boarded the boat and thanked God that true criminals had a streak of pride that often gave them away. He turned to look again at the name painted on the side of the boat: *Goo Goo,* just as it had appeared in the background of Grace's photograph. She had only gotten half of her subjects in the image, and Owen had to believe she'd done that on purpose. He would let her know as soon as he could how smart that had been. In the background was Goo Goo's ugly mug—just as Dasher had described him and pretty much the way Grace had drawn him. Goo Goo's ugly profile wouldn't be missing from the mug shot wall now.

And now Owen was about to surprise him before he could even try to make a bargain with the children as ransom. So long as the children were unharmed, this was perfect.

But all had to go as planned. The timing had to be spot-on.

Owen drew his pistol and inched onto the boat as Jake did

the same from the opposite side. They crept toward a window to look inside the boat.

A tapping came from the stern, and then a small foot appeared from under a cover. Owen hurried over and pulled off the tarp. The children had been gagged and tied to a stack of crates, but they did not seem harmed.

"Don't worry. I got ya."

They bobbed their heads.

"Now, when I get you loose, you have to be very, very quiet. Understand? Not a peep."

They nodded again.

"Good." He waved toward one of his lookouts.

The man hurried over, and together they got the children loose.

The boy started to cry.

Owen slapped his hand over the frightened child's mouth. "Quiet, boy. Mac, take them on out of here." When Owen let go, the children bit their lips and went with the officer.

Jake stood at the cabin door, taking aim, as Owen gazed into a porthole. Goo Goo and his gang sat around a table, leisurely playing faro. Knox probably wanted his men to learn how to cheat folks at illegal gambling, another vice of the city.

The men laughed and smoked, leaning back in folding chairs. They'd thought they had plenty of time—probably assumed the police were searching farther up near the west side docks. Who would look here? There had been an escape. It was the old case of making your pursuers think you'd run as far as possible, when you were really right under their nose.

Knox slumped in his chair, examining his cards. He had no idea what was about to happen. Owen paused and motioned for Jake to back off. Instinct told him something wasn't right.

The barrel of a gun struck his ribs. A gruff voice whispered in his ear. "Call off your goons and order them to bring the camera."

"A little late, aren't ya, Smokey?"

"Those urchins don't matter. We want that camera and you got it. Hand it over."

Jake had managed to sink into the shadows. *Stupid Dusters, senses all dull, thankfully.*

"My partner has it."

Smokey spun around but aimed his rifle at Owen again before Owen could move. "You got nobody."

Owen sensed his men advancing forward, slowly.

"Do you see a camera in my hands, man?"

Smokey shook his head. "Well, you make a better hostage than those kids anyway. They'd trade a cop, even a dead one, for the evidence, I figure. Nobody but a college-boy cop would go to so much trouble to run down the Dusters. Don't they tell you anything from up at Tammany, man? Dimwit! Get down there." He cocked his head in the direction of the cabin. "You and me's gonna show Goo Goo I was the one who caught you." He moved starboard.

"Afraid of Knox, aren't you? Is that any way—?"

"Shut up!" Smokey staggered, even more dangerous with that loaded weapon because of his drugged state.

Owen took a deep breath. "Hold on, Davis. Better to have that evidence than a dead cop, you know. The department will track down a cop killer, even for a college cop like me."

"You got it or not?"

"Jake, send that camera over here."

Jake was far smarter than any fuzzy-minded addict.

A shot rang out.

The idiot had fired aimlessly, hoping to hit a target he couldn't see. Owen turned and grabbed for the weapon, but Davis stumbled back and pointed it at him. Owen held his arms up. "You want the camera or not?"

That caught his attention.

"Jake, you hear me?"

"Sure thing, boss."

Something, a box of some sort, slid toward them and landed at the gunman's feet. Davis reached for it, and Owen grabbed the barrel of his weapon, wrenching it away. The boys playing cards scrambled on deck. New York's finest surrounded them, guns at the ready. If there was one thing the city's gangs did not like, it was being outnumbered. When cops outnumbered gangsters, the cops usually won.

But this time the gang leader was in jeopardy, so they put up a fight. Owen rolled to the ground to get out of the line of fire. Pain shot up from his ankle, but he couldn't be sure he'd been hit.

"Owen, your gun," Jake yelled.

The pistol Davis had forced him to drop earlier rolled toward him from the the starboard side. He got off a few shots.

"Hold up!" Jake yelled. "We got 'em!"

Goo Goo could not escape this time.

43

WHEN THE CHILDREN burst through the precinct doors, followed by several policemen, Grace joined their father in gathering them up and planting kisses on their cold cheeks.

"I got out of the ropes," Linden said, showing her his wrist. "I was quiet. A good boy. I'm going to be a policeman one day."

"Let me look at you all." They seemed fine and unscathed. Grace held the lad tight and closed her eyes, thanking God.

"You all go on home now," the police captain said. "We'll take care of the criminals and get your statements later."

Owen and another policeman limped in behind them. Linden ran over and hugged Owen's knees.

"Are you all right?" Grace asked, pulling Linden back.

"Fine. Just a twisted ankle. You all should go along home now." He smiled.

"Thank you," Grace said. "You do a good job chasing down criminals and robbers."

He chuckled. "Thank you for trusting the New York City police, Miss McCaffery. I know that was difficult for you."

It had been. And so was trusting God. But look what had happened. The best outcome.

Grace followed Mr. Parker and the children out to his carriage.

When they were all tucked in bed, Grace approached Mr. Parker. He seemed to have aged ten years. "Please, let me stay with them. If they have bad dreams, I'll be right here."

"Thank you, Grace. I'll be in my chair all night if any of them need me."

Auntie Edith paced back and forth in front of the parlor hearth, holding baby Douglas. "I was worried sick."

"Let me take the baby. Everything is fine now." Grace carried the slumbering lad upstairs.

Sometime later Grace found that she, like Mr. Parker, could not sleep. Still dressed in her day clothes, she came downstairs. Popping her head into the parlor, where Mr. Parker sat in front of a roaring fire, she offered to make warm milk. "And Edith?"

"Thank you, Grace. Edith's gone to bed."

When she brought two mugs back with her, she noticed the man had been crying. "Don't worry, Mr. Parker. The children were not harmed at all."

"I have no doubt about that. Linden's bright disposition seems untarnished, and the girls just seem more angry than anything else, a justified anger. And they are sleeping, yes?"

"All of them like bears."

"Good, good."

"Then what, if I may ask, is on your mind? Thinking about their mother?" She swallowed a mouthful of the warm milk, praying that she hadn't overstepped.

"I had a long talk with Reverend Clarke. He helped me see that God does not blame me for my past and that it's not too late to right wrongs. I'm donating the tenement I own in Chatham Square to the Tenement House Committee of the

Charity Organization. They are doing some fine work on the Lower East Side, making living conditions more acceptable. I'm donating funds as well, and Reverend Clarke says First Church will help too."

Thank you, God. I did not have to bring up the tenement. "Well, that's a good thing, no?"

"Very much. I'm not sad, not really. I have regrets, but mostly I am vastly overwhelmed how God forgave me. I am redeemed and no longer a slave to those old feelings of unworthiness."

She set her mug down on a side table and clasped her hands in her lap. "Oh, Mr. Parker, what a wondrous thing."

They sat quietly for a moment, watching the flames. Grace did not think that the fire's glow was what had transformed this man's expression. His entire face was smoother, his eyes brighter, the muscles in his jaw more relaxed. This was what she'd been searching faces to see, what she saw in her mother, Reverend Clarke, Mrs. Hawkins, and Owen. But she hadn't realized that the inner glow was something that could instantaneously come upon a person. It wasn't there, and then it was.

"Grace?"

"Aye, yes, Mr. Parker?"

"You're Irish. Perhaps you are familiar with the ancient Irish hymn 'Be Thou My Vision'?"

"My mother used to sing it to me at night." *Before the workhouse,* but she did not need to explain.

"There is a verse that speaks to me:

"Riches I heed not, nor man's empty praise,
Thou mine inheritance, now and always;
Thou and Thou only, first in my heart,
High King of heaven, my treasure Thou art."

"Beautiful, Mr. Parker."

"Ah, yes. I am no longer seeking man's empty praise. Tomorrow the children and I will plant coralbells."

A fitting tribute to Mrs. Parker. Grace was happy she'd told him about the flowers.

She went upstairs trying to remember the rest of the verses. The tune was firmly in her head but not the words.

"Ma, I will miss you so!" Grace clung to her mother in Hawkins House's parlor. Her mother was preparing to return to Ireland. S. P.'s business was finished, and the baby had received a leg brace to help his bones grow straight.

"And I you, my heart."

"Let's take a walk. Me, you, and the baby. I need to ask you about something."

"That's why we came early, darlin'. So we could have a wee bit of time together."

Grace was surprised when S. P. agreed. Owen McNulty had stopped by, and the two of them were engaged in police talk. The influence of Tammany Hall and other such topics the women had no interest in.

They stepped out into the cool, dry air. Ma looped a blanket over the wee one's head, hoisted him on her shoulder, and they headed toward Battery Park, a spot more pleasant to take a walk in than it had been in previous days. They paused where they could look at Lady Liberty holding her torch over the harbor.

"Ma, remember that old hymn you used to sing to me at night, 'Be Thou My Vision'?"

Her mother began to hum.

"There is a part I can't remember. The verse that begins 'Be

Thou my Wisdom, and Thou my true Word.' I can't remember the rest. Can you sing it to me?"

"Surely, I can. Let's sit on this bench. Patrick gets heavy."

They sat, and Grace leaned her head on her mother's shoulder and stared down at the baby. So beautiful. So innocent. So recent from the hand of God.

Ma began to sing.

"Be Thou my Wisdom, and Thou my true Word;
I ever with Thee and Thou with me, Lord;
Thou my great Father, I Thy true son,
Thou in me dwelling, and I with Thee one."

"Ma? Is it true that I can be God's dwelling place?"

"Oh, nothing truer than that, my child."

Then Grace knew, without a doubt. Her earthly father's criticisms did not matter any longer. Her abilities, whether lacking or not, did not determine her worth. Grace's great Father wanted her, loved her, believed in her. Mr. Parker had experienced a transformation. So could she.

Grace lifted her face to the clouds, where the sun splintered through, and felt a warm glow bathe her despite spring's chill. Yes, her mother was leaving, but she felt a contentment she could not explain. *Aye. Come, Lord Jesus, and dwell in me.*

EPILOGUE

GRACE SAT IN THE PARLOR, examining the photographs the police department had returned to her. She lifted the one that showed only half of Hazel's face. "I'm so pleased you saw that boat, Owen. I meant to mention it, but once the children were taken, it left my mind."

Owen, seated on the sofa next to her, clicked his tongue. "I was not completely surprised by it. Guess I patrol there so often, I knew something didn't belong. Besides, as often as those Dusters moved from the docks to the park, they had to have a boat. Smart thinking on your part to get that in the shot. I'm just glad the children are safe."

"Very fitting that they've promoted you to detective. If they had not, I would have had a word with that Captain Nicholson."

"I don't doubt that for a minute."

Grace examined her photographs again. Then she caught Owen's gaze and held it, losing herself in the warmth of his eyes, so happy she had let this policeman into her life. God knew. Now she did too.

Annie brought her a brown envelope.

"What's this?"

"Don't know. A messenger boy just brought it."

Grace opened it and pulled out a note.

Dear Miss McCaffery,

I've been cleaning out my desk, preparing to take my things to a new office. I came across your photograph again, and I thought perhaps you'd like to have it.

Yours truly,
Augustus F. Sherman, Ellis Island Registry

She pulled out the photograph.

Owen took it from her hands. "Hey, I met that girl on a trolley once."

Grace stared at the wee face, wrinkled and bearing a weight of worries. Her mother. S. P. Feeny. Men in uniform. A new job. A place to call home. Those had been the things frightening her back then. Those fears were gone now.

Owen tapped a finger on the image. "I haven't seen her for a long time. Have you?"

She smiled. "I have not." That Grace McCaffery had disappeared along with that tattered petticoat.

He leaned close to her, his sweet breath brushing her cheek. Her heart fell to her stomach as he lifted her chin with his index finger and brushed his lips across hers. Oh, what she would have missed if she hadn't given up her distrust of the police.

He leaned back a bit when the sound of someone's footsteps clattered in the hall. Hawkins House was a busy place, a happy and joyful lively place.

He glanced at her. "Where's that camera?"

"Why?"

"We need a new picture of the Grace I see now. Let's go out to the park."

"Now?"

"Sure. It's not far."

Spring flowers had begun to pop through the earth, and the trees were a vivid green. Nothing like spring to renew your spirit.

He stood across the walk, the harbor at his back. "Think this will work?"

"Hold your breath, count to three, and then click the shutter." She smiled.

Click.

He lowered the camera. "Beautiful."

A Note from the Author

Now that most everyone carries a camera-equipped smartphone, snapping a candid photo is commonplace. But at the turn of the twentieth century, amateur photographers taking pictures on the street was an alarming novelty. A comment in a contemporary newspaper opined about how this new invention might invade privacy. At the affordable price of only one dollar, soon everyone would have a box camera. So I wondered, *What if someone took a photograph of a person who did not want his picture made? What could happen, good or bad?* After I determined that I wanted to write about an Irish immigrant struggling to make her way in the huge city of New York, the germ of the idea about the Brownie box camera began to work on me.

The Brownie camera was a marvelous invention during a time when many of the modern conveniences we enjoy today were being created. What an exciting time it must have been. But for the streams of immigrants coming through Ellis Island (the ancestors of many of you reading this), it was also a scary time to be in New York—corrupt police, greedy tenement owners, various dangers from those preying on naive new arrivals. I've often asked myself how our ancestors survived at all.

I love research, and I value accuracy and honesty, so I must note here that I've taken a couple of liberties with the historical record. I hope readers will allow me these slight manipulations of the timeline. First, the John Ericsson statue in Battery Park was not erected until 1903. After spending some time in Battery Park, I admired the statue and imagined Grace pondering it, wondering why it was there. There are several statues and monuments in the park today, but at the turn of the century this one must have stood out. So I decided to include it, even though my story takes place in 1900–1901. Second, historians note that Ellis Island was closed after a fire in 1897 and did not reopen until December 17, 1900. I've stretched that a bit to allow Grace to arrive a couple of weeks earlier than that.

If you've never been to the Statue of Liberty or Ellis Island, I hope you'll consider making the trip. You will come away, as I did, with a greater appreciation of the sacrifices scores of immigrants made to come to America. Work is still being done on Ellis Island to restore some of the buildings and to maintain the museum. To learn more and perhaps become a part of the effort, visit www.ellisisland.org.

When I imagined how difficult life was for my character Grace, I admired her for fighting against the negative voices from her past. I know there are many people today who struggle with the results of emotional abuse. My heart goes out to them. Overcoming such adversity requires a drive to grasp for an anchor. I can think of only one worthy anchor. At first Grace did not know it was Jesus Christ she was searching for, but she saw the light of Christ in others and reached for it. My hope is that you and I will continue to shine that very same light so people like Grace will find the anchor they seek.

About the Author

CINDY THOMSON has been making up stories for as long as she can remember. Her first novel, *Brigid of Ireland*, was published by Monarch Books, and she is a coauthor of *Three Finger: The Mordecai Brown Story*, the only full-length biography of baseball Hall of Famer Mordecai "Three Finger" Brown. *Grace's Pictures* is the first in a series set in New York City at the turn of the twentieth century, following the lives of new immigrants as they struggle to find their place in America. Along the way they will find friendship and love and renew their faith in God.

Cindy is a mentor in the Jerry B. Jenkins Christian Writers Guild. She and her husband have three grown sons and make their home in central Ohio, where they enjoy rooting for the Cincinnati Reds.

Her greatest wish is that her writing will encourage, enlighten, and entertain her readers.

Visit her online at www.cindyswriting.com.

Discussion Questions

1. What was Grace trying to capture in her drawings and later in her photographs?

2. What part did the streetcar accident play in Owen's decision to become a police officer, and how did that help illustrate to him the difference in the classes?

3. Augustus Sherman, the Ellis Island photographer, said that he took photographs of immigrants at the immigration station because once they arrived at Battery Park, they shed their cultural garb. What is this symbolic of, and why do you think Grace did not do that with her tattered red petticoat?

4. What did Grace see in her Ellis Island photograph that she did not like?

5. While the Benevolents are a fictional group, this time in history gave birth to many real-life charities aimed at helping new immigrants. Why do you think groups like this often formed independently of larger institutions? What were they trying to accomplish that might have been unique?

6. The Hudson Dusters, a real historical gang, were viewed by the police at the time as relatively harmless. What peril did that gang represent that the police and the citizens of the time likely missed? And if they had taken the gang more seriously, what might have happened differently?

7. Why you think the Committee of Fifteen was formed? Did it have a chance to be effective? Why or why not?

8. How did the Brownie box camera change photography?

9. How did the voices in Grace's head change once she started working for the Parker household?

10. How did Mr. Hawkins's wise sayings influence Grace and eventually her perceptions of Owen?

11. What do you think was the purpose of the maid dances? Why do you think immigrants wanted to become Americans (and shed their old garments as soon as they arrived) and still hold on to their culture by holding dances like the Thursday night maids' dance?

12. In the end, how was Grace able to find what she'd been looking for in the faces of the people she admired?